THE
BRADBURY
CHRONICLES

THE
BRADBURY
CHRONICLES

Stories in Honor of
Ray Bradbury

EDITED BY
WILLIAM F. NOLAN AND
MARTIN H. GREENBERG

RoC

A ROC BOOK

ROC
Published by the Penguin Group
Penguin Books USA Inc., 375 Hudson Street,
New York, New York 10014, U.S.A.
Penguin Books Ltd, 27 Wrights Lane, London W8 5TZ, England
Penguin Books Australia Ltd, Ringwood, Victoria, Australia
Penguin Books Canada Ltd, 2801 John Street, Markham, Ontario, Canada L3R 1B4
Penguin Books (N.Z.) Ltd. 182-190 Wairau Road, Auckland 10, New Zealand

Penguin Books Ltd, Registered Offices: Harmondsworth, Middlesex, England

First published by Roc, an imprint of New American Library,
a division of Penguin Books USA Inc.

First Printing, November, 1991
10 9 8 7 6 5 4 3 2 1

Roc is a trademark of New American Library,
a division of Penguin Books USA Inc.

Printed in the United States of America

LIBRARY OF CONGRESS CATALOGING-IN-PUBLICATION DATA

The Bradbury chronicles : stories in honor of Ray Bradbury / edited by
    William F. Nolan and Martin H. Greenberg.
        p.   cm.
    ISBN 0-451-56134-1
    1. Fantastic fiction, American.   I. Nolan, William F., 1928–
II. Greenberg, Martin Harry.   III. Bradbury, Ray, 1920–
PS648.F3B7   1991
813'.0876608--dc20
                                                                91-18498
                                                                CIP

BOOKS ARE AVAILABLE AT QUANTITY DISCOUNTS WHEN USED TO PROMOTE PRODUCTS OR SERVICES.
FOR INFORMATION PLEASE WRITE TO PREMIUM MARKETING DIVISION, PENGUIN BOOKS USA INC., 375
HUDSON STREET, NEW YORK, NEW YORK 10014.

Naturally, for Ray

Contents

Introduction: A HALF-CENTURY OF CREATIVITY /
William F. Nolan   1

RAY: AN APPRECIATION / Isaac Asimov   4

THE TROLL / Ray Bradbury   6

THE AWAKENING / Cameron Nolan   14

THE WIND FROM MIDNIGHT / Ed Gorman   23

MAY 2000: THE TOMBSTONES / James Kisner   44

ONE LIFE, IN AN HOURGLASS / Charles L. Grant   60

TWO O'CLOCK SESSION / Richard Matheson   73

A LAKE OF SUMMER / Chad Oliver   78

THE OBSESSION / William Relling Jr.   93

SOMETHING IN THE EARTH / Charles Beaumont   105

THE MUSE / Norman Corwin   116

THE LATE ARRIVALS / Roberta Lannes   121

HIDING / Richard Christian Matheson   134

SALOME / Chelsea Quinn Yarbro   139

THE INHERITANCE / Bruce Francis   155

THE MAN WITH THE POWER TIE /
Christopher Beaumont   177

CENTIGRADE 233 / Gregory Benford   190

FILLING OUT FANNIE / John Maclay   203

LAND OF THE SECOND CHANCE / J. N. Williamson   208

THE NOVEMBER GAME / F. Paul Wilson   222

THE OTHER MARS / Robert Sheckley   232

FEED THE BABY OF LOVE / Orson Scott Card   248

THE DANDELION CHRONICLES / William F. Nolan   306

Afterword: FIFTY YEARS, FIFTY FRIENDS / Ray Bradbury   317

Introduction:
A Half-Century
of Creativity

William F. Nolan

Welcome to the party! That's what this is, a celebration.

All of us, all of the authors in this book, are here to celebrate Ray Bradbury's fifty years of professional writing. From 1941, when he appeared in the pulp pages of *Super Science Stories* (shortly after his twenty-first birthday), into 1991, he has produced an unbroken flow of books, stage works, television shows, and magazine stories.

Ray's ubiquitous output includes six novels, several hundred stories (printed in over a thousand anthologies and textbooks and in two dozen Bradbury collections), as well as a countless array of poems, essays, plays, articles, scripts, and reviews. Some 350 editions of his books have been translated in thirty countries around the world.

Bradbury's influence on other writers has been enormous and steadfast, particularly in the fields of science fiction, horror, and fantasy. His name comes up again and again when professional writers are asked which authors influenced them in the formative stages of their careers. (My first published story was a Bradbury pastiche.)

We all grew up reading his books, and just listing those early titles stirs a host of memories: ... *The Martian Chronicles* ... *Fahrenheit 451* ... *The Illustrated Man* ... *The Golden Apples of the Sun ... Dandelion Wine ... Something Wicked This Way Comes* ... and, of course, *The October Country*, where, according to Bradbury, "it is always turning late in the year ... where the hills are fog and the rivers are mist ... where noons go quickly ... twilights linger, and midnights stay."

He is October's friend. Ray's favorite holiday is Halloween and, in testimony, his basement studio is awash in monsters and skeletons.

More expansively, he is Imagination's friend—and he has never limited himself to any one area of storytelling. Ray has set his tales in California, Ireland, New York, Mexico, Mars, and Deep Space, while becoming poet laureate of the American heartland—the bard of Green Town, Illinois.

He's written of dwarfs and dinosaurs, mummies and Martians, of dark carnivals and dandelion wine, boyhood lakes and book burners, of fire balloons and flying machines, marionettes and million-year picnics, kaleidoscopes and magical kitchens, of ice cream suits and invisible boys, Irish ghosts and robot grandmas, mermaids and mechanical hounds, fever dreams and farewell summers, of astronauts and small assassins, drummer boys and Dublin beggars, trolleys and time travel, sea shells and star rockets ...

All of which are represented, at least in spirit, in this anthology celebrating Ray Douglas Bradbury's fifty years of creativity.

Among a stellar cast of contributors, Gregory Benford explores a theme linked to *Fahrenheit 451*; Charles L. Grant delves into the grim territory of Mr. Dark, from *Something Wicked This Way Comes*; Ed Gorman takes us into Bradbury's seedy carnival world in an affecting sequel to "The Dwarf"; Chelsea Quinn Yarbro and William Relling deal with Bradbury's vampire family from *Dark Carnival*; Cameron Nolan writes of the emerging sexuality of *Dandelion Wine*'s Douglas Spaulding, and Orson Scott Card takes us into the autumn of Doug's life, when he is a grandfather with a family of his own; Robert Sheckley, James Kisner, and Roberta Lannes rocket to the sandy deserts of the Red Planet in their own *Martian Chronicles*; F. Paul Wilson offers a chilling sequel to "The October Game"; Chad Oliver journeys into Bradbury's nostalgic summer-lake Midwest, and John Maclay picks up on a scene from *Death is a Lonely Business*.

There's more! J. N. Williamson sends several Bradbury characters on a bizarre journey into immortality, and Norman Corwin gleefully introduces us to Ray's feisty Muse. Richard Christian Matheson conjures up a deft little mood piece reminiscent of "The Invisible Boy," and from the files of the late Charles Beaumont comes a tale strongly linked to Bradbury's "The Meadow."

Here, too, exploring Bradbury country, are Christopher Beaumont (with his first prose story), Richard Matheson, Bruce Francis, and Isaac Asimov (with a Bradbury tribute).

Bradbury himself joins the celebration with "The Troll," a wickedly delightful new fantasy tale, and caps the book with a special "Afterword," in which he looks back on a half-century of remarkable creativity.

A toast, then, to the Maestro of Imagination, whose enduring works have affected us all, entertained us, enriched our lives, and illuminated our collective humanity.

Here's to *you*, Ray!

                                                        W.F.N.

Ray: An Appreciation

Isaac Asimov

Ray Bradbury and I were born in the same year, 1920, so we became septuagenarians more or less together, with white hair, an avuncular twinkle in our eyes—the whole business.

What's more, we both began to write science fiction when we were very young, and without any help beyond our own naive efforts, we made it. We made it in two different ways, however. I ran into John Campbell and made it in the Golden Age of Science Fiction. Ray sold only two stories to John; one appeared in *Astounding*, the other, for *Unknown*, ended up in *Dark Carnival*. Ray was the only great writer of the Golden Age to remain outside the Campbell stable.

It didn't do him any harm. He became world-famous while I was still struggling to achieve some sort of recognition in the science fiction world itself. I feel no bitterness about that because anyone reading Ray's early stories and my early stories can see the difference between them. (But please don't make the comparison. You'll think less of me.)

The trouble is that Ray lives in Los Angeles while I live in New York. I don't fly and, until comparatively recently, neither did he. The result is that although we knew each other well as literary figures, reading and enjoying each other's stories, we almost never met.

I did meet him once, about ten or fifteen years ago, when he came to New York (by train) in connection with a stage play being made of one of his stories. We were both on the David Susskind show together.

In 1989, we met in New York when he came to receive the Grand Master Award by the Science Fiction Writers of America, joining me and nine others (so far) in that great honor. Then, in 1990, we met again in Washington, where we had both been invited to attend a luncheon hosted by President Gorbachev of the Soviet Union, because our books were very popular in the USSR and we were his daughter's favorite writers. Gorbachev was kind enough to mention this in his speech on that occasion.

Ray and I met there at the Soviet Embassy and he asked me, "Are we the only two science fiction writers here, Isaac?"

To which I replied, "Yes, we are, but I think we two Grand Masters can carry the load."

He laughed, and agreed.

I don't really intend to rail against the Universe for so arranging itself that Ray and I can't meet more often. We are both members of the great science fiction fraternity. We both became members when it was a small group of disregarded enthusiasts. We have both watched it grow (and contributed to that growth) into a world phenomenon of great importance.

So we are brothers.

And we know it.

THE TROLL

Ray Bradbury

In November of 1941, Ray Bradbury's first professional short story, "Pendulum," appeared in Super Science Stories. *More than 300 others have been printed since then, over the past fifty years. This figure, however, does not truly represent Bradbury's full production of short stories, since he turned out at least 100 more that have never seen publication. For one reason or another, Ray felt they should remain in his files and not be sent out to market.*

"The Troll," his fictional contribution to this book, is one of these "lost" stories. Originally completed in 1950, year of The Martian Chronicles, *it has never been submitted anywhere. When I read the story in manuscript, I was delighted by its deft blend of fantasy and wit. But I felt that it needed a bit of polishing, and asked Ray to revise it for* The Bradbury Chronicles. *He happily obliged.*

You're bound to enjoy this wry encounter with Bradbury's grumpy, lovable Green Moss Summer Bridge Troll.

A word of caution: trolls can be *dangerous.*

W.F.N.

Once upon a time, when wishing *wasn't* having, there was an old man who lived under a bridge. He lived there for as long as people remembered.

"I'm a troll," he said.

When people passed on the bridge above he cried out, "Who goes there?"

When they told him, he would demand, "Where going?"

And when they had outlined their destination, he would say, "Are you a good, kind person?"

And when they said, "Oh, yes," he would let them pass.

He got to be quite a character with the people up in the village who said, "Go visit the troll. Don't be afraid. His bark is worse than his bite. He's much fun when you get to know him."

On summer days the children would hang over the stone rim of the bridge and call down into the cool spaces, "Troll, troll, troll." And the echoes would blow up cool and clear, "Troll, troll, troll. . . ." And then they saw his reflection in the slow running water, a wry, old face with a twisty green beard woven of moss and fresh reeds, it seemed, with green moss eyebrows and pointed wax-white ears. His fingers were horny and clawed and his naked body was clothed with reeds and green grass and verdigris, wet and gleaming.

And his reflection in the water would call back up to them. "What do you want?"

"Some crayfish, troll."

"Some snails, troll."

"Some tadpoles, troll."

"Some bright stones, troll."

And if they went away a while and didn't look, when they came back they would find some delicate, scuttling crayfish placed upon the bridge rail, along with some slow snails, a few wriggling tadpoles, and some bright pink and blue-white stones from the deepest part of the creek.

"Oh, thank you, troll."

"Thank you, thank you, thank you, troll," the child voices would call into the green coolness, into the water shadows.

Drip, drip went the water. No answer. The water slid under the bridge in the summertime, and the children went on their way.

But one summer day, as the troll was basking at his ease beneath the bridge, listening to the water purl between his soaking hooves, his eyes shut and at rest, he heard a great horning and tooting and something banged over the bridge above.

"One of those idiots with his new car," murmured the troll. "Damn fool, when he could be down here, in the water shadows all summer, watching the light on the stream, feeling it slide by with your hand or your hoof. Such rushing fools up there in that hot world!"

Not a minute later he heard two people pass on the bridge. By the tread of their shoes he knew it to be two men, and one of them was saying, "Did you see that red Jaguar? Boy, was he traveling!"

"Know who that was? Our fruitcake psychiatrist! You see his new office, most modern building downtown? He's come to get us nuts off the tree, cure our neuroses, put us back on the tree, or so he said on TV last night."

"Well, well," said the other. "He sure advertises! That car's a fire engine!"

"Believes in expression, no frustrations, so he said, loud and clear."

The voices passed.

The troll, listening idly, eyes shut, was only faintly stirred by the conversation. There was a nice long summer ahead, here in this midwestern town, and then when winter froze the stream to milk-glass, he would float south leisurely, like a clump of moss and reed, easing down toward the sea, to spend a few months in a creek under a bridge in the spring. It was not a bad life at all, one had one's perambulating stations, people respected you, and on occasion (here he licked his lips) you met up with a scoundrel, a thief, some perpetual criminal, and the world thanked you for services offered and services rendered. He thought of himself as a sieve hunkered here to strain the light and dark civilizations that passed above. He could guess the pace of murdering thieves forty paces away. None of them would last through an idling and suddenly violent summer.

This train of thought sat him up, musing. "Why," he wondered, "hasn't there been a really bad one through all June or July? Here it's getting almost August and I've had to make do on mini-frogs and crayfish. A frugal lunch, no dinner at all. Where, oh where is the dark flesh and rancid blood of a true, far-traveling villain?"

Hardly had he finished this half-prayer than he heard a sound of voices far off, and quick footsteps, a very defiant series of footsteps, hurrying down the road.

"I wouldn't go near there, if I were you," warned a woman's voice.

"Bosh!" a man said. "I'll find this so-called troll myself. I don't need your help."

"So-called troll?" The troll stiffened. He waited.

A moment later, a head popped over the rim of the bridge. A pair of beady black licorice eyes stared wildly down.

"Troll!" yelled the strange man. "You *there!?*"

Troll almost plunged into the water. He lurched back into the cool shadows.

"Is *that* what they call you, the damn-fool villagers here?" the stranger above wondered. "Or did you make the name up so you could blackmail pedestrians and grab their cash?"

Troll was so stunned, his mouth froze.

"Come on, speak up, come out, the game's up, cut the comedy!" shouted the stranger.

At last, Troll inched over and glared up at the loud man suspended in the noon glare.

"And who," muttered Troll, "are you?"

"I'm Dr. Crowley. Psychiatrist. Eminent. That's who," snapped the loud man, his face crimson from hanging upside down. "And since this is a very undignified posture, why don't you come up in the sunlight? Let's talk man to man."

"I have nothing to discuss with you, Dr. Crowley." The troll subsided against the bank below.

"Then, at least," barked the psychiatrist, "give me your name!"

"Troll."

The doctor snapped his fingers. "Come, come! Don't be ridiculous! Your *real* name!"

"Well, *Summer Bridge* Troll . . . or Green Moss Summer Bridge Troll, should you want the whole thing."

"When did this first come over you?" asked the irritable doctor.

"What?"

"To sit under *bridges.* When you were a child?"

"I've *always* sat under bridges."

"I see." The face vanished. Above, a pen scratched. A voice murmured, "*Always* sat under bridges. So." The face reappeared, perspiring. "Did you run away from home often, away from siblings?"

"Siblings!?" cried the troll, confused, "what in hell's that? I never *had* a home."

"Ah." The face vanished again. The voice murmured, the pen scraped. "Orphan. Psychologically dispossessed." Like a stringless puppet the doctor thrust himself down. "What would you say attracted you *most* about bridges. The shadows, the secrecy, eh? The stashed-away element, yes? Right?"

"No," said the troll, irritably, "I simply like it here."

"Like!" cried the psychiatrist. "There's no such thing as 'like.' Every thing has *roots!* You are probably suffering from a back-to-the-womb complex. Societal withdrawal. Paranoia. Leader complex. Yes, that's *it!* You hide down here and holler up at anyone who passes. Oh, I know about you. That's one reason why I came. I traveled a long way to investigate you and the people of this village with their superstitions. But especially, *you!*"

"Me?"

"Yes, the word spread there was a troll in residence who asks each fool crossing, 'are you passing good or loping evil?' "

"What's wrong with that?" demanded Troll.

"My dear fellow, everyone knows there is no dichotomy of bad and good. It's all relative."

"Sorry," said Troll, "I don't see it that way."

"Did you ever consider environment as a factor when you asked people if they were good or evil?"

Troll snorted peevishly.

"Or heredity. Do you research the genetics of the people you supposedly eat? You *do* eat people?"

"I do."

"Tut! You only *think* you do. That's an extension of your preoccupation with curing people of their so-called sins. You imagine that by snacking on them you can digest their crimes. What you do, however, is convince yourself that each time a local thief vanishes, you have dined off his bones."

"*Haven't* I?"

"No comment. Now, how long have you lurked down there?"

"One hundred years."

"Poppycock. You're seventy at most. When were you born?"

"I was never born. I just grew. Some reeds, some crayfish, snails, grass, lots of moss, fermented, coagulated, here in the rock's shade a century back, and here I was."

"Highly fanciful but hardly of any help to me," the psychiatrist declared.

"Who asked you to come here?"

"Well, truthfully, I came on my own. You lured me as a neurotic manifestation within a culture."

"You mean to hang up there and tell me I haven't done a good job, doc?!" Troll shouted so the echoes roared. "You came to make me doubt my work, make me unhappy, yes?!"

"No, no, I came simply to help you to arise and flourish, so you can live in this world and be happy."

"I *am* happy! I *am* content. Go!"

"You only think you are. I'll come to interview you each day until we solve your problem."

"The problem is yours." Troll quivered. His hooves flinted the rocks. "A year ago, doctor, a very bad man, a man who shot and robbed people, crossed the bridge. I said, are you good or evil, and thinking I wouldn't guess he told the truth, he laughingly said, evil. An instant later the bridge was empty as I sat down to dine. Now, do you mean to tell me I erred in flaying and deboning that man?"

"What, without researching his life, to scan his love-starved youth, his starved ego, his need for love, for comfort and help?"

"I loved him immensely. I helped myself to *him.* What if I told you I've breakfasted on ten hundred such men in my lifetime, doctor?" asked the troll.

"I'd say you were an obsessional liar."

"What if I proved it?"

"Then? You'd be a murderer."

"Good or evil?"

"What?"

"A good or an evil murderer, Doctor Crowley?"

The doctor's face dripped sweat. "It's awfully hot up here in the sun."

"Your cheeks *are* red. How old are you, Crowley? Look like a heart case. Better not hang there too long with your scratch-pad. Answer my question. Am I a good or evil killer?"

"Neither! Yours was a lonely childhood. Obviously, you retreated here years ago, to set yourself up as the town's moral tyrant."

"Did the town complain?"

Silence

"*Did* it?"

"No."

"They're satisfied to have me here, yes?"

"That's not the question."

"*They're* satisfied. They didn't send for you."

"You need me," said Dr. Crowley.

"Yes, I guess I do," said the troll at last.

"You *admit* it?"

"I do."

"You'll take my treatments?"

"Yes." The troll lay back in the shadows.

The doctor's face perspired in excess as his face blushed. "Glorious! Oh, but, god, it's hot!"

His spectacles blazed with sunlight.

"Fool," whispered the troll. "Why do you think I stay here? It's icehouse cool on the hottest day. Come down."

The psychiatrist hesitated.

"I believe I will," he said, finally. "Just for a moment."

His feet slid over the edge of the bridge.

In the late afternoon, three children passed above.

"Troll, troll," they called.

"Troll, troll," they sang.

"Troll, troll, troll."

"Give us a stone, give us a shell, give us a frog. Troll, troll, give us a gift, give us a nice gift, troll."

They walked off and then turned back.

And there, dripping in the little pool of cool water on the stone rim of the bridge, lay a shell, a tadpole, a fountain pen, a pad, and a pair of bright silver-rimmed spectacles.

The stream went under the bridge silently. And as they bent to call "Troll, troll!" they saw something that resembled a lazy cool mass of green reed and green grass and green moss float slowly and slowly south and south in the tide, even as the skies clouded and birds circled and the first smell of autumn touched the air.

THE AWAKENING

Cameron Nolan

Cameron Nolan is my best friend. She is also my wife. Additionally, I happen to think she's a sensitive, skilled writer.

She made her first sales, as a ten-year-old fifth-grader, to Archie Comics; these were followed by more than three dozen published juvenile pieces. Later, as a beginning adult professional, she worked as a staff writer for the popular rock magazine, Tiger Beat. She has a sizable amount of nonfiction to her credit, including five books and numerous articles. She's also been of primary help to me in my scripting career (with expert criticism and salable plots); we are currently collaborating on a Movie of the Week for television. On her own, she has written and produced a documentary on Los Angeles and is presently putting together a series of programs for cable television.

Very recently, Cam turned her attention to prose fiction, quickly producing four excellent short stories; she's now well into her first mystery novel. One of her four stories, "The Awakening," was written directly for The Bradbury Chronicles, and it deals with Dandelion Wine's Douglas Spaulding. In this expressive extension of the Bradbury classic, young Doug is poised on the brink of manhood; his inherent sexuality is about to be awakened.

I'm proud of my wife for writing this tender, powerful fantasy. It stands solidly with the best work in this anthology.

W.F.N.

Whack-whack-whack. Whack-whack-whack.

"You stay our of that room, you hear me, Douglas Spaulding?" his Aunt Henrietta yelled from the kitchen. "You sneak into Aunt Elmira's room again and I'll tan your hide. You understand, boy?"

"Yes, ma'am," he said.

His words were swallowed by the dusty darkness of the big hall. They should have echoed in the chill empty space, but instead they vanished whole into the textured dust of faded green brocade and worn red carpet. His nose was filled with dust motes and the heavy, sweetish smell of melted beeswax mixed with lemon essence. Layer upon layer of hot liquid beeswax applied each May to every inch of woodwork. "Spring cleaning," his aunts called it, which he always thought was funny, because instead of cleaning away dirt, they just added another layer to the top of it. Forty-eight years his relatives had lived in this house. Forty-eight layers of beeswax on nearly every wood surface in the cavernous building.

In his mind he always thought the walls quivered like red Jell-O every time he brushed against them. Sometimes in his dreams, dark red Jell-O walls would close in, suffocating him, as they reached out to cradle his body in gentle embrace. He would be frightened then, so frightened he would wake up, sweaty pajamas clinging uncomfortably to his body. He felt confused when he had those dreams, because he was scared, but he felt cheated, too. Like he'd awakened too soon. Like there was something very, very good waiting for him, if he could just get past the fear and not wake up. But he could never figure out what it was that he was waiting for.

He stood at the bottom of the stairs and peered upward. He could barely see the old gold-framed photograph of his Aunt Elmira hanging on the wall in the afternoon dimness of the upstairs foyer. She had been young then. Maybe ten. Maybe eleven. Swinging on a Victorian tree swing. Dressed in a poufy white dress, her legs outstretched, pantaloons down to her black buttoned leather slippers.

The pantaloons were white and edged with lace.

Her hair had been in long ringlets then. Not like the marcelled waves she'd worn when he knew her. But the little lines of gentle laughter that crinkled her eyes were already there back then, when the photographer took her picture. The same little smile, like she knew what you were thinking.

Sometimes when he came to visit here in this old house where only his unmarried aunts now lived, his Aunt Henrietta sat him down in the gloomy parlor on the scratchy horsehair ottoman that made his bottom itch and insisted that he look at all those brownish old pictures of his relatives. He couldn't ever imagine that those people were actually related to him.

Except his Aunt Elmira. She was just the same. He'd recognize her anytime. Anywhere.

He heard the distant *whack-whack-whack* of the butcher knife as it rained down on the chopping block in the kitchen. Then the knife sounds were followed by the high-pitched wail of the old-fashioned waterpump at the sink.

Vegetable soup. He'd dug the carrots and potatoes and turnips and onions himself in the back garden this morning. He'd dug two whole baskets of vegetables, although his Aunt Henrietta had asked for just one. She'd gotten real mad at him. Said that now she'd have to cut up all the vegetables at once and make two pots of soup and give the leftovers to the Christian Ladies Charitable Society so they could distribute it to the deserving poor.

He smiled.

He hated vegetable soup.

But the *good* thing about vegetable soup, he'd discovered this last summer, was that it took a long time to prepare. Chopping up all those vegetables for supper (and the Christian Ladies Charitable Society) was going to take his Aunt Henrietta an awful long time.

And she'd forget about him until the pot was on the fire.

Long enough.

He started to creep up the stairs.

The surface of the dark handrail quivered. Beeswax. Underneath those layers, he knew, were the fingerprints of everyone in his family, preserved for the ages like dinosaur prints in river rock. The dinosaurs were long dead, just like most of his relatives, but the prints lived on forever. The brownish photographs in the parlor felt cold to him, as if those people had never lived. But their fingerprints lived forever on this handrail. He could feel their pulsating warm life as he ran his fingers lightly over the wood's jellied surface.

Aunt Elmira's fingerprints were there. Underneath the beeswax. They'd always be there.

The stairs were easy. There were only two squeaking boards, each one covered with muffling carpet, and both easily avoided. The *whack-whack-whack* sounds began in the kitchen again. Potatoes. Aunt Henrietta always chopped up the potatoes after she finished with the carrots.

Flushed with courage, Douglas bounded upward, deftly avoiding the squeaks. He paused at the top landing to make sure there was no change in the rhythmic downstairs chopping sounds. Then he lightly moved along the hall to the last room on the right.

Her room.

The dark oak door was streaked with the afternoon yellow of the setting sun. The ornate brass doorknob gleamed. His heart started pounding, as it always did when he stood here. His breath was now shallow and fast and his head felt light. Time seemed to shift into a slower speed as he touched the knob hesitantly, then turned it with experienced confidence and slipped inside.

The sweet smells of Cara Nome cosmetics and Evening in Paris Eau de Cologne surrounded him, completely replacing the outside smells of dust and lemon-scented beeswax. Once the door was shut, he was taken instantly into another world—an enchanted world immensely better than any he could have invented in his imagination.

The soft white satin pillows on her four-poster bed beckoned in the autumnal twilight. He loved the bed's dark wood, so different from the gray-painted metal of his cot at home. He ran his fingertips, then his palms, slowly over the polished wood surface. He loved the smooth, cool feel under his hands. The feeling was . . . delicious. When he was home, when he was in his own bed in his little back bedroom, he often remembered the clean feel of the smooth wood on her four-poster bed.

No beeswax. She never allowed any beeswax in this room.

The passing minutes clicked off in his brain with the sure beats of his Aunt Henrietta's piano metronome. He was now dancing through the practiced steps of long-established routine.

It was time to leave her bed and go to her dressing table.

Tortoiseshell comb. Gold-backed brush and mirror with tiny little swirls cut into the metal. Real gold. Everything neatly arranged on the glass top. All from across the Atlantic Ocean.

From London.

From a prince.

She told him that once, when he was little. Said that a prince gave her the comb and brush and mirror as a gift. After she met him at a dinner party. When Douglas got back home he asked his mother about the prince (he'd never known anybody who knew a prince before). But his mother got angry at him and wouldn't speak to him until supper.

So he never asked about the prince again.

The minutes continued to click off in his brain. Like the vegetable chopping sounds he couldn't hear now, but knew were still continuing in the kitchen.

Whack-whack-whack. Whack-whack-whack.

The whacking sounds chopped the seconds into minutes. After the potatoes would come turnips. Then celery she would fetch from the root cellar. Then onions. Lots of onions. He'd made sure to get lots of onions this afternoon, because they took longer to clean and chop than anything else.

By now Aunt Henrietta would be chopping turnips. He had to hurry.

First the books.

Then the creams and perfume.

Then the kaleidoscope.

The books were kept in the space underneath the window seat.

Thick brown embossed covers. Stamped with gold letters. *Bernhardt Erickson's Health Culture Course,* they all said. He picked up Volume IX, placed exactly as he had left it when he looked here last time.

It opened automatically to the pictures.

Muscular Bernhardt Erickson.

With Aunt Elmira.

Doing exercises.

All sorts of exercises.

Standing up exercises and jumping around exercises and, most especially, lying down on the ground exercises. With wooden Indian clubs and metal bars and big leather-covered balls.

Outside of school, he'd never actually seen anyone do exercises before.

Especially his beautiful Aunt Elmira.

He could feel excitement building in his stomach as he looked at the pictures.

The photographs were hand-tinted.

Aunt Elmira's hair was unnaturally brown.

Her eyes were unnaturally blue.

Her lips were unnaturally red.

Her skin, all of her skin, all over her body, was unnaturally pink.

She was smiling that special smile of hers in every picture.

And she wore a closely fitting white knitted swimming suit he had never seen her wear in real life.

He'd never seen any woman wear a tight swimming suit like that.

All last summer, after he first discovered these books, he had looked for a woman who wore a white knitted swimming suit like the one his Aunt Elmira had on in these pictures.

He never found one that was even close.

Somewhere in this room, he knew, was that swimming suit. He kept telling himself (every time he visited her room) that next time he would search for that swimming suit. But so far he hadn't had the time.

Or maybe it was that he didn't have the courage.

The seconds continued passing as they were chopped into minutes.

He had to hurry.

He went back to her dressing table. Lifted her cold cream jar reverently. Twisted off the white enameled lid. And breathed in the rich odor of Cara Nome. Twice.

He put the jar back on her dressing table, exactly as he had found it.

He picked up the delicate dark blue bottle of Evening in Paris perfume. Took off the top and breathed in deeply. Took a tiny little bit on his finger and dabbed it on the inside of his left hand. Not so much that anybody else could smell it. Just enough so that he could smell it all night long, if he was careful not to wet that part of his hand when he washed for supper.

The kaleidoscope.

Now it was time for the kaleidoscope.

This was a scariest part. The kaleidoscope was on the floor of her wardrobe. In a padded wooden box. Behind her shoes. At the very, very back. Underneath her dresses and robes. The colored silk and satin and lace robes that had feathers hanging down. Feathers that tickled his face when he reached far in to get the padded wooden box.

He opened the thick, heavy doors of the wardrobe. Got down on his knees and breathed in the musty, musky smells. Her wardrobe was a rainbow of silky colors. So many clothes. So beautiful. Clothes she wore in a life nobody would ever tell him about.

His head felt funny. It usually did when he reached in her wardrobe for the padded box that held the kaleidoscope. Like after Bobby Harper punched him hard when he was in the fifth grade. His head felt funny then, too.

Whack-whack-whack. Whack-whack-whack.

Aunt Henrietta would be almost done with the onions now.

He found the padded wooden box. Opened it.

The tooled brass was beautiful. He'd never seen anything so beautiful as this kaleidoscope in his entire life. It was the most magical thing he'd ever touched. He started to put it to his eye so he could see the beautiful colors as they dizzily changed shape in the glass.

"Do you like it?"

He whirled around in panic.

He was caught.

It didn't matter.

It was *her.*

"You're dead," he said, matter-of-factly. "I found the newspaper clipping Mom hid behind the flour canister. It said you were shot dead by somebody's wife in a hotel room in Chicago."

"Yes." She shrugged. "That's true. But I needed to see you

again, Douglas, before I left for good." She indicated the kaleidoscope with her chin. "That was always my favorite thing when I was growing up. I used to visit it, too."

"*You* used to visit it?" he asked, amazed. "You mean you didn't always own it?"

She laughed in amusement. She had a wonderful laugh, he decided. Honest and warm and gentle. Kind. Someday, he'd like his wife to have a laugh like that.

Just like that.

Exactly like his Aunt Elmira's.

"It's an inheritance," she said. "It's been in our family for a long time. It was brought over here by one of our ancestors when our family first came to America." She paused. "You know, Douglas, the kaleidoscope actually belongs to you now."

"You *mean* it?" he said unbelievingly.

"Oh, yes. Someday . . . someday . . . it will be time to pass it on to our family's next generation. That means *you.*"

"Can I take it home now?"

"Not yet. Not quite so soon." She came over to him and stood very, very close. So close he could smell warm Evening in Paris on her skin. She gently touched his cheek with her finger, then rested her hand on his shoulder. "It's not yet time to pass it on." She thought for a moment. "You're twelve years old now. For a while—let's say another two or three years—leave it in its box here in my wardrobe. You can visit it whenever you're here."

"And Aunt Henrietta won't get mad at me?"

She laughed again. "Tell Aunt Henrietta that the kaleidoscope now belongs to you. It's your inheritance from me. Which she already knows, even though you're going to have to remind her. Tell her you're not going to take possession of it yet because you know that you're still more boy than man, but you *do* have the right to visit *your* kaleidoscope any time you want." She smiled that smile of hers, just for him.

He couldn't believe his good fortune. He ran his fingers lightly over the richly textured metal, felt the cool, smooth firmness.

"It's time for me to go now, Douglas," she said. "You stay here with the kaleidoscope. Just put the box back where you found it when you're through."

As she got to the door she turned to face him, the crinkly lines showing at the sides of her eyes.

"And by the way, Douglas, since I know you're interested in self-improvement, you might try the *other* set of health culture books. The ones in the oak chest over there."

Abashed, suddenly—inexplicably—ashamed, he still couldn't keep himself from looking at the wooden chest in the corner.

Her eyes glistened. "There are lots of pretty women doing exercises in those books." She laughed. "I wasn't the *only* model Bernhardt Erickson ever used, you know."

She smiled at him. With gentle love.

And then she was gone.

THE WIND FROM MIDNIGHT

Ed Gorman

I could make a solid case for the fact that there are at least five Ed Gormans. The first one works (as he has done for the past two decades) as an advertising executive in Cedar Rapids, Iowa, and (with Martin H. Greenberg) is co-editor/publisher of the respected genre quarterly, Mystery Scene. *The second Gorman turns out horror novels as "Daniel Ransom," with titles such as* Night Caller *and* The Forsaken. *The third writes hardboiled Westerns like* Blood Game *and* What the Dead Men Say. *The fourth is a busy crime novelist, creator of the "Jack Dwyer" detective series:* The Autumn Dead, *etc. The fifth edits anthologies:* Stalkers, Invitation to Murder, Westeryear, *three volumes of* The Black Lizard Anthology of Crime Fiction, *et al.*

Of course, they're all the same guy—a super-industrious fellow who didn't write his first novel until 1985, but who's whipped out a slew of them since then. Ed also happens to be a damn good short story writer, as his entry in this book clearly demonstrates.

Set in the 1950s, a direct sequel to Bradbury's moody carnival tale, "The Dwarf," it takes place just a month beyond the events in that tragic story. "The Wind From Midnight" is a suspenseful, haunting portrait of loss and recovery, written with the skill of a born storyteller.

W.F. N.

Even with the windows open, the Greyhound bus was hot inside as it roared through the rural California night.

Plump ladies in sweat-soaked summer dresses furiously worked paper fans that bore the names of funeral parlors. Plump men in sleeveless T-shirts sat talking of disappointing baseball scores ("Them goddamn Red Sox just don't have it this year; no sir they don't"), and the Republican convention that had just nominated Dwight Eisenhower. Most of the men aboard liked Ike, and liked him quite a bit. These men smoked Lucky Strikes and Chesterfields and Fatimas, and more than a few of them snuck quick sips from silver flasks at their hip pockets.

In the middle of the bus was a slender, pretty woman who inexplicably burst into tears every twenty miles or so. It was assumed by all who watched her that she was having man trouble of some sort. A woman this pretty wouldn't carry on so otherwise. Probably heading home to her parents after her husband walked out on her.

Traveling with the pretty woman was a sweet-faced little girl who was obviously her daughter. She was maybe five or six, and wore a faded white dress that reminded some of First Communion and patent leather shoes that reminded others of Shirley Temple. For the most part she was well-behaved, stroking and petting her mother when she cried, and sitting prim and obedient when mama was just looking sadly out the window.

But fifty miles ago the little girl had gone back to use the restroom—she'd had a big nickel Pepsi and it had gone right through her—and there she'd seen the tiny woman sitting all by herself in one corner of the wide back seat.

All the little girl could think of—and this was what she whispered to her mama later—was that a doll had come to life.

Before the bus pulled into the oceanside town for a rest stop, the little girl found exactly four excuses to run back and get another good peek at the tiny woman.

She just couldn't believe what she was seeing.

* * *

A lot of the passengers hurried up to get off the bus fast so they could stand around the front of the depot and get a good look at her. In the rolling darkness of the Greyhound, they hadn't really gotten much of a glimpse and they were just naturally curious.

She didn't disappoint them.

She was just as tiny as she'd seemed, and in her plain white blouse and her navy linen skirt and her dark, seamed hose and her cute little pumps with the two-inch heels she looked like a five-year-old who was all dressed up in her mama's clothes.

Back on the bus they'd argued in whispers whether she was a dwarf or a midget. There was some scientific difference between the two, but damned if anybody could remember exactly what that was.

From inside the depot came smells of hamburgers and onions and french fries and cigar smoke, all stale on the still summer air. Also from inside came the sounds of Miss Kay Starr singing "The Wheel of Fortune." Skinny white cowboys clung like moths to the lights of the depot entrance, as did old black men the color of soot, and snappy young sailors in their dress whites and hayseed grins.

This was the scene the tiny woman confronted.

She walked to a nearby cab and climbed into the back seat.

The cabbie knew where the carnival was, of course. There would be only one in a burg like this.

He drove his rattling '47 Plymouth out to the pier where the midway and all the rides looked like the toys of a baby giant.

He pulled right up to the entrance and said, "That'll be eighty-five cents, miss."

She opened her purse and sank a tiny hand into its deep waiting darkness. She gave him a dollar's worth of quarters and said, "That's for you."

"Why, thank you."

She opened the door. The dome light came on. He noticed for the first time that she was nice looking. Not gorgeous or anything like that, but nice-looking. Silken dark hair in a page boy. Blue eyes that would have been beautiful if they weren't tainted with sorrow. And a full mouth so erotic it made him uncomfortable. Why, if a normal-sized man was to try anything with a tiny woman like that—

He put the thought from his mind.

As she started to leave the cab, he just blurted it out. "I suppose you know what happened here a month ago. About the— little guy, I mean."

She just looked at him.

"He stole a gun from one of the carnies here and raced back to his hotel room and killed himself." The cabbie figured that the tiny woman would want to know about it, her being just like the little guy and all. To show he was friendly, the cabbie always told colored people stories about colored people in just the same way.

The cabbie's head was turned in profile, waiting for the woman to respond.

But the only sound, faint among the *crack* of air rifles and the roar of the roller coaster and the high piping pitch of the calliope, was the cab door being quietly closed.

A lady with a beard, a man with a vagina. A chance to get your fortune told by a gypsy woman with a knife scar on her left cheek. A sobbing little blond boy looking frantically for his lost mother. A man just off the midway slapping a woman he called a fucking whore bitch. An old man in a straw hat gaping fixedly at a chunky stripper the barker kept pointing to with a long wooden cane.

Linnette saw all these things and realized why her brother had always liked carnivals. She liked them for the same reason. In all the spectacle—beautiful and ugly, happy and sad alike—tiny people tended to get overlooked. There was so much to see and do and feel and desire that normal people barely gave tiny people a glance.

And that's why, for many of his thirty-one years, her brother had been drawn to midways.

He'd told her about this one, of course, many times. How he came here after a long day at the typewriter. How he liked to sit on a bench up near the shooting gallery and watch the women go by and try to imagine what they'd be like if he had a chance to meet them. He was such a romantic, her brother, in his heart a matinee idol worthy of Valentino and Gable.

She'd learned all this from his infrequent phone calls. He always called at dinner time on Sunday evening because of the rates, and he always talked nine minutes exactly. He always asked her how things were going at the library where she worked, and she always asked him if he was ever going to write that important novel she knew he had in him.

They were brother and sister and more, which was why, when he'd put that gun to his head there in the dim little coffin of a room where he lived and wrote—

Linnette tried not to think of these things now.

She worked her way through the crowd, moving slowly toward the steady *crack*ing sounds of the shooting gallery. A Mr. Kelly was who she was looking for.

A woman given to worry and anxiety, she kept checking the new white number ten envelope in her purse. One hundred dollars in crisp green currency. Certainly that should be enough for Mr. Kelly.

Aimee was taking a cigarette break when she happened to see Linnette. She'd spent the last month trying to forget about the dwarf and the part Ralph Banghart, the man who ran *The Mirror Maze*, had played in the death of the dwarf.

And the part Aimee had played, too.

Maybe if she'd never gotten involved, never tried to help the poor little guy—

Standing next to the tent she worked, Aimee reached down to retrieve the Coke she'd set in the grass.

And just as she bent over, she felt big male hands slip over her slender hips. "Booo!"

She jerked away from him. She saw him now as a diseased person. Whatever ugliness he had inside him, she didn't want to catch.

"I told you, Ralph, I don't ever want you touching me again."

"Aw, babe, I just—"

She slapped him. Hard enough that his head jerked back with a grunt of pain.

"Hey—"

"You still don't give a damn that little guy killed himself, do you?"

Ralph rubbed his sore cheek. "I didn't kill him."

"Sure you did. You're just not man enough to admit it. If you hadn't played that practical joke on him—"

"If the little bastard couldn't take a joke—"

She raised her hand to slap him again. Grinning, he started to duck away.

She spit at him. That, he didn't have time to duck away from. She got him right on the nose.

"I don't want you to come anywhere goddamn near me, do you understand?" Aimee said, knowing she was shrieking, and not caring.

Ralph, looking around, embarrassed now that people were starting to watch, shook his head, muttered profanely, and left, daubing off the spittle with his soiled white handkerchief.

Aimee started looking around for the dwarf woman again. She had this sense that the woman had somehow known the little guy who'd killed himself.

Aimee had to find her and talk to her. Just had to.

She started searching.

Mr. Kelly turned out to be a big man with an anchor tattoo on his right forearm and beads of silver sweat standing in rows on his pink bald pate.

At the moment he was showing a woman with huge breasts how to operate an air rifle. Mr. Kelly kept nudging her accidentally-on-purpose with his elbow. If the woman minded, she didn't complain. But then her boyfriend came back from somewhere, and he looked to be about the same size but younger and trimmer than Mr. Kelly, so Mr. Kelly withdrew his elbow and let the boyfriend take over the shooting lessons.

Then Mr. Kelly turned to Linnette. "What can I do for ya, small fry?"

Linnette always told herself that insults didn't matter. Sticks and stones and all that. And most of the time they didn't. But every once in a while, right now for instance, they pierced the heart like a fatal sliver of glass.

"My name is Linnette Dobbins."

"So? My name is Frank Kelly."

"A month or so ago my brother stole a gun from you and—"

Smiles made most people look pleasant, but Mr. Kelly's smile only served to make him look knowing and dirty. "Oh, the dwarf." He looked her up and down. "Sure. I should've figured that out for myself."

"The police informed me that they've given you the gun back."

"Yeah. What about it?"

"I'd like to buy it from you."

"Buy it from me? What the hell're you talkin' about?"

Mr. Kelly was just about to continue, when a new pair of lovers bellied up to the gallery counter and waited for instructions.

Without excusing himself, Mr. Kelly went over to the lovers, picked up an air rifle, and started demonstrating how to win the gal here a nice little teddy bear.

"A dwarf, you say?"

Aimee nodded.

"Jeez, Aimee, I think I'd remember if I'd seen a dwarf woman wanderin' around the midway."

"Thanks, Hank."

Hank got kind of flustered and said, "You think we're ever gonna go to a movie sometime, Aimee, like I asked you that time?"

She touched his shoulder tenderly and gave him a sweet, quick smile. "I'm sure thinking about it, Hank. I really am." Hank was such a nice guy. She just wished he were her type.

And then she was off again, moving frantically around the midway, asking various carnies if they'd seen a woman who was a dwarf.

Hank's was the tenth booth she'd stopped at.

Nobody had seen the woman. Nobody.

"So why would you want the gun your brother killed himself with, small fry?"

From her purse, Linnette took the plain white number ten envelope and handed it up to Mr. Kelly.

"What's this?" he said.

"Look inside."

He opened the envelope flap and peeked in. He ran a pudgy finger through the bills. He whistled. "Hundred bucks."

"Right."

"For a beat up old service revolver? Hell, you don't know much about guns. You could buy one like it in any pawn shop for five bucks."

"The money's all yours."

"Just for this gun?"

"That's right, Mr. Kelly. Just for this one gun."

He whistled again. The money had made him friendlier. This time his smile lacked malevolence. "Boy, small fry, I almost hate to take your money."

"But you will?"

He gave her a big cornball grin now, and she saw in it the fact that he was just as much a hayseed as the rubes he bilked every night. The difference was, he didn't know he was a hayseed.

"You damn bet ya I will," he said, and trotted to the back of the tent to get the gun.

"I'll need some bullets for it, too," Linnette called after him.

He turned around and looked at her. "Bullets? What for?"

"Given the price I'm paying, Mr. Kelly, I'd say that was my business."

He looked at her for a time, and then his cornball grin opened his face up again. "Well, small fry, I guess I can't argue with you on that one now, can I? Bullets it is."

The carnival employed a security man named Bulicek. It was said that he was a former cop who'd gotten caught running a penny-ante protection racket on his beat and had been summarily discharged. Here, he always smelled of whiskey, and Sen-Sen to cut the stink of the whiskey. He strutted around in his blue uniform with big half-moons of sweat under each arm and a creaking leather holster riding his considerable girth. His best friend in the carny was Kelly at the shooting gallery, which figured.

Aimee avoided Bulicek because he always managed to put his hands on her in some way whenever they talked. But now she had no choice.

She'd visited seven more carnies since Hank, and nobody had seen a woman dwarf.

Bulicek was just coming out of the big whitewashed building that was half men's and half women's.

He smiled when he saw her. She could feel his paws on her already.

"I'm looking for somebody," she said.

"So am I. And I found her." Bulicek knew every bad movie line in the world.

"A woman who's a dwarf. She's somewhere on the midway. Have you seen her?"

Bulicek shrugged. "What do I get if I tell ya?"

"You get the privilege of doing your job." She tried to keep the anger from her voice. She needed his cooperation.

"And nothing else?" His eyes found a nice place on her body to settle momentarily.

"Nothing else."

He raised his eyes and shook his head and took out a package of cigarettes.

Some teenagers with ducks ass haircuts and black leather jackets—even in this kind of heat for crissakes—wandered by and Bulicek, he-man that he was, gave them the bad eye.

When he turned back to Aimee, she was shocked by his sudden anger. "You think you could talk to me one time, Miss High and Mighty, without making me feel like I'm a piece of dog shit?"

"You think you could talk to me one time without copping a cheap feel?"

He surprised her by saying. "I shouldn't do that, Aimee, and I'm sorry. You wanna try and get along?"

She laughed from embarrassment. "God, you're really serious, aren't you?"

"Yeah, I am." He put out a hand. "You wanna be friends, Aimee?"

This time the laugh was pure pleasure. "Sure, Bulicek. I'd like to be friends. I really would. You show me some respect and I'll show you some, too."

They shook hands.

"Now, about that dwarf you was askin' about."

"Yeah? You saw her?" Aimee couldn't keep the excitement from her voice.

Bulicek pointed down the midway. "Seen her 'bout fifteen minutes ago at Kelly's."

Aimee thanked him and started running.

Linnette had a different taxi driver this time.

This guy was heavy and Mexican. The radio played low, Mexican songs from a station across the border. The guy sure wore a lot of after-shave.

Linnette sat with the gun inside her purse and her purse on her lap.

She looked out the window at the passing streets. Easy to imagine her brother walking these streets, always the focus of the curious stare and the cold quick smirk. Maybe it was harder for men, she thought. They were expected to be big and strong and—

She opened her purse. The sound was loud in the taxi. She saw the driver's eyes flick up to his rearview mirror and study her. Then his eyes flicked away.

She rode the rest of the way with her hand inside her purse, gripping the gun.

She closed her eyes and tried to imagine her brother's finger on the trigger.

She hoped that there was a God somewhere and that all of this made sense, that some people should be born of normal height and others, freaks, be born with no arms or legs or eyes.

Or be born dwarfs.

"Here you are, lady."

He pulled over to the curb and told her the fare.

Once again, she found her money swiftly and paid him.

He reached over and opened the door for her, studying her all the time. Did it ever occur to him—fat and dark and not very well educated—that he looked just as strange to her as she did to him? But no, he wouldn't be the kind of man who'd have an insight like that.

She got out of the cab, and he drove away.

Even in a bleak little town like this one, the Ganges Arms was grim. "Fireproof" was much larger than "Ganges" on the neon sign outside, and the drunk throwing up over by the curb told her more than she wanted to know about the type of people who lived in the place.

She couldn't imagine how her brother had managed to survive here six years.

Linnette went inside. The lobby was small and filled with ancient couches that dust rose from like shabby ghosts. A long-dead potted plant filled one corner, while a cigarette vending machine filled the other. In the back somewhere a toilet flushed with the roar of an avalanche. A black and white TV screen flickered with images of Milton Berle in a dress.

A big woman in a faded blouse that revealed fleshy arms and some kind of terrible rash on her elbows was behind the desk. The woman had a beauty mark, huge and hairy, like a little animal clinging to her cheek.

She grinned when she saw Linnette.

"You don't have to tell me, sweetie."

"Tell you?"

"Sure. Who you are."

"You know who I am?"

"Sure. You're the little guy's sister. He talked about you all the time."

She leaned over the counter, hacking a cigarette cough that sounded sickeningly phlegmy, and said, "*Linnette.* Right?"

"Right."

The woman grimaced. "Sorry about the little guy."

"Thank you."

"I was the one who found him. He wasn't pretty, believe me."

"Oh."

"And I was the first one who read the note." She shook her head again and put a cigarette in her mouth. "He was pretty gimped up inside, poor little guy."

"Yes. Yes, he was."

The woman stared at her, not as if Linnette were a freak, but rather curious about why she might be here.

"I was just traveling through," Linnette said quietly. "I thought I might stay here tonight." She hesitated. "Sleep in my brother's room, perhaps."

Now the woman really stared at her. "You sure, hon?"

"Sure?"

"About wantin' to take his room and all? Frankly, it'd give me the creeps."

Linnette opened her purse, reached in for her money. "I'd just like to see where he lived and worked."

The woman shrugged beefy shoulders. "You're the boss, hon. You're the boss."

Kelly was arguing with a drunk who claimed that the shooting gallery was rigged. The drunk had been bragging to his girl about what a marksman he'd become in Korea and wanted to do a little showing off. All he'd managed to do was humiliate himself.

Aimee waited as patiently as she could for a few minutes, and then she interrupted the drunk—whose girlfriend was now trying to tug him away from making any more of a scene—and said, "Kelly, I'm looking for a woman who's a dwarf. Bulicek said he saw her here."

The drunk turned and looked at Aimee as if she'd just said she'd seen a Martian.

Aimee's remark unsettled the drunk enough that his girlfriend was now able to draw him away. They disappeared into the midway.

"Yeah. She was here. So what?"

"Did you talk to her?"

"Yeah."

"About what?"

"What the hell's your interest, Aimee?"

"Kelly, I don't have time to explain. Just please help me, all right?"

Kelly sighed. "Okay, kid, what do you want?"

"What'd she say to you?"

"Said she wanted to buy a gun."

"A gun? What kind of gun?"

"The gun her brother stole from me."

"My God."

"What's wrong?"

"Don't you see?"

"See what, kid? Calm down."

"If she wanted to buy the gun her brother stole from you, then maybe she plans to use it on herself just the way her brother did."

Kelly said, "Shit. You know, I never thought of that."

"So you gave her the gun?"

Kelly seemed a little embarrassed now. "Yeah. Gave it to her for a hundred bucks."

"A hundred? But Kelly, that gun isn't worth more than—"

"That's what she offered me for it. So that's what I took, kid. I never said I was no saint."

"Where did she go?"

"Hell, how would I know?"

"Didn't you notice the direction she was going?"

He shrugged. "Down near the entrance, I guess." He looked chastened that he hadn't paid attention.

"Thanks, Kelly. I appreciate it."

And before he could say another word, she was gone, running fast toward the front of the midway.

There was a card table sitting next to the room's only window. It had the uncertain legs of a young colt. He'd put his portable typewriter on it—the one she'd bought him for his birthday ten years ago—and worked long into the night.

The room had a bureau with somebody's initials knifed into the top, a mirror mottled with age, wallpaper stained with moisture, a double bed with a paint-chipped metal headboard, and linoleum so old it was worn to wood in patches.

She tried not to think of all the sad lives that had been lived out here. Men without women; men without hope.

She made sure the door was locked behind her, and then came into the room.

She could feel him here, now. She had always believed in ghosts—were ghosts any more unlikely than men and women who only grew to be three and a half feet tall?—and so she spoke out loud to him for the first time since being told of his suicide.

"I hope you know how much I love you, brother," she said, moving across the small, box-like room to the card table, running her fingers across the indentations his Smith-Corona had made on the surface.

She decided against turning the overhead light on. The on-and-off red of the outside neon was good enough.

"I miss you, brother. I hope you know that, too."

She heard the clack of a ghostly typewriter; saw her brother's sweet round face smiling up at her after he'd finished a particularly good sentence; listened to the soft sad laughter that only she had been able to elicit from him.

"I wish you would have called me. I wish you would have told me what you had in mind. You know why?"

She said nothing for a time.

Distant ragged traffic sounds from the highway; the even fainter music of the midway further away in the darkness.

"Because I would have joined you, brother. I would have joined you."

She set her purse on the card table. She unclasped the leather halves and then reached in.

The gun waited there.

She brought out the gun with the reverence of a priest bringing forth something that has been consecrated to God.

She held it for a time, in silhouette, against the window with the flashing red neon.

And then, slowly, inevitably, she brought the gun to her temple.

And eased the hammer back.

At the midway entrance, Aimee asked fourteen people if they'd seen the woman. None had. But the fifteenth did, and pointed to a rusted beast of a taxi cab just now pulling in.

Aimee ran to the cab and pushed her head in the front window before the driver had stopped completely.

"The dwarf woman. Where did you take her?"

"Who the hell are you?"

"The woman. Where did you take her?" Aimee knew she was screaming. She didn't care.

"Goddamn, lady. You're fucking nuts." But despite his tough words, the cab driver saw that she was going to stay there until she had her answer. He said, "I took her to the Ganges Arms. Why the hell're you so interested, anyway?"

"Then take me there, too," Aimee said, flipping open the back door and diving in. "Take me there, too!"

Linnette went over and sat on the bed.

This would make it easier for everybody. The mess would be confined to the mattress. A mattress you could just throw out.

She lay back on the bed.

Her shoes fell off, one at a time, making sharp noises as they struck the floor.

Two-inch heels, she thought. How pathetic of me. Wanting so desperately to be like other people.

She closed her eyes and let the sorrow wash over her. Sorrow for her brother and herself, sorrow for their lives.

She saw him again at his typewriter, heard keys striking the eternal silence.

"I wish you would have told me, brother. I wish you had. It would have been easier for you. We could have comforted each other."

She raised the hand carrying the gun, brought the gun to her temple once again.

The hammer was still back.

"Can't you go any faster?"

"Maybe you think this is an Indy race car or somethin', huh, lady?"

"God, please! Please, just go as fast as you can."

"Jes-uz," the cab driver said. "Jes-uz."

Linnette said a prayer, nothing formal, just words that said she hoped there was a God and that he or she or it or whatever form it took would understand why she was doing this and how much she longed to be with her brother again and that both God and her brother would receive her with open arms.

She tightened her finger on the trigger and then—

—the knock came.

"Hon?"

Oh, my Lord.

"Hon, you awake in there?"

Finding her voice. Clearing her throat. "Yes?"

"Brought you some Kool-Aid. That's what I drink all summer. Raspberry Kool-Aid. Quenches my thirst a lot better than regular pop, you know? Anyway, I brought you a glass. You wanna come get it?"

Did she have any choice?

Linnette put the gun down on the bed and pulled her purse over the gun.

She got up and straightened her skirt and went to the door.

A long angle of dirty yellow light fell across her from the hallway.

The woman was a lot heavier than she'd looked downstairs. Linnette liked her.

The woman bore a large glass of Kool-Aid in her right hand and a cigarette in her left. She kept flicking her ashes on the hallway floor.

"You like raspberry?"

"Thank you very much."

"Sometimes I like cherry, but tonight I'm just in a kind of raspberry mood. You know?"

"I really appreciate this."

The woman nodded to the stairs. "You get lonely, you can always come down and keep me company."

"I think I'll try and get some sleep first, but if I don't doze off, I'll probably be down."

The woman looked past Linnette into the room. "You got everything you need?"

"I'm fine."

"If your brother's room starts to bother you, just let me know. You can always change rooms for no extra cost."

"Thanks."

The woman smiled. "Enjoy the Kool-Aid." She checked the man's wristwatch she wore on her thick wrist. "Hey, time for Blackie."

"Blackie?"

"Boston Blackie. You ever watch him?"

"I guess not."

"Great show; really, great show."

"Well, thank you."

"You're welcome. And remember about keeping me company."

"Oh, I will. I promise."

"Well, good night."

"Good night," Linnette said, and then quietly closed the door.

Ten minutes later, the cabbie pulled up in front of the hotel.

As always, this street reminded Aimee of a painting by Thomas Hart Benton she'd once seen in a Chicago gallery, a place where even the street lamps looked twisted and grotesque.

Aimee flung a five dollar bill in the front seat and said, "I appreciate your speeding."

The cabbie picked up the fin, examined it as if he suspected it might be counterfeit, and then said, "Good luck with whatever your problem is, lady."

Aimee was out of the cab, hurrying into the lobby.

She went right to the desk and to the heavyset clerk who was leaning on her elbows and watching Kent Taylor as Boston Blackie.

The woman sighed bitterly, as if she'd just been forced to give up her firstborn, and said, "Help you?"

"I'm looking for a woman who just came in here."

"What kind of woman?"

"A dwarf."

The desk clerk looked Aimee over more carefully. "What about her?"

"It's important that I talk to her right away."

"Why?"

"Because—because she's a friend of mine and I think she's going to do something very foolish."

"Like what?"

"For God's sake," Aimee said. "I *know* she's here. Tell me what room she's in before it's too late."

The desk clerk was about to respond when the gunshot sounded on the floor above.

Aimee had never heard anything so loud in her life.

"What room is she in?" she screamed.

"208!"

Aimee reached the staircase in moments, and started running up the steps two at a time.

An old man in boxer shorts and a sunken, hairy chest stood in the hallway in front of 208 looking sleepy and scared.

"What the Sam Hill's going on?"

Aimee said nothing, just pushed past him to the door. She turned the knob. Locked. The desk clerk was lumbering up the stairs behind her.

Aimee turned and ran toward the steps again. She pushed out her hand and laid the palm up and open.

"The key. Hurry."

The desk clerk, her entire body heaving from exertion, dropped the key in Aimee's hand and tried to say something, but she had no wind.

Aimee ran back to 208 and inserted the key. Pushed the door open.

The first thing was the darkness; the second, the acrid odor of gunpowder. The third was the hellish neon red that shone through the dirty sheer curtains.

Aimee was afraid of what she was going to see.

Could she really handle seeing somebody who'd shot herself at point-blank range?

She took two steps over the threshold.

And heard the noise.

At first, she wasn't sure what it was. Only after she took a few more steps into the dark, cramped room did she recognize what she was hearing.

A woman lying face down on the bed, the sound of her sobbing muffled into the mattress.

The desk clerk came panting into the yellow frame of the door and asked, "She dead?"

"No," Aimee said quietly. "No, she's not dead."

And then she silently closed the door behind her and went to sit with Linnette on the bed.

Aimee had been with carnivals since she was fourteen, when she'd run off from a Kentucky farm and from a pa who saw nothing wrong with doing with her what he'd done with her other two sisters. She was now twenty-eight. In the intervening years she'd wondered many times what it would be like to have a child of her own, and tonight she thought she was finding out, at least in a curious sort of way.

It was not respectful, Aimee was sure, to think of Linnette as a child just because she was so little, but as Aimee sat there for three-and-a-half hours in the dark, breathless room holding Linnette in her lap and rocking her as she would an infant, the thought was inevitable. And then the wind from midnight came, and things cooled off a little.

Aimee didn't say much, really—what could she say? She just hugged Linnette and let her cry and let her talk and let her cry some more, and it was so sad that Aimee herself started crying sometimes, thinking of how cruel people could be to anybody who was different in any way, and thinking of that sonofabitch Ralph Banghart spying on the little guy in the house of mirrors, and thinking of how terrified the little guy had been when he fell prey to Ralph's practical joke. Life was just so sad sometimes when you saw what happened to people. Usually to innocent people at that—people that life had been cruel enough to already.

So that's why Aimee mostly listened, because when something was as overwhelming as the little guy's life had been—

Sometimes the desk clerk made the long and taxing trip up the stairs and knocked with a single knuckle and said "You okay in there?"

And Aimee would say, "We're fine, we're fine." And then the desk clerk would go away and Aimee would start rocking Linnette again and listening to her and wanting to tell Linnette that she felt terrible about the little guy's death.

It occurred to her that maybe by sitting here like this and listening to Linnette and rocking her, maybe she was in some way making up for playing a small part in the little guy's suicide.

"Sometimes I just get so scared," Linnette said just as dawn was breaking coral-colored across the sky.

And Aimee knew just what Linnette was talking about, because Aimee got scared like that, too, sometimes.

The Greyhound arrived twenty-three minutes late that afternoon.

Aimee and Linnette stood in the depot entrance with a group of other people. There was a farm girl who kept saying how excited she was to be going to Fresno, and a Marine who kept saying it was going to be good to see Iowa again, and an old woman who kept saying she hoped they kept the windows closed because even on a 92-degree day like this one she'd get a chill.

"You ever get up to Sacramento?" Linnette asked.

"Sometimes," said Aimee.

"You could always call me at the library and we could have lunch."

"That sounds like fun, Linnette."

The small woman took Aimee's hand and gave it a squeeze. "You really helped me last night. I'll never forget it, Aimee. Never."

Just then the bus pulled in with a *whoosh* of air brakes and a puff of black diesel smoke.

In one of the front windows a five-year-old boy was looking out, and when he saw Linnette he started jumping up and down and pointing, and then a couple of moments later another five-year-old face appeared in the same window, and now there were two boys looking and pointing and laughing at Linnette.

Maybe the worst part of all, Aimee thought, was that they didn't really mean to be cruel.

The bus door was flung open and a Greyhound driver looking dapper in a newly starched uniform stepped down and helped several old ladies off the bus.

"I wished he could have known you, Aimee," Linnette said. "He sure would've liked you. He sure would've."

And then, for once, it was Aimee who started crying, and she wasn't even sure why. It just seemed right somehow, she thought, as she helped the little woman take the first big step up into the bus.

A minute later, Linnette was sitting in the middle of the bus, at a window seat. Her eyes barely reached the window ledge.

Behind Aimee, the door burst open and the two five-year-olds came running out of the depot, carrying cups of Pepsi.

They looked up and saw Linnette in the window. They started pointing and giggling immediately.

Aimee grabbed the closest one by the ear, giving it enough of a twist to inflict some pain.

"That's one fine lady aboard that bus there, you hear me? And you treat her like a fine lady, too, or you're going to get your butts spanked. You understand me?" Aimee said. She let go of the boy's ear. "You understand me?" she repeated.

The boys looked at each other and then back to Aimee. They seemed scared of her, which was what she wanted.

"Yes, ma'am," both boys said in unison.

"Then get on that bus and behave yourselves."

The boys climbed aboard, not looking back at her even once.

Aimee waited till the Greyhound pulled out with a roar and a poof of sooty smoke.

She waved at Linnette and Linnette waved back.

"Goodbye," Aimee said, and was afraid she was going to start crying again.

When the bus was gone, Aimee walked over to the taxi stand. A young man who looked like a kid was driving.

Aimee told him to take her to the carnival, and then she settled back in the seat and stared out the window.

After a time, it began to rain, a hot summer rain that would neither cool nor cleanse, and the rest of the day and all the next long night, Aimee tried to keep herself from thinking about certain things. She tried so very hard.

MAY 2000: THE TOMBSTONES

James Kisner

Over the past decade, since his first novel (Nero's Vice) *was published in 1981, James Kisner has sold another eight, including his latest (from Dark Harvest),* Dead Ladies of the Night, *a wild turn on standard vampire mythology. Jim's hair-raising short story, "The Litter," is a modern classic, and he's represented in a dozen major horror anthologies, from the* Masques *series to* Cold Blood.

With his contribution to The Bradbury Chronicles *Kisner moves from the horror genre to science fiction, offering a direct sequel to Bradbury's famed short story, "Mars is Heaven!" (printed in* The Martian Chronicles *as "The Third Expedition").*

Ray's story contains one of the most visually arresting concepts in SF: the discovery, by a rocket crew from Earth, of a small, Midwest town on the Martian desert. Mystic questions were posed: Was Mars a kind of heaven in space? Were the deceased mothers and fathers and relatives encountered by the Earthmen actually real?

The captain and crew of the third expedition find the answers, at the cost of their lives. But James Kisner tells us that one more man remains alive in the abandoned Earth rocket.

This is his story.

W.F. N.

Since he was inside a coffin, Greg Duncan assumed he must be dead.

It wasn't an ordinary coffin. Its curved lid was glass, and the bottom was stainless steel cushioned with foam that conformed to his body. The interior was lit by green crystals.

As he became more aware, he realized there were needles in his arms. He felt them pinch as he twitched in the coffin; if he were truly dead, he should feel no pain. At least, that had always been what people thought.

Maybe he was experiencing one of those near-death euphorias—the biological programs implanted in the mind to make the transition from life to death more acceptable to the psyche—such as the light at the end of the tunnel experience so many people had on operating tables, when they were "dead" for a moment or two.

Or maybe—by the slightest chance, he realized—he wasn't actually dead.

The ship's doctor, Arnold Cummings, had made no promises. Captain John Black had given him the option of taking drugs to ease the pain instead of being a guinea pig for a barely tested new vaccine. One way offered slim hope; the other none at all.

As the needle slid under his skin, Greg and the rest of the crew waited to see what effect the vaccine would have on the unknown disease he had contracted in space between Earth and Mars.

After the doctor pressed the plunger of the syringe, and the medication coursed through his veins, Greg remembered a brief moment of pain in his chest. Then, apparently he had technically expired, his body succumbing to the mystery virus that downed so many other space travelers.

But now he was awake, aware, resurrected. The vaccine must have worked. The doctor and the captain had kept him on life support systems just in case.

Or were they merely saving his corpse for dissection later, to see what had killed him? Maybe the IVs stuck in his arms were embalming fluids, not life-support nourishment.

A strange problem: How did a person know *for sure* he was dead?

Or alive?

Someone ought to be coming soon. There must be monitors that would tell the doctor that Greg was stirring in his tomb. He listened intently for footsteps or any other signs of life in the ship. But the silence was like a heavy blanket bearing down on him. No one was coming.

He was going to suffocate!

He panicked momentarily, overcome by claustrophobia and terror. He started to hyperventilate.

Then he remembered Captain Black's last words and brought himself under control.

"If you somehow overcome this thing," the captain had said, "press Sensor A, on your right. It'll set off an alarm, and we'll come running. Remember that."

Calmly now, he felt for the sensor membrane at his right side. Touching it would alert the others he was alive. He pressed his finger against the membrane and waited. A few seconds passed, then an LCD screen lit up over his face. Words blinked on the screen, character by character, forming a message:

SHIP UNOCCUPIED ... FAIL SAFE, PHASE TWO IN EFFECT ...

RECOMMEND EJECTION ... EJECT PROCEDURE: PRESS SENSOR B.

Fail Safe, Phase Two!

What the hell? Greg groped hurriedly, now driven by the Fail Safe imperative, until his index finger found the sensor at his left. He pressed it down hard. The glass top half of the tube slid away, the needles disengaged, and Greg sat up. An alarm sounded somewhere in the ship.

"Captain Black? Lustig? Hinkston? Dr. Cummings? The vaccine worked! I'm alive!"

His own voice echoing back to him chilled him. Then he remembered the LCD's message, "SHIP UNOCCUPIED ..."

Why in hell, he thought, would the entire crew leave?

That's why the Fail Safe, Phase Two was in effect.

He had to hurry, or he would die for sure this time.

Greg's limbs felt as if they were asleep and weighed a hundred pounds, and it was difficult to focus his eyes. He struggled to get to the door leading to the rest of the ship. His diseased body had been isolated from the crew for safety reasons.

Now he had to get that door open. It had a combination lock requiring four numbers be punched in on a keypad. Four numbers he couldn't recall.

Another alarm sounded.

The ship's intercom blared, "Fail Safe, Phase Three" in the computer's synthesized voice.

"Jesus!" he muttered. "Numbers. What are the goddamn numbers? Captain! Dr. Cummings! There's gotta be somebody on board!"

Numbers. It had to be something easy. It came back to him now; just in case a person was trapped, the combination was the year of his birth.

Greg punched in 1955 and the door slid open.

He was on the ship's lowest level where the rocket fuel was stored. He went over to the ladder and climbed up to the next level, where the bunks were, not one of them occupied. He shouted his crewmates' names again and again, as he ascended from one level to another, until he reached the bridge. There was no one on any of the levels.

There was no one at the bridge.

"Fail Safe, Phase Four," the synchronized voice announced.

His fingers numb from disuse, Greg fumbled at the main console, punching in data, trying to get the ship's computer to recognize *his* presence. Otherwise, he couldn't cancel the Fail Safe condition. He typed in his serial number, rank, year of birth and his code name.

He waited while the computer digested this information. The plasma screen blinked, and a line of type fluttered across the screen: *Gregory C. Duncan, 215678, Engineer First Class, 1955, Code Name Johnson, Deceased, March 12, 2000. Input?*

"Not deceased," Greg typed.

Ship log entry, March 12, 2000, Crewman Gregory C. Duncan believed deceased, placed in sterile isolation by authority Cpt. John Black, under sanction of Ship's Physician, Arnold Cummings.

"Not deceased," Greg typed again.

Input?

"I'm not dead, you son of a bitch!"

The screen went blank. Greg heard the hard disks spinning in the console.

Voice recognition affirmative, Greg C. Duncan. Input?

Greg sighed heavily. The computer was like any other machine: sometimes you had to cuss at it to make it work.

He typed very carefully, "Abort Fail Safe, Code A/Code 1/Code Green, Authority: Command by Proxy."

This was critical. If he had remembered the code sequence wrong, the ship would explode at Phase Five, a Fail Safe measure designed to keep Martians—or anything or anybody else in space—from learning the science inside the ship and using it against Earth.

The screen blanked off, then blanked back on.

Fail Safe Aborted, it replied. *Input?*

Greg pressed the "n" key for "no," and turned away. He felt incredibly exhausted, but he had more to do.

He had to discover what had happened to the other sixteen men in the crew.

Sipping a reconstituted orange juice, Greg glanced out the main portal. What he saw was a windblown, dusty reddish landscape barely illuminated by the sun.

It was Mars!

By God, they'd made it. That must be where the crew was now—outside, exploring the planet. He longed to be out there with them, kicking up the red dust, touching the alien rocks, perhaps even encountering life.

That was what space travel was all about, after all. To find life. To discover different intelligences. To assure humanity it was not alone in the universe.

Everyone on the ship must have felt as he did now, even though it didn't look too friendly out there.

Still, someone should've stayed aboard. Why would Captain Black allow the whole crew to leave?

Greg went to the opposite portal. More hostile landscape, evidently barren of life, yet he sensed something familiar was out there.

He adjusted the portal for a closer look, zooming in until vague whitish objects came into view. He shuddered as he recognized them: A row of very Earth-like tombstones, sixteen of them—with no names on them—set in the russet Martian soil.

His skin suddenly erupted in goosebumps and his stomach lurched as a terrifying thought occurred to him.

Could the crew be buried out there—all of them?

If they were *all* dead, who had buried them?

Without pausing to contemplate any possible answers, Greg went to the nearest weapons station and selected an atomic laser pistol with a holster and two napalm grenades to hang on his belt. He strapped on the holster and put the grenades in place. Now he was ready for anything.

But he was feeling increasingly tired. He needed to plan a strategy before he acted. Panic may have been responsible for what had happened to the rest of the crew. He sat down in the captain's chair, tensed for anything.

His head ached mildly. It occurred to him he should radio Earth, and he switched on the transmitter. It responded with a vague hiss.

He was on the wrong side of the planet. The only way he could communicate was to bounce the radio waves off one of Mars' moons—or wait for the planet to turn—which would be hours.

He went to the portal to look at those tombstones again. As he approached the portal, the glare of sunlight made him squint.

Everything was *different* outside! The barren landscape and the row of tombstones were gone. In their place were sidewalks, pavement, and cars from the 1970s. There were brick buildings. And storefronts. And newsstands.

There was also music playing out there, somehow penetrating the thick hull of the ship, creeping into Greg's brain.

Disco music?

He ran to another portal. He saw kids playing in the street, gaudy women strutting down the sidewalk, teenagers with boom boxes. Winos passed out in doorways.

It was a street in Harlem.

Sweat rolled down Greg's dark brown skin as he pondered the situation.

Harlem. Where he'd grown up. Where he'd run in a street gang till he was seventeen, then finally got his act together and decided to get out. He began studying, then won a scholarship to go to college. He learned aeronautical engineering. He had escaped the dehumanizing milieu that had brought down so many of his brothers.

Harlem. He thought he'd never see those mean streets again. There was nothing there, never could be, that would make him ever want to go back.

Except maybe to see his mother. But she had died in 1988, and his brothers and sisters who had stayed behind considered him a traitor to the family because he was educated.

What the hell was Harlem doing on Mars?

How had it appeared so suddenly?

A hallucination? Another biological program to fool the psyche?

He went to the ship's computer and punched in some hard questions. According to the computer, the view outside was real. The buildings were made of genuine brick; the sidewalks tangible concrete; and the people were real, living organisms. Strangest of all, the air outside was breathable.

How could the damned atmosphere change?

Greg shook his head, wondering if the computer had been tampered with. He asked it for coordinates and it confirmed that the ship was on Mars.

Then he typed, "Estimate age of outside structures."

From one-hundred years to five years. Input?

"You are being fooled," Greg typed.

Bad response or file name. Input?

"Illusion."

Bad response or file name. Input?

The computer was in a rut. Frustrated, Greg flipped it off and tapped his fingers on the console, trying to decide what to do. If the computer said it was real, then it was real. But the computer, though backed up with artificial intelligence to intuit, could still be wrong, just as a human being could be.

There was only one way to find out what was reality and what was sham.

He'd have to go out there.

The ship stood in a vacant lot between two crumbling buildings. Coming out of the bottom portal, Greg descended the landing stairs to the ground. As he set foot on the cinders covering the lot, he heard the portal shut behind him. In a few hours, the Fail Safe mechanism would kick in again if he didn't return.

Greg went out to the sidewalk for a better view. Up the street, he saw more of Harlem; down, he saw the familiar New York skyline, with its silhouette of the Empire State Building and other skyscrapers.

The air *was* breathable. But it stank with the smells of decayed garbage, rotten wood, rats and other vermin, human waste, exhaust fumes. There was more noise now, too: not only music, but the sounds of men cursing, women talking in high voices, and children yelling at each other.

For a few moments Greg just stood there, observing the endless parade of black people. *His* people. Curiously, they just passed by him, not seeming to notice his silvery space suit. Maybe they sensed he had an atomic pistol and grenades tucked inside his jacket. Maybe they thought him a bad-ass mother—someone not to be messed with.

That was fine. It would make it easier for him to move around.

He turned north and walked three blocks, weaving in and out of the milling people, expertly maintaining his own personal space as most New Yorkers did without even thinking about it. Not even the crazies—the street preachers, the junkies, the whacked-out pimps—paid him any attention. He was tempted to stop one of them and scream, "Don't you see I'm different?"

Or had they seen others like him? Who could he ask? Where did all this lead to?

"Hey, nigger!"

He turned, his ears bristling at the epithet he hadn't heard in a good ten years.

"You talking to me?"

"Yeah, I'm talking to you, Mr. Spaceman. Where the hell you been?"

Greg squinted at the short skinny man. He was in his early twenties, wearing a red shirt and navy blue slacks. He also wore a porkpie hat and his feet were clad in patent leather wingtips. His narrow face finally stirred something in Greg's memory—a former classmate. "Thomas," he said, "Reggie Thomas."

"Say, my man, you remember me." Reggie offered his palm to be slapped. Greg performed the ritual, feeling very foolish.

"You got a dollar?"

"No," Greg said.

"Too bad. Need a pack of smokes. Got a butt on you?"

"I don't smoke anymore, Reggie. This is going to sound strange, but what year is it?"

"Say what?"

"What year is this?"

"You stoned, man?"

"I don't do dope anymore, either."

"Don't smoke. Don't toke. What you do for fun?"

Greg grabbed Reggie by the shoulders and shook him. "Cut the jive-ass shit and tell me what year it is."

Reggie's eyes grew wide as he pulled away from Greg's grip. "Don't get so uptight, man. It's 1975."

"Where?"

"Everywhere I guess."

"I mean where are we?"

"Harlem. Man, whatever you been smoking, I want some of it."

"This isn't Harlem. It's Mars."

"You *must* be doing some kind of weed, man. Thinking Harlem is Mars. That why you wearing that funny suit?"

"How come nobody else notices my suit?"

"How the hell I know? You know the streets, man. Don't mess with nobody unless you prepared to back it up."

"This *is* Mars. I'm certain of it."

"I ain't got time to waste on you, man. I got to find somebody with a dollar so I can get me some Salems."

Reggie spun around and continued down the street.

"Come back! Explain this to me. You've got to talk to me."

Reggie flipped him the finger without looking back.

Greg started to follow him, but he spied someone else across the street he hadn't seen in years.

His mother! Without even pausing to consider that she had been dead for over a decade, he rushed across the street, disrupting traffic.

"Mama!"

Greg's mother was forty-eight, but appeared closer to sixty. She was a squat, heavyset woman with medium dark skin and liquid brown eyes. She was wearing a threadbare dress, and carried a handbag and a sack of groceries.

"Greg. Good to see you, honey."

"Let me take that sack." He was stunned, but accepting.

"Thank you, son. My back aches and my feet hurts." She smiled broadly at him.

He accompanied her back to the building where he had spent his youth, in a two-bedroom apartment three flights up. The stairway smelled of stale urine and other foul wastes, just as it had then.

The kitchen was exactly as he remembered it. A white enameled table sat in the center, surrounded by four wooden chairs with torn red padding on the seats. The cabinets had grime on them from cooking in close quarters; there were insect flecks on the edges from the hordes of cockroaches that infested the building; in the dark corners of the room were rat droppings.

Greg put the sack on the table and unloaded it. The groceries were simple, all-too-familiar fare: cans of red beans, a bag of generic rice, and a package of cheap hamburger.

"Making red beans and rice tonight," his mama said, taking a chair. "Your favorite. Got meat for it, too."

"It's not my favorite anymore," he said.

"What you mean?"

"Never mind. It was good when it was all we had to eat, but I don't have to eat that kind of food now. I can afford *real* food."

"Red beans and rice used to be good enough for you."

Greg had forgotten how his mother could make him feel guilty for saying something that in another family, in another culture removed from the reality of Harlem and places like it, would barely cause an eyebrow to raise.

He sat down across from her, noticing how her eyes seemed

always on the verge of tears, just as when he was young. From his present perspective, he now understood that careworn expression. His heart ached; he wanted to help her, to change her way of life, to change the past, but—he caught himself—how could he change the past? How could his mother even *be* here?

Because he wanted to believe it, he realized. Because she was the only person he ever missed from his old way of life.

Maybe she, of all people, would be honest with him.

"Mama, I just don't understand all this," he said carefully. "I mean, this just can't be. This is Mars."

"Mars?"

"Remember, Mama? I joined the space program after I got out of college. I'm here on the Third Expedition."

"What you talking about?"

"It's the year 2000. My crewmates are missing, except I thought I saw some tombstones earlier and—well, it doesn't make any sense."

She nodded sagely. "A lot of things don't make sense in this life, son. You just got to let the Lord handle it."

"The Lord don't figure in it, Mama. This *is* Mars. It has to be. But Harlem *can't* be on Mars."

Mama Duncan gave him one of those looks she had always used when she was protecting him from the bald, bad truth of something. "I ain't saying this is Mars, and I ain't saying it ain't, but you damn sure know I'm your Mama and I wouldn't tell you wrong."

"There's more to it than that, Mama. I don't know how to tell you this except to just come out and say it. You've been dead for twelve years." He watched closely for her reaction.

"Has it been that long?"

"You know it?"

"Course, I know it. That's why I'm here. I've passed on to my reward."

"You call this your reward? Living in Harlem? Spending the afterlife in a slum?"

"A person gets used to a certain way of living, and I guess it just keeps on going after you dead."

"That's not what the preacher used to say. He promised a heaven with streets of gold, not an urban blight. Don't you remember that? And your body—it's still wracked with the pains of life. Is that part of your reward too?"

Her face registered a variety of expressions, none of them clearly readable. Finally, she said, "Boy, you know the Lord works in mysterious ways. Maybe this is just a stepping stone on the way to a greater reward."

"I don't believe it."

She went over to him, resting her hands on his shoulders and massaging them gently. "You all tensed up. You think too much about things. You got to have faith that the Lord's got it all planned out just right."

His mother's hands felt warm and comfortable on his muscles.

"Son, why don't you stay over tonight, and we can just figure this all out tomorrow. I'll fix you a good meal, and we'll make some lemonade, and then you can just sleep like a baby, knowing your Mama's close by to take care of you."

Greg closed his eyes, imagining such an evening. . . . Back in the bosom of his Mama, like when he was a kid, and he had run to her when he'd gotten into trouble out on the unforgiving streets. It was, in its own odd way, a kind of heaven, despite the harshness of the environment. Maybe Mama was right. Part of the afterlife might be reliving some of your sorrows, so you could come to terms with them before passing on to—

He heard something rustling in the corner, something diseased and mean. His eyes snapped open.

"I can't stay here, Mama."

Her hands let go of his shoulders abruptly. "Why not?"

"Because this represents everything I left behind—the rats, the roaches, the stench of the slums, the hopelessness. I fought half my life to leave this, and I'm not about to be brought back down to this level."

Her voice was stern. "I'm your Mama, and I'm telling you you're staying."

He stood up violently, causing the chair to tumble backwards. "Goddamn it, Mama, I'm not staying. I *hate* Harlem."

"Son . . ."

At that moment, there was a ruckus out in the street. Mama Duncan went over and looked down. "Oh, my God! It's your brother Willie. One of them Tyler boys done pulled a knife on him. You got to help him!"

Putting his feelings aside, Greg went to the window. It was his younger brother Willie all right. "I'll go," he said.

"Save him, Gregory—so you and him can sleep safe up here tonight!"

He started to tell her one more time he wouldn't stay in this rat-infested dump if his life depended on it, but he was in too much of a hurry now.

Willie needed his help.

When he reached the street, he saw his brother, who was about fourteen, squared off against a much bigger teenager. They both had knives—Willie a switchblade, the other boy a big hunting knife.

"Willie!"

"You stay out of my fight, Greg."

Greg pushed his way through the gathering crowd. When he reached Willie, he pulled his brother away, taking the knife from him. "You go on home."

"Now everybody think I'm chicken!"

"What if they do? It's better than being maimed or dead."

Willie's glare burned into Greg's eyes. There was a street ethic involved here. Greg had violated it and shamed Willie in front of the other teens. They'd say he was a "toy" and a chicken. It was too late to amend that now. Willie would have to live it down—or prove his manhood some other way.

Greg started to follow Willie, but a voice stopped him.

"Hey, Spaceman," the other boy said. "This ain't the end. If you gonna take the boy out, then you take his place."

"What do you want from me?"

The big boy's face was twisted with hate. "I want to carve my initials in your belly, boy."

"I'm not a boy. You don't want to mess with me."

"I'll take you on, mother. Use the goddamn knife."

The crowd urged them on, some rooting for Greg, others rooting for his challenger, whose name was Richie.

"All right," Greg said, crouching with the knife in his hand. "I'll cut you, then it'll be over."

"You ain't cutting *me!*"

They danced around a bit, lunging at one another, neither connecting.

After a few seconds, Greg realized he was getting high on the excitement of the battle. The adrenaline pumping through him was better than speed or pot or anything else.

It was 1975, he reminded himself again. He tossed the knife back and forth between his hands, still taunting his opponent. His mother was upstairs watching, but she had died twelve years ago. He lunged, ripped the fabric on Richie Tyler's shirt, then retreated a few steps. No blood drawn.

This couldn't be reality; it was an extended nightmare. He was probably still in the glass coffin, his brain producing this elaborate scenario as it slowly lost oxygen.

Therefore, he reasoned, he *couldn't be hurt!*

Greg lunged again, this time more recklessly, enjoying the thrill of it. Even if he killed the other boy, it wouldn't lie on his conscience. It was an illusion, after all, a dream.

Richie Tyler suddenly moved in a blur, the hunting knife seeming to jump to his other hand, and before Greg could react, the blade had bitten deep into his forearm.

And, Sweet Jesus, did it hurt!

"You son of a bitch!" Greg stopped moving.

Richie seemed confused now. "Had enough, Mr. Chicken?"

"I'm just through screwing with you." He reached inside his jacket and pulled out the atomic pistol. "You're not real, anyhow." He aimed at Richie's stomach and pulled the trigger, expecting the boy's guts to explode.

Instead, Richie melted.

As he dissolved, he no longer looked like a human being. His features shifted back and forth until they were just a blob, and his body became a puddle of amorphous goo.

Greg looked around at the crowd. Some of the other faces seemed less substantial now. He stared down at the muck that had been a black teenager seconds before. Things started clicking, almost, but not quite, coming together in his mind.

Then his mother broke through the circle of onlookers. "You in a buncha trouble now, Gregory. Come upstairs. I'll hide you from the police."

"Will you, Mama?" The pain in his head, previously a minor annoyance, now roared. He knew now, damn it.

"You know I will, son."

"The Lord works in mysterious ways," Greg muttered.

He *knew!*

"That's a fact ..."

His mother never finished the sentence because Greg blew her head off, and the body to which it had been attached melted.

The crowd hissed, starting to tighten the circle around him. Greg blasted several of the crowd, transforming them into ugly stinking puddles of bubbling protoplasm, and creating an opening through which to escape. He lobbed a napalm grenade into their midst and ran toward the waiting spaceship.

The Martians that survived pursued him.

The skyline started to blur in his vision as Greg sprinted down the middle of the street, blasting illusionary cars and hallucinatory people out of his way.

The Martians were certainly clever bastards. Unable to fight atomic weapons, they had gone into Greg's head and pulled out the memories they thought would draw him into their trap.

God only knew what would have happened if he had stayed overnight with his "Mama."

They would have killed him, probably in a horrible fashion—just as they had done to the rest of the crew. He wondered what illusion had been created for them, and how they had been lulled into believing it. What could possibly fool sixteen rational, military-trained men so completely? Why had they trusted the illusions?

He saw the spaceship shining in the waning sun only a block and a half away.

The spurious city around it was wavering, melting ... revealing the reality beneath—the true Martian landscape Greg had seen when he first awoke from his death-like sleep.

He twisted around and tossed his other grenade. The Martians emitted toad-like sounds as their shifting flesh was burned by jellied gasoline.

A few more feet to the ship ... He was going to make it! Then he stumbled over a tombstone, dropping his pistol.

There was no name on the stone, but he knew now there were

only sixteen possibilities. He picked himself up and ran toward the ship, realizing too late he had left his weapon in the dust.

Greg climbed up the steps, punched in a code on the lock, and entered the portal. It closed behind him. He made his way quickly to the bridge. He looked out a portal and saw the Martians hovering around the first tombstone, examining the weapon he had lost.

He sat at the console, punching in some numbers. Maybe he could lift off before they thought to blast the ship. Greg heard the rockets starting to kick in.

He heard noises below.

An atomic pistol blast.

The rush of air coming into the ship as it depressurized.

The disheartening sound of the rockets being disabled.

He'd be able to take a few of them out with the other pistols in the weapons cabinet. But he'd only be putting off the inevitable.

He armed himself and switched on the radio. Phobos was in the right position now; he could warn Earth.

"This is Greg Duncan, Engineer First Class, last surviving member of the Third Expedition. Others all dead. Mars—Mars is Hell!"

He didn't wait for a reply; he could only hope the message reached someone.

He heard the Martians skittering up the inside ladders. One of their ugly heads popped up through the bridge access and Greg blew it off, smearing it all over the computer's side panel.

More Martians came through.

Greg kept firing.

There were so *many* of them!

Before they descended on him, he managed to activate the Fail Safe, setting it to go directly to Phase Five.

It would be over in sixty seconds. There'd be a new crater on the Martian landscape several miles across, glistening with the pooled remains of dead Martians.

Then he laughed because he was going to die.

Again.

ONE LIFE, IN AN
HOURGLASS

Charles L. Grant

After being awarded a Bronze Star by the U.S. Army, Charles L.
Grant left the service to become a high school English teacher in
1964. He taught for a full decade, began selling magazine fiction
in the late 1960s, and in 1975, became a fulltime writer.

His first science fiction novel was published a year later. Grant
produced three more novels in this genre before turning his main
attention to horror, where he soon achieved solid and lasting success. Such novels as The Nestling (1982) and The Pet (1986) are
modern classics, and his Shadows series of edited horror tales are
World Fantasy Award winners. (Grant is also a Nebula Award winner for his science fiction.)

Charlie's special domain is Oxrun Station, the fictional town he
created in 1977 (beginning with The Hour of the Oxrun Dead), a
middle-class village in western Connecticut which has served as an
ideal background for most of his quietly horrific works.

"One Life, In An Hourglass," however, is set in Bradbury country—in Green Town, Illinois, the arena where Cooger and Dark's
Pandemonium Shadow Show arrived to set up its tents one night
in late October (as told in Bradbury's Something Wicked This
Way Comes). Elegant, smooth-tongued, hypnotic Mr. Dark pre-
sided over this carnival of evil, and it is his pervasive and lasting
influence, once the carnival has come and gone, that motivates
Cora Fallman in Grant's offbeat tale.

The setting may be Bradbury's, but the mood and neatly sardonic plot are pure Charles Grant.

W.F. N.

Demons walked the halls in the long hour past sunset, and gargoyles leered through the bedroom windows, moving with the branches of the deep maple outside. The carpet had been woven from human hair, still growing at the edges. The mirror over the dresser had been forged from cold flame that continued to escape from a crack in the lower corner. Dust turned grey along the baseboards. Water dripped in the kitchen. In the closet, behind the clothes, eyes that were slanted, swaying, each a different color, all of them staring.

In the milk-glass scalloped cover of the ceiling light, the dark shadows of corpses. Spiders, moths, a horse-fly, gnats; cleaned out once a month and there once again by the end of the week.

The lingering stench of dried blood.

Cora put the book down beside her on the mattress, adjusted the two pillows behind her back, and rubbed her eyes until the pain forced her to stop. When her vision cleared, sparks and flares faded, everything was gone but the dead insects; when her vision cleared, she was alone.

A small, second-floor apartment in a large house on Parleroad Lane. Front room, kitchen, bedroom, bathroom. Old wallpaper, old furniture, old sounds when the floorboards were trod upon in the silence.

She stretched her legs out, making them rigid, relaxing them, wiggling her toes. Not bad legs, she decided, examining them by the light of the dime store lamp on the nightstand. A little fleshy around the thighs, not as taut as she'd like, but not bad legs for a woman a zillion years older than she wanted to be. The rest of her wasn't all that bad, either. Her arms, when she lifted them, had no discernible flab; her breasts, when she peered down at them, were too small to develop much sag; her tummy had just the slightest bulge in spite of the garbage she usually ate for dinner. What the hell. All in all, not at all bad.

It just wasn't great.

Her palm itched; she scratched it lightly so it wouldn't tickle.

Then she scratched hard along her scalp, hair once in a while snagging on a nail, finished by clasping her hands behind her head, blowing out a breath as warm as the air around her, lifting her knees and looking between them to the dresser, the mirror, the flowers she had taped around the thin wood frame. Most of them were dead. A few brittle petals scattered among the bottles of perfume and nail polish, the tray that held bobby pins and paper clips and a single-garnet necklace and whatever else she couldn't be bothered to put away.

A slip hung halfway out of a half open drawer.

She couldn't see it, but she knew that the pleated skirt she had worn that day lay on the floor, huddled where it had been dropped.

Pigsty, she thought without a moment's concern.

It didn't matter; she wouldn't be here that long.

She swung her legs over the side of the bed and sat up, stared at her feet, sniffed, stared at the wall, and listened to the hushed voice of the street creeping in through the open window—the trees whispering to each other, someone walking a dog and talking to it loudly, music from down the block, cars up on Main Street.

She listened.

She reached up under her t-shirt and scratched at her ribs.

For crying out loud, Cora, make up your mind.

Something in her throat, then—a sob, maybe, or a laugh. Whatever it was, it marked her indecision. Her apprehension. Her belief that this was the year it would happen. All the waiting was over. All her nightmares turned to dreams. Never before, not since the first time she had returned to Green Town, in autumn, in October, had she felt this way. The other times were only wishes; this time, she was certain.

It frightened her.

What if . . . ? she wondered, and wouldn't let herself wonder anymore.

Hello, child, he had said.
I'm not a child, I'm sixteen.

* * *

She stood and stretched her arms toward the ceiling, spread her fingers, and waited until she felt the muscles edge toward the lip of a cramp. A sigh when she heard whispering in the front room. She stood with a shake of her head and walked into the front room, dropped onto the overstuffed couch, crossed her legs.

"Okay," she said. "What do you think?"

An overstuffed armchair to the left of the couch, both facing a console television Keith had given her as a surprise. A copper-and-glass coffee table cluttered with magazines, opened mail, old catalogues, several cut-glass tumblers with hardened milk on the bottom. The table had been Johnny's gift—to force, he had said with a sailor's rolling laugh, this crazy room back into the twentieth century. It hadn't. The standing lamps were fringed, the walls papered with twining daisies and stalwart ivy, the sideboard by the window Victorian ornate. The seashell ashtray on the table next to the couch had been carried back from Maine by the ever-anxious Rex. He had thought it cute; she had never used it.

"Well?"

On the wall beside the television, the fireplace. Pure ornament now, because it had been plugged up by the landlord before she'd returned the third or fourth time, she couldn't really remember. On the mantel were several framed pictures—Johnny and her, Keith and her, Rex and her, Drake and her, and one of her alone, down in the back garden the day she'd turned sixteen.

And on the mantel as well, four hourglasses. Faceted crystal. Round walnut top, square walnut base. The first three were full of grey at the bottom, their tops long since empty; the last one had nearly run out, running slowly.

So very slowly.

Well, Miss Sixteen, he had said, I would say you're about the most beautiful creature I have ever seen in my life.
Liar, she had answered with a giggle.
He smiled.
She shivered, out there in the meadow, Mother's shawl around

her shoulders. Shivered again when he brushed a tender thumb
across her cheek.

Miss Sixteen, he had whispered.

Cora, she had answered, half closing her eyes, lips opening just
a little. Cora Fallman.

Ah, he said, and you can call me Mr. Dark.

Her foot tapped the air impatiently. "Well?"

Pewter everywhere—mugs and bowls and vases and trays and
small pitchers and a creamer she had discovered in a Quebec
shop last summer.

No one spoke.

Her foot stilled.

"Helpless," she muttered, slapping the cushions, pushing herself to her feet. "What good are you?"

Not much, she answered for them, the ghosts and memories
of her past, and returned to the bedroom where she posed in
front of the dresser mirror, pouting, pursing her lips, a sideways
coy glance, chin tucked against her shoulder, chest out and elbows back, finally standing back and ordering someone, for God's
sake, to make up their minds before she lost hers.

It isn't mind, it's nerve, something said into her ear.

She nodded.

Nerve is right, but nervous is better.

Yet, if she didn't leave now, didn't go out there as she'd done
a hundred times in thirty years, he might leave without her.

Quickly, before she could change her mind, she pulled herself
into a sweater, a fresh pair of jeans, low boots, and a down jacket.
A check to be sure all the windows were locked, a furtive glance
at the last hourglass and a faint shudder of fear, and she hurried
down two flights of stairs, paused in the vestibule to check her
pockets for the house key, then out to the sidewalk, into the
night.

She didn't run, but the streets passed her by; she didn't look
around, but she knew the houses just the same—the big ones,
the old ones, the here and there new ones that somehow instantly fit, as if Green Town wouldn't permit even a single shin-
gle to clash. Pumpkins on the porches. Ears of maize tied to the
doors. Witches and black cats in cardboard in the windows.

It had always been that way. Always. It was what she liked about the place—the world went to the moon, the world went to Mars, the world sometimes went to war, but Green Town never changed. It had found what it needed and threw out all the rest; it found what it liked and somehow made it adapt.

Sometimes, though, it was disconcerting.

Once, she had arrived from New York City, and the change nearly terrified her; once, she had driven in from Dallas and had nearly driven right back out again.

But she had stayed nonetheless.

Each time, she had stayed.

Until Halloween was over, and she was still alone, and had to go.

Come with me, Cora Fallman.
I will. God, yes, I will.

Rolfe's moon meadow was empty.

She stood there, the town far behind her, and watched the sky for a while. Too soon, of course. She knew that. Yet she couldn't take a chance that he might come early, look around, not like what he saw, and leave again on the wind. So she waited, stamping her feet, rubbing her hands, cursing herself for forgetting her gloves. She walked a little to get the blood going, wandered over to the railroad tracks and knelt beside the northbound rail. A palm on cold iron. No vibration. Nothing there.

"Okay," she said to the black tree-wall on the other side. "No big deal, I'll come back tomorrow."

No big deal, she thought as she trudged across the crumbling furrows, kicking at stunted stalks of corn long since gone to harvest; the hell it isn't.

Sleep came with dreams.

The hourglass ran.

When she woke up, the dreams were still there, scuttling away into the corners as she rubbed her eyes and realized her lips were pulled back in a grin.

Tonight.

She knew it.

Good Lord, it was tonight.

She laughed in the shower, swallowing water and sputtering laughter. She laughed downstairs at breakfast, for the first time in ages not angry that her home had been turned into a boarding-house by a family she didn't know, the only rule of sale being that they save her an apartment in the attic. She dressed as gaily as possible for a walk downtown, intending to say goodbye at last and not at all feeling sorry.

Tonight. Good Lord, tonight.

But when she reached Main Street, her mood was tempered by dark clouds creeping around the edge of town. No, not rain. Not today. It wouldn't dare. By contrast, the circle of blue above the shops, the bars, the First National Bank, was almost too bright to look at, the air like thin ice, the breeze that teased her around each corner a chilly caress she didn't mind.

"Hey, Cora!"

Amazingly, perhaps miraculously, the United Cigar Store was still there. The wooden Cherokee Indian, however, had been taken inside; protection against vandals who had painted it orange five Halloweens before.

Not everything remained the same; not everything could be saved.

"Cora, hey!"

At the corner she turned and smiled as a young man, lank and blond and red-cheeked and running, waved at her to stop, hang on, hold up a minute. He had to grab a lamppost to keep from skidding into the street, and she grabbed his hand to steady him while he exaggerated gasping, his other hand clamped dramatically to his chest.

"I've been calling you for ages," he said. "Where were you, dreamland?"

She shrugged. "Looking around, that's all. Memories. You know."

They had met when she'd stepped off the bus in front of the barbershop three days ago. A collision, actually. He'd been carrying a crate of fruit to the greengrocer down the block, and she'd been trying to make sure she wouldn't trip over her own well-traveled suitcase. Fruit and underwear, then, all over the pavement. Anger to laughter. Hands helping her to her feet, chasing after a nightgown that had decided to ride the wind to Indiana.

Dinner that night.

Lunch the next day.

She felt no guilt at all since she hadn't known, not then, that she'd be leaving him so soon. And even if she had known, there would have only been relief—Parker Arnold wouldn't end up like Keith and Rex and all the rest.

A finger tapped her forehead lightly. "Hey, in there."

She giggled. "Sorry."

She took his arm and let him lead her across the street, accepting an invitation to a late lunch at one of the new places a few blocks on. Why not? she thought. A free meal, a few laughs, and when I'm gone, he'll find someone else he thinks he loves.

You are not going, young lady, and that's final.
Mother!
Stop your caterwauling! You sound like a spoiled child!
Mother, you're not going to stop me. He loves me.
You're only sixteen, don't be foolish.
I am not being foolish.
And you are not going.

They sat at a table near the window, in the Ploughman's Lunch, and watched the pedestrians dodge the traffic, each other, and hold the line against the increasing wind. She couldn't see the clouds, but even inside she could feel the storm coming.

Him, she prayed. Please let it be him.

"Too bad," Parker said, using his fork to point at the weather outside.

"It won't last."

"I mean, the rain. Sure looks like it."

A slight pressure against her knee. She almost frowned.

He sighed. "It would have been great."

Sometimes, even in the short time that she'd known him, Parker could exasperate her with his enigmatic speech. She figured he read too many plays from the 1940s—lots of meaningful pauses and symbols and such. He was a teacher, after all; it was probably in his blood.

She poked him with a spoon. "Would you mind explaining just what the hell you're talking about?"

He winced.

She stuck out her tongue playfully. He didn't like swearing; it almost made him cute.

"The carnival thing."

The pressure against her knee increased just enough for her to realize it was no accident.

She ignored it. "What carnival thing?"

He fumbled in his back pocket, nearly knocking over his water glass, pulled out a folded sheet of paper, and dropped it next to her plate.

She gaped at it.

"It won't bite, you know," he said with a laugh.

Yes, it will. Lord, yes, it will.

Carefully, as if it were a cursed Egyptian scroll, she smoothed it out on the tablecloth. Closed her eyes. Felt her breath catch and hitch in her lungs. Felt her heart try to claw its way free.

Cooger and Dark's Pandemonium Shadow Show

She didn't have to read any more.

A woman walked past their table, turned, and looked over Parker's shoulder. "Excuse me," she said. "I don't mean to be forward, but . . . don't I know you?"

Cora blinked shadowtears from her eyes and looked up.

The woman, in a topcoat and veiled hat, the veil pinned up, was too heavily made up for her age to be ignored. Fifty-five, sixty, and obviously not what she saw in the mirror. She smiled when Parker twisted around to look up at her, smiled at Cora expectantly.

"I don't think so," Cora answered politely.

The woman's smile trembled, a white-gloved hand pointing to her own breast. "Eileen Islin. Thirty years ago. We worked in the bank?" The smile vanished, snapped off. The woman stepped away. "Oh, of course not, forgive me." She held her black purse tight against her side. "Forgive me," she said to Parker. "I didn't mean . . ." Another look. "I'm sorry, but you look *so much* like her, I thought . . . I'm sorry."

And she was gone.

Cora let her eyes close.

"Now that," said Parker, "was one weird lady."

No, she thought. Just one with a memory too close for comfort.

It was bound to happen sooner or later, this time. She should have stayed in her rooms the way she usually did. But Parker had drawn her out, let her see the town again, and she hadn't been able to resist. Again. As she hadn't resisted with Keith and Rex and Johnny and Drake.

Suddenly she yanked her napkin from her lap and dropped it over her plate. Stood. Made a false hasty check of her watch. "Oh Lord, I just remembered something," she explained as Parker began a protest. "I'll call you later, all right?" A sweet smile, a kiss to his cheek. A whisper in his ear: "I'll call you, don't worry."

The clouds were closer, heavier, the circle of blue shrinking as the wind raced through her hair.

She tried not to cry out, to dance, to wave her arms, to kiss every man she passed as she raced home. She tried not to smell every autumn blossom in every garden, not to return every Halloween pumpkin's grin. She tried not to weep when she burst into the living room and stood before the mantel.

The last hourglass was nearly empty.

"Soon," she whispered to it. "Soon."

But not soon enough.

She paced through each room, willing the sun to make its move, willing the moon to begin its climb.

She paced and laughed and clapped her hands and felt the joy; paced and laughed and clapped her hands and felt the cold.

Mother, let me out!
You will stay in there, child, until you come to your senses.
Mother, please! He's waiting!
Go to bed, Cora. There's nothing more you can do.

She didn't know how to dress and so didn't bother to change. It didn't matter. He would take her no matter what. Gloves this time, however, and a muffler to keep the wind from sluicing down her neck.

She hurried without running.

She listened for the sound of the calliope and train.

The storm flicked lightning over the western horizon.

Impatience grabbed her at last, and she ran across the deserted meadow, leaves flying like startled bats around her head, glaring up at the sky, glaring at the empty tracks, pressing her fists to her temples to stop the pounding there.

When exhaustion finally stopped her, dropped her to her knees, she ordered herself to be patient. It was the only way. She had waited this long, she could wait a few minutes longer.

The cold of the ground seeped through her jeans. The wind finally slowed, though the lightning moved closer. She watched the flaring white warily, having seen it before, knowing what it could do, and what it had done. It shouldn't be here. Not this year. He was coming, not the fire.

"I'll be waiting, Miss Sixteen."

"Yes."

"But if you fail—"

"No, don't say that!"

"I'll be waiting nevertheless. Sometime, but always here."

"But—"

And he had laughed and he had kissed her and he had pressed into her hands an exquisitely wrought hourglass of crystal and wood: and he had whispered that Time would be hers always so long as she knew how to fill it and protect it with the fire of their love.

"Corny," she whispered and grinned to the ground, to the approaching storm, to the dark. "God, that was so corny."

The fire of their love.

How sweet sixteen that was.

How agonizingly true.

"So where are you?" she demanded of the dark and Mr. Dark. "Where the hell are you?"

A glow, white and bobbing at the meadow's far edge.

Holding back a cry, she leapt to her feet and pushed at her hair and dusted the weeds and dirt from her knees and watched the light bounce toward her, flaring at the belly of the storm overhead, blinding her for a moment, cutting a silver path across the meadow. She wanted to run toward it, but commanded herself to remain calm. He mustn't see her as too anxious; he mustn't know his power.

"Cora?"

She almost screamed.

The light grew, and grew brighter.

"Cora?"

It wasn't him.

Damn, it wasn't him!

Before she could duck, veer away, somehow find a hole in the night to cover her, the flashlight swept over her face, away and abruptly back. Parker's footsteps on the ground sounded like the dirge of hollow drums.

"Hey, there you are!"

Cora felt the tears and didn't bother to hide them.

"Cora," Parker said, wrapping an arm around her waist. "God, I'm glad I found you. You ran away so fast this afternoon, I didn't get a chance to tell you where the exhibit was. I waited at the library for over an hour before—"

"Exhibit?" She pushed him away, but gently, listening to her voice grow too suddenly old. "What exhibit?"

"The flyer I showed you," he said, as if she should have known. "You know, that carnival exhibit. Didn't you read it?"

No, she thought. Lord, no, not all.

He chuckled. "I didn't think so." He hugged her again around the waist, and this time she didn't, couldn't remove his hand. "So I went to your rooms, and the landlady let me in because we were so worried when you didn't answer. As soon as I saw you weren't there, I had a thought. I don't know why, but I did." His face, grinned, in a burst of lightning, as he passed the beam over the meadow. "Pretty smart, huh?"

Not here, she thought: he won't be here, not this year.

A finger nestled under her chin. "Hey, don't cry. I didn't mean to scare you. Honest."

Not here.

He put something into her hands, turning her so that the wind was at his back, so that he sheltered her. "This came for you after you'd left."

Weary; so weary as her fingers, no longer young, no longer nimble, tore the gaily wrapped package open and held its contents to her chest.

"Hey," he said, putting the beam on her prize. "Hey, you've got some of those on the mantel, right?" The beam shifted, and she averted her face, covered it with a free hand. "Sorry again. But it's beautiful, you know. The hourglass, I mean. That wasn't sand in the others, though, was it? It didn't look like it."

"No," she said quietly, to hide the years that sped toward her on the lightning.

He laughed. "Looked like ashes, actually. My aunt has my uncle on the mantel. Morbid, I'll tell you."

"Yes," she whispered.

He leaned closer, the beam tightening, brightening. "Damn, this one's empty. I think you got gypped."

For the first time that night, there was thunder.

She almost laughed at the melodramatics of it, and the storm.

His grip on her waist strengthened, the smell of him now and of his autumn-cold clothes. "Cora." Hoarsely.

She inhaled slowly, deeply, and felt the warmth, felt the heat; she lowered herself and him to the ground where she fumbled off the top of the hourglass *he* had sent her. He had. So he still loved her. And this just wasn't the time, this just wasn't the year.

"What . . . what are you going to put in it?" Parker wanted to know, lightly kissing her brow.

The hourglass between them.

The heat of her as she kissed him back.

"It's dumb," he said breathlessly, pulling away for a second. "It's really dumb, but I really think I love you."

"And I do love you," she answered, bringing him back. "For a time."

Embracing him, and kissing him.

"For a time."

Letting him know the fire of her love.

TWO O'CLOCK SESSION

Richard Matheson

Not many fantasy writers become legends in their own time, but Richard Matheson certainly lives up to the title of his published bibliography, He Is Legend. *Of course, this title honors one of the author's best-known science fiction/horror novels,* I Am Legend, *a long-established classic.*

Matheson's award-winning 900-page Collected Stories, *issued in 1989, contains 86 of his 100-plus shorter fictional works. He has published another ten novels, including* The Shrinking Man, A Stir of Echoes *and* Bid Time Return. *Additionally, he has written more than 80 scripts for television, many for Rod Serling's* Twilight Zone, *plus individual TV films such as* Duel, The Night Stalker, *and his recent (1990)* Dreamer of Oz. *Also to his credit, some 20 feature films, headed by* The Incredible Shrinking Man, The Legend of Hell House, *and* Somewhere in Time.

In 1950, Richard Matheson's first printed story, "Born of Man and Woman," earned him immediate recognition, and he hasn't slowed down since.

Ray Bradbury was an admitted early influence. The story Matheson has written for The Bradbury Chronicles *(dealing with the rite of passage beyond death) subtly echoes "The April Witch," wherein Bradbury's Cecy sends her mind soaring out into other bodies.*

This one will stick like a burr in your memory.

W.F.N.

The breakthrough came at two forty-one. Until that time, Maureen had done little more than repeat the bitter litany against her parents and brother.

"I have nothing to live for," she said then. "Absolutely nothing."

Dr. Volker didn't respond, but felt a tremor of excitement in himself. He'd been waiting for this.

He gazed at the young woman lying on his office couch. She was staring at the ceiling. What was she thinking? he wondered. He didn't dare to speak. He didn't want to break in on those thoughts, whatever they might be.

At last, Maureen spoke again. "I guess you didn't hear that," she said.

"I heard," Dr. Volker replied.

"No reaction then?" she asked, an edge of hostility in her voice. "No sage comment?"

"Like what?" he asked.

"Oh, God, don't start that again," she said. "Respond with an answer, not another goddamn question."

"I'm sorry," Dr. Volker said. "I didn't mean to make you angry."

"Well, it *did* make me angry! It made me—!" Her voice broke off with a shuddering throat sound. "You don't care," she said then.

"Of course I care," he told her. "What have I ever done to make you think I don't care?"

"*I said I have nothing to live for.*" Maureen's tone was almost venomous now.

"And—?" he asked.

"What do you mean *and?*" she snapped.

"And what does that make you feel like?"

The young woman shifted restlessly on the couch, her face distorted by anger. "It makes me feel like *shit!*" she said. "Is that precise enough for you, God damn it! I feel like *shit!* I don't want to live!"

Closer, Volker thought. A shiver of elation laced across his back. He was glad the young woman was turned away from him. He didn't want her to know how he felt.

"And—?" he said again.

"Damn it to hell!" Maureen raged. "Is that all you can say?!"

"Did *you* hear what *you* said?" Volker asked as calmly as he could.

"About what? About having nothing to live for? About wanting to *die?*"

"You didn't use the word *die* before," he corrected.

"Oh, big deal!" she cried. "I apologize! I said I don't want to live! Anyone else would assume from that that I want to die! But not you!"

"Why do you want to die?" Volker winced a little. He shouldn't have said that.

Maureen's silence verified his reaction. It became so still in the office that he heard the sound of traffic passing on the boulevard. He cleared his throat, hoping that he hadn't made a mistake and lost the moment.

He wanted to speak but knew that he had to wait. He stared at the young woman on the couch. Don't leave me now, he thought. Stay with it. *Please.* It's been such a long time.

The young woman sighed wearily and closed her eyes.

"Have you nothing more to say?" he asked.

Her eyes snapped open and she twisted around to glare at him. "If I said what I wanted to say, your hair would turn white," she said, almost snarling the words.

"Maureen," he said patiently.

"*What?*"

"My hair is already white."

Her laugh was a humorless bark of acknowledgment. "Yes, it is," she said. "You're old. And decrepit."

"And you're young?" he asked.

"Young and . . ." She hesitated. "Young and miserable. Young and lost. Young and empty. Young and cold, without hope. Oh, *God!*" she cried in pain. "I want to die! I want to die! I'm going to see to it!"

Dr. Volker swallowed dryly. "See to what?" he asked.

"God damn it, are you stupid or something?" she lashed out at him. "Don't you understand English?"

"Help me to understand," he said. His pulsebeat had quickened now. He was so close, so close.

Silence again. Oh, dear Lord, have I lost her again? he thought. How many sessions was it going to take?

He had to risk advancing. "See to what?" he asked.

The young woman stared at the ceiling.

"See to what, Maureen?" he asked.

"Leave me alone," she told him miserably. "You're no better than the rest of them. My father. My mother. My brother."

Oh, Christ! Volker clenched his teeth. Not the goddamn litany again!

"My father raped me, did you know that?" Maureen said. "Did I tell you that? Tell you that I was only seven when it happened? Tell you that my mother did nothing about it? That my brother laughed at me when I told him? Did I tell you that?"

Volker closed his eyes. Only about a thousand times, he thought.

He forced himself to open his eyes. "Maureen, you were on to something before," he risked.

"What do you mean?" she demanded.

Oh, no, he thought, chilled. But he couldn't stop now. "You said you wanted to die. You said—"

The young woman twitched violently on the couch, her head rolling to the right on the pillow, eyes closed.

"No!" Volker drove a fist down on the arm of his chair.

One more failure.

When the young woman sat up, he handed her a glass of water.

Jane Winslow drank it all in one, continuous swallow, then handed back the glass. "Anything?" she asked.

"Oh . . ." He exhaled tiredly. "The usual. We're right on top of it, but she backs off. She just can't face it." He shook his head. "Poor Maureen. I'm afraid it's going to be a long, long time before she's free to move on." He sighed in frustration. "Are you ready for the next one?"

She nodded.

At three o'clock she lay back on the couch and drew in long, deep breaths. She trembled for a while, then lay still.

"Arthur?" Dr. Volker said.

Jane Winslow opened her eyes.

"How are you today?"

"How *should* I be?" Arthur said bitterly.

Dr. Volker rubbed fingers over his eyes. Helping them was difficult. My God, how difficult. He had to keep trying though. He had no choice.

"So, how's life treating you, Arthur?" he asked.

A LAKE OF SUMMER

Chad Oliver

Back in the long lost summer of 1951, when I was editing the Ray
Bradbury Review, *I asked Chad Oliver to be a contributor. He
promptly agreed, happy to be part of a tribute to a writer who had
helped shape his own beginning career in science fiction and fantasy.*

*And indeed, in 1951, Chad's career was just beginning. He had
made his first professional story sale just a year earlier, and was
still a year away from publication of his first novel,* The Mists of
Dawn. *(Seven more Oliver novels have seen print since then, including two award-winning Westerns.)*

*Texas born and bred, with a proud love for that sprawling state,
Oliver has actually followed a double trail in his creative life. He
continues to be highly regarded as a science fiction writer with 70
short stories and novelettes to his credit, in addition to his six SF
novels, but his primary career has been as a professional anthropologist. He still teaches this subject at the University of Texas at
Austin as a full professor. He is a recipient of the University's
Presidential Award for Teaching Excellence. Having spent a year
in East Africa as a research anthropologist for the National Science
Foundation, Chad is also the author of an introductory textbook,*
The Discovery of Humanity.

*Ray Bradbury's poetic celebration of the American Heartland
was first expressed in his initial collection,* Dark Carnival, *in 1947—
a book that profoundly affected young nineteen-year-old Chad Oliver. He, too, had grown up loving forests and lakes and small
towns, and when asked for a contribution to this book, Chad turned*

his thoughts back to such nostalgia-haunted boyhood towns to create "A Lake of Summer."

Welcome back, Chad, to Bradbury country.

W.F.N.

There is a lake of summer that is just small enough for a boy of twelve to swim across in an emergency. When the wind blows and the whitecaps foam, it is big enough for the waves to touch strange shores.

There is a young time when all things are possible. Not all of them are good things. But some of them are better than anything that comes later.

A lake of summer when you are twelve holds more than sunfish and crawdads and painted turtles and flat green lilypads with sweet white flowers. It contains miracles if you can find them. It holds deep wavering shadows that are far older than the years of a boy's life.

It was that kind of summer for Douglas.

It was a summer when anything might happen.

It began when they told him about Larson.

"It was a winter fire," the people said. They were the ones who always knew everything. They lived near the lake the whole year round. "Wiped out the farm and Old Larson both. Ain't nothing there now. Just charred junk." They said it almost with pleasure, as though Larson had been asking for trouble.

"The fire got it all?" Douglas could not talk above a whisper. The world he knew had shaken under him.

"Everything," the people said.

"Even the cats?"

"Don't rightly know." Who cared about half-wild cats that had lived in a sagging barn?

"Even the mules?"

"I think one lived through it," somebody said. Mules were worth more than cats. They were noticed.

"You stay away from Larson's place," Mom said. "I don't want you going there, not ever again."

That seemed odd. She had never said that to Douglas before. All the kids went to Larson's farm, always had. If it had burned, if it was all gone, what was the danger?

Douglas did not lie to his mother about important things. Not unless he absolutely had to. His way was to say nothing at all.

The very first chance he had, two days after arriving at the lake of summer—its name was Sky Lake, but not to Douglas— he went to Larson's.

He had to walk, of course. His feet had not hardened yet from a summer without shoes. He hated walking to Larson's in his sneakers. It felt all wrong.

The way was as known to him as the rhythms of his heart. The winding narrow road, more sand than dirt, bending to the left, curving around the lake toward the far side. The woods crowded the road. It was never called a forest. It was always the woods, pure and simple.

Douglas skirted the prickly brush, alive with wax-red berries. He breathed the dry scent of old pines and the smell of summer sunlight.

It didn't take him long. Perhaps an hour. There was nothing on the road. No cars; they were very rare in these parts. No wagons. No men or women or children. It was almost always that way. The rutted road to Larson's was forever the same, if forever meant six years in the life of a boy.

Not this time.

The people with the eager mouths had told the truth, or what they believed to be the truth.

Something in Douglas knotted and came close to death. It was the first enormous loss he had ever known. It hurt.

The small unpainted wooden farmhouse where Larson had lived alone for God only knew how many years had vanished. There were some black charred beams and a dark square outline in the dirt. No grass grew there. Two of the corner posts on the weathered barn were still in place, though blackened by fire. The roof had collapsed, the plank-board walls had caved in. The hay bales were long ashes, mostly blown away by the wind. There

was no sign of the cats. They had loved that barn. It was close
to heaven for a mouser.

The slat-fenced corral was more or less intact, but the kid-
tolerant old mules were gone. There was no tractor, of course.
Douglas looked at the rusting harrow and cultivator and plow,
and his heart sank. Larson had never been much for spit-and-
polish, but his farm equipment—the tools of his life—was always
in operating condition.

The rickety grape arbor seemed okay, but the fruit trees had
an oddly wild look to them and weeds were choking Larson's
small fields and gardens.

Douglas listened for the clucking hen who had needed no
rooster to protect her chicks from the cats. The rooster had strutted around as though he were lord of the earth, but that fearless
hen ran the barnyard. There was no chicken, hen, or rooster.

The sun-splashed silence was deafening.

"Larson!" Douglas called. "Larson!"

It was never "Mr. Larson," and never "sir," although Douglas
had been taught his manners. He didn't even know whether Larson was the old man's first name or his last. Larson was always
just called Larson, though sometimes letters came that spelled
his name with an "e" rather than an "o," and that was the way
of it.

"Larson!"

There was no answer. Douglas had not expected one.

"Larson," he said more quietly.

Then he turned and started back toward the cabin on the lake.
His shoe-heavy steps were slow in the afternoon sun.

Larson was a part of the magic of Sky Lake. There could be
no lake of summer without him.

All winter Douglas dreamed about that lake. It was in Michigan, not far from the Illinois border, but it was also in another
world, a world as remote from Douglas' hometown as the planet
Mars.

Douglas dreamed of specific things.

First, always, there was the frogsound. At night, with his window open on the lake side, he could sometimes hear lapping
waves when the wind was right. He could *always* hear the frogs.

Their wonderful croak-singing was loud and continuous. It circled the lake with a protective enchantment. The friendly music of the frogs was very important. It prevented the terrible swamp dreams from coming. There was no greater pleasure in Douglas' life than drifting off to sleep with the soothing frog songs in his ears.

Then there was running barefoot through the clean white sand to the clear lake waters with the sun turning your still-thin body brown. The slope of the lake was gentle. You could run until the water—cool, but not cold—was up to your waist, and then launch yourself like a torpedo. Douglas had a rowboat. The paint was flaking and there was enough of a leak so that he carried a coffee can for a bailer. No matter. He liked to row the boat backwards so that he could see where he was going. He would surprise the small sunning turtles on the lilypads and rocks near the shore. When they scuttled into the water, Douglas would ship his oars and dive over the stern of the rowboat.

Magic! Open your eyes underwater. A translucent world, the sunlight filtered by water, stalks undulating in the currents, fish sometimes, big old sunfish twisting out of your way, their orange and blue bodies glistening. And the turtles! How frantically they swam, diving down, always down, but they were not fast. Douglas could catch them easily unless he lost sight of them in the murky depths. Catch them from behind and they can't bite you. . . .

He didn't hurt the turtles, just kept them for a time and fed them bits of fish and dead flies, then let them go. Once, he had taken a washtub filled with turtles back to his house in Illinois. Mom hadn't been very happy, and Dad had made him keep the washtub in the basement. Douglas had been very careful with his little turtles; the largest was no bigger than his hand. He cleaned the water every day and gave them plenty of food. Nobody told him that turtles *had* to have sunlight. All of them died. They stank. He buried the peeling shells and the dead eyes and all the oozing stuff in his backyard. He did not cry, but he was sorry.

There was a hammock on the screened porch of the cabin. The porch faced Sky Lake, as did the porches of all the other cabins. The lake of summer was the focal point of this universe. Besides, that was where the breeze came from.

For a dime, Douglas could get a dripping cold RC Cola and a Milky Way from the general store. He could climb into the hammock with one of his old *G-8 and His Battle Aces* pulps carried in the car with him from Illinois. It did not matter to him how many times he had read the stories. He loved the way the magazines *smelled.* Think of it! A sip of RC, a chewy chunk off the Milky Way bar to mix it with, the lazy murmur of a summer afternoon, and there you were with G-8 and Nippy Weston ("the terrier ace"), Bull Martin ("former All-American halfback"), and the faithful manservant, Battle. (What *was* a manservant, anyway?) You were in the cozy apartment in the end hangar at Le Bourget with the Spads roaring through the gray skies of France and the Germans cooking up some new devilment to obliterate the Allies in the trenches . . .

Larson was in those dreams, as constant and eternal as the frogsounds and G-8 and the ever-unwary turtles.

There he was. A tall man, gangly, an old beaked cap covering his thin, whitening hair. Patched bib overalls and clodhopper shoes that were as hard as rocks. Larson had only one eye, which was a pale blue, and his lined and leathery face was crooked and askew in a pleasant sort of way. Larson was still strong enough to jerk a mule to its knees. He was the kind of man who can fix anything in his world with baling wire—a broken harness, a wood-burning cookstove, a wagon with a dragging spoked wheel.

He would have been called Popeye, whom he somewhat resembled, but Larson did not like the name. Generally, people avoided Larson, except for the kids, and nobody wanted to offend him. Larson was not a weak man, and when he got annoyed he had been known to teach some hard lessons with his anchor-rope fists. He would certainly have been called Swede, except that the Swedish population in the Sky Lake area was so thick that if you hollered "Swede!" half the county converged on your door.

So Larson he was.

Remember the pies? Larson had no children of his own; at any rate, he never spoke of them. Douglas had no idea of whether he had ever been married or not. He thought not. Larson was born to be an eccentric old bachelor. He loved kids as only a childless man can, had a way with them, and somehow when you walked up to Larson's farm there was often a fresh-from-the-oven pie waiting. Apple sometimes, but usually one of those sweet black cherry pies with just a touch of cinnamon on the flaky crust.

Grown-ups didn't quite know what to make of Larson. He was different, that was for sure. He was a loner, and therefore he was suspect. With kids, it was simple. You went up to see Larson because he treated you like you counted for something, and you had fun. He would let you go in his old barn and lie on the hay bales. His cats would spit at an adult, but, with Douglas they came and curled up and purred in the hay. You were always welcome, always free to come and go as you pleased. When Larson was busy with his chores, he might ignore you except for a wink from that one good eye. When he had the time, he would show you the marvels of a farm. Douglas came from a small town, but he was no farmer's son. Larson could tell you stories about animals and plants that became a part of you forever. And, sometimes, there was the pie.

Now, sitting restlessly in his hard wooden chair in the cabin while Mom listened to the Kraft Music Hall on the battery-powered Philco, Douglas felt that something precious had been stolen from him. Bing Crosby was nothing to him, just background noise, and Bob Burns and his buzz-burp bazooka failed to amuse him.

He didn't care what they said about Larson. Larson was as much a part of his summer life as the sunshine and the scent of pine needles.

Dead? Burned? No. No!

If Larson could die, anything could die.

"I don't believe it," Douglas whispered, although he had seen the evidence with his own eyes. "I don't believe it."

"What did you say?" Mom asked, turning the radio down for a moment.

"Nothing, Mom. I'm going to bed."

He slowly climbed the worn wooden stairs to the sleeping loft, and he was very careful blowing out the coal oil light.

He closed his eyes and waited for the frogsound to soothe him. It was late when he slept, and his dreams were empty.

On a day when that summer was more than half over, but before Dad came up from Illinois for his annual ten-day vacation, Douglas took the rowboat out on Sky Lake.

He did not have the strength that would later come to him, but he rowed expertly under a cloudless blue sky. Rowing did not require power; it needed skill and fluid motion, and Douglas had that. His shirtless body was as tan as varnish over a dark knotholed board. His bare feet squished in the seeping water by the red coffee can.

When something is taken from you, you do what is possible with what you have left. Turtle hunting was still possible.

He rowed steadily more than halfway across the lake of summer, angling slightly toward his right. There was a cove there with lots of lilypads and the projecting rocks that the turtles liked. Sky Lake was a lake Douglas could swim across if he had to, but it was not tiny. Douglas was a good swimmer and he could barely make it. It took time to row across that lake. How much time? Does any boy carry a watch on an afternoon in summer?

When he got close to the cove, he turned the boat around, working the oars against each other, enjoying the slight slipping rattle of the oarlocks. He moved stern-first, pushing the water in the opposite direction from normal rowing, so that he was facing where he was going.

You had to see turtles to catch them.

He had a great day.

The little turtles had sectioned green shells with splashes of color along the edges. They dozed in the sun, nearly always off guard, protected by their ancient armor. When they saw Douglas coming, they took their sweet time scrabbling into the water. He could almost grab them off the rocks, but not quite. He could have used a long-handled net, but that was not the point of the game.

Douglas loved diving into the cool clear water, his brown body going in as straight and true as a knife. He liked holding his breath and swimming in the green hush of the underwater world. His arm strokes were more coordinated than the wild flapping of the turtles' stubby clawed little legs. He almost never missed. He had a large bucket crawling with turtles in the boat. He needed a bucket with a lid to keep things under control.

It was such fun that it was hard for him to imagine that other boys did not do this. Grown-ups? The idea was impossible. Girls? They never had the opportunity. This was kid stuff, but it was more than that. It was something for a special boy, not just any boy. Douglas did not dwell on that, but he knew it.

Catching turtles has a way of releasing time. An afternoon can vanish in an instant. This one did. Clock time does not count. It has no meaning here.

The first real change Douglas noticed was that the turtles had stopped their sunning and were slipping into the water before he arrived. The next thing he was aware of was a feeling of cold. The sun was no longer drying the drops of water on his thin shoulders. He wished that he had brought a shirt.

There was no need to turn the boat around to get back to the cabin. He simply has to lever the oars in a more orthodox way.

But suddenly there was a wind. It was a strong wind, blowing toward the cove. Before he could be ready for them, the waves came swelling across the lake. The lilypads bounced and shook, went under and struggled back, only to be drawn under again. The waves began to smack the shore with a crashing he could hear even above the whining wind.

Douglas looked up. The blue sky was gone. There was a boiling blackness.

This was not the friendly darkness of night, a velvet canopy laced with stars. No, this was black and churning. It had hate in it.

Sure enough, the lightning came. It started with a single jagged bolt, smashing straight down, hissing into the water. The instantaneous crack of thunder was like a plank slammed against his ears.

"Now, Douglas, you be careful out there." Mom's voice. How long ago?

Then the storm really hit. It was a solid wall of wet flashing fury. Douglas had never been out in such a storm. His rowboat was tossed around like a cork in a draining bathtub.

Douglas knew that he could not row back across the lake. He certainly could not swim against those waves. He could not stay where he was, a lightning rod bobbing in a leaking rowboat.

And there was something else.

He did not want to beach the boat on the swampy shore of the cove. He had never liked the shoreline there. That was where the bad dreams started. Even in sunshine, with his Daisy BB carbine to protect him, he had always hurried his steps when he circled the cove. There was oozing muck there. Strange ferns arched over crawling things. The willow brush grew in twisted clumps. The tall poplars were dead in their upper branches. They cracked and snapped even in the still weather. They would be showering dead wood now.

Douglas was quite certain that something terrible lived in that place. Not all the time, maybe. But sometimes.

If it had a name, it was a name Douglas had never heard.

It was there now.

Waiting.

Douglas knew that in his bones.

Douglas wiped the driving spray out of his eyes. He recoiled from another stunning smack of sound and electricity that hit within thirty yards of his boat.

There was nowhere else to go, nothing else he could do.

He remembered to dump the turtles. He unfastened the bucket lid and separated it from the bucket. He didn't want the turtles trapped in a sinking coffin with no way out.

Then he just went with the flow. Wind, rain, and smashing waves picked his boat up and hurled it against the cove shore. He felt it hit. It struck hard, but the shore had a spongy yielding texture to it.

Douglas jumped out. He sank in muck up to his knees. He beached the boat as well as he could. It was heavy with water.

Another crooked shaft of lightning sizzled the swamp. The hammer afterblow of the thunder dazed him.

Douglas ran. Or tried to. His bare feet were sucked into the ooze. He felt things crawling between his toes. Imagination? Maybe.

It was tough to walk, let alone run.

He was shaking and crying.

Running?

Perhaps not. But he moved as fast as he could, dragging himself away from the churning lake and toward whatever it was that was waiting for him deep in the dark shoreline of the cove.

* * *

It was not a blur. Douglas experienced each event with an intense clarity.

He heard the snapping of each dead poplar branch. He felt every drop of slashing rain separately. His bare skin reacted to each shift of the howling rain. His feet sensed every change in the structure of the earth: squishy ooze that was colder than it should have been, sharp rocks that cut and sliced, flat grass that gave him a welcome surface to move on.

Strained as he was, he knew that his two most urgent problems were time and distance. Time was suspended in the fury of the storm. No matter how hard he tried to cross it, the swamp seemed endless. He knew he was moving, moving toward the deep swaying woods, but somehow he could not close the distance. It was always the same time and the same place.

The wall of wind was solidly at his back now, shoving him. Even the lightning bolts seemed behind him, held by the lake. It was as though he were being driven. Like a cow. Herded. Toward what?

The awareness of the thing that prowled the shoreline between the swamp and the deep woods permeated every cell in his body. It was not a conscious knowledge. It was way down deep.

Douglas was more afraid than he had ever been.

It wasn't that something was *after* him. No. Something was *waiting* for him. That was worse.

But he had no choice. He kept running, trying to run, fighting, a stab of flame in his lungs, getting closer to the wet pine smell of the woods, eyes half-shut, and then—

A bony hand grabbed his right shoulder.

Douglas screamed.

Some primitive nerve network got through to him before the voice did. A dry musty smell. An old beaked cap that the rain did not touch. A warm clean odor, like freshly washed denim overalls hanging in the sun.

Then the voice.

"Take my hand, boy." Only the trace of an accent. "Chust come along and nothing will hurt you."

Not a ghost voice. Not a skeletal voice.

Larson's voice. His real voice. His only voice.

Douglas grabbed the offered hand. It was hard, sure, tough as anchor rope on a big ship, always had been that way, but it was a hand of flesh and blood. The bones were covered.

Fear flowed out of Douglas like a violent upchuck. Joy suffused him.

Never mind the storm!

Forget the thing that wandered hungrily through the stinking swamp.

He had Larson back.

Larson!

"Larson." He whispered the name.

Larson heard him. Douglas did not know how, in such a storm. There was so much wind, so much noise . . .

But he did. And he said exactly one word in return: "Yes."

Douglas let himself go. He didn't think. He felt no fear. There was a silly grin on his wet face.

Why, everything was just as it should be!

They moved without effort. Douglas knew where they were going and did not question it.

Of course.

Back to the farm.

One pale blue eye twinkled at him across the worn kitchen table. The room was hot, dry, and cozy. Fresh split wood crackled and hissed in the stove. There was a very large slice of black cherry pie on a thick, glazed plate.

Real-for-sure rain pelted the roof. It sounded like marbles dropped on a metal washtub. It sounded like the hail of acorns that ushered in the fall.

Douglas had dried off. He had even managed to comb his sun-bleached hair back with his fingers. Larson had given him an old long-sleeved shirt that had once been blue. It had patches on it. It felt wonderful.

Douglas neither probed nor doubted.

He accepted.

He was totally safe in this place.

He wanted to stay forever.

Gradually, the rain slowed down. Douglas was almost sorry to see it go. The thunder receded. It was far away now. The pie was eaten, the plate shiny. There was a sense of expectancy that was not entirely welcome.

"Yew cannot stay," Larson said. There was a sadness in his voice. Douglas did not know whether it was for Larson or himself. "We must get you home before morning. Your mother, she will be worried."

Worried! That was the understatement of the year.

"I *am* home," Douglas wanted to say. He wanted to say it very much. He knew better than to voice the words.

"Can I see the cats?" he said.

Larson smiled. His teeth were crooked, but there were no stains on them. "Just for a little. There are kittens."

Outside, then. Still dark. A dripping world where stars were just beginning to be born.

The hay-smell in the old wood barn. It was fresh-cut hay, juicy, no decay in it. The cat was there with four kittens. They hardly had their eyes open. Douglas did not know how he could see them so clearly in the dark. He touched the kittens, gently, one by one. He stroked Mama between her velvet ears. She purred.

Out through the farmyard. He didn't have to worry about rusty nails here. Larson kept them picked up. Douglas smelled the mules, heard them shuffling.

The sand road under his bare feet. An instant, an eternal instant, no more, no less. A half-moon silvered the running clouds. He could see the cabin where his mother was. There were buttery lights in the windows.

"Larson, are you okay?" Douglas knew that he could not come any closer than that without risking something infinitely fragile.

Larson smiled. "I have pleasure," he said.

"Will I ever see you again?"

Larson did not answer him at once. He held out his hard knotted hand for his shirt. They both understood that Douglas could not show up in the cabin with that shirt on. There were some questions that were best avoided.

"I do not know, Douglas," he said finally. Douglas was surprised. Larson had not called him by name before. "I think it is up to yew, what yew become."

The words were so thick in Douglas' throat that he almost

choked. He could not say any of them. All that could be said had been said.

Douglas started for the cabin, breaking into a trot. The night air was cool against his bare skin.

He turned once and looked back.

Larson was not there.

Douglas did not have to be told that if he retraced his steps there would be no farm up that bending sandy road. It was not there always.

Just sometimes. For some people.

The reality was a fire-gutted ruin and an old man who no longer lived. One reality.

Douglas felt strange. His heart was hammering as he practically fell through the back door of the cabin. There was heat from the woodstove, light from the lanterns with their glass chimneys. All the neighbors were there.

"Mom," he said.

The tears came. He did not know why.

There was a confusion Douglas did not even try to sort out. Even though it had once been his, this was a world he did not fully understand.

Tense men were gathered in clumps and circles. They had been planning a search in the morning. Some of them carried rifles. Now, they did not know what to do.

Women bustled about, not giving any orders but obviously running things. They cooked and comforted and fussed.

The neighbor kids, all wadded up wide-eyed in the corners, stared at him with a mixture of relief and regret. They did not often get to stay up so late. He saw some envy in their eyes.

Douglas was scared. Not as frightened as he had been in the swamp. More scared than he had ever been with Larson.

Mom. "Where *have* you been? I've been worried sick." Rubbing her hands together, wanting to comfort him, not knowing how.

"The storm," he said. The words ran together. "It came up so fast. I had to beach the boat. I got lost in the swamp." Sort of true. Not completely a lie.

Mom. "You're all dry. Even your pants. I don't understand how . . ."

"I found shelter." Try to sound like a real woodsman. "A big fallen tree I could get under. I just waited until it was all over, and then I came home as soon as I could." Oh, sort of true!

"You're going to have some hot oatmeal right now, young man." In her view, oatmeal could cure anything, maybe even death itself. "Douglas! Don't you *ever* scare me like that again."

"I'm sorry, Mom."

Now she could embrace him. He could feel her trembling. They tried to ignore the gawkers.

He ate the oatmeal. He didn't want it. He was full of black cherry pie. It seemed to him that he ate buckets of oatmeal.

He could not tell them anything, of course. Not even Mom.

He shivered. It was not from cold, and certainly not from hunger. He felt loved but not entirely *safe*. Peculiar.

Mom. "You're going to march right off to bed this minute. Catch your death, that's what you'll do if you don't take care!"

Douglas eyed the people in the cabin. He had never seen the cabin so crowded. They all seemed to be strangers, although he knew their faces. He remembered his manners. "Thank you," he said. "Sorry."

He almost ran up the old stairs, his bare feet sensing the grain of the worn wood.

He shucked his shorts, yanked on his pajamas. They were clean and a little stiff, like from too much starch.

He piled into his bed, pushing the wooden shutter on the window open. He had to hear the lake.

He closed his eyes. The trick was to get to sleep before Mom came up and before the frogsound stopped. The frogs were at it late because of the heavy rain. Soon, it would be morning. It would be too quiet then.

He tried not to be frightened. He felt something slipping away from him.

Don't let it go. Don't ever let it go. Hold on to it. Make it a part of you. Never think about it but never forget it.

He pulled the frogsound inside of him, letting it soothe him.

He kept his eyes tight shut.

"Larson," he whispered once.

And then Douglas slept, and he dreamed the dreams that were forever dreams.

THE OBSESSION

William Relling Jr.

Bill Relling has been a truck driver, camp counselor, carnival ride operator, stock boy, warehouseman, librarian, musician, hospital orderly, magazine editor, and junior high school teacher. All prior to 1983. Since then he's been a fulltime writer in Los Angeles, with fiction appearing in such volumes as The Year's Best Horror Stories. His first horror novel, Brujo, was published in 1986, and he's sold several more over the past five years, including a mainstream thriller, Azriel, and a new story collection, The Infinite Man.

Relling admits to a warm fondness for Ray Bradbury's outré "Family" of creatures featured in a series of delightfully offbeat short stories: "The Homecoming," "The Traveler," "The April Witch," "West of October," and "Uncle Einar." It is this latter story, concerning Bradbury's bizarre gentleman with sea-green wings, that prompted Bill Relling to contribute a Family story to The Bradbury Chronicles. Again, we meet the gentle, unassuming Einar, who is thrust into a very unusual (and highly amusing) situation in which he encounters an old enemy seemingly bent on his destruction.

A deft mix of ancient myth and modern hype, "The Obsession" is fresh, funny, and far out—a worthy addition to Bradbury's Family Chronicles.

W.F.N.

Promotional spots, fifteen seconds long each, began to air twenty-four hours before the show's broadcast. The spots were straightforwardly and simply done: close-ups of the Host peering directly into the camera as he intoned in a stentorian voice, "Tomorrow, an All Hallow's Eve special. The Prince of Darkness, *live* on our next show." His spiel was as effective as a carnival pitchman's.

The show's producer, Mr. Harker, was a small, balding toad of a man. When a researcher brought to his attention the story in the *New York Post* concerning the discovery of an honest-to-goodness vampire living in Mellin Town, Illinois, Harker rushed the information to the Host.

"It's the perfect Halloween theme!" cried the producer. "Imagine—Dracula himself right here on our stage! Why, compared to the show we did with the skinhead transvestite born-again heroin addicts, we'll have ten times the audience of that one easily!"

"I'll have to think about it," the Host mused.

The producer was crestfallen.

"I've thought about it," said the Host a moment later.

The producer beamed.

Negotiations began. Deals were offered. Lawyers were hired. Contracts were struck.

The date for the show was set. October 31.

The entire production staff was moved from New York to Chicago for Halloween week. It was an accommodation to their guest, who preferred to be as close to home as possible.

On October 29, the Host burst into the office that had been assigned to Harker. The Host was livid. He hurled a tabloid newspaper onto the producer's desk and demanded shrilly, "Have you *seen* this?"

Harker opened the tabloid: the current issue of the *National Inspirer,* hot off the press. The top headline story had to do with the trainer of a well-known animal actor—the most famous mutt in the world—admitting that the canine star had to undergo two years' worth of psychotherapy for depression following the cancellation of his network television series. The producer looked up at the Host and said, "Do you want me to check into booking the dog or the shrink?"

"Not *that* story, you boob!" shouted the Host. "*This* one!" He jabbed a finger at the lower left corner of the front page. There was a garishly colored photo of the Host, above which was printed: RATINGS SLIDE FOR THE "MOST HATED MAN ON TELEVISION"

The producer blanched. "Well, sir . . ." he began.

"How can they *print* such lies?" the Host steamed.

"Well, sir," said Harker carefully. "You *have* done one or two shows lately that some people might've found a teeny bit . . . offensive."

The Host stared at him, uncomprehending.

"Like that one where you had those 300-pound male burlesque dancers bumping and grinding down to their G-strings," continued Harker. "Or when you had the bulimic teenagers come on and share their favorite recipes, and then demonstrate to the audience just how purging is done."

"What in God's name are you babbling about, man?" said the Host. "I don't care about *offending* people. I care about *this.*" He snatched the paper from the producer's hands, folded it, then with his fingertip drew an invisible underline beneath the word "RATINGS."

"*This* is what I came to talk about," said the Host. "You promised me big numbers for this Halloween show. I want you to know, I'm *holding* you to that promise."

The producer's forehead had begun to bead with perspiration.

"So," said the Host, "how are we doing with the arrangements for our *other* guest?"

"He arrives tomorrow," Harker answered quickly. "From Amsterdam via London. Only you and I know that he's going to be here."

"I'm holding you personally responsible," said the Host. "If it happens that we *don't* manage to have the two of them on the show together at the same time, it's your ass."

"Yes, sir," gulped the producer.

* * *

"But Einar," said his wife Brunilla. *"Television?"*

"It's the only way I can be sure that the Family's side of the matter gets heard and understood," Uncle Einar replied.

Brunilla Elliott shook her head stubbornly. "He's such an awful person," she complained. "He tricks people and belittles them and baits them until they lose their tempers. He plays to that audience of his like Antony at Caesar's funeral."

Uncle Einar sighed tolerantly, realizing that his wife was, after all, only human. Her membership in the Family was solely by virtue of her marriage to him. "Now, now, my dear. He's not as bad as all that."

"He's pretty bad, Papa," said Ronald, the eldest son. "Remember the show where he had on the gay white supremacists? When they broke his nose?"

"He was really asking for it that day," said Stephen.

"Or how about the time he had on those two movie critics?" Michael chimed in. "The tall, thin one and the short, fat one. They'd been the best of friends all their lives, till the day they went on his show."

"I remember," said Meg, Einar and Brunilla's only female offspring. "Before the show was over, he'd gotten the two of them so angry that they were trying to choke each other to death."

Brunilla was shaking her head again. "You see, Einar," she said. "Even your children think this is a very risky thing for you to do."

Uncle Einar shifted in his chair, causing his silken, sea-green wings to rustle like dry leaves. He looked at the members of his family one by one: wife, son, son, son, and daughter. "I'm afraid it's too late to back out now," he said firmly. "A contract is a contract."

And that was that.

Uncle Einar was accompanied to Chicago by his son Ronald and his nephew Timothy. They drove from Mellin Town in a hearse they borrowed from Timothy's brother, Bion, who owned the local mortuary. Uncle Einar hated to travel by car. He did it now only because it was his flying that had precipitated the troublesome situation in which he found himself.

First had been The Accident. One November morning many years ago, in the early hours before dawn, while heading back to Europe following a Homecoming in Mellin Town, Uncle Einar had crashed drunkenly into an electrical tower. A shower of blue sparks surrounded him like fireflies, a high-tension wire lashed his face like a bullwhip, and his right wing was badly crumpled. He fell to earth, unconscious.

He awoke at dawn and took refuge in a nearby forest, where he was discovered by Brunilla Wexley, the owner of a local farm. Brunilla took Einar home with her and nursed him back to health. Days later, after his damaged wing had healed, he waited for nightfall and took off for Europe once more. And promptly crashed headlong into one of Brunilla's maple trees.

It was then that Uncle Einar realized the awful consequence of his accident. His delicate night perception was gone.

He could never again fly after sundown, because the peculiar telepathy that warned him of the trees and towers and houses which stood in his flight path was lost. But by that time he and Brunilla, who lived alone, had fallen in love. Uncle Einar decided to remain with her, and a few months later they were married.

Then, just three weeks ago, had come The Incident.

Because his injury had restricted him to taking to the air only during daylight hours—when he was more likely to be mistaken by fearful and ignorant human beings for something dangerous or harmful: a bat, a UFO, a monster—Uncle Einar gave up flying altogether. For years he coped broodingly with the misery of being earthbound. Until last March, when he and his children devised a way for him to embrace once more the singular rapture that flying gave him.

On a bright and blustery, first-weekend-of-spring, midwestern day, Uncle Einar accompanied the children to Kite Hill. There he tied a tail of cotton rags to his belt behind, took the end of a length of twine between his teeth, and rose joyously up and up into the March wind.

Taking turns holding the ball of twine, Meg and Michael and Stephen and Ronald became the envy of their playmates. Proud possessors of the huge and magical green "kite" that dipped and soared majestically! The only ones aware of its true nature!

Uncle Einar flew throughout the spring and summer, until

school began again and Indian Summer came and went, and the first nip of winter could be tasted in the air. Until that afternoon when he and Stephen went to Kite Hill for one last flight of the year, just the two of them.

As Uncle Einar sailed on the chilly October breeze, he could see a quarter of a mile below him the railroad crossing at the outskirts of Mellin Town. He saw the little girl—not much older than Meg—whose bicycle had broken its chain and sent her tumbling to the tracks. He watched as she tried desperately to free her foot which had become wedged between rail and tie. He could hear her screams for help above the keening whistle of the too-rapidly approaching train.

Without a thought Uncle Einar swooped from the sky like some enormous, green-winged bird of prey. He snatched the little girl to safety by a hairsbreadth. And was seen doing so by the train's engineer and the brakeman and a dozen other witnesses.

By the end of the following day, news of the existence of The Man Who Could Fly had spread, quite literally, around the world. Media representatives descended upon Mellin Town like a swarm of locusts. Each news story that subsequently emerged was more wild than the last. Vampires in Illinois! Monsters Live Among Us! The Apocalypse Is Nigh!

"My God," said Timothy as he steered the hearse through the gates of the television studio. Hundreds of irate demonstrators and curious celebrity-seekers had to be shunted aside by security guards in order to allow the car to pass through. "I hope you know what you're doing, Uncle Einar. And I hope it'll bring an end to this nonsense once and for all."

"I hope so, too, Timothy," sighed Uncle Einar. "I hope so, too."

"Ladies and gentlemen," said the Host, spreading his arms melodramatically. "It is my shuddery pleasure to present to you the most fearsome being ever to grace the stage of this or any other talk show. I give you the Prince of Darkness, the original Count Dracula himself—*Einar Elliott!*"

The audience hissed. Watching from the offstage wings, Timothy and Ronald cringed. Uncle Einar twisted in his chair, reflexively pressing his wings together. He blinked at the bright stage lights that stung his eyes.

The Host took a seat beside him. "It's true, isn't it?" said the Host. "You *are* the original Count Dracula?"

Uncle Einar shook his head. "It's possible that I may have been an inspiration for the character. But there is no 'Count Dracula.' The man who wrote the novel—Abraham Stoker— made him up."

"But there really was someone named 'Dracula,' wasn't there?" the Host asked.

"Oh yes," replied Uncle Einar. "There was a fifteenth century Wallachian prince named 'Vlad the Impaler,' because of his habit of impaling his enemies on the end of sharpened stakes and watching them bleed to death. But Vlad was one hundred per cent human. He was not—I repeat *not*—a member of my Family. He's your relative, not mine."

Someone in the audience booed. The Host held up a hand to silence the heckler, then turned back to Uncle Einar. "But you just said you were the inspiration for the book . . ."

Uncle Einar nodded reluctantly. "Bram and I . . . Mr. Stoker, that is . . . we were . . . acquainted. Back when I was living in England."

"And when was that?"

"Many years ago."

The Host produced a paperback copy of *Dracula.* He opened the book to its flyleaf and held it up to show the audience. "Do you know when *Dracula* was first published, ladies and gentlemen? In the year 1897!" He turned to Uncle Einar. "I must say, you don't look to me to be nearly old enough to have been Bram Stoker's acquaintance, much less his inspiration."

Timothy winced. Ronald muttered softly, "Oh no. He's tweaking Papa's vanity . . ."

"It happens that I'm a good deal older than I appear to be," said Uncle Einar.

The Host arched an eyebrow. "You are?"

Uncle Einar nodded. "On my last birthday I turned two hundred and eighty-eight."

The Host was smiling smugly. "Are you trying to tell me that you're *immortal?*"

"Not exactly," said Uncle Einar. "Eventually the members of the Family do pass on. We simply tend to be long-lived."

"*Obviously,*" the Host said, his tone of voice oily with sarcasm.

The audience chortled, then broke into appreciative applause.
The Host nodded to them, acknowledging.

"Let's talk some more about your Family, Mr. Elliott," he continued. "Is it true that some of them actually sleep in coffins
during the day and come out only at night?"

Timothy and Ronald exchanged looks of apprehension.

Uncle Einar frowned uncomfortably. "Well . . ."

"And that some of them can actually assume the shapes of
animals?"

Uncle Einar said, "Well . . ."

"And that they actually imbibe *human blood?*"

The audience gasped.

Ronald whispered to Timothy, "Uh-oh . . ."

Uncle Einar sputtered, "If you'll allow me to explain—"

"The *truth*, Mr. Elliott!" challenged the Host. "The truth is
that you and your Family are *vampires!*"

A woman in the audience shrieked. Another moaned.

The crowd's wallah drowned out Uncle Einar's protestations,
"No, no, you're getting it all wrong—"

The Host turned away from him to look into the camera. "A
vampire defends his lifestyle. Right after this important message."

During the commercial break, Uncle Einar fumed while the
Host supervised the addition of three more chairs to the set.
Ronald and Timothy took two of the seats, at Uncle Einar's right
hand, just as the stage manager was counting down the last seconds till the show went on the air once more.

A flashing sign cued the audience to commence applauding.
The stage manager pointed a finger at the Host, who smiled at
the camera and said, "We're back. We've been joined by two
members of Einar Elliott's Family, the young men sitting to Mr.
Elliott's right. They are, respectively, his son Ronald and his
nephew Timothy. Both of whom appear to be quite ordinary
human beings."

"Which is exactly what they are, by any standard you wish to
apply," said Uncle Einar. "But they are also members of the
Family, in good standing."

"Tell me, Ronald," said the Host. "What's it like having a
father who's a vampire?"

Ronald made a face. "He's not a vampire."

"He sleeps in a coffin, doesn't he?"

"Not anymore. Not since he met my mother."

"Ah," said the Host. "Your mother. She's human, isn't she?"

"So what?"

"So doesn't that make you and your siblings . . . *half-breeds?* Neither fish nor fowl?"

"What in heaven's name are you talking about?" asked Einar.

The Host turned to Timothy. "Tell me, boy. How are you and your Uncle Einar related?"

"Uncle Einar and my father are brothers," answered Timothy. "Does *your* father have wings as well?"

Timothy shook his head. "Uncle Einar is the only one in the Family who has wings."

"This is exactly the point that I wanted to make," said Uncle Einar. "The Family comes in all shapes and sizes. We have all sorts of different powers and abilities. Yes, there are some who sleep in coffins during the day and come out only at night. And there are some—like Timothy's sister Cecy—who have the ability to place themselves within the minds of other living creatures, to see and smell and hear and feel what they do, to *become* those creatures. And yes, some of us do nourish ourselves with the blood of human beings. But we don't kill anyone—we haven't for hundreds of years. We have other sources—Timothy's brother, for example, who works as an undertaker in our town and saves the blood of the people he's embalmed, when they've got no use for it anymore. We've found a way to co-exist with human beings. We've been co-existing for centuries, living with you side-by-side without your being aware that we were any different from you. That's why I've come here, to assure you that you have nothing at all to fear from us."

Unexpectedly, a portion of the audience erupted into spontaneous applause. The Host glowered at them. The applause subsided.

The Host turned his grim expression to Uncle Einar. "Nothing to fear from you, eh? It so happens, Mr. Elliott, that I have waiting *another* guest to whom you are personally responsible for a great deal of grief and tragedy."

Uncle Einar's eyebrows drew together, a look of puzzled wariness.

The Host turned back to the audience. "Ladies and gentle-men, may I present to you from Amsterdam, Holland, a man whose ancestors have been the sworn enemies of Einar Elliott and his Family for more than a hundred years! Please welcome *Mr. Barnard Vorhees!*"

The Host led the audience in applause. Timothy and Ronald looked to Uncle Einar. Their eyes grew wide when they saw how he had paled at the mention of the name.

Ronald whispered with concern, "Papa, who *is* he . . . ?"

Uncle Einar's gaze was fixed upon the man who was emerg-ing uncertainly from backstage. Barnard Vorhees was a stocky, middle-aged man of medium height, with a ruddy complexion and curly, brown hair peppered with gray. He wore an ill-fitting tweed suit and heavy brogans. The Host directed Vorhees to the empty seat beside him.

Vorhees settled himself, looked about, then locked his eyes onto Uncle Einar's. Uncle Einar straightened slightly in his chair, his wings bristling.

"If you would, Mr. Vorhees," urged the Host, "tell our audi-ence who you are and what your connection is to Mr. Elliott."

The man turned away from Uncle Einar to face the Host, who motioned for him to look out toward the audience. "My name is Barnard Vorhees," the newcomer said. He spoke with a soft, Dutch accent. "I live in Amsterdam. I am the great-grandson of Dr. Hans Vorhees, the famous nineteenth-century vampire hunter."

"If I may," interrupted the Host. He held up his copy of *Drac-ula* again as he spoke to the audience. "Mr. Vorhees's great-grandfather was also living in London at the time this book was written. He is probably better known as the character whom *he* inspired, Dr. Van Helsing."

Vorhees had turned to look once more at Uncle Einar. "My great-grandfather, my grandfather, and my father devoted their lives to one purpose—the utter destruction of Einar Elliott."

The audience stirred.

"And what happened to them?" asked the Host.

Vorhees took in a deep breath. "All three died in an insane asylum. Where they had been placed because their obsession had driven them mad."

A hush fell over the audience.

The Host prompted Vorhees, "And the reason why you agreed to let us bring you on the show . . . ?"

"To destroy the evil in our midst," uttered Vorhees. He turned to the Host, eyes glittering with madness. "Your show goes out all over the world. I've seen it many times, often enough so that I feel as if I know you very well. When I was offered this opportunity to rid mankind of a terrible monster—"

Vorhees suddenly leaped from his chair. In the same motion he pulled from his coat a long cedar stake, sharpened at one end, and a large mallet.

Uncle Einar, the Host, Timothy, and Ronald were frozen in their chairs. Several members of the audience began to scream.

Vorhees cried out maniacally, "Die, fiend!"

Before anyone could stop him, the man hurled himself at the Host, knocked him from his chair to the floor, and pounded the stake into the center of his chest.

The Host gurgled, blood trickling from the corners of his mouth. He clutched at the stake futilely, shuddered, then lay still. Vorhees came to his feet, standing astride the body of the murdered man. He lifted his arms, fists clenched in triumph.

Pandemonium erupted.

In an instant, the set was thronged with frantic stagehands, production assistants, camera personnel, security officers, and autograph seekers. A pair of uniformed guards seized Vorhees, dragging him away from the dead man. Uncle Einar, Timothy, and Ronald moved as far off to one side as they could, trying to stay clear of the phalanx of individuals that crushed the stage.

A quiet voice behind Uncle Einar's shoulder muttered, "I honestly didn't think he'd go through with it."

Uncle Einar, Timothy, and Ronald turned around. There stood Mr. Harker, the producer. He looked at them and smiled. "You have no idea how long I've prayed for somebody to kill that son of a bitch," he said. "I only wish I could've gotten up enough nerve to have done it myself."

Harker led Uncle Einar, Timothy, and Ronald to his office, secluding them until things quieted down. As they settled themselves on a sectional sofa opposite Harker's desk, Ronald was saying, "You mean Mr. Vorhees didn't hold any grudge against Papa at all?"

"He forgave your father years ago," answered Harker, "when he made up his mind that everybody in his family was simply crazy. However, when I invited him to come on the show, I found out about his own little obsession. He couldn't tell me vehemently enough how much he despised the man I worked for. The show has quite a following in Europe, you know." Harker nodded to Einar. "Vorhees didn't want to come at first, because he didn't have anything against you, and because he was genuinely afraid of what he might do if he ever found himself in the same room with my boss. My *ex*-boss, that is. I had to talk him into it."

"Unbelievable," said Uncle Einar.

"But true," responded Harker. "Incidentally, Mr. Elliott, I thought you handled yourself extremely well. You presented the case for your Family most eloquently."

"But Mr. Harker," said Timothy, "if you're the one who talked Vorhees into coming on the show, doesn't that make you an accomplice?"

"I don't think Mr. Harker has much to worry about," said Uncle Einar. "How was he to know what Vorhees might do? After all, the man is clearly insane."

Timothy said doubtfully, "I suppose . . ."

"I'm grateful for your concern, Timothy," Harker said, reassuring him, "but there's really no need for it. I'm not the least bit worried. In fact, I feel like celebrating. I'd like all of you to be my guests for dinner." He stood up and motioned them toward the door. "I think a little champagne might be in order, don't you?"

As he got up from the sofa, Timothy said, "Uncle Einar doesn't drink . . . wine."

Harker slapped his head, a gesture of *How stupid of me.* "I'm sorry," he said. "I forgot."

"I think I can make an exception this one time," said Uncle Einar, stretching his wings.

SOMETHING IN THE EARTH

Charles Beaumont

This story by the late Charles Beaumont (best remembered for his superb work on Rod Serling's Twilight Zone) *has never been reprinted in any form since its appearance in a 1963 issue of* Gamma, *a short-lived West Coast fantasy magazine of limited circulation. As managing editor, I selected the story from a file of Beaumont's unsold work because he was then too ill to write new fiction. (Stricken with a case of extremely premature Alzheimer's disease, he died in 1967 at age 38.) In his all-too-brief thirteen-year career, Chuck wrote two novels, 80 short stories, many articles and essays, and dozens of TV and film scripts (see his* Charles Beaumont: Selected Stories, *1988).*

As a friend and mentor, Ray Bradbury exerted a strong influence on Beaumont's early fiction; "Something in the Earth" clearly reflects that influence. Bradbury's "The Meadow" features a frustrated, angry old night watchman who tries desperately to keep a film studio backlot set (his "meadow of the world") from being destroyed—just as the equally frustrated old man in Beaumont's futuristic story fights to preserve his own small piece of the world. In basic content and poetic approach, the two stories are closely related, and it seemed most appropriate that "Something in the Earth" should achieve its first book publication in the pages of this anthology.

W.F.N.

The old man came into the room and sat down on the edge of the bed and put his hands together. He sat there without moving for several minutes while his wife waited patiently. Then the old man said, "They're going to kill us."

His wife reached out and touched his wrists. "I'm sorry, dear," she said.

"Kill us, rip us up and cut off our legs and our arms, burn us to little black cinders . . . then, forget we ever existed."

"Hateful people!"

"Yes. Tomorrow we'll be dead and gone and that'll be the end of us."

His wife raised herself in the bed and stroked his forehead with damp fingers. "That's a shame," she said.

The old man got up and walked slowly to a window. "I can't understand it," he said.

His wife settled back onto her pillows. "Well, you know, if you'll think back, dear—it *has* been a long time since anybody has come to see us."

The old man said nothing.

"Over a year, I'll bet. Aunt Jeaness was the last, and she came only because I wrote and asked her."

"You—asked her?"

"You looked so sad, dear. I couldn't stand to see you that way."

The old man remembered how he had taken the woman out into the forest and showed her every tree, and had her stand quietly so she could hear the insects and the birds. It had been almost like the beautiful days, when the children came from the cities, from miles away, to feel grass and small wet leaves.

The old man tried not to think of those times. He looked at his wife.

"What I mean, dear, is—well, isn't it just possible that they might have their reasons?"

"Of course, yes! They explained very carefully; with graphs and charts and whole books bloated with statistics. I told them,

'Why not go and build your houses on Mars, build them on the moon, anywhere!' Impossible: no choice. They must build *here*; and we must die."

The wife clenched her fists. "Stop saying 'we'! I'm tired of it. Not you, not me! Just the trees."

The old man's eyes widened.

"Do you mean that?"

"I mean it. For all these years I've lived with you in this place and never a complaint from me, never. Now we've got to leave and I'm glad and—"

"The mountains!" the old man cried. "You didn't care when they took away the mountains! When we watched them dry up the rivers and level the fields and put their cities over all the earth— You've lied!"

"I love you."

"And when the world was turned to stone, all but this little corner . . ."

The old man turned and rushed from the room. He ran down the hall of the house and out into the night. He ran until each breath was a sharp pain inside him. Then he stumbled and sat down and tried to think, but he could only cough.

When he breathed normally again, finally, the thoughts came. They came, and his hands moved across the soft grass, feeling the dying leaves, tracing their slender veins with his fingers.

He rose and walked to where the forest grew thick with tall trees. He walked past the trees, putting out his hands and touching the rough bark surfaces, running his palms along the hardened syrup, caressing the small twigs but taking care not to injure them. The ground was soft beneath his feet with the softness of damp tufted grass and fallen leaves.

He walked.

They will murder us, he thought. Eat us with tin teeth and spit us out into flames and we will die, slowly. When we're gone, they will lay over our grave a tomb of steel and stone. And then *they* will live here, and in all the world there will not be a blade of grass nor a single tree! And children will be born and raised who will never know the robin's song, whose hands will know only the feel of cold metal.

He walked and tried to disregard his head which throbbed with pain; from time to time he stopped while the smaller creatures flew out of the dark to be near him. And when he stopped he listened, too, for the gentle rustle of other creatures, running away or—the braver ones—edging cautiously closer. From the corners of his eyes he caught the tentative movements. But he made no sign.

They will kill you too, he thought. Once they kept big parks where you might go; the parks are gone, so they will kill you.

The old man stooped and picked up a twig not yet saturated with damp, still brittle; he turned the twig over and over in his hands, remembering.

Now he talked aloud to the trees in the forest. And his voice was soft in the wind that came through the thousand high branches.

The trees seemed to listen—and the voices of all the forest creatures ceased; now there was only the sound of the old man's soft voice.

"Once in the earth," the old man said, "we were everywhere. We stretched across the mountains clear to the deserts and to the very edges of the great waters. And only our friends moved among us, those who loved us because we were their shelter and their food and their life. You—" the old man paused and thumped the bole of a giant sequoia "—you remember. When the vines hung from your arms and the animals ate from you!" He walked to another tree, not a sapling, but one young in the years of trees. "You don't remember. But you've been told! Small boys once climbed upon you, and swung from those arms!"

The horned moon became visible at last to the old man's eyes. He stared at the cool light.

"Idiot!" he whispered. "You'll be next. You don't believe me? When we're gone and their buildings fill the ground, do you think they'll stop? See, look at what they're doing to Mars—poor, tired, dried-up planet. They've just started there. It won't take long before the sands disappear and the red is turned to iron. Wait! You'll see!"

He continued through the wood, tapping the wrinkled twig against his palm. He thought of his wife, and sighed.

I mustn't hate her, he thought. How could I expect a woman from the cities to understand? How could I have hoped? But—I did think she loved us, just a little. . . . When I used to take her out in the mornings, before she grew ill, and be careful to say nothing so she could watch the sun—*our* sun—come up slowly through us, so she could feel us come to life—I thought . . . but in all this world, I am the only one! The only one!

The smaller limbs and branches high above moved in a slow, sad dance to the night breezes that soughed over them. Leaves fluttered softly, turning over and over, caught by the wind.

The old man stopped a while to rest, for his heart had begun to pound.

She was right. I knew she was. No one has come to us as they used to. Not even the old ones who lived when we were every-where, who watched us die . . .

The old man looked at his hands, which had once been young and had turned to parchment and were then made young again by the cities' men and were now beyond the help of their shining tools and glass ribbons. The hands would never be young again; they would only grow older and more wrinkled.

His heart regained its normal beat, and he walked to the edge of the forest, to where the great stone wall rose; then he turned around and started to walk back, another way.

A terrible thought came to him: *And if I had not been born here, where my father lived, perhaps there would be no one*—No. No, there had to be one.

My father kept us alive. Twice they wanted to kill us—he told me—and twice he stopped them.

He was not alone . . . But now . . .

One man against the world . . . You took your machines and stamped the mountains flat for your cities. You drained the riv-ers and the seas and set your people to live on the dry beds. And when you made food from the air, you ruined the fields, and the cities grew where the grass and the wheat and the corn had grown! And you made your water and spread canals under the earth so the deserts could keep your buildings!

I told them. You took even the great forests. The bird and animals, not the ones raised with you but the *free* ones—these you slaughtered.

The world is nothing but a vast city. Can't you spare the one last corner that was not made by your hands? Let the trees go on growing and remembering, let the animals run unafraid . . .

But they brought out their books of numbers for me to see.

And tomorrow they come for us, with their tractors and their saws and their explosions, to kill us. And there's nothing I can do.

Something happened to the wind.

It came rushing suddenly down from the sky, straight down, through the branches and upon the old man, chilling him. It caught up the flying creatures, the dark ones and those who were excited points of fire in the night always, and sent them whirling with the dead grass and leaves. The wind came into the old man's ears, into his head.

He listened.

Then, he stopped looking old. His back straightened, and his head ached no longer: it was clear now, clearer than it had ever been.

The old man looked about him, while the wind quieted itself and went away. Then, he found what he was looking for.

It was the tallest tree in the forest. And ancient, hardened long since from wood to marble. The hard crystal shreds of bark were strong and easily supported the old man as he began to climb.

He climbed quickly, not feeling tired or worried. The heavy thoughts were gone; they left when the wind had whispered; so he climbed with the lightness of a young boy, from hand-hold to hand-hold, up finally to the first fat branch, over this; and the rest was not work at all. It made his thoughts rush back over the long years, when he was truly young.

After a little while, the old man had reached the topmost branch.

He looked out across the glowing cities which stretched beyond the end of his vision, in all directions.

Then he laughed . . . and waited.

"They'll write ugly letters and scream and put up petitions!" the Undersecretary had said, but he was wrong. He read books.

The President, who lived in the here and now and did not read books, had said, "Ridiculous nonsense!" He was right.

There were a few letters, of course, but all quite insincere, from the older colleges. The strongest of these read:

WE OF THE FACULTY AND STUDENT BODY URGE THE PRESIDENT TO
WEIGH THIS MATTER WITH HIS USUAL DISCRETION AND KNOW-HOW
BEFORE HE MAKES ANY DEFINITE MOVE.

The others were inconsequential.

"You see, Herman," the President said, "nobody cares. Nobody gives a damn. Do you give a damn, Herman?"

The Undersecretary admitted he didn't.

"There's Markeson though," he said.

"The custodian? Of course. The man was born there. Why shouldn't he want to stay? Human nature. He doesn't realize that every school in the world has a whole building full of the finest reproductions of every tree that ever existed. *Permanent* reproductions, you couldn't tell from the original. Bugs, too. All kinds."

"You explained this to him?"

"I told Jerred to, or somebody. What's the difference? We'll find him another spot. Plenty of work around. APU, WVP, UNF."

"Yes."

The President explained that the group planned for the new site would include a subsidiary of U.S. Rockets.

The Undersecretary read his instructions and called up the crews and told them to go out and destroy the last forest on earth.

Some time later the chief engineer of the crew asked audience with the Undersecretary. He looked confused.

"I beg your pardon, sir," the chief engineer said, "but something peculiar has happened."

"Yes?" the Undersecretary said.

"About the new site for U.S., sir?"

"Yes, yes?"

"Well, we've run into difficulties."

"Difficulties?"

"The trees, sir. They won't saw."

"Of course they won't. They're petrified, old. You knew that."

"Not all of them. The wooden ones won't saw. We tried drills, and they didn't work."

"What about explosives?"

The chief engineer flushed. "We tried all of our equipment, all morning. Planted VO3 under one tree and blew it, and it didn't hurt a leaf. I'm scared."

The Undersecretary said something under his voice, and called upon the President.

"Ridiculous!" the President snorted. The Undersecretary transmitted the message and went to other work.

The chief engineer returned later, looking worse.

"Well?"

"VO5, Blue Test, Red Test, everything."

"And you failed?"

"May I suggest," the chief engineer said, "that the Undersecretary and the President go back with me and see for themselves?"

They all went to the forest.

The crew of workers were huddled in a group on the other side of the wall, smoking and talking in low frightened tones.

"Now, see here," the President said loudly. "The job has got to be done by tonight. By *tonight!* I've got other crews waiting to put up the buildings, lay the foundations. What have you accomplished?" The President looked around. Then he cried angrily. "Here, give me that!" He snatched an axe from the limp hand of a pale man and went over to a small poplar. "Must the President of United World do his own work?" He swung the new axe in a wide arc. The sharp heavy edge smashed against the tree trunk and then ricocheted back, upsetting the President's unsteady balance.

"I see," he said. "Well, it must be something in the earth. The F-Bomb—that's it. Polluted the earth or something last war. Wait, I'll go talk to the custodian."

The President slapped his hands together and commenced to walk, with other men, for the small cottage hidden in back of round bushes and slender eucalyptus shoots.

He knocked, and the door was opened by an old woman who looked sick. She clutched a bedsheet to her.

"Madam, I wish to speak with your husband, Mr. Markeson."

"Gerald isn't here. I don't know where he is," the old woman said sadly. "He went away last night and he never came back.

All I said was I loved him!" Her eyes were wide with astonishment.

"I've never seen him angry before. Will you look for him, please, and bring him back to me? Tell him I want to understand. Tell him I'll try, very hard."

The President paused a moment, gave instructions that the old woman be taken to a safe place, then walked back across the leaves and grass, quickly to his men.

"I found him, sir," said one of them.

"Well, bring him here!"

"I can't, sir. He's up a tree."

"Up a tree?"

"Sitting on a branch, sir. He said he didn't want to come down. He wants to talk with you."

They went to the tree.

The old man called down from the dizzy heights. "Go away. Leave us alone!"

"Now, now," called the President.

"You might just as well pack up and leave," the old man shouted. "Nothing you can do. Nothing in the world."

The old man laughed long and hard. "Go ahead. Do your work. Try. Try to kill us!"

Three men were dispatched to climb the tree, but they didn't know how or couldn't. No one could climb the tree.

The President said, "We're going to have to blast it all out, Mr. Markeson. Come down or you'll be killed."

The old man laughed.

An aircar was advised to pick him up, but the aircar crashed into a weeping willow, and fell to earth. The same thing happened to others.

The President, who had sat down, took off his coat and applied a handkerchief to his forehead.

The shrill old voice carried. "Can't you see? They told me— do what you like."

Finally, the President said, "See here, Mr. Markeson. You're holding up production. This center is essential. Either get out of that tree—or take the consequences."

The old man looked at the animals who waited hidden from

the men; he looked at the ungrieving forest, at the expectant sky. "Do what you like," he repeated.

The President shrugged, and the men walked off and did not return.

Machines covered the sky. They dropped shields about the city's walls to protect the buildings. The old man watched them intently, feeling not the least bit uncomfortable, though he didn't know what they were doing.

Then the flying machines opened their riveted stomachs and released glass balls, filled with pink vapor.

They dropped to the ground, where they burst open, letting the wind take up the pink mist and blow it through the trees.

The explosion took away the old man's breath. It made him close his eyes tight and hold fast to the branch. But soon the shaking and the noise passed, with the foul smelling smoke, and when he looked, nothing had changed. The trees stood as they had always stood, and he could hear the animals and the insects.

Soon the men came back, blinking, shaking their heads, talking very little and in short words. The President was along, lagging in back.

"See?" shrieked the old man, bouncing, laughing.

"Something in the earth," the President mumbled, but not so softly that the old man didn't hear.

Then a new voice came up to the tree. "Gerald!"

The old man saw his wife. She was out of breath and her ripped gown was covered with burrs. "What's happening?" she cried hysterically.

"I don't know. . . . Something. I've prayed for it, but I can't tell you what it is. Go with the others, leave me."

The pale woman put her hands to her mouth and nodded.

Soon they were all gone; and when he was alone at last, the old man put his head against the treetop and fell into a quiet sleep.

He dreamed of the world before the cities had gone mad. He lay on the white sands of a lonely beach by a river and watched grazing sheep on the other side of the river. It ran fast, and sang through golden fields and deep green forests, and broke into wild brooks and streams within the forests. And in the distance, he could see mountains under the sun . . .

Then the old man woke. He shivered once and looked across the cities: then he stared with wide eyes.

He stared at the cities as they broke and crumbled. As the air grew fat with screams of many people. As the roots of giant trees, greater than he had ever seen, came up from the stone and spread and toppled the mighty buildings. As the water came flooding in through the steel canyons. As the mountains pulled the earth apart and rose and made room for the fields and the forests.

THE MUSE

Norman Corwin

*One name stands, Everest-tall, in the history of dramatic radio—
the name of Norman Corwin. In the 1940s and 1950s, Corwin's
poetic, soul-stirring radio works reflected awesome talent, unflag-
ging energy, and a personal commitment to excellence unmatched
in the field. His hour-long World War II radio drama,* On a Note
of Triumph, *broadcast throughout the world in 1945 in celebration
of the allied victory in Europe, remains one of the genre's undis-
puted masterworks. It was one of many he produced, wrote,
and directed. Corwin proved to be a major moral and artistic
force in shaping network radio in America. He followed this
monumental radio career with film scripting (winning an Oscar
nomination for his screenplay on* Lust for Life), *television
work (with his own show,* Norman Corwin Presents), *teaching
and lecturing—and, always, writing. He has more than a
dozen books to his credit, as well as numerous magazine articles
and essays.*

*Ray Bradbury counts Norman Corwin among his closest friends;
each greatly admires the achievements of the other. Corwin's affec-
tion and admiration for his longtime friend shines through in this
wry, tongue-in-cheek contribution.*

The tone is light, but the love is deep.

W.F.N.

116

Her name is Polyhymnia. Greek. Likes to be called Polly. I found out she was Ray's muse, through the offices of my friend Spyros Nonstopoulos, who runs a Greek restaurant named the Moussaka Experience on West Pico. Spyros is a deep thinker, versed in the classics, and he claims he is able to get in touch with ancient Greek gods, or members of the Muse establishment, any time he wants, simply by ingesting his own concoction: a compote of psari plaki, steifado, and matzo meal, laced with equal parts of unpasteurized Ouzo and *Cannabis sativa indica.* I asked if I could try it.

I awoke with a hangover. I was in a loft on Olympic Boulevard, sitting on an ottoman. Across the room, draped on a musnud, was a weary looking female of indeterminate age. I introduced myself. She said she was Polyhymnia, no last name, and volunteered that her occupation was Muse of Religious Poetry. She was in town, she said, because she worked for Ray Bradbury, and had to be around when he called, which could be any time of day or night.

I was thrilled, because I had for years been president of the West Los Angeles chapter of the International Ray Bradbury Fan Club. But religious poetry? *Religious?* I was puzzled, and asked politely what her background had to do with Mr. Bradbury or his work. She looked at me condescendingly, and answered with a slight Hellenic accent, that Ray is a poet, that poetry is art, that art is the best religion, and besides, the vocation of being muse to strictly religious poets had become a drag because nobody writes hymns anymore and bishops are in the main a dull bunch. Therefore she had *asked* to be assigned to Bradbury. Others of the muses, particularly her sisters Calliope and Euterpe, challenged her for the privilege, since they all had been brought up on Bradbury by their mother Mnemosyne. (Her father does not read.) But Polly held out, and made such a scene about it that the others retreated.

I asked her whether she had any regrets about the portfolio. None at all, she responded, a little too quickly. "It's exciting. You never know, with that man. He sometimes resists my suggestions. After all, I've been around for a spell, and I know what I'm doing."

Since she seemed to want to unburden herself, I asked how much of what it takes to fire up Bradbury comes from her, and how much from his own native genius. "Oh, his own native genius," she said ruefully. "I am constantly struggling against it, pitting my genius against his, and half the time I am vetoed."

I asked if she could give me some instances of where he did take her suggestions. "*The Martian Chronicles*," she snapped.

"That's not what Ray says. He says the idea of sewing together some of his Martian stories was put into his head by an editor at Doubleday named Walter Bradbury, no relation."

She laughed scornfully. "And who put the idea in *Walter* Bradbury's head? I was *there*. I accompany Ray to most places he goes. Except that I won't get on an airplane. They scare me. For a long time I persuaded Ray to be scared too, not only of airplanes but automobiles, but now he rides in both. People change. It's a shame.

"Ray is very generous in giving credit," she went on, "except to me. He takes inspiration from me, sinks his talons into my ideas, puts them to work, and gets so absorbed he forgets I'm around, so I go home. Then suddenly he'll awake in the middle of the night and summon me. And by the rules of the sacred sorority, I must show up, tired or not."

"And his wife Maggie doesn't mind?"

"She sleeps right through it. What I do is, I hover over him, I distill divine thoughts, I weave a sort of afflatus, I devolve an inspiration, I convey them to him in the traditional low whisper, and he makes notes. He thanks me, and I transit myself back to this loft, to try to catch up on lost sleep. On the day shift, I usually hang around his office until he gets stuck, then he calls me on the intercom. While he's busy at the typewriter exploiting my concepts of the previous night, or of that morning, I fool around with some of his thousands of artifacts, read his fan mail, browse through the special editions of his stories, which keep coming out every other month. Sometimes he asks me to come along with him for lunch or dinner, where I have to remain invisible, but he never thinks to take me to a Greek restaurant."

"Ah, well, I have a good Greek restaurant for you. The Mouss—"

"I've even inspired him in the middle of a salad. It might be only a pun, or a fast retort, or a rhyming partner that had eluded him in a poem he's been grappling with. And he grapples, may I add, mostly when he tries to make it alone, when he denies my heritage and minimizes my function."

"I understand your annoyance," I said, "but you must also understand that Ray is a proud man, and that whatever debts he may owe to others, like Shakespeare, Melville, Dickens, Dickinson and Tom Wolfe (the one from North Carolina, not the fop in the white suits) he has gratefully and cheerfully acknowledged. But you, after all, are a nebulous spirit, a sort of ectoplasm really, and if you are usually invisible to others, you must be invisible to him at times."

"I am astonished," she said sharply, "that you could have been president of a chapter of the R.B. Fan Club, and not know more about the man you honor. Who inspired Ray to read Charles Dickens and Emily Dickinson in the first place? Who whispered in his ear, 'Go, my boy, drink deep of the Pierian spring. *Spurn* Arrowhead and Evian—leave them to admen and menu-writers!' He *listened* to me then, Ray did. He acknowledged me. He drank deep of Pieria water. He blossomed. He flourished. But as soon as he began to make it big, to become a national then a world figure, with people like Bernard Berenson, Truffaut and the Gorbachevs sending him valentines, he figured he could make it on his own."

"And hasn't he?"

Polly was silent for a moment. "Are you still president of the West L.A. chapter?"

"No."

"Good."

"I was defeated by the faction that believes Ray should dress more formally."

"Doesn't matter. Your ignorance of the nuclear Bradbury is appalling. Ask yourself when you get home tonight: where do his ideas come from? How can one man, unassisted, write about worlds within worlds, and worlds outside worlds, and a 300-pound diva, and a million-year picnic, and a season of sitting, and the town where no one got off, and the day it rained forever, and punishment without crime, and a mechanical grandmother, and Christus Apollo, and a wonderful ice cream suit, and Irish anthem sprinters, and ghostly parachutists, and a tyranny of bookburners, and an aphrodisiac foghorn, and a Buddhist temple dissolving into a log cabin, and death in Mexico, and a train station sign viewed from an ancient locomotive passing through after midnight, and a girl long ago who jumped rope and sent Ray weeping to the shower ... Do you think any one writer, who incidentally also lectures and gives interviews and writes prefaces and sits on panels, that any one writer can do all that without a combination Coach, Guardian Angel and Girl Monday-through-Friday helping him? In other words, an active, even hyperactive *Muse?*"

"Yes," I answered. "Bradbury can do all that. And *nobody* needs to help him!"

I don't know where Polly got the pie. I had not seen it before, and I've wondered ever since what a pie was doing on, under, or even near the musnud that Polly was draped over. Anyway, I got it full in the face. Polly then disappeared. I wiped lemon meringue from my forehead, eyes, nose, jowls and necktie, and left the loft.

No more Spyros's recipes for me. And in case that bitch of a Muse of Religious Poetry is interested, I'm running again for president.

Sheesh!

THE LATE ARRIVALS

Roberta Lannes

Amazingly, at eighteen, Roberta Lannes sold her first short story to nothing less than the prestigious Paris Review, *then placed two more stories with literary quarterlies before becoming a fulltime teacher. She has taught art, English, journalism, creative writing, and photography, and, along the way, has functioned as a painter and graphic designer.*

Roberta resumed her writing career (while still continuing to teach) in 1986 with a memorable appearance in the seminal Cutting Edge. *She has since had new works printed in several more anthologies (*Lord John Ten, Alien Sex, *etc.) as well as in magazines such as* Fantasy Tales *and* Iniquities.

Bradbury's *Martian Chronicles was an early influence. The lost Martians in their delicate crystal cities triggered a strong emotional response. But the* expression *of that response had to wait until she was asked to write a story for this book.*

"The Late Arrivals" forms a brief sequel to Bradbury's larger saga, in which a final rocket from Earth sets down on Mars. In the course of the narrative, her protagonist meets Bradbury's robot family, the Hathaways, as well as survivors from the devastated Martian society. Their personal interaction forms the heart of the story.

This gentle fantasy is not typical Lannes. Up to now, much of her fiction has been dark and hard-edged. But, returning to Bradbury's red sands, she reveals a nostalgic warmth that is both touching and tender.

Herewith, a fine new Martian chronicle.

W.F.N.

Rollie Painter struggled out of his mother's arms onto the fine blue Martian soil. Legless, with short seal-flipper arms, Rollie's usual source of locomotion was the scooter his father had built for him on Earth. The scooter was still packed away on the rocket with an endless array of other things Rollie seemed to have a constant need for, but these things were of little importance to his father. Even Momma grumbled quietly that she had to wait for her kitchen things; longing to be at work instead of carrying her son about. Dad's stuff always came first.

Stephanie, his sister, stood atop "her mountain," as she'd claimed it, staring blindly into the sunset. Mars had only been home for a few days, yet Stephanie said she felt she'd known it her entire fourteen years—as if she'd been destined to live on Mars, that she belonged here. Rollie pulled his way up her mountain and wiggled close to her. She absently put her arm around him and smiled.

"What's it like to you, sis?" Rollie's little arms went bumpy with goose flesh as he looked out over the glistening web of Martian canals, stringing their way over the hugest expanse of rolling blue velvet hills he had ever seen.

Rollie knew she sensed things no one else in her family did. Invisible things. Intangible things.

"Oh, Rollie. You can't tell Momma or Dad."

"Cross my flips and hope to die. What? What?" His heart skipped.

"The Martians. They're still here. Not far." She wiped at the permanent veil of tissue that kept her from seeing anything more than light or shadow.

Rollie turned to look at the long-dead city behind them. Its crystal spires were the last still intact on the planet. They glinted in the sunlight; rusty orange, gilded ochre, and purest white. Beneath them, dust-covered tile streets awaited new footprints. He shifted beside his sister, thinking. Wondering.

Stephanie clucked her tongue. "No, Rollie. They said we couldn't go into the city without them. Maybe tomorrow."

"Come on, sis. They're busy with setting up the new place. Momma's too concerned about her kitchen to worry about us. We have hours of daylight left."

"They said to stay in sight. You know what they'll do if we don't obey them."

Rollie squinted at the site of his new home, then back at the city. "They can see the city from the house. Let's go."

Stephanie grinned. "All right then, hold on." She lifted him up and carried him, his eyes helping to guide them into the city.

Rollie squirmed, delighted to be somewhere so ancient, yet so intoxicatingly new. "Feel any Martians yet?"

Stephanie's boots crunched over the gritty layer of sand atop the walkway. "They're here, but they don't trust us. I sense one or two close by. Do you see any marks in the sand?"

"Nope. What do they look like?"

"Oh, Rollie, they are more beautiful than any human. And they are pure of heart."

Rollie stiffened. "Stop! I see something. Inside that building. The one with all the books. It's dark, but I thought I saw someone moving around." His stomach clenched.

"They won't hurt us."

Rollie squirmed out of her arms onto the ground, then shimmied his way to the door and peered in. Like a shadow against a dark wall, an absence of light or substance in the shape of a man, the Martian moved across the sea of neatly shelved books with their fine snaking letters. It did not speak, but somehow Rollie knew it moved only as close as it felt was safe.

"Sis. I see one." He pulled his compact body upright against the door jamb.

Stephanie scooped Rollie up into her arms. "Hello." They spoke in unison.

The figure remained still. Rollie whispered to her. "He's wearing a robe of wine-colored panne. His skin is nearly the same color, though more brown. His eyes. Oh, sis, his eyes!"

The Martian came closer. "I called to you and you've come. You are the newcomers."

Rollie was captivated by the Martian's eyes.

Stephanie gasped. "You don't speak aloud. I hear you in my mind. How is that?"

"You sense thoughts and feelings in your own kind, do you not? I merely make my thoughts ... available." The Martian drew close. "Tell me, what became of your vision?"

Rollie was frozen in his sister's arms. The deep liquid gold of the Martian's eyes was like molten amber lit from within. He thought he should be frightened, but he wasn't.

"We, Rollie and I, were born after the great war on Earth. My father was protected during the chemical and nuclear fallout because he worked in a secure underground lab. My mother was not. We were genetically tainted."

"Does it hurt?"

"Not physically. No. Now that we left what remained of humankind. Where we came from, people were awful to us."

The Martian stood eye to eye with Stephanie. "The humans who ravaged our people and our planet went back to fight their war. I was glad to see them go. And now you have left them behind." He tilted his head. "This is better."

Rollie beamed. He had always longed to know things others thought, as his sister did, and now he was hearing another being in his mind. Wonder of wonders.

"Yeah, we left," he said. "We came in a family rocket. Just us four. We got away from the meanies, the greedies, and the sickies. Our parents are back—"

The Martian gave a short cry, then disappeared into the darkness.

"Roland Dennis Painter! What mischief have you led your sister off on now?" Dad's voice caused the diaphanous walls of the city to vibrate and chitter.

Rollie was snatched from the arms of his sister. His father held him tightly, roughly. Then he was off with Rollie, dragging Stephanie by the wrist.

"You two will pay for this disobedience. Oh, yes. Your mother was frantic when she found you missing. Lucky for us this Martian soil takes footprints so easily."

"Dad, it's my fault. It's always my fault. Don't blame Stephanie. I fooled her. Don't ... you know. She just ..."

His father stopped at the edge of the city; his face was the rose of plum flesh in the waning light.

"Stephanie is nearly a woman with a mind of her own. She

certainly knows better by now. As should you. You are both going to do penance."

Rollie endured the tortuous silence through dinner, knowing that soon after they would receive their punishment. He glanced at Stephanie, who kept her head lowered, barely touching her food. . . .

After they'd been scolded and then beaten, they were left tethered outside the new house. They sat on a space blanket, suffering in anticipation of whatever terrifying wrath the imaginary horrors of the Martian night might bring upon them. Those thoughts festered in them now, souring the possibility of sleep.

They were instructed not to speak, or the beatings would resume. Blustery winds blew fine blue dust into their eyes and their noses. The air was colder than either of them could ever remember. Huddled close to his sister, aching and bruised, Rollie felt his usual guilt and remorse, but Stephanie didn't share these. She wanted to run free, exercise her curiosity, grow up and out. If she was angry at him for what had happened, he was not aware of it.

Stephanie felt the visitor first. "He's here. The Martian," she whispered to Rollie.

Rollie rolled over and saw the tall figure that covered the stars, the golden eyes like two hot coins.

"I am sorry you have both been hurt because of me. I have lost much of the intuitive ability. I should have sensed you would be in danger. I should never have called to you."

Rollie thought about how he and Stephanie had gone into the dead city for their own reasons, that if the Martian had called to them, he wasn't aware of it.

The Martian nodded, reading Rollie's thought. "Perhaps it felt to you as your own desire." The Martian touched the tether that ran from the two children to the struts of the metal hut. "I would like to free you. You do not belong in chains."

"Go away," Rollie whispered. "If my dad hears us, he'll come out and . . ."

Then . . . footsteps from deep in the belly of the house.

The Martian did not move. Light spilled from the open door

as Dad stepped out. He squinted into the darkness, unsure of what he saw in the scythe of white.

"You two all right out here?" He cupped a hand at each temple, like blinders, to help him focus on the darkness that cloaked his huddled children.

"We're not supposed to speak. You told us not to," said Rollie.

"Well, I want to know." The wind whipped his robe about his tall pajama-clad frame. He didn't sound as if he really cared about them. The Martian's presence had roused him.

Stephanie was trembling. "It's cold, Dad. Too cold."

Rollie nodded. "We could freeze out here. Let us back in. I won't be dragging Stephanie away anymore."

Dad crossed his arms over his chest. "Well, I've heard that before. Rollie, if this happens again, I'll disable that scooter of yours and you won't be *able* to get far. Understand?"

"I understand."

As they hesitated at the hut door, they both looked back toward the Martian. There, stars twinkled brilliant in the night sky.

He was gone.

The next afternoon, Dad took the scooter out of the rocket, but fiddled with it so that it wouldn't operate. Rollie knew what his father was doing and it made him angry. Stuck in the shade of the rocket as the others carried equipment and household things to the hut, Rollie began to think of ways to get back to the city. He was trapped until it cooled off. The sun had heated the soil until it burned like fire underfoot. He yearned to find the Martian again, but he would have to wait.

Stephanie followed Momma, wincing at the pain and loneliness she sensed in her. As she helped to move their things inside, Stephanie turned toward Rollie, who appeared to be no more than a shadow within a shadow to her, smiling encouragement. His sister had always insisted that someday, somehow, life would be what they wanted it to be. Rollie knew how small the chance was for that.

He wanted to cry, to release the tears that burned at the corners of his eyes, but he dare not show his father he'd won. Yet, his father had won long ago. After the war, he married Rollie's mother; a victim of radiation poisoning who would otherwise never have found someone to care for her. He won when he sired two mutant children no one else would ever want, then binding them to him with fear and promises he only half met, giving them just enough to inspire some faith in him. Rollie hated him, felt sorry for him, and inexplicably loved him.

The dim light grew darker beside him. A shape loomed: the Martian.

"Go away!" cried Rollie. "My father . . . I don't want him to hurt you."

"He will not harm me. He would be afraid of me. The thought that we may still exist on Mars frightens him. My name is Moor. I wish only to help you and your sister."

"Geez. How?"

The Martian squatted down and put a long-fingered hand on Rollie's smooth flipper. "I can't tell you just yet. Please know that I will find a way."

"I dunno." Rollie felt unsure. "How can I trust you?"

Moor bowed his head, then looked to Rollie with his gilded eyes. "There are *other* parents. They could care for you."

"Yeah? Like us?"

"Yes. In a way. A mother and father left here on Mars. Their family is gone."

"Why would they want us? We're mutants."

"You are no more a mutant than I. We are alien, but only in visage. In our hearts, we are brothers."

Rollie smiled. "I like that." Then he saw his father step out of the hut.

Moor faded back into the shadows and disappeared, as Rollie's father trudged toward the rocket in the heat, going after fresh supplies. Waves rippled off the fine blue soil, shifting the air.

Rollie gestured to Stephanie, whispering to her. "He was here. I talked to him."

"I know," she said. "I sensed his presence."

Dad motioned to them. "Stephanie, come help with this load. Quit wasting time talking with your brother. We have work to do."

She shrugged. His anger eating at him, Rollie rolled his eyes and sneered. "What's wrong with talking? It's just not *right*, the way you treat us!"

"Young man, I think you just earned another night outside. And no dinner."

"Dad . . ." Stephanie whined.

"That's enough. You, too."

As they lay huddled together, tethered to the hut, Stephanie wept softly. Rollie wished he had arms to hold her. Dust adhered to her wet face, and she coughed.

Momma peered out at them periodically. Rollie was furious at her. She was hopelessly ineffectual. When he was younger, he'd seen her as a goddess, a savior with a sweet smile and soft words of consolation. But she was weak. So many times he'd prayed she would find her spine, her strength, and fight for them. And too many times his hopes had been dashed.

Cloaked in darkness, they fell asleep. Rollie dreamed he had arms and legs and was taller than Stephanie, who could see as clearly as he. They ran down the washed-silk blue hills until they came to the Martian sea. Moor waited for them to climb into his great ship with its gossamer sails to carry them to safety far, far away. There waited the others. They didn't look like Martians, though. They looked like the people in the pictures he'd seen on Earth of the early immigrants. Warm, grateful, happy people. Loving people. They embraced the two children and welcomed them into their family. . . .

Stephanie nudged him, hard. Rollie awoke, looked up, and saw four dark shapes with glowing eyes.

"Do not speak aloud. We have come to take you to a place where no one will hurt you."

Stephanie's eyes twinkled with reflected starlight. Rollie thought of his dreams. Behind the Martians stood a tall sand ship, much like the one in his dream.

"Come with us."

Stephanie drew Rollie into her arms. "The chains." Rollie could hear them clacking together softly.

Moor reached out and touched the plastine links. They fell away. He ushered the two children onto the sand ship where, safe and secure, they slept until dawn.

* * *

They awoke to familiar faces staring down at them.

Instead of the stern looks Rollie and Stephanie expected, the figures were smiling warmly, lovingly.

"Welcome home," said their mother. "I made some ginger-bread. I know how you love it." The children nodded, their mouths falling open, unbelieving.

Moor was gone, but another Martian who called himself Zzx stood behind their parents.

"You look surprised to see them."

Rollie's throat was closed tight with fear as he tried to speak. His voice was no more than a whisper. "Momma? Dad? We just woke up here. I don't know how we got on this ship. I guess the Martians just came and stole us out of our chains and . . ."

Stephanie squeezed Rollie's shoulder. She put her mouth to his ear and told him quietly: "They aren't Momma and Dad. They're . . . Martians."

"I don't understand," he said.

"I . . . I sense they're in camouflage," she told him. "Like they're wearing *masks* of our parents. Maybe they can change; become whatever they like. What do you say to giving it a chance; seeing how it goes?"

He nodded, wearily. He was tired and hungry.

Momma scooped Rollie up in her arms as if he were weightless and walked with him into the hut. Stephanie followed, Dad holding her hand, smiling down at her without a trace of malice.

The hut *seemed* the same as the one they'd slept next to the night before, but slightly off; as if someone tried to copy it, but created it a fraction out of scale. Smaller.

"I'll have gingerbread and milk out in a minute." Momma went into the kitchen as Dad sat down across from them.

"What do you say to a trip into the dead city this afternoon?"

"Dad? You all right?" Rollie was unconvinced.

"Sure, never felt better. In fact, I fixed your scooter."

Stephanie reached out to Rollie and held him. "I don't like this. Where are Momma and Dad . . . *really?*" She looked to the Martian standing at ease by the door.

Zzx unfolded his long arms from across his chest. "Home. The one we took you from last night."

"And these?"

"A mother and father who will love and cherish you. Who will care for you the way children should be cared for. Who will let you flower and find your bliss in this life. Please. Just believe. It is for the best. We all need one another. This is the way."

Rollie squirmed, looking frightened. "But our real parents . . . they'll come looking for us. Dad'll *kill* us! We *have* to go back before they wake up."

"Your father and mother awoke to another Rollie and Stephanie. They will never know you are gone."

Stephanie protested. "No! Momma has the gift of sensing, too. Not like mine, but good enough. She'll know the difference."

Rollie closed his eyes. He hoped desperately that Momma might find the strength to let them go and be happy. Maybe she would see she had no choice left but to protect them with her silence.

This was it. They *had* to stay.

He heard the electric whir of his scooter. Dad returned, wiping sweat from his brow.

"Come on outside and see."

"Don't take too long," Momma said. "We'll be eating in a few minutes."

Stephanie carried Rollie outside and settled him onto the scooter. It was exactly like his scooter, yet somehow *better*. He pressed his finger stubs to the raised handles and took off across the cornflower blue sand.

He wanted to shout for joy! How wonderful to feel the air whooshing past him, the sun on his face, the speed. He jumped small sand drifts and spun around and around until he was dizzy and giddy with laughter. In the growing distance, he saw his father become a speck at the back door of the silver box of a home, Stephanie beside him. Dad had his arm around her. Her face was turned up to him.

Rollie rode his scooter over the low hills until they were lost to view.

Wouldn't his new parents worry about him? The fear and guilt washed over him. How familiar the feelings were. How constant they had been all his life. Now, as he rode swiftly away, it occurred to him that he might never have to feel them again. Martian parents might not be anything like human ones. He grinned. It felt so good to feel hopeful when anything was possible.

Suddenly, a ruined town ahead surprised and distracted him. As he raced in, the purr of his scooter echoed softly between the walls of the once human-built replica of Anywhere, U.S.A. A town street. Stores and offices. Open windows coughed out tattered curtains. Screen doors yawned and jittered in open doorways. He heard the sound of running.

"You. There!" someone was calling to him.

Rollie squinted in the hot sun. It was a boy. In his late teens, maybe twenty. Rollie met the boy in front of a drugstore.

"Who are *you?*" Rollie wished Stephanie was there to tell him what this stranger was thinking. What he *was.*

"My name's John Hathaway. What's yours?"

"Rollie Painter. You live here?"

"No. I live with my mother and sisters about a mile away. Where do you live?"

"I dunno. I sort of drove off. A few miles away, I guess. I thought we were the only humans left here on Mars. At least that's what my father told me."

"Seems he was wrong. Come on. You can meet my family. This will be great. Friends! Finally!" John seemed genuinely happy to find Rollie.

The young man walked beside Rollie as he scooted out of the town. Rollie marveled at how John walked so easily over the broiling sands. John talked of the old days; rockets landing, all the people coming, then leaving for Earth, and how at last, only Captain Wilder's rocket returned to report there was no life beyond Mars.

"How long have you been here?" Rollie noticed a house in a fold of sand at the base of a low hill.

"Well, at least all my life, maybe more."

Rollie was confounded by John's response, but the sight of two pretty girls coming out of the house turned his mind to other things.

"Marguerite, Susan," John shouted. "I found a friend. His name is Rollie Painter. He has a family here, too."

The girls, young women actually, swept around Rollie. They

had golden hair and perfect smiles. Seeing them made Rollie wish he had legs and arms.

They introduced themselves and invited Rollie in. He shook his head and looked to the east, where he'd soon have to return.

"I can't come in right now. I'd better get home. They'll wonder where I've gone. But I'll bring my sister next time. How's that?"

"A new friend. How wonderful!" exclaimed Susan. "I must go tell Mother!" And she rushed into the house.

John patted Rollie on the back. "I'm glad we met. I'll be looking for you."

All the way back, Rollie thought about the people he'd met. Were they really human? Stephanie would know, and tomorrow they could visit. He wanted to see Marguerite again. He recalled the way she looked at him as he drove off. He wondered what life might be like in ten years; whether he and Stephanie might find love among the aliens. His heart raced all the way home.

When he returned, the bread was hot and ginger-smelling on the table. No one scolded him for being out so long, and Momma gently smacked Dad's hand for grabbing for a slice of gingerbread with his fingers. Stephanie grinned at Rollie, who swooned at the taste of real cold milk.

"Who wants lemonade for lunch?" Momma winked at Rollie.

"I do. You know I like it best of all."

Dad hadn't let them drink lemonade. Said it was "too acidy." It had been just one of many favorite things he had put an end to over the years.

Now Dad said: "I could go for a nice tall glass with lots of ice." He smiled, the white of the milk gracing the sides of his mouth with crescent moons.

Together, they plotted how to reach a nearby dead city and talked of all the places on Mars they would someday explore. Rollie kept expecting things to turn horrible at any moment, just as they had all his life. Yet they never did. Even when he told them about the others, Susan and Marguerite and John. In fact, Dad said they'd like to have them all over for dinner. It was like that. And it kept getting better.

For lunch there were tuna sandwiches with real bits of cucumber. And there was lemonade that tasted better than Rollie could ever remember. Sitting with his new family, Rollie sighed, marveling at the sound of laughter that floated up from the table and tinkled in the air like the ice cubes in their tall glasses. If he could, he thought, he would pinch himself. It was *that* good.

Miles away, under the same hot sun, Painter and his wife sat having lunch with their children. Momma broke down in tears every now and then, hurrying into the washroom to dry her eyes.

Dad didn't understand, but he said he was glad to see that his children were finally being sensible and respectful. He had so much for them to do, and no time to waste. No, sir. They would someday thank him for what he was doing for them. Yes, they would. He'd brought them all the way to Mars, hadn't he?

HIDING

Richard Christian Matheson

Bradbury's influence now spans generations, as demonstrated in the case of the Mathesons, father and son. Just as Bradbury's work impacted in the 1950s on Richard Matheson, Ray's fiction also made a deep impression, decades later, on Richard Christian Matheson.

The younger Matheson is best known in television and films, where he has been extremely successful in building a major scriptwriting career, but as his 1987 collection of short fiction, Scars, *conclusively proves, he is equally adept in prose. His first novel,* Created By, *offers further extension of his powerful, no-words-wasted storytelling.*

"Hiding," the tale he contributes to The Bradbury Chronicles, *echoes Bradbury's "Invisible Boy" in its basic mood and not-quite-fantasy approach. Both stories sharply define female characters who experience a similar sense of loss, yet "Hiding" is very much the product of Richard Christian Matheson's personal sense of wonder.*

Here's a taut, tart, poetic little tale, showcasing R. C. Matheson's special talent for emotional compression.

W.F.N.

They'd been married two months when the first fight streaked down their lives like black dye.

She'd never truly understood him; the delicately sensitive movements of mood and need that blew him, kite-like, from one moment to the next. Ever changing. Ever vulnerable.

But she tried to understand because she loved his tender heart; how he gently encircled her face in sweet hands as they made love. The way his shy smile would pillow her when they drank cappuccino together in bed and he could make her laugh at invisible animals; silly voices.

She giggled around him.

Morning talks, naked and sleepy, were like a kid's party for two; complete with exotic treats, pantomime hats, and invented places.

And though he could never be sure she meant it, she cared about his feelings; his secret coastline. Sometimes as he slept, a contented infant under thick wool, she would slip from bed and stare at his paintings on the bedroom wall; feathery watercolors, intense with hope. Windows to perfect places.

Fragile places.

Hectic dreams in yogurt colors.

She marveled at his imagination. His exquisite sensitivity. How he could touch a surface or color and tell her what it was thinking. How he could hold a cat and it would curl into a lulled nautilus in his warm arms; a child held by its mother.

It was why she regretted the argument.

It was the first time she'd ever raised her voice around him, and he sat so pale, he seemed to be filling with snow. Then, he wordlessly slipped from his morning spot, leaving the newspaper open, his cappuccino left to die.

He went up the stairs.

It was the last she saw of him.

He was still in the house. But she couldn't find him. She knew he was in there; sensed he was only hiding. Grieving from the disagreement. Healing from the momentary trauma.

But he wouldn't let her find him.

At rare moments, as she searched, she'd think she'd glimpsed some aspect of him dashing around the curved mahogany banister at the top of the stairs; a flutter of trouser leg, an evasive elbow.

Once, several days after he'd disappeared, she even sensed the ironically upturned corner of his mouth, a piece of a melancholic smile, in movement. Suddenly sweet.

Suddenly gone.

Weeks stood on one another's shoulders and reached to months. She would continue to leave food out, to sustain him and let him know she still loved him. She would leave notes, at first angry, demanding he come out. But when they did no good, she feared they'd driven him more deeply into the shadows and creases of the house.

Hoping it wasn't too late, she began to leave tender notes. Notes that told him she loved him. That she would wait for him. That she was sorry.

There was never an answer. But the food still disappeared and the plate, glass, and silver were always washed afterward by unseen hands. The cloth napkin was never soiled, the gingham checkerboard always pleasingly refolded, resembling a soft pattern of red bricks.

Though others never heard it, and, in fact, assumed he had merely left her for another woman, she often sat entranced by the sound of his singing, cloaked by wood and plaster, seeping beautifully through the walls.

He sang for hours, and his muted arias rose on sweet pain, perfect pitch. She tried to record the angelic mourning as evidence she wasn't mad, that he was in the walls, hiding.

But nothing much came out. Just the suggestion of melody, compressed and small, audible only to a believer.

And what few there had been, were now falling away, skeptical and pitying. Their faith and sympathy had winnowed and fled, unable to further indulge the sad fantasy that no longer made sense.

That really never did.

The phone didn't ring. The mailbox sat empty.

Seasons passed, forever gone; irreplaceable ledgers of the solemn two-story home that housed a lonely woman and her husband who hid somewhere she could never get to fast enough.

Her family suggested selling the house.

She couldn't bear the idea of strangers trying to find him by rapping on the walls, listening for a telling presence. She couldn't stand that they might accept him but ignore him. That he might die of neglect or loneliness. She decided to stay with him in the house; they would live under one roof, though they'd never see each other.

For her, it was better than nothing at all.

And she always remembered what his mother had said. How as a child, whenever his feelings were hurt, he would hide until he felt better.

"He'll come out when he's ready," she had whispered. "Just speak quietly and be patient. Loud voices scare him."

She never spoke loudly again.

On Christmas Eve, she wrapped his presents, using the bright-colored paper and ribbons he'd always loved. She tiptoed down the stairs and left them under the tree. Then, she went back to bed and stared at the walls, wondering if he were watching her, too. Wondering what he did for Christmas.

She turned off the light and reached over from the bed, placing her hand gently to the wall's warm surface. She stroked it, slowly, lovingly, fingers tracing its smooth flatness, remembering how she used to touch him.

She began to cry, trying to make no sound, trying not to startle him and scare him away.

"I love you so much. Please come back," she whispered. "I'll always be nice to you. I'm sorry."

Her hand pressed the wall, as if it were a huge palm and she fell asleep, protected beside it.

She went down in the morning, rubbing sad eyes.

His presents were gone.

But he'd left something for her; the first message he'd ever sent from the other side of the walls, from the corners and shadows where he hid.

It was an envelope, and he'd tied it with a bit of the ribbon she'd wrapped his gifts with. She opened it eagerly and inside, found a simple note. It read, "Soon."

She smiled, feeling excited.

She tried to imagine how he would look. A bit older but the

same. In her mind, they gazed longingly at each other and he held out his arms to her, wanting to trust again.

"I love you," he would say. "And I missed you."

"I love you," she would say.

But for now, she got the logs going in the fireplace and put on Christmas music. And as the cat climbed on her lap she spoke softly to it.

"He's coming back," she whispered. "He's really coming back."

SALOME

Chelsea Quinn Yarbro

*In the 1960s, Chelsea Quinn Yarbro functioned as a theater man-
ager, playwright, children's counselor, cartographer, composer, and
editor. In the 1970s she emerged in her ultimate career role, that
of novelist. The first of her darkly original historicals, Hotel Tran-
sylvania, featuring the vampire nobleman Francois Rgoczy, Count
de Saint-Germain, was published in 1978. It launched a series
blending historical romance with horror, extending from
seventeenth-century Antwerp into the modern world, chronicling
the adventures of the ageless, charming Count de Saint-Germain.*

*Obviously, Quinn (as she prefers to be called) knows her vam-
pires. Therefore, it was entirely fitting that when asked to contribute to* The Bradbury Chronicles *she chose to write about the
character, Timothy, from "The Homecoming." In the Bradbury
original, Timothy was the odd boy out in his bizarre clan since, as
a young vampire, he had no taste for blood. A vexing problem
indeed.*

*Quinn Yarbro picks up Timothy's story after he has matured to
manhood. She deftly and deliciously propels him into a complex
emotional relationship with a woman who has no idea of what her
new lover is really like.*

*Can a young man, who also, through no fault of his own, hap-
pens to be a vampire, find true love? Read "Salome" and find out
for yourself.*

W.F.N.

She had the apartment now almost the way she liked it. The sofa faced the window so in the afternoon the sun warmed it, the small bench in front of the bedroom vanity was upholstered in plush. There was still too much clutter on the window sills and she had not figured out what to do with the antimacassars, but for the most part Salome was satisfied. Leigh-Ann, who shared the place with her, made allowances for most of Salome's whims, which suited them both very well.

There was, however, the question of Leigh-Ann's new boyfriend. His name was Timothy and he was fresh out of graduate school with a shiny new Ph.D. in sociology.

"He's a very nice man," said Leigh-Ann to Salome as she dawdled over a late salad. "He's been with the company for about three months. He's in marketing research, doing regional demographics." At twenty-eight, Leigh-Ann was just coming into her own style, and much to her surprise, she was learning how to look pretty.

Salome, who had eaten earlier, did her best to ignore the green leaves and the sharp smell of the vinegar.

Leigh-Ann caught another hapless shred of bibb lettuce on her fork. "He's agreed to come to dinner on Friday night." She paused. "I said I'd make linguine a la Caruso. That's with chicken livers. You like chicken livers, don't you?"

Salome lowered her head in acknowledgment. She had a great fondness for chicken livers and Leigh-Ann knew it.

Leigh-Ann smiled a little. "Well, I don't want you to think I'm leaving you out of my plans, Salome." She finished up her salad and got up from the table. "You'll like him. He's a very sweet guy. I don't know what it is about him, but he gets to me." As she rinsed off her dish in the small kitchen, she added, "I know I said I wouldn't get involved with someone at work. But Timothy isn't like most of the men I've met there. For one thing, he's single, *and* for another, he's straight. That's too good an opportunity to turn down."

There was nothing Salome could do to distract Leigh-Ann from her speculations about this Timothy. Clearly, Leigh-Ann was determined to spend time with Timothy and nothing she could do would change that. She decided it would not be dignified to try.

"Don't get huffy about him, Salome," Leigh-Ann requested. "You don't know him yet. This isn't anything like . . . well, before. I've admitted you were right about Jack after all. He wasn't the kind of man I'm looking for. But Timothy isn't anything like Jack was. You'll see when you meet him. He's gentle and kind and very close to his family."

Salome went into the living room and took her place on her favorite chair.

Timothy was slight, not much more than medium height. He had dark, soulful eyes and straight brown hair that tended to fall over his brow. He carried a bottle of very good wine and a dozen blood-red roses. His clothes were neat and a little professorial— a tweed jacket over an open-collar oxford cloth shirt and flannel slacks. "I found the place without any trouble," he said. "Your directions were terrific."

"That's good to know. People always get lost here in the hills. The roads are so confusing, and the signs aren't easy to read." Leigh-Ann stepped back to give Timothy more room. "Come in, please."

"Thanks," said Timothy.

Salome gave him an intense inspection as he came through the door, and decided she was not pleased with what she sensed. There was something about Timothy that raised her hackles.

"I'm so glad you asked me over, Leigh-Ann," said Timothy as he held out the wine and the flowers. "You were so nice . . . I mean, I never expected . . ." He faltered and blinked once as if the light were suddenly too bright for him.

"This is very nice of you. Thank you very much." Leigh-Ann glossed over the awkward moment as she took the gifts and held the door wider. "And mind Salome; she's not supposed to go out."

Timothy bent and scratched Salome's head. "Don't worry. I like cats."

This was an effrontery Salome was not willing to endure. She backed up, prepared to hiss, then bolted for the living room where she settled herself on her favorite chair with her back to the newcomer.

Leigh-Ann shrugged. "Give her a little time to get used to you. She's almost ten and pretty set in her ways."

"That makes her pushing seventy in human years, doesn't it?" said Timothy, following Leigh-Ann toward the kitchen. "Your food smells wonderful."

"Thanks." She looked at the wine, inspecting the label and trying to appear she knew more than she did. "Do we need to put that in the fridge?"

"I guess it wouldn't hurt," said Timothy with a diffident smile. "I don't drink wine, usually."

"We'll chill it," Leigh-Ann decided, and popped the bottle into the refrigerator. Only a major effort of will kept her from rattling on about the wine, the way her day had gone, anything to fill the silence.

In the living room, Salome began—with supreme indifference—to wash her tail.

"I've made some appetizers," said Leigh-Ann when she was sure she wouldn't run on about it. She was fudging the truth a little, since most of them had been purchased at the gourmet deli at the other end of the block. "And I have some sherry, if you'd like it."

"Iced tea would be fine, if you have any," said Timothy. He stared at Leigh-Ann as she took the tray of finger sandwiches and cheeses from the refrigerator. "You didn't have to go to all this trouble for me."

Leigh-Ann blushed. "Oh, it's not just for you, really. I don't do much entertaining here, and when I do, I like it to be special. You know."

"Would you like me to carry anything?" Timothy offered, looking around the kitchen.

"Well, there are two goblets there on the counter. You could bring them along, if you like. And there's some cranberry juice in the fridge. I'm sorry, but I don't have any iced tea."

He took the goblets at once, and retrieved the cranberry juice. "Ready when you are."

"Great." She led the way past the dining area—the table all

laid out with the real silverware and good dishes—to the living room. "Please. Sit anywhere you like. Except on Salome."

"Never on Salome," Timothy agreed, choosing the far end of the sofa, the part where the sunlight rarely touched. Part of him seemed to blend with the darkness that hovered there. "She's a very pretty cat." He set the goblets down with care and placed the jar of cranberry juice beside them.

"Yes, she is," Leigh-Ann said at once, as she put her tray on the coffee table. "She was the best of my old cat's last batch of kittens. We were supposed to get rid of her with the others, but I just couldn't. I badgered Mom and Dad for two weeks solid before they let me keep her. I said I wanted to take her to college with me."

On her chair Salome stretched out one leg and lazily went about cleaning her claws, all the while watching Timothy. She was struck by a shadowiness about his eyes, something that made his features hard to see.

"I don't think she likes me very much," said Timothy as he reached for one of the little sandwiches. He sniffed it once, just as Salome might have done.

"Oh, don't mind her. She's like that with everyone until she's used to them," said Leigh-Ann.

Timothy cocked his head. "Then I guess I'll have to come back again, for Salome."

Leigh-Ann smiled. "Sure. For Salome."

On her chair Salome made it clear that she was not deceived by either of them; she curled up again and dropped the end of her tail over her nose.

"There's a crab salad in the little round pinwheels," said Leigh-Ann, trying to keep their conversation going. Once again it was an effort to keep from babbling. "And the others are chicken, I think."

Timothy gestured his approval. "Crab salad's always nice." He leaned back against the cushions in an attempt to appear relaxed. "This is a great building, and well kept up for being so old. You don't find many of these old three-story places around anymore."

"It was built in 1911," said Leigh-Ann. "They made it into apartments just after World War Two. That's why the units are so big. I'm glad I got the top apartment. There's just one bedroom, but the view makes up for that."

Salome heard the nervousness in Leigh-Ann's voice and mewed in sympathy. She lolled on her side and looked at Leigh-Ann upside down over her shoulder.

"Well, it's a very special place. You have a very pretty apartment." Timothy patted the arm of the sofa twice.

"Oh, that's nice of you to say." Leigh-Ann reached out for the cranberry juice. "Let me pour some of this for you."

"Thanks," said Timothy, holding out both goblets as she removed the cap on the jar.

As Leigh-Ann finished pouring, she very nearly dropped the jar. As it was, a splash of the red juice fell on her toast-colored carpet. "Oh, damn," she whispered. "It's going to stain, I just know it."

Timothy was on his feet at once. "Let me get something to clean it up." He took an impulsive step toward the kitchen, then stopped. "What should I use?"

"I don't know," said Leigh-Ann miserably. "Cold soda water, I guess. There's a tea towel by the sink." She knelt down and reached for one of the cocktail napkins to try to soak some of it up.

Salome came down from her place on the chair and ambled over to the fruit juice stain, sniffing with great care. She never much liked the smell of juice, but things on the carpet were always worth a glance or two.

As Timothy came back from the kitchen, a bottle of Pelligrino Springs water in one hand, the tea towel in the other, he said, "Don't worry about it too much. Things like this were always happening when my family had parties." There was a nostalgic lilt to his voice as he handed the water and the towel to Leigh-Ann. "We had these annual family reunions, Homecomings. There was always so much to clean up, but no one really minded."

Leigh-Ann was scrubbing at the stain; she bumped Salome with her arm and apologized to the cat. "Sorry. Get out of the way, Salome."

Tail up, Salome sauntered away. If Leigh-Ann was determined to act like a drudge, Salome knew there was little she could do about it, or wanted to do. She jumped back onto her favorite chair and made herself into a tucked-up package, her half-closed eyes lingering on Timothy as he bent over Leigh-Ann; Salome did not like that at all.

The only good thing about dinner, in Salome's opinion, was the amount of chicken livers that were left over at the end of the meal. Both Leigh-Ann and Timothy had indulged so heartily in the appetizers that they had little room left for the actual dinner. Artichokes, linguine a la Caruso, and spinach salad were only picked at.

"It was very nice of you to have me over, Leigh-Ann," said Timothy as they dawdled over coffee. "I hope you'll let me come again."

"Because of Salome?" teased Leigh-Ann, who was feeling more relaxed at last.

"It can be. I'd rather it was for you, too." He drained the last of his coffee and put the cup aside. "Do you want me to help you wash up?"

"No, thanks," Leigh-Ann said at once. "I'll do that." She blushed a little and shot one guilty look toward Salome, who was now draped over the lid of the stereo turntable. "I'm sorry about the cat. She's not very sociable tonight, I guess."

"Don't worry about it," said Timothy as he got to his feet. "She'll warm up to me in time, if you'll let me have the chance." He held out his hand to Leigh-Ann and brought her to her feet.

To Salome, kisses looked almost enough like licking to be fun. She regarded the two caught in each other's arms, her yellow eyes bright with curiosity. What was it about Timothy that was so unlike other humans she had seen over the years? It was hard to tell, which made her all the more suspicious of it. She got down from the turntable cover and hopped onto the sofa, stopping to sharpen her claws on the arm before strolling toward the couple.

"I don't want to apologize for doing that," Timothy said softly as he released Leigh-Ann from his embrace.

"There's no reason to," she said, her breath coming more quickly than usual. "I . . . I liked it."

"So did I," said Timothy, moving reluctantly away from her. "Enough that I better leave."

Leigh-Ann nodded twice. "If you think that's best."

He smiled at her, a warm, shadowy smile that made Leigh-Ann's heart race and brought a low, musical growl to Salome's throat. "There," he said, looking toward the cat, "you see? She's got the best sense of any of us."

"Yes," said Leigh-Ann with regret.

Timothy was already walking toward the door, his hand extended so that Leigh-Ann could hold it as they went. "I'd like to come again next week. If you don't mind. That is, if you're free. Say, Saturday night? We could go out. Maybe see a movie. I don't want you to think you have to fix dinner for me all the time."

"We could stay in and order a pizza," said Leigh-Ann.

Timothy grinned. "Tell you what: I'll pick up something and surprise you." His kiss was briefer but no less intense than the first had been. When it was done, he took her face in his hands and looked down into her eyes. "Dream about me, okay?"

After he left, Leigh-Ann lounged about the apartment for a short while, gathering up dishes and piling them in the sink as if performing an arcane ritual whose significance she had never understood. She kept up a stream of conversation with Salome as she worked, as if that would make Timothy's being gone more bearable. "Did you notice that he only had one glass of wine? That was a very expensive bottle if all he wanted was one glass. Maybe he's just cautious. Maybe he's the kind who takes a couple sips and it goes right to his head. Maybe he wanted to make a good impression on me."

Everything was stacked, the pans were soaking, and Leigh-Ann announced she would finish the cleanup in the morning.

Salome followed Leigh-Ann closely, adding her own comments when Leigh-Ann fell quiet. It was disquieting to see Leigh-Ann in such a state, caught in the grip of something that Salome knew was dangerous for her. She watched Leigh-Ann with troubled eyes, recognizing the fascination that claimed the woman as surely as she recognized something of sinister innocence in Timothy. She rubbed against Leigh-Ann's legs and continued to try to convince her, now with exhortations, now with blandishments. She was vexed when Leigh-Ann stroked her and called her a curmudgeon.

In the bath, Leigh-Ann luxuriated in the unusual pleasure of scented bubbles and watched Salome try to catch them on her claws. "I know it's silly, buying this bath stuff when it's so expensive, but I feel very special tonight. I think that's what I like about Timothy. He makes me feel very special, as if there's no one quite like me in the world."

Salome muttered in exasperation, but whether it was at the futility of catching bubbles or the frustration of dealing with Leigh-Ann's infatuation with Timothy, it was impossible to tell.

That night, and the next night, and the night after that, Leigh-Ann dreamed of Timothy. Her dreams were so real to her that she wondered how she was going to face Timothy at work on Monday. As she finished her spartan work-morning breakfast of wheat germ and low-fat yogurt, she told Salome about it while the cat picked at her breakfast of chicken scraps and cat crunchies.

"It would be so easy to fall for him. He's got that gentle way about him, and he's nice." She drank the last of her tea and smoothed the front of her blouse. "I'm afraid I'm going to do something reckless, just because I don't want to be single anymore. I want to ... oh, get involved, I guess. Not the way I did with Jack; really involved, day to day. But I don't know enough about him yet. Not enough to decide about that. I don't even know if he's really interested in me."

That, Salome knew, was not the problem. What troubled her the most was her certainty that Timothy was very seriously interested in Leigh-Ann, his attraction originating in that hidden part of his eyes where something lurked that was not what Leigh-Ann wanted so badly. She sat in her best sphinx posture and regarded Leigh-Ann steadily.

"You haven't got any good reason not to like him," Leigh-Ann persisted. "You're always jealous if someone pays attention to me. You don't want me distracted from taking care of you, do you, you old duchess?"

Salome endured the indignity of being picked up and held on her back while Leigh-Ann rubbed her tummy. In a short while it began to feel good and she started to purr.

"That's what it is, isn't it? You don't want to share me with anyone. Timothy likes cats, you heard him say that himself. You're being possessive because you think I won't care about you as much if he's here. How could I not care about you? You're my cat. I'm not going to let anything happen to you. But you won't suffer if I have another person around—why, you'll have two people to pamper you instead of one. You'd like that, wouldn't you?" She rubbed Salome's tummy one more time, then put her down. "Look at this. You're shedding all over my jacket. Serves me right for picking you up."

For the rest of the week Salome and Leigh-Ann had supper alone. Salome listened as Leigh-Ann told her about work—spending much too much time on reporting what Timothy said and did each day—and then curled up beside her to watch whatever was playing on cable until the nighttime news signaled the end of their day.

But while Leigh-Ann slept and dreamed her disturbing dreams, Salome only cat-napped. Through the silent hours she patrolled the bed, taking up one post and then another, keeping guard over Leigh-Ann. She was alert to every sound, every creak and rattle in the apartment. She could sense something hovering just beyond her sight, something lurking in the darkness.

"I haven't often had dreams . . . so . . ." Leigh-Ann said with a faint, embarrassed laugh as she checked her lipstick toward the end of Saturday afternoon. She had changed into soft jersey slacks and a silk blouse only ten minutes ago, putting off her preparations as long as she could to keep from becoming too nervous about the evening. "It's awful. I'm acting like an idiot. You'd think I was fifteen with a crush. Only this is worse. It's so . . . specific." She ran a comb through her shiny hair.

Salome watched closely, her eyes tracking the motion of the comb as if anticipating catching it. She made a plaintive sound before she got down from the clothes hamper and set about washing her face. It was worse than she supposed. She had never seen Leigh-Ann with her cheeks flushed and her eyes so bright. This Timothy was a fever in her, an infection. Salome was determined to reveal the terrible truth about him at any cost.

Timothy arrived less than half an hour later, bearing two bags full of fragrant little paper containers of Chinese food: here were Kung Pao chicken and Empress prawns and oyster sauce beef and Mu Shui pork with six rice pancakes and tea-smoked duck and baked fish in black bean sauce and bamboo shoots with three kinds of mushrooms in lobster sauce . . .

As Timothy set them on the coffee table, Leigh-Ann could not help laughing. "We'll never finish it all," she protested as she went to the kitchen for bowls and serving spoons.

"Well, I didn't know what you liked, so I got a little of every-thing. There's pot stickers in here, and Bao in this package, too." He started opening the containers and putting serving spoons in them. "The biggest one is rice. Just steamed rice, nothing fancy."

"There're ten different dishes," said Leigh-Ann, hating herself for adding up what this gesture must have cost.

Salome sniffed at the package containing the tea-smoked duck. That, at least, was not redolent of hot sesame oil, and therefore fit for her consumption. She gave a genteel hint that she would like a bite, but neither Leigh-Ann nor Timothy paid any atten-tion to her. She repeated her request a little more emphatically.

As Timothy ladled prawns onto his rice, he said to Leigh-Ann, "Have some of this. You'll like it. It's really good. And I'll make you one of the Mu Shui pork rolls." He pulled two pair of chopsticks out of one of the bags. "I hope you know how to use these things."

"I can manage them a little," said Leigh-Ann, accepting the pair he offered her. "I don't get much practice with them, but I do know how."

"Good." He put his bowl on the coffee table and seated himself on the floor, crossing his legs and looking very much at home. "I see most of the cranberry stain got out. That's good." He pulled a pillow off the sofa and used it as a cushion against the legs of Sa-lome's chair. "I wish I knew what you were thinking now," he said suddenly as he picked up his bowl, chopsticks poised.

Color suffused Leigh-Ann's face. "It would probably . . . it isn't all that important." She busied herself in pulling some of the baked fish off the bones.

"Do you mind if I give a little of this to Salome?"

"Go ahead," she said.

He smiled at Leigh-Ann, then turned to the cat, meeting her yellow eyes straight on. "Come on. You like fish, don't you, girl?"

Salome sniffed carefully at the bit of fish that was offered her.

"I'm not a Borgia, kitty," said Timothy patiently. "If you don't like black bean sauce, maybe we can scrape it off for you." He reached out and Salome drew back, showing all her teeth and making a challenging hiss.

"Salome!" Leigh-Ann's rebuke startled the cat, and she looked chagrined for an instant. "Don't be like that. Timothy is being very nice to you. To both of us."

That was what Salome trusted the least about him. He was going out of his way to court not only Leigh-Ann but herself as well. Indignation swelled in her. That she should be so underestimated! She was a cat, not a mere human! She looked at him narrowly, not conceding anything. She was not going to be made a fool of by this Timothy person. Still, there was no reason to deny herself because she knew there was something wrong with Timothy; there was nothing wrong with the food he offered. Finally she hooked a small bit of fish on one claw and held it up for inspection. The fact of the matter was that the fish smelled delicious, and whether Timothy was bribing her or not, Salome could not resist it. She ate the piece of fish.

"That's a good girl," said Timothy, and returned his attention to Leigh-Ann.

Salome contented herself with some more fish and a few bits of duck before she set about a thorough washing, all the while watching Timothy.

"I have . . . well, I guess you could say that my family is unusual," said Timothy as he and Leigh-Ann finally gave up on the tremendous meal.

"Don't you think most people feel that way about their families?" Leigh-Ann asked, wanting to encourage him.

"Not the way I mean," Timothy said slowly. He ventured on, "I'm not much like them, actually." He looked down into the cup of strong tea he held. "I always wanted to be, but . . ." He lifted one shoulder, then gave her a quirky smile. "They understand. They don't hold it against me."

"How could they?" Leigh-Ann asked with a trace of shock. "How could they dislike anyone as . . . as nice as you are."

"Oh, they don't dislike me, they just know I'm different. I'm not the same sort." He gulped down his tea and refilled the cup. "Or I'm not very much the same sort. I don't live the way they do. I'm . . . not built for it." He smiled a little, the smile very sad.

"Well, we can't all be strong or . . ." She realized she didn't know what made him different from his family. "Besides, you're probably more like them than you know."

There was something in the way he said, "Probably," that made Salome look up sharply. In that word there was the voice of the thing that was hidden. She glimpsed it, joyous and fierce, in the depths of his eyes, and then it was gone.

"Yes," he went on, musing aloud, "since I met you, I've thought that maybe I *am* more like them than I assumed I was."

"Maybe you're a late bloomer," suggested Leigh-Ann, letting herself lean comfortably against his arm when he slid it around her. "Wouldn't that be nice?"

He nuzzled her neck before he kissed her.

Leigh-Ann had been restless since she fell asleep. Salome sat all tucked in at the end of the bed and watched her turn over yet again, heard her mumble a few words, one of which was certainly *Timothy*. The cat yawned and gathered her ankles together, dropping her chin on top. She relaxed and gathered her strength. Ordinarily such a soothing posture would have put her to sleep quickly, but not tonight.

Somewhere out on the hillside a dog barked, to be echoed by two or three others. Salome lifted her head, watching the window with her bright yellow stare. Tonight something would happen. She was absolutely certain of it. She was too much a predator not to recognize a hunt when she saw one; at last she knew what it was she saw in Timothy's shadowed eyes.

There was a scrape against the shingles, a rustle in the tree that stood beside the building, a soft footfall as Timothy stepped onto the narrow little balcony outside Leigh-Ann's bedroom.

Salome stood up, alert and ready. She patted at Leigh-Ann's shoulder, taking care not to use her claws yet.

Timothy pulled the sliding glass door open, then paused to brush off his jacket. He stood, indecisive, then made his way toward the bed, more tentatively than stealthily.

At that, Salome's fur stood out and she glared at the intruder, daring him to come one step nearer.

"Salome," whispered Timothy. "What's the matter?"

Salome uttered a low, warning growl in her throat and stood more squarely between Timothy and Leigh-Ann. She would not be bullied by this human in a brown suede jacket, and that was all there was to it. Her eyes blazed.

"I'm not going to hurt her, Salome. I wouldn't do that." Timothy held out his hand, but drew it back at once as Salome took a swipe at it with her claws extended. "Hey. Don't do that, okay?"

Leigh-Ann sighed deeply and wrapped her arms around her pillow. Salome did not glance away from Timothy, not for an instant, as she adjusted her stance. Her fur was electric and her eyes shot sparks.

"She's not going to wake up, not until morning," said Timothy, his voice apologetic. "I can't do what some of my relatives do, but I can manage that much." He came a step closer and looked down at the cat. "Why don't you let me do this, and then I'll get out of here."

This time Salome spat at him.

Timothy hesitated near the side of the bed. "What's the matter with you, kitty? It's not as if I'm going to do anything bad to her. Not even my uncles can do that, and they're a lot more dangerous than I am." He crouched down beside the bed so that he could be more on the same level as Salome. "I like Leigh-Ann, Salome. I really do. This is one of the ways my family shows it when they like people, or some of them do." He stared directly at the cat now.

Salome's ears went flat back and her tail scythed over the comforter.

Timothy was determined to explain. "I didn't think I could do this. All the time I was growing up, it just didn't seem to be in me. I know I'll never be the way they are—my family—but I'm a little bit like them, and that's something. For a long time everyone thought I wouldn't become . . . I never thought I'd . . ." He started to reach out for Salome, then thought better of it. "I know you want to protect her. I want to protect her, too."

Salome's scorn was complete. What audacity! She crouched low and moved a few inches closer to him, muttering imprecations.

"You see," said Timothy, hunkering down on his heels, "I'm not as bad as you think. I'm not going to drain her or anything like that. Until I met Leigh-Ann, I didn't know I'd be able to do this at all. All the time I was growing up, I never wanted to, or needed to. At least I didn't think I did." He laced his fingers together and stared at where his hands were joined. "The Family didn't care that I wasn't . . . well, the way they are."

Leigh-Ann moved against her pillow, her eyelids fluttering, her lips opening enough for two breathless syllables to escape.

"You see?" Timothy challenged Salome. "Look at her. She wants me. She's got me in her dreams already. She wants to make the dreams real. It would make her very happy."

With a gesture of utter contempt, Salome lashed out with her front paw. Her claws caught on the suede collar of Timothy's jacket. It was mortifying, to have to pull her paw free when what she had intended to do was open his cheek in three neat furrows. Her distress came out in a long, sinuous yowl. To make it worse, while she was struggling to pull loose, he stroked her.

"You'll get used to me, Salome," Timothy promised her. "Leigh-Ann is used to me now, but she doesn't know it yet. She's learning about me in her dreams. Look at her. See the way she's lying there? Just the way she breathes tells you she's dreaming of me, doesn't it? In a month or two, when she's had a little time to adjust, then I'll let her stay awake, and she can live her dreams with me." He got to his feet. "You ought to be able to understand me, if my family can. We're more the same than you realize. I'm not as much a night creature as you are, and I'm not as relentless a hunter, but we have a little in common, don't you think?"

Salome launched herself at his shoulders, her paws full of daggers.

Timothy fell back, bringing his arms up to shield his face and to force Salome to release him. He strove not to shout as he struggled with the outraged cat. As he pulled at her, Salome wriggled furiously and grabbed for his left arm. Before he could recover his balance, he blundered into the wall.

The sound was loud enough to break through the barrier of Leigh-Ann's unnatural sleep. She stirred, then rose on her arms, staring in fright at the battle taking place less than a foot from her bed. She shook herself in an effort to come awake.

Salome shrieked and dug her teeth into Timothy's hand.

"Hey!" he bellowed. "I don't want to have to hurt you, cat!"

At last Leigh-Ann came awake, a hand to her eyes, terror starting to stretch her mouth into a scream.

Timothy flung himself and Salome onto the bed, hoping desperately that Leigh-Ann would not do anything senseless. He wrapped his free arm around the cat, to buffer their fall.

Now Leigh-Ann was sitting bolt upright in bed, blanket clutched under her chin, her face drawn in fear. Only when she realized that it was Timothy, and that he was locked in combat with her cat, could she make herself move and speak. "What's going on here?" She was in that precarious state where fright turns to anger.

"Leigh-Ann," Timothy said as he wrestled with Salome. "Get this damned cat off me."

Salome renewed her assault with more determination than ever. She was not about to permit Timothy to triumph now. Her teeth sank deeper, with better purchase; she felt the blood run into her mouth.

"Let go of him," cried Leigh-Ann seizing her cat's middle and tugging. "*Salome!*"

The cat was shocked to hear Leigh-Ann sound so afraid, and so determined. In her confusion, she let go of Timothy's hand and in the next instant was flung across the room. She landed on her feet, her fur bristling, teeth bared.

Leigh-Ann was leaning down from the bed. "You leave him alone! Do you hear me?" Then she looked at Timothy. "Oh, God. Look what she's done to you. You're bleeding." Then she stared at Timothy. "What are you doing here?"

Timothy's half-smile was self-effacing. "I came to see you." He watched as she daubed at his hand with the sheet. "That's another stain because of me."

"Don't be silly," she said, frowning as she worked. "What on earth came over her?"

"She was trying to protect you," said Timothy, sitting more comfortably now. "She saw someone coming into your bedroom and she defended you. That's some cat you have there. Most dogs wouldn't do as well."

"But she hurt you," said Leigh-Ann.

"Not as much as you think," said Timothy, and smiled at her again, this time with dawning passion.

As Leigh-Ann slipped into Timothy's arms, Salome turned away in disgust. That Leigh-Ann would choose Timothy! It was so unthinkable that she put it out of her mind and concentrated instead on the strange, sweet taste of the blood she licked off her claws and whiskers.

THE INHERITANCE

Bruce Francis

Before he left Los Angeles with his family to live in the wilds of Vermont (having purchased a house he painstakingly renovated into a local showpiece), Bruce Francis was editor/writer for an entertainment industry magazine. His short fiction has appeared in the Shadows *series of anthologies and in* Lord John Ten—*and his first novel,* Scenic Route *(a surreal shocker) was published in 1990.*

At one time, prior to his move back East, Bruce had the largest Bradbury collection on the West Coast. He still retains an intense admiration for Bradbury's unique talent. A book celebrating Ray's fifty years of creativity would be incomplete without an entry from Bruce Francis.

In his contribution to this anthology, Bruce uses Bradbury's story "The Lake" as his takeoff point. Yet this work is not *a pastiche. It is sharply original in answering the question of what really happened to Tally when she failed to return from the dark waters of the lake.*

Bruce Francis displays strong narrative talent in a poignant, penetrating tale of revelation and triumph.

You'll remember "The Inheritance."

W.F.N.

I never forgot her. Over the years, the lake called to me with her voice. I heard its waters sing in my blood. And one day, I knew, I would return to it.

To Tally.

That day I locked the car. I suppose that had been foolish, but the seaminess of the place seemed to call for it. Though late in the season, there was more activity than I'd expected. Games, concessions, decrepit rides. For every two that were boarded or chained, one remained open. Video games and pinball machines buzzed and dinged. Rusty tin food huts sizzled. Flapping tents belched smoke from beneath their sagging sides, looking like hollow-cheeked heads of giants, buried up to their necks along the beach. I could hear the calling of gulls, but only faintly beneath the racket of generators. Gasoline fumes saturated the salt air, all but masking the aromas of sun tan lotion and french fries.

I walked toward the beach through the buckled tarmac of the parking lot. A group of youths with pasty skin leaned against cars, alternately braying laughter and looking sullen. One of the boys, his index finger hooked around the neck of a beer bottle, said something as I passed them, but I kept walking.

I passed beyond the shops, across the boardwalk, and down the few steps into the sand. Here, with the arcades at my back, the scene before me was much as I'd remembered it. Probably much like anyone would remember it on any given day in early autumn. But for me, it was important for it to be like this.

I watched small children scrabble like crabs as they chased the surf away from the shore, giggling, racing frantically as it chased them back a moment later. It was cool and the breeze made it cooler. Bathers kept their shoulders below the surface and were quick to pull on windbreakers as they left the water to huddle beneath umbrellas and pavilions. I didn't hurry. I gave myself that time to watch them. And as I watched, it occurred to me that in all my memories, what was now most noticeably different was the color of the water. I had always thought of it as green, the color of an old Coke bottle, a color that seemed to teem with life. Now, as it curled in against the sand, I noticed that it was actually blue, almost medicinally pure-looking. Maybe it was just a quality of the gray afternoon light, or a certain early autumn slant to the sun as it flashed on the water.

I don't know how long I stood there. After a time, I became aware of the nearly constant sound of car engines starting in the parking lot behind me. Out on the beach, the last few determined waders hurried from the surf and began towelling off. I looked along the shore, scanning its long crescent in either direction. A light mist was settling. Down the beach stood the lifeguard station that marked the spot where, seventeen years ago, the attendant had carried Tally from the water. So small, I remembered. After ten years in the water, small enough to have been nearly lost in the folds of the canvas sack draped across his arms, nearly weightless but for the water that ran from the cloth. There had been so little of her there in that stranger's arms. A trace of gold from the locket that she still wore. Another trace of gold in her hair. Beyond that, what the lifeguard had taken from the lake could have been so many sticks bundled together with sea-weed. That day, the lake had given up only a little of what Tally had been; it surrendered nothing of what she had become.

She waited in a world where time did not exist, moving with the tides, learning from them, knowing that I would one day return. Knowing that this time I would stay. That is what I had come to know over the long slow curve of years that once again found me there at the water's edge.

I walked to the waterline where the sand was wet and hard and made walking easy. I didn't care that the tide slipped in close enough to froth and bubble over my shoes. I kept my head down as I passed the lifeguard station, and I felt my heart quicken when I saw the imprints of a child's feet in the sand. "Down the beach, where the water gets shallow." That was where he had found her. I followed the small impressions in the sand, the sound of my breathing replacing the steady churning of the surf. Remembering the sand castle I had come upon so long ago, I thought the footprints might be a sign, a path to follow. But a few yards on they suddenly veered away from the water, heading up the beach. I peered after them, trying to trace their path where the sand became dry. Far off, I saw the figures of a child and his parents as they climbed the rocks of the breakwater.

This time, there was no sand castle. As I walked on, I began to wonder if I had overlooked something. Suddenly, alone on that stretch of beach, I had lost that beacon. Twice I nearly turned back, but both times I told myself that she would lead me to her. I began to think of it as a test of faith, this pilgrimage a trial of my devotion.

Still, doubts nagged at me. Was I seeking the spot where Tally had died? I had believed so. But why would she have come so far from where we had always played? Here the strip of sand narrowed, then became stone and rock as the beach gave way to a jetty. What would have brought her here? I had always believed that she had been silently taken by the currents off the beach. "Don't get caught in the undertow," our parents had always warned. But this part of the lake was unknown to me.

Inland from the jetty, a bluff stood above the water, forming a promontory overlooking the rocks below. Clumps of reeds sprouted along its crest, nodding in the breeze. As I climbed the boulders that formed the jetty, I turned and looked back over the beach. The mist had folded in upon itself, thickening into a fog. The tide was coming in, the surf sending its scalloped advances high up along the shore. Neither allowed any sign of my passing to remain.

I turned and climbed the last few feet to the crest of the ridge. I knew the place the instant I saw it. A few yards beyond the jetty the sand resumed, encircling a broad pool at the foot of the cliff. There the water was glassy and still, sheltered from all but the highest tide by mounds of rock and boulders. The last high tide had left lank streamers of seaweed plastered against the rocks and the carcass of a fair-sized fish, its one visible eye concave and dull. This, I knew, was where Tally had died. The footing was treacherous as I made my way toward the tidal pool. I felt a child's fear, the sense of helplessness as I imagined a small ankle twisted or broken on one of the slippery rocks, a bare foot snared in a stony crevice, caught there and held as the water rose . . . I pushed these thoughts away.

I picked my way around the edge of the pool to a large flat boulder that lay beneath the outcropping of the bluff above. The water lapped gently below me as I huddled near the top of the rock where it was still dry, my legs tucked up against my chest, my chin resting on my knees, staring out across the pool past the reef of stones, focusing on the spot hidden in the mist where I heard the sound of the surf falling upon the shore. I closed my eyes. At my back, the face of the bluff gathered the sound and directed it around and down upon me. I made my breathing assume the same interval as the waves. This was the sound that had called me here. This was the voice that had answered so many years ago when I had called to Tally. I had heard it then, but it had taken all these many years since to understand it.

I first heard it the day Tally died. I can see her on that day, her blond hair filled with the sun and the wind from the open window of my father's old Plymouth as we rode together to the beach. Those beach trips were always the same; as my father drove and smoked cigarettes and listened to the radio, Tally and I would bounce and tumble around in the back seat until he'd yell at us to quiet down. "If you two can't rein it in, I'm gonna turn this thing right back around," he'd threaten. We'd always strike some deal. We'd be quiet if he promised any of the usual enticements: an ice cream cone before lunch, hot dogs at Shine's, where they wrapped them in bacon and cheese, a creepy sea story, a story about the Navy, a story about his tattoos. Of course we always got the ice cream and the hot dogs and the stories, and never once did we turn around and go back home, the big threat taken less seriously each time we heard it.

Sometimes there were others ... Larry Blackwood, Michael Vermillion, Tommy Nutter. Sometimes my mother came along too. But the best times were when it was just the three of us. Me and my father and Tally. That was when it was special. Somehow, watching Tally bite into a big swirl of frozen custard made mine seem colder and sweeter. Watching her break her hot dog up into small cheese-stringy nuggets made my own last a little longer. And hearing her squeal at one of my father's stories made it seem just a little bit scarier.

The best of those days began early, always weekdays during summer vacation on a day when my father wasn't on the road. While the grass was still wet with dew, we'd load the trunk with the big umbrella and towels and beach toys. Then we'd drive down to the pharmacy before they opened, where my father would use his pocketknife to snip the twine on the stack of morning papers outside the door. He'd leave a nickel on the window sill, and we'd be off.

We had the lake to ourselves those mornings. Sometimes my father would bring his surf casting rod, and Tally and I would cut up the slimy bait and pretend to be sick. Other times we'd wander up and down the beach looking for treasures along the surf line while my father sat on the boardwalk, reading the paper and drinking coffee from his chipped Old Spice mug.

I can't remember now why we weren't in school that day, but I remember everything else. It was a weekday late in May, but too early for Memorial Day because there were no crowds and some of the places along the boardwalk still had not opened for the season. The morning was too cold for swimming, so we ran along the beach, sticks in hand, flipping seaweed back into the surf, queasily mashing jellyfish underfoot, and writing letters in the sand so tall that only airplanes could have read them. Tally made a pouch with the front of her windbreaker and we gathered shells. I dug them from the sand and rinsed them in the surf while Tally held the pouch open, clinking as she walked, as if her joints were made of china. When she could hold no more, we climbed the beach to sort through our haul. It was still too cool to want the shade of the umbrella, so we took the old tartan blanket into the sun and lay on our stomachs beneath it, pressing our bodies into the sand until we had our own cocoons, warm and hard and close-fitting. There we lay, side by side, shoulder touching shoulder, judging our shells for size and shape and color and most important, for their sound. We named one for each of the seven seas, or at least I tried to. Tally giggled as I struggled to remember the names. "My father would know," I told her. "He'd know in a second."

"But your father isn't going to have Mrs. Welch for geography next year . . . *you* are." Tally made her voice low and husky and looked at me sternly as she said, "Harold Douglas, you will stand and name the oceans of the world for the class." She laughed and flicked a spray of sand at me with her fingertips.

"Stop it, Tally," I complained, but not about the sand or the teasing. Suddenly, I didn't want to think about geography or the oceans of the world. I especially didn't want to think about next fall or school at the new junior high.

"God, Hal, just think of how different everything will be next year," she said, as if reading my thoughts. "Riding the bus to school . . ."

Instead of walking together, I thought.

". . . six different classes, six different teachers . . ."

No more sitting across from each other in the same classroom as we had every school day for as long as I could remember. No more secret signals or rolling our eyes behind the teacher's back.

". . . all the new kids that'll be there."

The yellow buses would bring children from all over the county, from other towns and the outlying farms, not just from our neighborhood like at the grade school. Maybe Tally and I would have some of the same classes. But maybe we would not. And where we no longer sat together, some of these new children would sit beside Tally. And, gradually, some would become her new friends. And, perhaps, one of these would become her *best* friend.

All at once I hated these children, children who were still strangers, but who, even as Tally and I lay beside one another on the beach, were certain to one day come between us. I pictured them as hateful, faceless creatures, stumbling blindly through dim, cavernous hallways of metal and tile.

Inwardly I moaned at the excitement I heard in Tally's voice. She talked on, her thoughts racing ahead to a future filled with school dances and basketball games and cheerleading . . .

I resisted, stubbornly trying to go back and freeze in my mind those moments before she'd begun all this talk of how different things would be. Didn't she know what she was saying? I wondered. Didn't she care? I squeezed my eyes shut tight and tried to make her words fade, make her voice melt away beneath the sound of the surf. As I listened to the waves curling in upon the shore, I envisioned each one from its beginning somewhere far down the beach to its end at some distant point far along from where we lay. Each wave different, I saw, and not, as I had always thought, the same wave, repeating and repeating forever. I felt the sun's warmth on my back as it climbed the sky from somewhere down below the distant lake shore. Even nature, it seemed, was conspiring to bring change to all that I had ever known.

I felt Tally squirming next to me. I opened my eyes to see that she had peeled the blanket from our backs, and was now shrugging off her windbreaker. I watched as she tossed her head, admiring the way that each separate hair seemed filled with gloss and light. Gone were last summer's pigtails, untied and shaken loose at some point the previous fall or winter or early this past spring. Though I must have noticed at the time, it seemed I had never before seen her hair without those childish braids. Now she wore it short, but not boyish, and I studied the way each strand followed the same gentle curve back from her face, brushing from her forehead to the top of her cheek, from the bottom of her earlobe to the back of her neck, where it tapered to a vee in the hollow between her shoulders. There, a wisp of down gave way to the eggshell sheen of her skin, for now still pale, but by summer's end, the color of a walnut shell. At some point, without my noticing, Tally had become gentle slopes and curves and roundnesses where I was still all jutting angles and knobs and points. I marveled at the skin on her shoulder, the faint spray of freckles, how its shape and its texture seemed to invite touch. In all the years growing up together, after all the games of tag and the piggyback rides and the impromptu wrestling matches, for the first time ever, I wanted—no I needed—to touch Tally. And for the first time ever, I was afraid to.

Suddenly, the change Tally had spoken about was no longer the far-off start of a new school year, or somewhere on the other side of a summer storm, or a week or even a day away.

Tally kicked her feet, tossing the blanket aside and raising a small sandstorm. I felt a veil of sand settle on my back and scalp. She had stopped talking, and I felt her watching me.

"Caspian . . ." I muttered.

"What?"

"*Caspian,*" I repeated. "The sea I was missing—the Caspian Sea."

"You didn't hear a word I said, did you?" She smiled and shook her head. "Let's go down to the water." She stood for a moment, blocking the sun that was nearly overhead. "C'mon, Hal, it's getting hot."

I followed a few steps behind, not failing to notice that even Tally's walk had somehow acquired all the confidence that had disappeared from my own in recent months.

The water was like ice. A small wave broke against Tally's shins, and she turned to me with a rigid smile, hands clenched and elbows flapping, then back to the water again. With a sound that was part laugh, part scream, part shiver, she ran ahead into the surf, splashing wildly as she plunged beneath the next wave. She beckoned and called, but I only stood and let the cold water lap at my feet. She teased and taunted and dared from the water, but I just waved back from the shore.

"Fine, then—" she called at last, "—you just go ahead and think about the oceans. I'll be swimming in them." She tucked her head, rising as she arched her back, and sliced the water with her hands, her feet vanishing beneath the surface with one last indignant kick. The water swirled for a moment where she had disappeared, then became calm again. I waited for her blond head to break the surface, but only the waves moved on the water.

I counted, holding my breath until I could hold it no longer. Still no Tally.

I ran into the lake, churning the water into a froth as I raced for the spot where she had slipped beneath the surface. I turned in a circle, scanning the lake and the shore and back to the lake. No. The water was up to my chest, but I didn't feel the cold, only the fear that rose like a knot into my throat. "Tally!" I called. And again. *"Tally!!"* Not even an echo came back to me. I had no voice left with which to call. The knot had risen and choked it away.

Tally's face rose from the surface on a jet of water, inches from my own, sputtering and wheezing as she tried to laugh and catch her breath at the same time.

I felt my hands ball into fists and I smacked the water between us. "Goddammit, Tally!" I shouted, but my voice broke, ending in a yelp.

Tally's eyes widened. "Don't you swear at me, Harold Douglas," she managed to say, laughing even harder than before.

I turned away feeling foolish and dejected. I tried to stomp off toward the beach, but the water prevented even that feeble display of temper.

Tally tugged my arm. "Come on, Hal, don't be mad. I didn't mean to scare you."

"I wasn't *scared*," I lied. She knew me too well.

"I just wanted you to come into the water. I just wanted you with me, that's all." She smiled, and all traces of the mocking laughter were gone. All my anger melted away. No longer resisting, I simply stood there feeling her small hands around my wrist, wanting her to say those words again.

Instead, she flashed a grin as she darted away, backhanding a plume of water that caught me square in the face. I took off after her.

We romped in the surf, Tally dividing the water like some golden fish, me sloshing and lumbering behind her. While we swam and played, the sun grew bigger and hotter as it rolled across the sky, making our shoulders pink with its fire. Shadows along the beach did their long, slow somersault as noontime passed, and the day stretched gloriously on. Summer was just beginning, I told myself, trying to put aside those earlier thoughts. And for a while, I succeeded. For a while there was nothing in the world but Tally and me, the lake and the sky.

I followed Tally out to where the swells formed, where the currents intersected, where the lake stored its power. There she made me crouch in the water as she climbed on my back, and using her hands on my shoulders as a springboard, launched herself atop the next swell at the precise moment it crested into a wave. She rocketed away, paddling fiercely as she rode ashore. We did this again and again, our bodies growing more attuned to the right moment, each time Tally paddling less but riding farther. As she splashed back out to where I waited, I could see that her thighs had become red and tender, chafed by the sand each time she slid aground. Finally, she insisted that I take my turn and crouched in front of me, reaching around to guide me close as we waited for the next swell. She was shorter than I, and where the water hadn't covered my shoulders, Tally had to stretch to keep her chin above the surface. I botched the first take-off, fearful that I'd push her head beneath the water. I fared better with the second, surprised by the strength in her legs and back, though I failed to paddle hard enough to keep afloat. Tally had not yet taken her stance as I moved behind her for my third attempt, and I happened to glance down at her shoulders where the sun was caught in a cluster of gleaming water droplets, clinging to her skin. In a rush I felt the return of the sensation I'd had earlier on the beach, that sudden need just to touch her. This time, though no less afraid, I didn't stop to think as I knelt behind her and placed my hands on her waist instead of her shoulders. I drew her to me, suddenly pleased that she didn't resist, surprised to find how naturally my ungainly features matched her perfect ones. I let my arms encircle her waist and pulled her closer still, feeling her warmth. I could smell the salt water in her hair. I felt my right hand drift out, touching her knee, then back, trailing gooseflesh in its wake. Tally shivered against me. I could have held her like that forever. I should have. Impulsively, my fingertips drew back along her leg to where the hem of her swimsuit met her thigh, feeling the curve where the red, chafed skin gave way to white. I watched the beads of water glisten on her shoulder. I almost tasted one.

Suddenly, Tally was clawing at my arms, fighting to stand, to pull forward and away from me. She made a terrible, unhappy sound like nothing I had ever heard. I didn't struggle against her, but even after she was up and away from me, she still flailed her arms, swiping at the air and water between us. When she finally stopped, she stood facing the shore, her back to me, her hands clenched in fists just above the water's surface.

"Tally—" I started.

She spun to face me. I saw color climbing high on her cheekbones, her eyes starting to tear, but flashing with anger. But more than anger . . . Her look was filled with betrayal and sadness and disappointment.

I think I probably opened my mouth to say something, but I don't know what it would have been. An unusually large swell moved past me and lifted Tally, putting her off balance. I reached my hand out to help steady her, but she slapped it down and away. She turned and walked in toward the shore, her head down as she wrung the water from her hair. I only watched her for a moment. After that I felt ashamed to have even my eyes on her.

I wandered down the beach, keeping to the shallows where the water swirled around my ankles. I don't know if Tally ever looked back to see me, but I kept hoping I'd hear her running to catch up to me or that I'd suddenly feel her touch my arm or hear her call. But none of these things happened.

After a while, I saw Donny and Del Schabold ahead of me

splashing in the surf. I joined them for a time, but the twins annoyed me with their bickering and their silliness, the two-year gap between our ages suddenly looming to separate us like some great expanse. They whined and sulked when I told them I had to go. I promised to return later, though I knew I would not.

When you're twelve, there are no mortal wounds. Especially when the wounds are made by words or small selfish acts. At twelve you can still "take back" something you've said or done, and suddenly honor and balance and dignity are magically restored. So I hoped it would be when I returned to Tally. I would offer to take back what I'd done. A brief but humbling moment of remorse. I would be penitent. Then the forgiving could begin. Then everything would be just as before.

Down all the years since, I've wondered what would have been if I'd had the chance to say those words to Tally. Probably, the events of that day would have become just another dim recollection, at most, the tastier bits in a stew of childhood memories. Who really remembers when life became changed forever? Who can point to a single day or a moment that made all the difference? Few, I suppose. But I can.

Tally was not on the blanket or beneath the umbrella or, as far as I could see, anywhere along the shore. The beach was dotted with other bathers by that time, but I saw no sign of her blue and yellow swimsuit. Her windbreaker still lay in a small mound where she had shed it earlier. I trudged up the beach, trying to make some sense of the trails in the sand, deciding that she must have gone up to the boardwalk. I wandered the strip, peering into the shops and the eateries and the game arcades. I stopped for a moment and rocked on the big-linked chain that hung across the entrance to the rides at the end of the pier, scanning back along the boardwalk at the few figures that strolled there. Tally was not to be seen. I repeated my circuit, walking faster this time. I was suddenly famished from all the exertion, thirsty from the salt-water. The smell of french fries became a torment, the sight of lemonade sloshing in big glass coolers, agony. But I had no money, and besides, I couldn't eat without Tally. That, I had already decided, was to be part of the forgiving ritual. The sun's glare had brought on a headache and my eyes burned. I reached the end of the loop where I had come up from the beach. From there I stared down along the sand to the water. I could see our beach umbrella, but nothing else. Nothing that could have been Tally. Once again I checked the buildings along the boardwalk, jogging this time, panting, feeling each breath hot in my throat. The faces of a few of the browsers seemed to have looks of concern or alarm as they watched me pass. Two or three started to say something, but I continued on unheeding. I quickened my pace to a run, making it all the more difficult to negotiate around the milling shoppers. An old man sidestepped nervously, wagging a cane in my path. This time I ran past where the buildings gave way to the open boardwalk and the view of the beach. I ran to the bike rental shack, but the attendant said he'd just had his only two rentals returned. Neither had been a pretty twelve-year-old—with pigtails, I had almost told him—in a bright blue and yellow swimsuit.

I felt a stitch throb to life in my side; my mouth was gummy and dry. With nowhere else to check, I ran toward the parking area with the dawning horror that not only had Tally disappeared, but I had not seen my father back there on the boardwalk, either. He could have been behind the doors of one of the long, dark bars that I hadn't bothered to check. Or he might have crossed the highway to one of the rambling shacks called the Silhouette Vacation Court. But a part of me kept imagining that Tally had found him and told him what I'd done. Would she have done that? Would she have told on me? After what I'd done, maybe. It hurt to admit it, but maybe. My father thought the world of Tally. I hoped when I finally found him, he hadn't been drinking. If he had, there'd be hell to pay. I suddenly dreaded the ride home that night.

I ran along the line of cars in the parking area, but the Plymouth was not there. Back and forth, up and down, as if under the ridiculous assumption that I had somehow overlooked it. But this was not the Fourth of July, when the lot would be a blazing sea of sun-blasted car hoods. There were fifty or sixty cars at most, all of them visible and distinct in one long sweeping glance. And my father's two-tone green Plymouth was just not there.

It had become such an unhappy day, I remember thinking. Wasn't twelve the beginning of the time when I was supposed to be seeing new things everywhere? I seemed to be suddenly existing in reverse. My life had become an ugly game of hide and seek, everything I trusted slipping away to some secret hiding place that I feared I would never discover. At that moment, whatever small amount of composure or reason I'd maintained simply bubbled away into a child's hysteria. I was flooded with a stream of irrational thoughts: My father had taken Tally home, so upset that he had simply abandoned me; they were hiding somewhere, maybe even watching me at that very moment; they had gone to the police to report my behavior . . . any second now I would hear their sirens. I looked off down the highway, expecting to see flashing lights come up over the rise.

There, out beyond the far edge of the parking lot, past the line of scrubby little trees that squatted along the beach service road, parked in the shade alongside an old Esso gas station, was the Plymouth.

I took off at a run, almost colliding with a Studebaker that was angling into a space. I saw the figure of my father emerge from the shade, looking like a Wyeth pirate; shirtless, pant legs rolled up to his knees, a bandana rolled and knotted at his forehead. I leapt the line of bushes, not even seeing them, but clearing them by a mile. The car's doors and trunk were all thrown wide, and I could see an open tin of Simoniz on the front fender. Suddenly the mystery was solved—no one waxed a car in the afternoon sun, even I knew that! I ran harder, the soles of my feet stinging as they slapped the earth. His back was to me; he hadn't seen my approach. I wanted to shout. I could not have been happier to see anybody.

Except Tally.

I slowed at once.

What did he know about what had happened with Tally and me?

"Dad?" I said quietly. It seemed a very long time since I had used my voice. He didn't hear me. I cleared my throat. "Dad!"

He turned at once, looking startled, sweat streaming from his face. He held a bottle of Carling in his hand.

"Dad, I can't find Tally."

For a moment, he just stood there with an almost stuporous expression, perhaps weighing the words for their importance. Then he was suddenly all action. He pitched the beer bottle into the weeds behind the gas station and slammed the trunk lid shut. "Get in the car, kid," he said.

We pulled away with a screech of tires, a rooster-tail of sand arcing out behind us. The can of Simoniz and its lid slid along the fender then dropped away.

I was frightened by this sudden sense of urgency, by my father's intensity. I blurted out a story about what had happened, saying only that we'd had a fight and I'd gone off down the beach, and when I'd come back she was gone.

"A fight about what?" he asked.

"School," I lied.

I repeated the story to the fat balding man at the shabby little building that was the tourist information booth. And again a little later to the supervisor of the lifeguards. In all, I probably repeated that story a dozen times that afternoon, never once varying the way it was told. Never once telling the real truth. The truth, I reminded myself, would wait until Tally could be there to tell it. As the day wore on, it began to appear as if the truth would never be told.

I heard Tally's name on the lips of the gathering crowd. They whispered among themselves as they peered out over the lake. It seemed unfair to me. They had never known her. She was *my* friend, not theirs. My *best friend*. What right did they have to speak her name, as if she were merely some new amusement?

A big klaxon horn on a tripod was dragged out, its shrill bleat sounding every few minutes. A firetruck and police cars arrived. Lifeguards were sent out again and again into the waves, and strong swimmers were recruited from the crowd of onlookers. At some unspoken point, one felt by all gathered, there came an awareness that the focus of the search had shifted. No longer did they hope to find a sunny little twelve-year-old named Tally. Now they only hoped to recover her body.

As the day ebbed away into dusk, a panicky gloom descended and there grew a palpable sense of defeat. Most of the crowd lost interest and drifted off to their dinners or their card games. Someone, either out of deeply misguided officiousness or unforgivable cruelty, summoned Tally's mother. Her sad, resounding wails replaced those of the klaxon. She cried as she struck my father's chest, his arms stiff, his hands clenched helplessly at his side. Through all her grief, I felt her hate. Hating my father for losing her Tally, hating me for simply being alive. I wandered away, believing that I deserved to be hated. I stood feeling the still-warm planks of the boardwalk beneath my bare feet, looking out across the water. One by one, the glare of the emergency crew's spotlights switched off, and as I listened to the waves and watched the darkness consume the last remnants of that amazing and fearful day, I whispered Tally's name over and over and over again.

Of all the petty fears I had felt on that last day with Tally, none came to pass. Instead, some things far worse took their place.

Tally was but the first and most immediate of that summer's casualties. The others were slower and subtler, though no less insidious in their arrival, all spreading forth from that day like parts of the same black tide that had taken her away.

There followed a feast of accusation, a veritable banquet of blame. And there was enough to go around for everyone involved.

A few accusations were directed at me, though by virtue of my age I was absolved of any real share of the responsibility. Others were not so fortunate.

Some hapless lifeguard, a college kid, had his life ruined.

Tally's mother one day simply walked away from her home of nearly ten years. A widow, Tally had been her only child, her whole world.

But it was my father upon whom most of the disdain fell, and for whom, ultimately, it was most damning. All through that summer, I remember the nights in my bedroom, hearing my mother from downstairs as she spoke to my father, her voice never raised in anger but filled with disgust and contempt and loathing. The next morning I would awaken to the sound of my father weeping. It was a strange and pitiful sound the first time I heard it, but it became familiar as the summer wore on. He stayed away at his work for weeks at a time instead of days, and when he returned home, he drank more than ever. Even his beloved Plymouth suffered; it grew dusty and disused, still displaying the white curlicue of wax on the front fender, looking

like the crest of a small wave. By August, my parents' marriage
had dissolved into a poisonous silence. My last recollection of
my father is the sight of him seated stiffly in the office of my
mother's attorney, staring hollow-eyed as he meekly signed the
divorce papers put before him. The following day, my mother
and I visited the lake that one last time, and the day after that,
we were on a train bound for the West.

I left "Hal" behind. It had really only been Tally who'd called
me that, anyway. To my father, I'd been "kid." To my mother,
I was always Harold. To my new friends in the West, Harry.

Harry became an attorney. Harry managed to forget the lake,
or at least put it out of his mind for a time. Harry married a
beautiful young woman named Margaret. Harry and Margaret
took their honeymoon in the land of Hal.

And that was when the sadness began again.

After my ten years away, Tally came in from the lake to welcome me home. Her half of a sandcastle awaited me . . . with the
small footprints going back out, into the dark water. After that,
if not always, the lake held me in its grasp.

Margaret and Harry returned to the West. There I watched as
Harry went about establishing his practice. I watched as they
started a home. I watched as Harry made love to Margaret and
as Margaret sweetly loved Harry back. And a little at a time, like
a small trickle at first, I watched as the lake slowly seeped back
into his consciousness. I saw its tides tug at his heart and erode
his mind. I saw his practice fall into disorder, I saw their home
slide toward neglect, I saw their marriage go childless. Still Margaret loved him. Loved me.

The night before my father died, I had a dream. It was the old
house and I was a child again. I heard my father calling from my
bedroom. I walked, then ran, through long hallways before I could
find the door. When I entered the room, he was drowning in a
whirlpool made by the bedclothes. They became winding cloths.
I reached for him and he pulled me along behind him, down into
silence.

The call came the next afternoon as I sat staring at the rain
outside the office window. My father was dead. A boating accident.

I returned alone that time. Margaret had never met my father, so it didn't seem callous for her not to attend. Besides, I had insisted.

It wouldn't have mattered. No one else was there. Somebody had made the arrangements, though. Someone who knew him. He was buried in the Garden of the Apostles, in a plot that lay beneath the shadow of Saint Peter's net. It was a fitting place for a sailor, a man of the seas. A drowning victim.

I wasn't fooled. But I nodded in agreement with their suppositions and their speculations. Boating accident. In all the world, there was no more unlikely a victim of a boating mishap than my father. No, I knew. Tally had called. His blood heard the call. She had called to me, but for a time he would do.

I visited the place where he had lived out the past years, along the highway across from the lake. One of the shacks that had once been the Silhouette Vacation Court. The place smelled of stale beer, dirty clothes and bug spray. I sifted through the squalor, keeping only the broken glass display box that held his navy ribbons. Once, long ago, the water had given him honor. I left the rest of the junk behind. Anybody desperate enough to live there next would be desperate enough to need it.

One day in court, not long after returning from the funeral, I opened my briefcase and discovered that it was brimming with water. Not clear rainwater or water from the tap, but the blue-green water of the lake, sandy and shot through with tendrils of weed. I slammed the briefcase closed and stalked from the courtroom without any explanation.

They hospitalized me. Twice.

I convinced Margaret that a change of locale was what we needed, and the doctors concurred. Lake Bluff, I suggested.

Lake Bluff, Margaret agreed.

Poor, loyal Margaret. Always there, always agreeable, always believing that somehow she could help bring about the change we both hoped for. For seventeen years she watched as the lake currents ate at my soul. For most of that time, I'm sure, she blamed herself for my unhappiness. I never told her about the lake or about Tally. I know that she followed me at times, fearful, I suspect, of what I was capable of doing to myself. I'd have thought she would have welcomed an end to the burden of living with me. But those times, the times when I visited the lake, I only sat in the car listening to the surf and the gulls and feeling the breeze. I waited, but none of those days were right. I had not yet heard the final call.

It came one night with the rain. I lay halfway between sleep and wakefulness, and where my hand dangled over the edge of the bed I felt the touch of something cool and wet. I didn't react immediately, unsure that I had actually felt anything at all. Then a drop rolled down my forefinger and off the back of my hand. I heard it fall into a puddle below. I switched on the light and there, next to the bed, lay a small pool of water. I glanced up, suspecting that a leak had begun, but the plaster on both the ceiling and the walls showed no sign of moisture. I looked back down to the puddle, and saw at its edge a small piece of green-brown leaf. I tasted the water on my fingertip. Salt.

She had come during that brief time both her world and mine were connected by water. By the rain. I lay back, listening as it fell on the roof and ran down the outside walls of the house. In my mind, I let the drops melt me and carry me away, following her, coursing through creeks and streams and rivers. I saw her ahead of me, floating, drifting, beckoning me to follow. "I want you to come into the water," she called to me again, down all the years. "I just want you with me."

It was time.

I opened my eyes. The fog had swept past, rolling inland. The night was clear before me. The moon fell on the water where it broke into splinters of light. It coated the slick surface of the rocks and shone whole in the still water of the tidal pool. Far out in the lake, where the swells formed, it glistened off the back of something that played there, splashing in the dark waters. I heard myself sigh as I slid from the rock. I felt myself lifted by the water, impossibly buoyant as I drifted toward the ridge that separated the tidal pool from the body of the lake. A gentle push with my legs and the tide surged beneath me, carrying me over the rocks, down and out through the surf, moving me effortlessly toward the moonlit figure ahead.

I held my breath. As I drew closer, the motion of the water created illusions, played with my vision. I could see features and shapes moving slowly, gleaming in the moonlight. I saw a slender arm arc from the water, its small hand clenched in a fist. A leg broke the surface, splashed for a moment, then disappeared. A broad, smooth plain of flesh rose and fell, sending out small waves of its own.

She screamed.

"Tally!" I cried.

The figure in the moonlight began to move, turning slowly toward me in the water. I could see Tally's face turned skyward beneath a confusion of shining surfaces. She was crying, the light caught in tears streaming over her face. Her sobs were soft, but deep and hurtful, the low, hoarse moan of surrender. She turned to look at me, pleading with her eyes. My father lifted his face from where it had been pressed against her shoulder.

For the first time I felt the numbing cold of the water.

"No!" I cried, pushing forward against the sandy bottom. But the water that floated me so easily moments before, now dragged at my limbs, drawing me down. My father stood and Tally's pale, small body slipped partially from his embrace. His chest heaved as he turned away from her.

"No, Dad . . ." I heard myself say. He covered his face with shaking hands. Then the hands clenched into fists that beat against his temples. Behind him, Tally began to swim away, trying to quiet her sobs.

He turned back and strode after her, the water rolling in broad black curls against his thighs. When he stood above her in the water, she turned to face him, still catching her breath in sobs. He leaned close to her and gently stroked her head, her neck, her shoulder. Then she began to cry again, softly. He lifted her from the water and drove a fist against the side of her face.

I thrashed in the water, unable to reach her, unable to help and finally, unable to watch any longer. I tried to cover the sound of her voice with the lake sounds, but this time I could not. Tally screamed in my mind. I heard my own voice, shouting, crying, calling to her, to my father, but above it all, Tally's screams.

Until finally they were extinguished beneath the sounds of the lake.

This was what she had called me here for. How many nights since that May had she died again and again in these dark waters? Waiting for me to come, waiting for me to know. How many nights until the lake finally freed her? This was the last, I knew.

She had called me here to see. I owed her that.

I looked to where my father stood, staring at what his hands still held beneath the surface of the water. When he finally released her, she floated away from him, drifting slowly to where I waited with outstretched arms. But by then she was a part of the lake. I felt her pass through me as I tried to hold her, but she was no more than the warmth from some rare summer current. I turned, looking behind me to where the surf rode that current ashore. There, high on the bluff above the water, sat the Plymouth; it wavered briefly as if painted on the mist, then washed away. When I turned back, my father had begun to swim in a wide circle around the spot where I stood. I felt the current he made turn me, and I followed him with my eyes as he stroked the dark water, watching the moon on his back, slipping past, faster. The circle drew tighter, my father nearer. The lake rose above me, its sides spinning in a glassy funnel, carrying me out past the swells, out to where the lake released its power. I heard it hum and gurgle about me, I waited for the funnel to collapse. Still, my father rode the crest above me, where the lake seemed to rise to the sky. At last he dove down into the maelstrom, spinning down and away into the lake's dark eye. And just before the water closed over my head, I heard Tally call my name from the far-off shore.

I watched the beams of flashlights as they criss-crossed in the darkness. Margaret held me tight as she kissed and whispered and cried softly through the layers of blankets and towels. I couldn't move. My limbs were numb with cold, leaden with exhaustion. I lay there and watched the sky above as a wind came and tore bits of the fog away, carrying it back out over the lake. I wanted to raise my hand to touch her face, but my fingers only twitched.

Did I know the child? someone asked. The child they'd heard calling for help. The call that had led them to me. I think I nodded. I tried to. *Where had she gone?* they wanted to know. The child that had saved me. The child they never found.

"Don't ever leave me," Margaret pleaded softly.

"I won't," I promised, if only silently.

* * *

Tonight, as we lay beside each other in bed, I turn the pages of a magazine I don't really see, pretending to read, listening instead to the far-off sound of waves on the lake shore. If I listen for it, it's always there, but it no longer calls. Death has lost all its charm for me. Now it's just the sound of time passing. Time.

Almost a year now, since that night. Not a long time in which to heal, but after waiting twenty-seven years for forgiveness, it's a start. And, I've had encouragement.

I close the magazine and turn to look at Margaret, something I do often now. I follow her shape with my eyes, from where her feet lie beneath the covers to where one hand dangles limply across the roundness of her belly as she shifts in her sleep. There, a book of baby's names lies open. Margaret smiles in her sleep. Someone has said something I could not hear. Someone has touched her in a place I could not feel. I'd thought of her as a stranger all those years, and now I marvel at how familiar her features have come to be. I know how her skin feels where the light follows the curve of her shoulder. Now, when I need to touch her, I'm not afraid to. I do. She opens her eyes and smiles, looking mildly surprised to find that she's been asleep. She glances down at the book. "What kind of a name is Tally?" I hear her ask.

I look away. "Tally," I whisper to myself. As I lay here numbly, wondering if she has really asked me such a question, an answer comes to me. "Something that's made its mark. The sum of all that's gone before. I think that's what Tally means."

She closes the book and pulls the blanket up to cover our backs. "It's a nice name," she says as she reaches for the light on the nightstand. The room becomes dark and Margaret curls against me.

Never have I felt as brave or as vulnerable. Though the lake no longer calls to me, there are nights when I think I can still hear something out on its waters, something raging there in the cold. On those nights I know that I am protected. I listen to the sounds within her as she sleeps, the rush of small tides and small currents. Someone swims there now, inside her.

Someone I already know.

Maybe that black tide has finally gone out forever.

There is the warmth of her breath on my ear as she whispers, "I love you, Hal. I always have . . . and I always will."

THE MAN WITH THE POWER TIE

Christopher Beaumont

He's been a professional scriptwriter for a full decade, but—until now—Christopher Beaumont has never attempted prose fiction. "The Man With the Power Tie" is his first short story. In it, he displays the same manic wit and flamboyant talent that marked the fiction of his father, the late Charles Beaumont.

The route Chris took to reach the pages of this book was lengthy and circuitous. He began as a teenage television actor, performing in such shows as The Brady Bunch, Bonanza, *and* The Streets of San Francisco. *He also made numerous commercials for airlines, auto manufacturers and fast food chains. At twenty-eight, Chris left acting to take a film cutter's job, quitting two years later to become a bartender. Since he wanted to break into scripting, the bar job allowed him to write days and work nights. Which paid off. After selling an episode to* Fame, *he was subsequently hired as the show's story editor. This eventually led to his becoming producer/ writer on two TV shows of his own,* Bridges to Cross *and* Downtown. *He recently sold his first screenplay and now looks forward to a career in feature films.*

Like his father, he was influenced by Ray Bradbury's work— especially one particular short story, "The Man in the Rorschach Shirt." When asked for a contribution to The Bradbury Chronicles *Chris chose to write a sequel to Bradbury's saga of psychiatrist Sammy Brokaw, who left his wife to move through society wearing an incredible shirt whose complex pattern offered a different world* to each individual. Chris Beaumont tells us that Sammy had a son, Simon Brokaw, who also became a psychiatrist.

Thus, the saga continues. . . .

W.F. N.

The bus was a good twenty-five inches from the curb, but it was clear that the driver wasn't about to do any better. Dr. Brokaw glared and then moved his Florsheimed foot out over the rushing stream of water that banked the curb and stepped up onto the metal platform. He grabbed the handrail and held on tight as he tried to gain his balance. He might have succeeded, too, were it not for the woman who decided she "absolutely, most definitely" was on the wrong bus and had to get off, *now!* She was a force of nature, not an ounce under three hundred pounds, and if she wasn't going to listen to the driver's orders to "exit out the back only!", well, she certainly wasn't going to pay Brokaw any mind. He managed to stay on his feet, and that would have been a clear victory were it not for the fact that his shoes, socks, and cuffs were now completely drenched.

What a day, Dr. Brokaw thought to himself, trying to keep his calm, sighing against the chaos that had marked his morning thus far.

Breakfast had been a total disaster. A slipshod series of failed attempts at the pristine, stainless steel order with which the good doctor preferred to start his days.

The morning paper, it seems, had been shot from the eager arm of a dervish, thereby stripping his *Times* from its see-through protection and exposing its headline: "Rain in L.A." Brokaw had lifted the soggy lump with pinched fingers, but the damage was complete. There would be no Bible reading today, no chapter and verse of to whom, to what, to where and when. No ersatz communiqué from the community of man to help Brokaw create the illusion of membership in same. And, far more important to the doctor, there would simply be no order to his morning.

Robe, slippers, kiss to Katy en route to paper retrieval, coffee, breakfast, paper perusal, morning chat with Katy and review of day's duties, shave, shower, suit and tie, second and final morning kiss to Katy, drive to office. This was Brokaw's playbook. This was his personal battle plan in his crusade against that Beelzebub known variously as entropy, confusion, mess, muddle. Whatever the appellation, the result was always pain and, God knows, he was privy to enough of that during his work day. He didn't need it at home.

Dr. Simon Brokaw, "Sam" to what few friends he had, was a shrink, and a damn good one at that. His father had been a shrink, and he was carrying on in the best shrink tradition. With one major difference. Simon wasn't going to let it do to him what it had done to his father.

"Goodbye forever!" Those were the last words his mother heard as she stood on the runway with her six Pomeranian dogs, watching Sam's father run to catch his twilight plane, destination: another life. She didn't know that she was pregnant at the time or she might not have been quite so understanding. But she was, and so Simon was born to a flesh and blood mother, but a father made of pieced together photographs and unraveled threads of terse remembrances. Not to mention a life lesson in what happens when one lets go of one's battle plan against disorder.

Thus, Brokaw's day was off to a lurching start at best. He dumped the soggy deadweight into the trash compactor and turned to face his granola and de-caf. He exchanged a few words with his wife as he tried his best to regain the rhythm of his routine. But the beat was off, and no matter how he tried to relax, his frustration continued to grow. Maybe if he had ever learned to appreciate the healing powers of good, which is to say, bad, food—piping hot toast with sweet marmalade, bacon and eggs, warmed syrup over buckwheat cakes; all the things designed to make a life short, but happy. Maybe then he could have breathed deep the loving scents of what Katy was cooking for herself on this otherwise disastrous morning. Maybe that would have given him back his center. But food had always been little more than a necessary evil for Brokaw. A transference of energy, certainly nothing to be lingered over. He never really understood his wife's passion for cooking. All those gourmet meals she cooked were, in truth, wasted on him. He would have been just as happy with peanut butter on white bread.

Brokaw left his cereal half-finished and walked purposefully to the rear bedroom and bath. With every step, he concentrated on getting back on track, and such was his skill that he managed, in only fourteen short and simple steps, to throw himself totally and completely out of synch.

Nothing worked. Most of all, Brokaw. He broke the floss, nicked his chin, dropped the soap, gagged instead of gargled, parboiled his fingertips, and froze his toes.

No wonder, then, that he chose the wrong tie.

Not really the *wrong* tie. Just not the tie he thought he had grabbed from the rack. He had reached for the dark blue paisley that had always seemed to speak from a place of assurance and calm, a soft breeze, just passing through, promising not to disturb a thing. The teardrop pattern a Bach fugue of order and art.

What was presently wrapped around his neck was anything but calm. The colors were right, blues and maroons. But the design was ... Brokaw didn't have a clue as to what the design was. Only that it was closer to jazz than to classical, and closer to Coltrane than to Cannonball Adderley.

It had been a Christmas gift, delivered to his office, but neither he nor Katy could figure out who had given it to him. The wrapped package was without a "To-From," and all their other gifts had been accounted for. Brokaw was nervous about running into his dubious benefactor unawares and so, for this reason among others, he had not worn it before.

But such was Brokaw's confusion on this particular morning that he had already completed his usual Windsor knot before realizing what he had done.

He tried to work his thumb into the space under the top loop of fabric, but he had done his job too well and there was no room in which for him to maneuver. He tried an underhand approach, but this just seemed to make the knot tighter. Frustration growing, he was about to begin a search for the scissors when he heard the sound of Katy's car horn, signalling the time.

They always left the house together. She in her Peugeot, he in his BMW. She onto the San Diego Freeway into Culver City, he down Wilshire Boulevard to his office in Beverly Hills. It was a neat little metallic ballet they danced Monday through Friday, each and every morning at precisely seven-thirty.

"See you tonight, sweetheart," she said, leaning out the window as he made his way toward the driveway.

"Tonight," he volleyed, trying to hold on to his famous reserve.

"New tie?" she called out, tapping the brakes and smiling at the unlikely pattern of dark blues and reds across his chest.

Brokaw just shrugged in non-answer. "You'll hit the traffic if you don't get going," he said.

"I *like* it!" she replied before backing out of the drive. "The tie, not the traffic," she finished with a chuckle and then pulled away onto the rain-soaked streets.

Brokaw forced a smile and then turned toward the garage, briefcase in hand. But whatever hopes he had for saving the morning vanished in that moment with two, dim orbs of soft light, reflecting off the front wall of the garage. He checked the sky to see if perhaps the sun was breaking through, sending two, special delivery rays of velvety illumination into an all but inaccessible corner of his garage. But, consistent with his day's luck, it was exactly what he thought; the last gasps of life in the car battery. The storm that had soaked his morning paper, and set his day askew from the get-go, had begun the previous afternoon, dark clouds necessitating headlights on the way home from the office. Headlights that had lived, in one short night, a full and complete life, sucking dry the juice of the one instrument that could have set his life back on track. The smooth ride, the soft, fragrant leather, the eight, acoustically placed speakers releasing a steady stream of Bach, might have put things back in their proper order. Might have . . .

The voice of the Automobile Club was courteous. It was programmed to be courteous. And truthful, as well.

"Due to the inclement weather and the increase in service calls," said the computerized voice-simulator, "there will be a minimum, one-hour delay in emergency roadside service. Please stay on the line and a service representative will be with you just as soon as—"

Brokaw hung up and dialed a taxi service, but the three and a half cabs still working L.A. seemed to be in similar straits.

And that's how he ended up here, standing ankle-deep in water, waiting to get onto a city bus headed down Wilshire Boulevard on this finely fickle morning.

"Thank you," said the doctor as he accepted the hand of the man now standing at the top of the landing.

Once inside the bus, Dr. Brokaw immediately regretted his decision. He hadn't been on public transportation in over twenty years, and as he looked around the crowded conveyance, he began to feel the closeness that had always caused him such distress.

It was noisy, smoky, the air foul with sweat. Someone was eating a hot dog, and the stench turned Brokaw's face sharply into the cold wind blowing through the only open window.

And the people. So many of them, so close. How could they keep from screaming, pressed up against one another like that?

In his youth, such thoughts would have embarrassed the doctor. He was, after all, a psychiatrist; a profession claiming to be deeply, seriously concerned with people. But over the years he had reconciled himself to the idea that the best way to help was from a distance.

Why, even the physical set-up of an office—not just his office, but any good psychiatrist's office—was a study in distance: the patient afloat on a sea of pillows, nothing but velvet swells or leather whitecaps for support, as he or she hoists anchor and sets out upon that chartless journey with nothing but a disembodied voice for counsel.

Which was, perhaps, just as well. For, truth be told, had his patients been able to study the shallow waters behind his eyes, they might have known that his advice came not from the briny seas of experience, for he had none, or at least close to none. Instead, all his words of well-worn erudition came from reading other words of well-worn erudition which were, of course, written by good doctors who had read yet other words of well-worn erudition written by . . . And not an ounce of life in the lot.

A young female patient had once put it to him squarely: "How could a psychiatrist, who, by definition as well as by law, must have completed college, post-graduate work, medical school, as well as years of specialized psychiatric study; how could that person, who must surely have had some sort of support system, if even an abusive, high-pressure one, in order to have completed such a course of study; how could that person truly understand a patient who had no such support system? I don't think they really can," she had said in answer to her own question.

Dr. Brokaw had answered her immediately.

"That's a nice fantasy," he snapped with a smile in his voice, and that shut her up but quick. An accusation of "fantasy" was a shrink's Stealth Bomber, and Brokaw knew it wasn't exactly hoyle. But he also knew that the young patient was attacking a gap in his defenses and he wanted none of it.

Oh, there were times when he regretted the price paid for his crow's-nest perch behind life's couch, but they were few and far between. He had heard too many stories from his mother about his father's fall from greatness at the hands of feeling. Brokaw wasn't proud of his numbness, but it beat hell out of twilight planes on dusky fields, and trips of madness cloaked in shirts bespeckled with windows onto other worlds that did or did not exist.

The shirt ... He hadn't thought about that in years. His mother had told him about it once when he was very young. A crazy story about some accursed shirt that was the beginning of the end for them.

Funny, he thought to himself as he smiled. It takes the collected nausea of a busload of L.A.'s great unwashed to send me tripping down memory lane in search of a father, and a ...

Shirt.

He remembered now. It had played a starring role in countless dreams that he had had as a young boy. Sometimes the hero, other times the villain, most often cloaking the illusive, winged acrobat, swinging just out of reach, beckoning Simon Brokaw to quick! leap! from the cliff into his waiting arms. And always he would awaken with a start, his heart pounding like a real, this-is-not-a-drill, fire alarm. And it would take him hours to sort out the nameless feelings that crowded his still-racing heart before he dared return to sleep and to that phoenix that threatened, promised, to return to the landscape of his young life.

Little by little, Simon had tamed the tigers of his carnival heart, dowsing the hoops of fire and sending the crowds home for milk and cookies. All three rings were quiet now, only the sounds of canvas flapping against the wind, ropes straining to hold on in their old age. The wooden bleachers worn but ... willing ... ?

Willing?

Brokaw tried to sideswipe this train of thought, but the momentum gained too much speed, too quickly.

. . . Willing to take just one more crowd of crane-necked eye poppers, one more gaggle of peanut-crunching, popcorn-munching riffraff royale, eager to get a look at, a glimpse of . . . the one, the only, the incredible, the stupendous . . . You've heard about it, you've read about it, it's more than a mere sartorial statement of acrobatic excellence, my friends. More than a tailored tribute to the flying trapeze. He's more than an acrobat. It's more than magic. Not since the legend of Dr. Lao. Not since the fearless Flying Wallendas. Ladies and gentlemen, may I direct your attention to the center ring? Drum roll, please . . . mesdames et monsieurs, I present for your cultural and *ed*-u-cational edification, wearing a doublet of indubitable powers . . . the one, the only, the . . .

"Nice tie, mister."

"Huh?" said Brokaw, snapping out of his trance, straining to focus on the woman standing no more than two inches away from him.

"I said, nice tie. Kinda sad, though, don't you think?"

"Sad? My tie?" queried Brokaw. "I . . . don't think so."

"Oh, yes," she said. "Saddest tie I ever seen." Her clear, blue, glistening eyes, peering from an ancient, snow-white visage, looked deep into Brokaw's face. Searching for what? Brokaw didn't know.

The bus pulled into traffic with a lurch, sending arms and legs searching for purchase. The woman grabbed hold of Brokaw's tie and held it close, her fingers rolling the silken fabric carefully.

"My boy," she whispered. "My sweet boy, gone to Heaven." Tears instantly appearing, turning the blue of her eyes a darker, richer hue.

A shot of something. What, Brokaw didn't know. All he knew was that a burning shaft of pain, and loss and emptiness, the likes of which he never knew existed, just cut through his soul, ripping his heart in two and spilling molten lava, which now ran searing toward his fingertips.

"Please! Don't," he said, pulling away as best he could.

"Good to cry," she said sweetly. "You should know that."

Again she caressed the tie, and again the lightning bolt shot through Dr. Brokaw, reducing him to a shivering bundle of nerves.

"Listen," he said, raising his voice more in fear than in anger, "I don't want to have to tell you again . . ."

"This asshole bothering you, ma'am?" The voice belonged to a tree trunk in full leathers. Tattoos on both arms. Hair to his shoulders and minus any neck to speak of. "Because, if he is . . ."

"Oh, no," said the woman. "Actually, I'm bothering *him*." And with that, she turned, pulled the string to let the bus driver know to stop, and made her way toward the proper exit.

"But not any longer," she said, still smiling as she cast a final glance to the shaken Dr. Brokaw.

Several passengers exited and Brokaw snatched a seat next to a well-dressed man in his early forties, fast asleep, his head resting against the window, a *Wall Street Journal* for a pillow. Catching his breath, Brokaw strained for comprehension of what had just happened. What on earth had happened to him when that sad, old woman touched the fabric of his tie and started to remember her pain, and . . .

. . . in his first appearance under the big top since coming out of retirement, ladies and gentlemen, would you please put your hands together and give a warm welcome to the one, the only, the . . .

"Mind if I take a closer look?"

"What?"

"The tie. I happen to be something of an expert."

"What is it with this tie?" asked Brokaw, his voice displaying more than a touch of exasperation.

"Well, we'll see, won't we?" said the man, and before Brokaw could lean back out of range, he rested the pads of his fingertips upon the pattern and almost immediately drew in a deep gulp of air.

Simultaneously, Dr. Brokaw was filled with a rush of feeling unlike anything he had ever experienced. A wave of . . . what? Romance was the only word that fit: lush and totally without rhyme or reason. Exactly the kind of runaway emotion that he had spent hour upon "hundred and twenty-five dollar" hour advising against in the strongest possible terms, was now rushing through his body, making it hard for him to find his breath.

"Paris," said the man, a twinkle of remembrance in his loving utterance of the sacred word. "My wife and I honeymooned there. City of light. City of love. City of . . . Hemingway was right, wasn't he?"

"I don't know," said Brokaw, still struggling for air. "I've never been there."

"You're there now, aren't you?" asked the man knowingly.

"I don't know," said Brokaw, his hand instinctively going for the tie. "Am I? I don't know what's going on. Why am I . . . ?"

"Feeling?" finished the man. "I don't know. But any fool can see that you are."

"But I . . ."

"Don't like it," finished the man again. "Yes, anyone could see that, also."

Brokaw struggled with the knot, succeeding only in tightening it beyond release. He stood, angrily surveying the bus, finally spotting an empty seat in the very back.

"Thank you," said the man, before Brokaw could escape.

"How did you know that would happen?" asked the doctor, his every fiber searching for a trace of logic to explain the last fifteen minutes of his heretofore becalmed life.

"I didn't," whispered the man, honestly. "I was just drawn to the pattern. Whatever secrets it holds, they are yours."

"But I don't *want* them, dammit!"

And, with that, Brokaw began to make his way through the crowd to the corner seat in the back of the bus.

. . . you will think your eyes deceive you, but they don't! You will look for mirrors and manipulation, but you will find none, I promise you. Ladies and gentlemen, I invite you to sit back and enjoy a wonder to surpass all wonders. I present for your approval, the one, the only . . .

"That's funny."

Brokaw's head snapped to address the speaker, his tongue ready to issue forth a warning to fend off any further interest in his accursed tie. But instead of a snarl, he found that his lips were curled in an involuntary smile.

And a good thing, too, because the speaker was an eight-year-old princess, golden brown of hair, chocolate brown of eye, ample of cheek, and hearty of laugh. She pointed to the swirling lines that danced across the length and width of the tie and, light in her eyes, began to assign a series of names to match her fancy.

"Snails . . . no, whale's tails! No, horseback trails!" She giggled, her laughter growing with each advancing theory.

And Brokaw had no choice but to match her, giggle for giggle. It was an odd feeling, the pleasant tickle of the laughter, battling his self-imposed abstention from anything smacking of spontaneity.

"Fishes . . . no, dishes! No, wishes come true!" The young girl's giggles now becoming screams of laughter, spreading like a warm, welcome shower over the still-sleepy faces of the crowded passengers.

Brokaw, holding his side, trying to control the gales of laughter, begged her to end this battle raging inside him.

"Please . . . stop."

But his earnest appeals only fueled the flames of the growing laughter which continued to pass through him like a heavy rain, drenching his parched soul to its very roots, and scaring the man half to death.

But, which half?

"Please . . ."

. . . and so, without further ado, I would like to introduce . . .

Brokaw stood, and began to stagger toward the exit, gasping for air.

"Beverly Drive," announced the driver, and Brokaw yanked at the string to indicate his stop.

"Skaters . . . no, Taters. No, Darth Vader's Raiders," she squealed, especially proud of herself, and earning a high round of guffaws from the others.

Brokaw stumbled through the crowd and was about to make good his exit, when he stopped, the pain of his laughter suddenly exploding in his chest.

. . . the one, the only, ladies and gentlemen, for your aerobatic edification. The Doctor of Dare . . . *Mr.* . . . Sammy . . . Brokaw! . . .

Silence.

Then . . .

"Beverly Drive!" came the driver's repeated cry. But Brokaw simply continued to stare at the young princess.

"Thank you," he whispered finally, his own tears welling in the corner of his eye. His own smile forming, unbeckoned, on his very own lips. His own swell of emotion casting the moment in his memory, newly re-opened for business after a much-too-long winter.

The doors started to close, but Brokaw put an arm out to change their mind for a last wink and a leftover giggle before he stepped out onto the sidewalk and watched the bus pull back into traffic.

For a long moment Dr. Brokaw's legs remained planted on that sidewalk, at the corner of Beverly and Wilshire. He just stood there, soaking in sounds that rang new to his ears. Like a hostage given his liberty at last—eager to feel the rush of freedom's fine air, but wary of straining, pulling, snapping muscles that have lain dormant too long to mention—the good doctor finally dared to draw a breath that reached deep down to his roots.

He cast a sideways glance downward, spying on the neck-wise accessory that had turned a twelve-mile trip into an Ahab journey off the edge of the Earth.

"Fishes . . . no, dishes. No, wishes come true," he whispered to himself, and smiled a smile, steadier than his first.

There was construction going on, refacing the building that housed his office, and Brokaw had to step around the "cafe on wheels" that was parked curb-side on Beverly.

"Mmmmm . . ." he said luxuriantly, in response to the rich blend of pleasures working their way deep into the center of his brain.

"What is that smell?" he asked of the pleasant-faced man responsible for the culinary incense billowing from the lunch-wagon. The man sported an apron, splattered with mayo and catsup, and Brokaw took him to be the Manny of the "Manny's Meals" emblazoned across the nose of the coach.

"Bacon and egg sandwich," he barked. "Best in town."

"I'll take one," said the good doctor.

"Of course you will," replied Manny, who turned to shuffle his deck of delectables.

Inside the building, Dr. Brokaw stepped into the elevator, wiping the last smudge of mayo from his lips.

Joining him was the tenant from the office down the hall. Silver haired and ruddy faced, the man kept odd hours and so the two of them ran into each other only rarely. Their conversations had been pleasant, but perfunctory.

Only once had they ever gone beyond salutations, and that was when this man, a writer of some sort, told Brokaw that he had once met his father. It had been a chance meeting, years before, somewhere along the boardwalk at Venice, but it had stuck in the man's memory. He even admitted to Brokaw that the encounter had found its way into a bit of his prose. At the time, Brokaw's reaction to any mention of his father was limited to mild discomfort, and so he pursued the matter no further, allowing the two of them to return to their practice of exchanging pleasantries about the weather and such.

"Well . . ." said Dr. Brokaw, smiling now. "Nasty weather."

"We needed the water, though, didn't we, eh?" came the reply.

"That, we did," said Dr. Brokaw, watching the other man loosen the buttons on his raincoat.

An easy silence the rest of the way up.

The doors opened and the two of them stepped into the hallway and started toward their respective doors.

"By the way," added Dr. Brokaw, his voice turning the man's gaze back toward him. "I don't think I saw you over the holidays. Merry Christmas."

"Thank you," said the man, his smile traveling the full territory of his face. "And Merry Christmas to you, too."

That was when Dr. Brokaw spotted the tie that had been hidden under the man's raincoat. It matched his exactly. Color, design, everything.

Everything?

The man caught the shift in Dr. Brokaw's look, but said nothing.

"You?" came the question, creeping from the doctor's suddenly parched throat.

The smile from across the hall took on a hundred thousand, unseeable colors and hues. But not a word to spoil the picture. Only a wink as he turned to continue on his way.

Dr. Brokaw started to speak, but then thought better of it. He had traveled far enough for one morning. Far enough to know that the roads, while perhaps not safe, not ever safe, were at least open.

CENTIGRADE 233

Gregory Benford

Basically, he considers himself a scientist; he is presently a professor of physics at the University of California in Irvine. Yet Gregory Benford is also one of the premier names in science fiction. He sold magazine fiction in the 1960s, and his first novel, Deeper Than the Darkness, *was published in 1970. Ten years later, his now-classic novel,* Timescape, *won several world awards, including the Nebula. More recent works, such as* Great Sky River *and* Tides of Light, *have established him in the genre's top echelon.*

Benford's abiding concern for the impact of science, of its philosophical implications on human beings, is evident in the story he has written for The Bradbury Chronicles.

Echoing Bradbury's Fahrenheit 451, *in which the act of reading is no longer part of normal society and books are burned, Gregory Benford's futuristic narrative also concerns the idea of printed works being put to the torch. Yet his treatment of this idea is surprising and original, striking off in an entirely new direction.*

Follow one of science fiction's brightest talents into a future only he could imagine.

W.F.N.

It was raining, of course. Incessantly, gray and gentle, smoothing the rectangular certainties of the city into moist matters of opinion. It seemed to Alex that every time he had to leave his snug midtown apartment, the heavens sent down their cold, emulsifying caresses.

He hurried across the broad avenue, though there was scant traffic to intersect his trajectory. Cars were as rare as credible governments these days, for similar reasons. Oil wells were sucking dry, and the industrial conglomerates were sucking up to the latest technofix.

That was as much as Alex knew of matters worldly and scientific. He took the weather as a personal affront, especially when abetted by the 3D 'casters who said things like, "As we all know, in the Greater Metropolitan Area latitudinal overpressures have precipitated (ha ha) a cyclonic bunching of moist offshore cumulus—" and on and on into the byzantine reaches of garish, graphically assisted meteorology.

What they *meant*, Alex told himself as cold drops trickled under his collar, was the usual damp-sock dismality: weather permanently out of whack thanks to emissions from the fabled taxis that were never there when you needed them. Imagine what these streets were like only thirty years ago! Less than that. Imagine these wide avenues inundated to the point of gridlock, that lovely antique word. Cars *parked* along every curb, right out in the open, without guards to prevent joyriding.

"Brella?" a beggar mumbled, menacing Alex with a small black club.

"Get away!" Alex overreacted, patting the nonexistent shoulder holster beneath his trenchcoat. The beggar shrugged and limped away. Small triumph, but Alex felt a surge of pride.

He found the decaying stucco apartment building on a back street, cowering beside a blocky factory. The mail slot to 2F was stuffed with junk mail. Alex went up creaky stairs, nose wrinkling at the damp reek of old rugs and incontinent pets.

He looked automatically for signs that the plywood frame door to 2F had been jimmied. The grain was as clear as the skin of a virgin spinster. Well, maybe his luck was improving. He fished the bulky key from his pocket. The lock stuck, rasped, and then turned with a reluctant thump; no electro-security here.

He held his breath as the door swung open. Did he see looming forms in the murk beyond? This was the last and oldest of Uncle Herb's apartments. Their addresses were all noted in that precise, narrow handwriting of the estate's list of assets. The list had not mentioned that Uncle Herb had not visited his precious vaults for some years.

The others had all been stripped, plundered, wasted, old beer cans and debris attesting to a history of casual abuse by neighborhood gangs. At the Montague Street apartment, Alex had lingered too long mourning the lost trove described in the list. Three slit-eyed Hispanics had kicked in the door as he was inspecting the few battered boxes remaining of his uncle's bequest. They had treated him as an invader, cuffed him about and extorted "rent," maintaining with evil grins that *they* were the rightful owners and had been storing the boxes for a fee. "The People owns this 'parmen' so you pays the People," the shortest of the three had said.

There had been scanty wealth in any of the three apartments, and now—

The door creaked. His fingers fumbled and found the wall switch. Vague forms leaped into solid, unending ranks—books!

Great gray steel shelves crammed the room, anchored at floor and ceiling against the earth's shrugs. He wondered how the sagging frame of this apartment building could support such woody weight. Alex squeezed between the rows and discovered wanly lit rooms beyond, jammed alike. A four-bedroom apartment stripped of furniture, blinds drawn, the kitchen recognizable only by the stumps of disconnected gas fittings.

But no—in the back room cowered a stuffed chair and storklike reading lamp. Here was Uncle Herb's sanctuary, where his will said he had "idled away many a pleasant afternoon in the company of eras lost." Uncle Herb had always tarted up his writing with antique archness, like the frilly ivory-white shade on the lamp.

The books were squeezed on their shelves so tightly that pulling one forth made Alex's forearm muscles ache. He opened the seal of the fogged polymer jacket and nitrogen hissed out. A signed and dated *Martian Chronicles!* Alex fondled the yellowed pages carefully. The odor of aging pulp so poignant and undefinable, filled him. A first edition. Probably worth a good deal. He slipped the book back into its case, already regretting his indulgence at setting it free of its inert gas protection. He hummed to himself as he inched down the rows of shelves, titles flowing past his eyes at a range of inches. *The Forever War* with its crisp colors. A meter-long stretch of E. E. "Doc" Smith novels, all very fine in jackets. *Last and First Men* in the 1930 first edition. Alex had heard it described as the first ontological epic prose poem, the phrase sticking in his mind. He had not read it, of course.

And the pulps! Ranks of them, gaudy spines shouting at customers now gone to dust. Alex sighed. Everything in the twencen had apparently been astounding, thrilling, startling, astonishing, even spicy. Heroines in distress, their skirts invariably hiked up high enough to reveal a fetching black garter belt and the rich expanse of sheer hose. Aliens of grotesque malignancy. Gleaming silver rockets, their prows no less pointed than their metaphor.

The pulps took the largest bedroom. In the hallway began the slicks. Alex could not resist cracking open a *Collier's* with Bonestell full-colors depicting (the text told him breathlessly) Wernher von Braun's visionary space program. Glossy pages grinned at their first reader in a century. To the moon!

Well, Alex had been there, and it wasn't worth the steep prices. He had sprained an arm tumbling into a wall while swooping around in the big wind caverns. The light gravity had been great, the perfect answer for one afflicted with a perpetual diet, but upon return to Earth he had felt like a bowling ball for a month.

Books scraped him fore and aft as he slid along the rows. His accountant's grasp of numbers told him there were tens of thousands here, the biggest residue of Uncle Herb's collection.

"Lord knows what was in the others," he muttered as he extracted himself from the looming aisles. The will had been right about this apartment—it was all science fiction. Not a scrap of fantasy or horror polluted the collection. Uncle Herb had been a bug about distinctions that to Alex made no difference at all. No novels combining rockets and sword-wielding barbarians, no voluptuous vampires, to judge from the covers.

Alex paused at the doorway and looked back, sighing. Bright remnants of a lost past. He recalled what awe that Brit archeologist had reported feeling, upon cracking into Tut's tomb. Only this time the explorer *owned* the contents.

He made his way into the chilly drizzle, clucking contentedly to himself. He shared with Uncle Herb the defective gene of bibliophilia, but a less rampant case. He loved the crisp feel of books, the supple shine of aged leather, the *snick snick snick* of flipped pages. But to *read*? No one did that anymore. And surely the value of a collectable did not depend on its mere use, not in this Tits 'n Glitz age.

In less than an hour, Alex reclined on a glossy Korean lounger, safely home, speaking to Louise Keppler on his wall screen. Her face showed signs of a refurb job still smoothing out, but Alex did not allow even a raised eyebrow to acknowledge the fact; one never knew how people took such things. Louise was a crafty, careful dealer, but in his experience such people had hidden irrationalities, best avoided.

"You got the index?" He wanted to close this deal quickly. Debts awaited, and Uncle Herb had been a long time dying.

"Sure. I ran it through my assessing program just now."

Alex nodded eagerly. She was swift. He shivered and wished he had paid his heating bill this month. His digital thermometer read Centigrade 08. A glance at the window showed the corners filmed by ice. "I hope we can agree on a fair market price."

Louise smiled, eyes at last pinning him with their assessing blue. He thumbed a close-up and found that they were true color, without even a film to conceal bloodshot veins, the residue of the city's delights.

"Alex, we've dealt before. You know me for no fool."

He blinked. "What's wrong?"

"*Books*, Alex? Early videos, yes. First generation CDs, sure— nobody realized they had only a seven-year lifetime, unless preserved. *Those* are rare." Her mouth twisted wryly.

"These are even earlier, much—"

"Sure, but who *cares*? Linear reading, Alex?"

"You should try it," he said swiftly.

"Have you?" she asked sardonically.

"Well . . . a little . . ."

"Kids still do, sure. But not long enough to get attached to the physical form."

"But this was, well, the literature of the future."

"Their future, our past—what of it?" Her high cheekbones lent her lofty authority. She tugged her furs about her.

His knowledge of science fiction came mostly from the myriad movids available. Now that the genre was dead, there was interest in resurrecting the early, naive, strangely grand works—but only in palatable form, of course—to repay the expense of translation into movids.

"They do have a primitive charm," he said uncertainly.

"So torpid! So unaware of what can be done with dramatic line." She shook her head.

Alex said testily, "Look, I didn't call for an exchange of critical views."

"Quite so. I believe you wanted a bid."

"Yes, but immediately payable. There are, ah, estate expenses."

"I can go as high as twelve hundred yen."

"Twelve—" For the first time in his life Alex did not have to act out dismay at an opening price. He choked, sputtered, gasped.

Louise added, "*If* you provide hauling out of that neighborhood and to a designated warehouse."

"Haul—" He coughed a last time to clear his head. Twelve hundred was only two months' rent, or three months of heating oil, with the new tax.

"My offer is good for one day."

"Louise! You're being ridiculous."

She shook her head. "You haven't been keeping up. Items like this, they were big maybe a decade back. No more."

"My uncle spent a *fortune* on those magazines alone. A complete set of *Amazing Stories*. I can remember when he got the last of it, the rare slab-sheeted numbers."

She smiled with something resembling fondness. "Oh yes, a passing technical fancy, weren't they?"

"Expanded right in your hand. Great bioengineering."

"But boring, I'm told. Well past the great age of linear writing."

"That doesn't *matter*," Alex said, recovering slowly and trying to find a wedge in her composure. He drew his coverlet tightly around his numb legs. Should he jump up and shout, to gain some psychological edge and also bring blood back into his frozen feet? No, too obvious. He summoned up a stentorian bark instead. "You're trying to cheat me!"

She shook her head slowly, wisely, red curls tumbling. He had to admire her craft; she appeared completely at ease while she tried to rob him. "You don't understand post-literate times, Alex. We've dealt before in posters, antique cars, oldie-goldies, gravmets. Those are real collectables. Books aren't."

"There's a wealth of *history* in that apartment. A complete set of everybody, the masters of the high period. Anderson to Zelazny. Pournelle and Aldiss, Heinlein and Lem, everybody."

"And worth damn little. Look, I know the situation you're in. Let me—"

"I don't want charity, Louise." He did, actually, but the best guise was to pretend differently.

"Those other apartments of Herb's, they had really valuable goods." Her eyes drifted off camera, lost in memories. "Unfortunate that he did not secure them better."

"Those were good neighborhoods when he started buying up apartments for storage. With rent control that was a smarter way to use them, after all." If he kept her talking he might think of a way to jack up her price.

"Still is," she said reflectively. "I knew Herb well, and he was a savvy collector. A fine man. I told him to junk the books long ago."

This kind of scuffing around the topic was standard for dealers, but Alex found it only irritating now. He remembered rumors that Uncle Herb had kept several mistresses in the business, and suddenly he suspected that Louise, with her distant gaze and pursed lips, was recalling some fevered trysts.

Her eyes clicked back from the infinite and became analytical. "Okay, fifteen hundred yen. Top offer."

"Absurd!"

"Call me when you calm down, Alex."

And she was gone, trickling away on the wall screen.

He calmed down with a movid. His favorite reader had a buffed leather jacket and a large tubular spine. He inserted a cylinder of *The Lust of the Mohicans* and contentedly watched the opening segments of the period piece drama on his enveloping walls,

sitting amid the revelry and swank. Entertainment was essential
these forlorn days, when all who could have already fled to
warmer climes. Even they had met with rising ocean levels, giving the staybehinds delicious, sardonic amusement.

Alex tired of the main plot thread, distracted by his troubles. He
opened the book-like reader and began scanning the moving pictures inside. The reader had only one page. The cylinder in its spine
projected a 3D animated drama, detailing background and sub-
stories of some of the main movid's characters. He popped up side-
bar text on several historical details, reading for long moments while
the action froze on the walls. When he turned the book's single
sheet, it automatically cycled to the next page.

Alex had been following the intricately braided story-streams
of *Mohicans* for months now. Immersion in a time and place
blended the fascinations of fiction, spectacle, history, and philos-
ophy. Facets of the tangled tale could be called up in many forms,
whole subplots altered at will. Alex seldom intruded on the action, disliking the intensely interactive features. He preferred the
supple flows of time, the feeling of inexorable convergence of
events. The real world demanded more interaction than he liked;
he certainly did not seek it in his recreation.

The old-fashioned segments were only a few paragraphs of
linear text, nothing to saturate the eye. He even read a few,
interested at one point in the menu which an Indian was sharing
with a shapely white woman. Corn mush, singularly unappeal-
ing. The woman smacked her lips with relish, though, as she
slipped her bodice down before the brave's widening eyes. Alex
watched the cooking fire play across her ample breasts, pertly
perched like rich yellow-white pears in the flickering, smoky
glow—and so the idea came to him.

"Alex," the Contessa said, "they're *marvelous*."

"Absolute rarities," he said, already catching on that the way
to handle these people was to act humble and mysterious.

"Hard to be*lieve*, isn't it?" The Contessa gave her blond tresses
a saucy little flip. "That people *were* that way?"

Alex had no idea what way she meant, but he answered, "Oh,
yes, nothing exceeds like excess," with what he hoped was light
wit. Too often his humor seemed even to himself to become,

once spoken, a kind of pig irony—but the Contessa missed even this much, turning away to greet more guests.

He regarded them with that mixture of awe and contempt which all those who feel their lights are permanently obscured under bushels know all too well—for here was the mayor and his latest rub, a saffron-skinned woman of teenage smoothness and eyes eons old. They gyred into the ample uptown apartment as if following an unheard gavotte, pirouetting between tight knots of gushing supplicants. The mayor, a moneyed rogue, was a constant worldwide talk show maven. His grinning image played upon the artificial cloud formations that loomed over his city at sunset, accompanied by the usual soft drink advertisements.

Impossibly, this glossy couple spun into Alex's orbit. "Oh, we've heard!" the mayor's rub squeezed out with breathless ardor. "You are *so* inventive!"

The mayor murmured something which instantly eluded Alex, who was still entranced by the airy, buoyant woman. Alex coughed, blinked, and said, "It's nothing, really."

"I can hardly *wait*," the perfectly sculpted woman said with utterly believable enthusiasm.

Alex opened his mouth to reply, ransacking his mind for some witticism. And then she was gone, whisked away on the mayor's arm as if she had been an illusion conjured up by a street magician. Alex sighed, watching the nape of her swanlike neck disappear into the next knot of admiring drones.

"Well, I'll talk to you longer than that," Louise said at his elbow.

She was radiant. Her burnt-rust hair softly flexed, caressing her shoulders, cooing and whispering as the luxuriant strands slid and seethed—the newest in biotech cosmetics.

Alex hid his surprise. "It was much longer than I expected," he said cautiously.

"Oh no, you've become the *rage*." She tossed her radiant hair.

"When I accepted the invitation to, well, come and do my little thing, I never expected to see such, such—"

"Such self-luminosities?" Louise smiled demurely in sympathy. "I knew—that's why I strong-armed the Contessa for an invitation."

"Ah," Alex said reservedly. He was struggling to retain the sense that his head had not in fact left his body and gone whirling about the room, aloft on the sheer gauzy *power* of this place. Through the nearest transparent wall he saw brutal cliffs of glass, perspectives dwindling down into the gray wintry streets of reality. Hail drummed at him only a foot away. Skyscraper, he thought, was the ugliest word in the language.

Yet part of a city's charm was its jagged contrasts: the homeless coughing outside restaurant windows where account executives licked their dessert spoons, hot chestnut vendors serving laughing couples in tuxes and gowns, winos slouched beside smoked-glass limos.

Even in this clogged, seemingly intimate party there were contrasts, though filmed by politeness. In a corner stood a woman who, by hipshot stance and slinky dress, told everyone that she was struggling to make it on the Upper West Side while living on the Lower East. Didn't she know that dressing skimpily to show that you were oblivious to the chilly rooms was *last* year's showy gesture? Alex snuggled into his thick tweed jacket, rented for the occasion.

"—and I never would have thought of actually just making the obvious *show* of it you did," Louise concluded.

Incredibly, Louise gazed at him with admiration. Until this instant he had been ice-skating over the moments, Alex realized. Now her pursed-mouth respect struck him solidly, with heady effect, and he knew that her lofty professionalism was not all he had longed for. Around him buzzed the endless churn of people whose bread and butter were their cleverness, their nerves, their ineffable sense of fleeting style. He cared nothing for them. Louise—her satiny movements, her acerbic good sense—that, he wanted. And not least, her compact, silky curves, so deftly implying voluptuous secrets.

The Contessa materialized like one of the new fog-entertainments, her whispery voice in his ear. "Don't you think it's . . . time?"

"Oh. Oh, yes."

The crowd flowed, parting for them like the Red Sea. The Contessa made the usual announcements, set rules for the silent auction, then gave a florid introduction. Sweating slightly despite the room's fashionable level of chill, Alex opened his briefcase and brought out the first.

"I give you *Thrilling Wonder Stories*, June 1940, featuring 'The Voyage to Nowhere.' Well, I suppose by now we've arrived."

Their laughter was edgy with anticipation. Their pencils scribbled on auction cards.

"Next, *Startling Stories*, with its promise, 'A Novel of the Future Complete in This Issue.' And if you weren't startled, come back next issue."

As more lurid titles piled up, he warmed to his topic. "And now, novels. *Odd John*, about a super-genius, showing that even in those days it was odd to be intelligent. Both British and American first editions here, all quite authentic."

Louise watched him approvingly. He ran through his little jokes about the next dozen novels. Utopian schemes, techno-dreams.

Butlers circulated, collecting bids on the demure pastel cards. The Contessa gave him a pleased smile, making an O with her thumb and forefinger to signal success. Good. The trick lay in extracting bids without slowing the entertainment.

"I'm so happy to see such grand generosity," Alex said, moving smoothly on. "Remember, your contributions will establish the first fully paperless library for the regrettable poor. And now—"

They rustled with anticipation.

A touch more of tantalizing to sharpen matters, Alex judged: more gaudy magazines. A fine copy of *Air Wonder Stories*, April 1930, showing a flying saucer like a buzz saw cutting through an airplane. Finally, an *Amazing Stories* depicting New York's massive skyline toppling beneath an onslaught of glaciers.

"We won't have that, will we?" Alex asked.

"Nooooo!" the crowd answered, grinning.

"Then let the past protect us!" he cried, and with a pocket lighter bent down to the stack he had made in the apartment's fireplace. The magazines went off first—*whoosh!*—erupting into billowing orange-yellow flame.

Burning firewood had of course been outlawed a decade ago. Even disposing of old furniture was a crime. They'd tax the carbon dioxide you exhaled if they could. But no one had thought of this naughtiness . . .

The crisp old pulps, century-dried, kindled the thick novels. Their hardcover dust wrappers blackened and then the boards crackled. Volumes popped open as the glue in their spines ignited. Lines of type stood starkly on the open pages as the fierce radiance illuminated them, engulfed them, banished them forever from a future they had not foretold.

The chilly room rustled as rosy heat struck their intent faces. Alex stepped away from the growing pyre. This moment always came. He had been doing this little stunt only a few weeks, but already its odd power had hummed up and down the taut stretched cables of the city's stresses. What first began as a minor amusement had quickened into fevered fashion. Instant fame, all doors opening to him—all for the price of a pile of worthless paper.

Their narrowed faces met the dancing flames with rapt eyes, gazes turned curiously inward. He had seen this transformation at dozens of parties, yet only now began to get a glimmer of what it meant to them. The immediate warmth quickened in them a sense of forbidden indulgence, a reminder of lush eras known to their forefathers. Yet it also banished that time, rejecting its easy optimism and unconscious swank.

Yes, there it emerged—the cold-eyed gaze that came over them, just after the first rush of blazing heat. The *Amazing* caught and burst open with sharp snaps and pops. On its lurid cover New York's glaciers curled into black smoke.

Revenge. That was what they felt.

Revenge on an era that had unthinkingly betrayed them. Retribution upon a time which these same people unconsciously sought to emulate, yet could not, and so despised. The Age of Indulgence Past.

"Let's slip away," Louise whispered.

Alex saw that the mayor and his newest rub were entranced. None of these people needed him any longer. His treason was consummated, Uncle Herb betrayed yet again.

They edged aside, the fire's gathering roar covering their exit. Louise snuggled against him, a promise of rewards to come. Her frosty professionalism had melted as the room warmed, the radiance somehow acting even on her, a collector.

As Alex crossed the thick carpet toward the door, he saw that this was no freakish party trick. The crowd basked in the glow, their shoulders squaring, postures straightening. He had given these people permission to cast off the past's dead hand.

The sin of adding carbon dioxide to the burdened air only provided the spice of excitement. Unwittingly, Alex had given them release. Perhaps even hope.

With Louise he hurried into the cold, strangely welcoming night.

FILLING OUT FANNIE

John Maclay

A former advertising executive, John Maclay (with his wife, Joyce) runs his own small-press publishing company in Baltimore, Maryland, and has issued a score of impressive books under the Maclay & Associates imprint. These include three of the World Fantasy Award-nominated Masques *series.*

Primarily, however, John is a writer—with more than 100 short stories, two novels, a book of essays, and a verse/short story collection in print over the past decade. In 1986 he edited the much-discussed atomic doomsday anthology, Nukes. *His own work has been anthologized in many volumes from* Scare Care *to* Urban Horrors.

John's contribution to The Bradbury Chronicles *is directly tied in to Bradbury's crime novel,* Death is a Lonely Business. *One of the book's most colorful characters is the immense, opera-loving Fannie whose dead body is found in her upstairs apartment, the victim of a killer who preys only on those who are lonely.*

In crafting this touching vignette based on the final moments of Fannie's life, John Maclay shows us that the killer in Bradbury's narrative didn't really know the truth about his victim.

Fannie was anything but lonely.

W.F.N.

She knew that she was dying.

All three hundred and eighty pounds of her, lying there on the linoleum floor, fading eyes staring up at the cracked ceiling of her L.A. tenement room. No more eating now, no cartons of ice cream nor jars of mayonnaise scooped out with a spoon; their result, these pounds, now destined to rot away to nothing but a slim, spare skeleton in the grave. Not even a melody of her beloved opera to accompany it, the recording of *Tosca* having been snatched from the still-revolving turntable by the possessor of the eyes which still looked down upon her, waiting. Waiting as she suffocated under her own flesh, as he'd known she would when he pushed her from her massive chair. Death: it would come soon, with a last outward breath, not unlike the high note of a Puccini aria back in her own singing days in Chicago. A breath which would leave her empty at last.

What had spooked her during the past few weeks had come again to, and at last inside, her door. Though a wry laugh was as out of the question as a final note of song, her moon-face did break into a smile as she thought about it, which made her watching assailant recoil in wonder. It was just this: how wrong it all was, how wrong about her *they* had been.

Even her oldest friend, the faded film star Constance Rattigan, who'd thought she knew her like a well-worn script. "Remember what somebody told Scott Fitzgerald," Fannie once had said, when Connie, on a visit from her huge, empty beach house, had started off again about how her three hundred and eighty pounds were recompense for her long-lost love. Nineteen forty-nine now, thirty-odd years back to their time together in Chicago, both of them past fifty, and Connie still harping on that! "You're too old to have theories about people." And Connie with her play-acting, her posing as her own maid and chauffeur: did she think she was the only one who could have secrets?

Wrong. Even the young writer, whose marvelous business it was to see and know. Fannie could even now imagine him constructing it after she was gone, from the newspaper she'd told him to look for in her beloved icebox, the circled advertisement directed to the lonely, the lovelorn. She'd answered that ad, yes, but not for the reason the young man would think, of finding her love of decades before; rather, simply, for contact with someone who obviously wanted it. Just as she'd lured the writer himself, with her siren song of opera, that man who did also specialize in anomalies.

Lured them. Yet not for her to become, as in the case of the young writer, a character, a curiosity. And certainly not, as the face which now loomed over her wrongly evidenced, because she wished to be put out of some imagined misery, have some loneliness ended in ... death.

Fannie took another breath. The blind man would know. Henry, the blind man, would know but never tell. Maybe there had been Lonelies, failures, who'd been rightly visited by the self-appointed Angel of Nothingness. But not she, Henry would know. It didn't require a sixth, or a seventh, sense to divine what her three hundred and eighty pounds of flesh had told him, what was apparent in every extra cell of her being. He whose senses of smell, hearing, taste and touch had been so heightened by his deprivation.

And another: Jimmy, dead Jimmy, drowned in his bathtub, suffocated by water much as she now, ironically, was lying there being crushed by herself, Jimmy had known. Known, when he stood, leaned, in front of her massive chair—closer—that she had not let her life be a failure—closer—that she hadn't been lonely—*closer*—that only in the haunting, sublimely beautiful melodies of her beloved Puccini was there pure tragedy, that the composer himself had never given up, had been penning *Turandot* to the day of his death.

But Connie, and the writer, and her ... killer, now: they'd gotten close, only not close enough.

Three hundred and eighty pounds. Three eight oh. Fed by jar after jar of mayonnaise, spoonful by spoonful, why spread it on bread, why not just eat it, leave some for tomorrow, no, why not finish the job, send out for another jar in the morning? Twenty years here in the L.A. tenement, rare excursions to the balcony, the telephone, ten years since the street. And decades back to Chicago, where she'd been an impossibly slim one hundred and

twenty, one-third of a Fannie, even less, my God! Only her so-
prano voice, unchanged, a reminder. Three eight oh minus one
two oh, grade school, two six oh. *Divided by ten . . .*

The first one had been in Chicago, scarcely two weeks after
love lost, when her body was still as slim as her voice, and her
later moon-face a piquant, round flower. Connie would have said
she was desperate, not herself, so Connie would never be told;
but in such crises of the heart, action was always better than
eating *at* oneself, that was the secret.

Eating. By the time of the second one, she'd gained ten
pounds, the face a little fuller, earthier, angles of shoulder, hip,
slightly softened. No mayo yet, just larger meals, late snacks,
figure not watched but encouraged. If you lost something exter-
nal, Fannie thought now, you replaced it. If you lost something
inside, why, you simply added to yourself.

Sustenance. Two kinds. Max Bodenheim, that Village character, bless him, had done something called *Replenishing Jessica,*
and he was right. You needed it from the outside, but internally
what was the sense in not matching it, emptiness of self filled as
well as emptiness of arms? Flesh to flesh, then perhaps even a
souvenir created, a place that would be forever the other's and
her own. Starting on ice cream now—the third one—and the first
spoon of whipped egg from the jar.

Or maybe . . . making room. Now the move to L.A., one hundred and fifty pounds, young-matronly; to that sunny and open
place of indolence, of tolerance for what she would inexorably
and happily become. Fannie smiled. Go West, Young Woman.
Territorial expansion, pun intended. And soon after her arrival,
sure enough, the fourth one, then more . . .

Then legion. She'd lost count. No huge beach house, like Connie's, needed to live in: only a room, a chair, and something to
keep the round white jars cold. No exotic mansion needed to
lure them: just the sensuous, siren song of opera, and the machine to spin the magic discs. Up the stairs they'd come: Sam,
and Pietro, even Lawrence Tibbett, to sample her sweet wine.

Lost count. But her body hadn't. Two hundred and sixty
pounds gained. Divided by ten, equaled *twenty-six—*

Fannie lying on the linoleum floor now, dying. Staring up at
the cracked ceiling, at the warped eyes of the one who at last

had read her wrong. She'd always hated *Tristan,* the *Liebestod,* as if death could be a lover, or love be a death. Ridiculous. A lover was a lover; love led to more. And that he'd thought she was a Lonely ... all those warm afternoons spent lost in the motion, in the sultry air and the aroma of her perfume, heaven wasn't out there, earth was heaven ...

The young one, too, the dreamer whose thoughts often, characteristically, turned to space. Space: she could have shown him that, could have put him into the vast heaven of herself. Someday, perhaps, he'd realize how special she'd truly been, that she hadn't wanted to be written about at all, she'd only wanted ...

Men. Number twenty-seven, and twenty-eight, to ... sleep with. Then, more mayonnaise, ten pounds each—to the magic four hundred!

And with her last breath, Fannie wondered how close to the size of the round earth, or the universe itself, she eventually might have grown.

LAND OF THE SECOND CHANCE

J. N. Williamson

Any wordsmith who can turn out 38 horror novels in just over a decade is a writer to be reckoned with. Jerry Williamson not only accomplished this awesome feat (with novels as vigorous and variegated as The Black School, Ghost, The Longest Night, Monastery, *etc.), but during this same period edited four anthologies (highlighted by the justly famous* Masques *series), and wrote more than 100 short stories!*

A longtime Bradbury enthusiast, Jerry tackled his assignment for The Bradbury Chronicles *with particular fervor. The story he has produced involves several characters from the Bradbury canon: Clemens, the astronaut from "No Particular Night or Morning" (who is haunted by the ghost of his fellow astronaut, Joseph Hitchcock, who died in space); Tom, whose grandmother was an android robot, from "I Sing the Body Electric!"; Margaret, the character no one would listen to, from "The Screaming Woman"; Elma, Sam Parkhill's wife, from "The Off Season," who helped her husband run their hot dog stand on Mars; Harold, whose childhood friend, Tally (she of the sand castles), was drowned in "The Lake"; Timothy, from the final Earth family to arrive on Mars in "The Million-Year Picnic"; and the nameless lieutenant from "Dark They Were, and Golden-Eyed."*

What Williamson does with this odd assemblage of characters results in a very unusual, thought-provoking tale of the future, as they face a Satanic creature of Jerry's own dark devising, the Ice Doctor.

We'd all like a second chance at life, but at what cost?

W.F.N.

The five men and two women came from their various worlds and various times to the luminescent lodestone, the free-floating edifice centered in the artificially nourished heart of New Earth's greenest hill. They were here because people who knew of such things had individually assured them they were dying, and they were here to see what might be done about arranging a substitute for death.

They intended to replace it. Here, they meant to squint at the Reaper's pale face until the cruel and evasive eyes stared back—then, thumbing their noses, they planned to scoot around that forbidding scowl and sprint straight for the haven each of them sought.

The until then only dreamt-of land of the second chance.

This was what they had in common, these seven people; the quest for another opportunity to live and get it right this time, despite the heart-stopping knowledge of the Ice Doctor's special method that each was to use in order to cheat death.

And they shared a silent truth. It grew from the furrows and creases of each wintered face, asserting that years beyond desirable counting ago, every man or woman of them had swallowed the seed of the dying experience. Not their own; someone's, individually precious. Because they'd supped on shadow, sipped snifters brim-filled with the spirits of isolation, devoured platters littered with the broken bones of hope—and capped the banquet off with the bitter dessert of adjustment—dying was nothing new. Why, they'd nibbled at every course of the Reaper's miserable harvest, then Adjusted, Picked Up the Pieces, Gone On, Seen it Through.

Then they had queried the cosmos; *why?* and *for what?*, and heard no reply.

It was old Tom—whose grandmother had once called him sad

and funny—who dubbed their deliverer of the hill (please, God!) the Ice Doctor, both because it reflected the hints of truth about his methods and because his invitation had not included his name. Yet, they'd come, each picked up and fired like photons through the wormholes of the inconstant universe to ride the bounding transversal waves at zigzagging right angles—surfers of time, defiant of the ages, especially their own.

Inside the hill pumped green by steroidal injections of grassy chlorophyll, the aged men and women were being trundled in wheelchairs or on moving carpets toward their first encounter with the Doctor of Ice. All they'd need do was sleep, he'd told them—that was all. And awaken one finest of days to be slipped into a new, *healthy* body! "How does it fit under the arms? What about here—and over *here*? Now, then—run and play, and don't worry about darkness!"

So, for determined Margaret Leary, haunted Clemens, widowed Elma Parkhill, aging Tom, trapped and desolate Harold, and even the grown/grown old Timothy, dying was no fruit for fear—it was another chance! Life-hardened Elma it was who said living itself had become a botherment and that she'd wait until hell was frozen to see the blue sand ships float once more toward her and Sam's hot dog stand. Clemens had told Joseph's ghost that dying wasn't so bad—it was *death* that might be forever!

Before them, the Ice Doctor spread his thin arms like parentheses. "Just in time!" he greeted them. "Welcome to you all!"

He had arrived suddenly from a large room into which Timothy had had a glimpse of metallic tubes arrayed before a window wide open upon the vista of New Earth. Without understanding why, Timothy shivered when he peered closely at their host.

Black, oiled-satin hair smoothed back. Carnation in the lapel of a suit bright enough to read by. Shaking a marionette's head in greeting, so very affably that the old lieutenant (whose name no one knew) felt it could come loose.

"Mine," said the Ice Doctor, "is an advanced process of neuro-suspension which cannot fail." Teeth were bared when he spoke. "The future is yours, and it won't cost you a penny."

"That's a start," Elma sniffed from her wheelchair prison.

"Sir." The uniformed lieutenant showed traces of military

bearing about his aging shoulders. "I have seen the future, and it's not all it's cracked up to be."

"Ah." The Ice Doctor's pale, pocked face had brows like sticks of licorice. His grimacing mouth freed a voice like a theater organ. "But you've never seen *my* future—that of New Earth!"

"I saw the past," stooped Harold added. "In Lake Bluff. It came in a gray sack on a deserted beach. I saw—"

"*This,*" their host finished, waving an arm.

The seven saw a picture take form on a viewscreen behind Doctor Ice. Grainy. Colors so faded it appeared black and white. But a half-constructed sand castle lapped by the lake's kitten-tongue made white-haired Harold blink uneasily. Above the sand structure, snow-bright against the hungry fall sky, rose a girl-child with pigtails of gold atrail on her shoulders. She was laughing silently.

"*Tally.*" The attorney's forehead cobwebbed. He glared at their host. "Stop this. Please."

And sand alive with writhing water-weed swept over the screen to darken it.

"She drowned." The Ice Doctor watched Harold. "You saw Tally's small footprints coming in from the lake—*after* they found her, years later. But they *returned to* the lake." His organ accents played pianissimo. "What do you wish, Harold?"

Eyes damp, Harold said simply, "To find her. To complete the castle beside Tally. Fulfill my . . . early dreams."

"Then you need a *newer* Earth. The cold first, then the warmth!" Their host wobbled his head, turned to observe Clemens. That old rocket man saw, on the screen, that he was staring once again into the spackled universe; then he spotted Joseph Hitchcock—no more than a twisting speck, a blotch of skeleton in a space suit walking his skinless legs as his body turned, grew, turned. Instinctively, Clemens threw his hands out and caught himself on what he believed to be the jagged hold of a steel bulkhead. And Hitchcock called mournfully, as he did always, *No people. No planets. No body. Only—the gap.*

"And believing was once enough for you," Doctor Ice reminded Clemens. A wave razed the rocketman's specter from the screen. "You hoped! While Joseph sat on the floor after the meteor struck your ship, you told him you could still see Earth in your mind. When Hitchcock said if he couldn't see a man for a day, the fellow was dead, *you* thought him too much the realist. What happened to your belief, man?"

Old Clemens considered that. Remembered looking for his friend in the blackness and star-blur when Joseph went for his solitary stroll in space, and all he'd heard was Hitchcock's empty voice in his helmet radio—for a while: *No more ship. Space. No hands, no feet.*

"I saw the gap, too," Clemens confessed. "Saw I was on my way to no particular night, then realized I was heading for no particular morning. The indetermination . . ."

"You, madam!" the doctor cried, pointing to she who clutched a walker. The viewscreen pictured a vacant lot baked hard by the July sun on old Earth. A muffled scream seeped to the surface, to the ears of the frightened child Margaret Leary once was. "Your father and neighbors finally believed you and came to dig her up. True?"

"Not till they'd left me all alone with my terror!" Piqued, shoulders beetled, once-pretty Margaret craned her neck to see the others. "Dad had to drink his iced tea, my friend Dippy thought I was a ventriloquist!" Tears popped out, wet memories. "If poor Miss Nesbitt hadn't sung a song from where they buried her alive, she'd still be in that hole—because they *never* believed me!" The memories ran upon her cheeks. "I have no song to sing, no one for whom to sing it."

The Ice Doctor folded his arms. "What is it you seek, then, with no song in your heart? Margaret, what happened to the child who cared so greatly?"

She hung from the walker as if it was her private gallows. "Without belief in me, *I* no longer believed. They buried me alive like Helen Nesbitt!"

"It was I who heard your screaming, Margaret," the Doctor of Ice said softly, grinning, "and I have answered. Now, come!" He gestured for them to follow him. "To my laboratory, all of you!"

They did follow, into the room Timothy had glimpsed, a place alive with stainless steel tubing and myriad objects of high science and higher mystery. Against one wall, an electric switchboard shone. From another, pictures loomed—of skeletons ajiggle, mazes gone to magic as one regarded them, of dragonflies and beetles and possibly *dragons* X-rayed and X-Y-Z-rayed. Of scientific diagrams with minute illustrations of processions of odd and wondrous beast-beings. Doctor Ice beckoned from a far window. "Come in, come in! Is it not wonderful?"

Tom and Margaret exchanged glances asking, "What does he mean to *do?*" and, seeing their reflections in the gleaming tubes, "Will he blow us across time like men shot from *cannons?*"

But Elma had sped to the window in her wheelchair to squint out at the vista of New Earth. The others joined her, peered far below the floating laboratory at partially built structures nesting amid small fires in the run-wild woods. Much of the ground had been cleared, but more—much more—remained to be done. Elma reminded herself of her husband Sam Parkhill, dead in his madness, lowered into the Martian ground behind the hot dog stand that nearly cost them both their lives, and knew she must hear out this saturnine man of machines and promises.

But why would he help them, free, and who did he think he was, anyway?

"Grandmother," Tom was saying, balanced on his crutches like a leaf not yet fallen, "made me believe in machinery. She'd say *Fly* to a kite, and it flew. Men threw big shadows, she said, then ran to fit them—because the shadows were always longer." He touched his fingertips to the nearest steel tube. "She said we needed 'compensating machines,' but I never found one for her loss, or my many failures."

And into the mood of doubt, the lieutenant told his story. "We landed on Mars, found an American-style town where no one lived. On patrol in the hills, I met dark people with yellow eyes, then reported them to the captain."

"But," Doctor Ice murmured, "he cared only about remapping; mining sites."

"And I wondered about the earlier Earth settlers." The lieutenant nodded. "Where they went. If their eyes might have turned yellow, their skins dark, like the Martians. Wondered if they'd drifted in the spring valley waters and emerged one morning as the new players of pipe and flute." He lowered a cupped hand from his brow. "I wondered secrets about the blue hills and mist bathing the tips of the sloping mountains."

They saw that his eyes were yellow, his skin dark.

"My name was not recorded. I couldn't even see my face clearly because the springs had been tainted by too many of our images." The lieutenant stood erect. "I wish for a time when the invaders have left the Martian ghosts to play the ancient music from the stones. My identity was taken, and I want it returned—improved. Altered for all time, as I have been."

"I couldn't wait a million years for customers, and I can't wait that long for Sam!" Elma Parkhill snapped. "Look out there, people—there's nothing for any of us!"

"Madam," the Ice Doctor interjected, "there's nothing for you *now*." He nodded in Timothy's direction, and waved a long arm toward a laboratory viewscreen.

Five people—father, mother, three boys; one of them was the boy Tim—were staring into the canal where Dad had said they'd come to fish. "Life on Earth never settled down to doing anything very good," the father said as the Timothys, young and old, listened intently. Dad said science had leapt too far ahead, that folks were "lost in a mechanical wilderness." It had killed Earth, and *they* were the new Martians now, Dad announced. Then the images on the screen faded.

"Time passed," aged Timothy explained, "and an Earth remnant came to take us home. But it wasn't home anymore. So," he said, sighing, "I've spent my life with those who didn't know where I was truly from. Sometimes I think that I—and Elma and the lieutenant—drowned in the canal. And, like old Harold's Tally, are living somehow."

"How lonely," Doctor Ice purred, "you all are."

Timothy bathed his cataract glasses with tears. "Since Mars couldn't really be Heaven and I don't know what is, I decided to check out this—this land of a second chance you're advertising, doctor. Now I think we'd appreciate an explanation. How do you know it will be livable down there, and what do you propose to do to us?" Timothy's eyes were clear now, and level. "Also, sir—*why?*"

The tall man's head wobbled, his gaze finding each of them. "I stand before you as a man who has dwelled on all your worlds, in all your times, and—upon the Earth beneath us, when it is ... ready ... for you. I have lived there! As for why I issued my invitations, ladies, gentlemen"—the Doctor of Ice bowed slightly from the waist—"it is because I have known you, *watched* you, moved among and observed you on my screens, and *waited* for you."

"Why?" Elma Parkhill asked brusquely.

He smiled at them, hugely, beamed upon the seven oldsters with eyes like lumps of bright, black coal. "Because you are the vanguard, the advance company for the many millions I hope to divert to the New Earth." His eyelids closed only for an instant. "Call me a humanitarian, if that is what you wish. Or call me a man of business—who understands that there are some people who truly do not want to die, because they believe they have never lived."

"*How?*" Clemens whispered. For now, it was their only question.

And the Ice Doctor's organ voice rumbled, "We are in the midst of relics of cryonics. *Early* cryonics."

"The freezing process?" asked a startled Tom. "How did it go? Got a terminal disease? Let us plunge you into frosty coffins to sleep the decades away until you awaken one bright morning to be cured! Is that it?"

"Well . . ." The Ice Doctor paused. "Is that so dreadful to consider?"

"But why would future people thaw us out?" Margaret said. "To feed ourselves, we'd have to be reeducated."

"I think it's the way shadows are thrown for old folks to fit," Tom offered. "They're too long for us."

"Refrigerated." Harold shuddered. "Like a popsicle! All we'd have left are dreams."

"Yes!" Elma snapped. "It demands all sorts of stuff and nonsense."

"Yet dreams," replied the Ice Doctor, "seem to be your principal possessions now—no offense."

"I couldn't rely on rocket engines or my captain not to wreck my life," the lieutenant observed. "How can I depend on your science or you? No offense!"

Clemens: "My friend Joseph would still be haunting me. Spirits can't tell the differences between time and space. Right?"

The doctor's lips twitched. "Not to flutter pages of the King James at you, but there is only one place mentioned there where old Hitchcock might not get at you. Tell me, Mr. Clemens—why should one ghost be haunted by *other* ghosts?"

Though Margaret Leary laughed, Tom pointed a shaky finger at their host. "You told Harold, 'The cold first, then the warmth.' Weren't you only referring to what you called 'early cryonics'? What's different about your procedure?"

Scrubbing his palms, the Doctor of Ice spun on his heel. His knife-sharp nails on the steel tubes threw sparks as he strode to a large cabinet set against the other wall. They followed him. He fiddled with complicated locks. A clanging sound, and the cabinet doors sprang open. "Your transport to the New Earth is in here."

Tom glanced toward a dubious Elma with fresh hope. "Grandmother took the force of a speeding car meant for my sister Agatha and they both survived because of science."

"I'll listen," Elma agreed, and no one turned to leave.

"My procedure is a truly grand advancement of the ingenious methods begun late in the twentieth century," said the doctor. "I will replace your blood with a variation of the substitute *profusatype* and my own solution of glycerol."

"Yummy," Elma sniffed.

Doctor Ice pretended not to hear. "Cryonics patients once were inserted in a camper-size sleeping bag and lowered on a pre-cooled stretcher into one of the tubular vacuum bottles. Tube and body were chilled to a liquid nitrogen temperature of 320 degrees below zero—Fahrenheit. Then the patient was stored in the container, head first."

Harold's nose wrinkled. "This is not . . . well . . . your plan for *us?*"

"Oh, no." The Ice Doctor smiled. "By no means." He thrust his fleshless arms into the cabinet again, reaching. "*Absolutely* not—in a manner of speaking."

Then he straightened, turned back, and they were staring apprehensively at a most ingenious contraption.

At the lieutenant's first glance, it seemed to be the model for an unknown solar system. Something hung at the center: a round machine. Connected by narrow lengths, seven objects with their names stamped in the shiny surfaces revolved around it. Round and round, slowly. Objects, resembling buckets; white pails, open at one end.

The seven buckets were the size of human heads.

Doctor Ice watched the realization move from guest to guest. "Precisely!" he cried.

"Goodbye." Elma tapped the accelerator on her chair. "I'll show myself out, thank you."

Tom and Timothy roused themselves, the latter stopping her. "But we don't know how we got here. How *can* we go home?"

With no ready answer for that, the horror in their faces deepened. One by one, they turned to face their host.

"*Patience,*" he begged. "I would not keep you against your will. That would be meaningless to me. Yet ... you wouldn't want to miss out, would you? How does being sixty again sound, fifty? And forty is twice-five sweeter than fifty ... and so on down the line to the point at which age is no more a matter of significance than a sip of elderberry wine!"

"Shan't listen," Elma swore, wheelchair in park.

The doctor drew within two paces of Tom, and veered to face Margaret. "Consider. Your bodies are little more than crutches themselves now." His eyes found Elma. "Time to put on fine, *young* bodies." An index finger stabbed the air like a conductor's baton. "The cold is only momentary. Then, the warmth!"

"Do our h-heads go in the buckets *before* we're dead?" asked the lieutenant. A nod from Ice. "We *stay* alive but asleep—till a predetermined future moment?" Another nod. "And we'll get healthy new bodies then?"

"You've got it, got it, got it, and you all can *have* it!" exclaimed the Ice Doctor, enthusiastically. Briskly. he connected the system of white pails to an outlet and a soft humming drifted into the lab. The complex of buckets revolved soothingly round the central mechanism. "Afraid of the isolation, the aloneness? You'll communicate mind to mind if anyone awakens, sleep again as one! Never felt at home anywhere except Mars or midwestern America? You'll be together on New Earth—*your* planet! Make of it what you will!"

"Depending upon the kindness of strangers," Margaret said doubtfully, "especially for assistance in donning a new body ..."

"Margaret, you shall *awaken* in new raiment—*automatically!*"

The doctor's fingers danced a polka on the humming planets. "That is my surprise for you, and I will attend to it *myself!* You'll never even know it's happening. Mrs. Parkhill ... Elma ... can you see the violet streams through the window, the light blue hills? You have but to ask and, when you awaken, a part of this planet will be Mars *recreated*—for each of you who yearns for it!"

Timothy and Margaret returned to the wide window and Doctor Ice flowed on. "Those from other worlds will visit, come as customers at the Parkhill hot dog stand and other youthful enterprises." Tapping Harold's shoulder, he lowered his voice to a whisper. "Look closely and you may already see Central School under new construction, the ice cream store, an empty lot. Evanston, and the house where Barbara lived; Bluff Station and ravine trails; a lake and a beach—in Michigan. And who can say what young woman awaits *you*, Mr. Clemens? Better run through a few scales, Margaret, for you shall have your song! And ... Harold? There shall be castles of sand to begin anew with a pigtailed child beside you!"

The shining laboratory was steeped in remembering. Longing. Dreaming.

Elma astounded them by being the first. "I'm asking," she said. "I'm yearning."

"Do you think I might find Grandmother, or recreate her?" Tom asked. He was using his crutches to steady his body, and his hopes. "Perhaps other machinery will help me locate her. 'Everything you ever say, everything you ever do,' she told me, 'I'll keep, put away, treasure.' That seemed enough." He coughed. "We're surprised by time, by age, aren't we? Always."

"But once for each of us," the Doctor of Ice said truthfully, "we can regain our composure. Come, Tom!" he said with his busiest tone. "Your choice!"

The old man and the others watched the solar system wind slowly on itself and saw the purity of dreams in the sterile emptiness of the pale white buckets.

"I must learn if someone has remembered," Tom said. "I need a gold key turned in my breast, too, to set me in motion."

The light showing through the tears in his eyes, their host led them the rest of the way to readiness. "It won't hurt," the Doctor of Ice said softly. "There will be no pain."

Dormant as green plants suspended by an off-season of the soul, two women and five men drowsed. Challenged time huffed outside the nearly hermetic lodge in the heart of the hill while seven white vessels moved metronomically around a sun that sustained life in aloof and awful silence. *Tick-tick,* clicked a remarkably powered robot, detached as a manservant. Sustaining its own artificial existence by immuring itself in routine, it calibrated its calculations, enacted its duties, perfectly. *Tick-tick,* clucking to itself as time muttered.

Mostly strings, ceaselessly soothing music played lullabye and psalm, woodwinds soughing breeze-gentle counterpoint. *Tick* and *tick.* Incremental as infants growing from womb-seed, the solar system closed another complete cycle, began around again like time-lapse photography.

Once every ten or ten-hundred years, a voice spoke poetry into the frozen solitude. A songbird began its lyric of solicitude, and then *announced spring.*

Tick—and seven old, old brains . . . came alive.

A panel covering each receptacle slid back, soundlessly. A human face waited within each, rested, eyelids atremor. *Eeeeeee,* machinery creaked for them, made dry lips crack open, mutter soundlessly.

And open eyes stared into other open eyes.

"Morning," Tom said in his mind, projecting it into theirs without effort.

" 'Lo," Margaret answered, lids fluttering for focus.

And "Good morning," Elma murmured mind-to-mind, catching sight of Harold, Timothy.

"Here—we're *here*," the lieutenant managed; and from Clemens, "We *made* it!"

Then they remembered the great window in the Ice Doctor's dark laboratory.

It wasn't possible for all of them to see out, not at once. But then the centrifuge moved again, regained its miniature pace like a carousel . . . and gradually, slowly, each of the captive canisters was rotated into a position of inspection.

Elma's shrill, despairing thought penetrated the others' minds. "Oh, dear God."

Clemens, second to see, conveyed only his grief, no words. Timothy, the third, had time to plead, "Don't make me see," before he saw.

And as the planets revolved, each of the seven peered out at New Earth; at heartbreak, irrecoverable error, darkest deception.

The shacks of the temporary workers were gone, but they had not been replaced. No marvelous Martian structures or towers of tribute to Earth's architectural genius stood. All was weed and ruined dream. Small fires they'd glimpsed on their arrival at the shining lodestone in the hill had blinked out as if Doctor Ice's scores of miracle workers had never quarreled with decay and flora run rampant. Perhaps they never had.

"The shacks were an illusion," Harold thought—and so all of them thought. "None of the ground was cleared," added Elma Parkhill, bitterly. "The viewscreens were blank," the lieutenant realized, "save for what our minds and memories put on them." Tom remembered: "He said we were the vanguard for millions he hoped to 'divert,' and he chose us because we believed we had 'never lived.' What did he divert us *from?*"

For a time they fell silent, dwelled in their private prisons of betrayal, even as the centrifuge turned more and more slowly, *crrreeaaaaking* now, shutting down. The robot calibrator glanced at himself, whirled, and left without so much as announcing the hour or date. When it had departed, the lights inside the laboratory dimmed like theater lights warning an audience of an impending final act.

"He took all our remembered loneliness and loss, our dreams *and* our fears," Timothy's mind merged with the rest, "and made them *one*. He gave us our only guarantee of survival, but it was a lie. And he—"

Tom completed the thought they shared: "He diverted us from finding the land of the second chance, by helping us imagine that our frustrations and grief were more special than anyone else's."

"Look!" Clemens thought. "*See!*" There before him, before all of them, they saw the rocket man Hitchcock, traipsing across the

inner depths of space—and he was smiling behind his viewplate!
"Joseph is *alive!*"

Sam could be there, Elma told herself in private hope—and to
the others, "He *must* be *somewhere!*"

There was no machine like Grandmother, Tom knew, drawn
toward the rocket man, seeing a hot dog stand, too, and smelling
the steamy flavors simmering in his nostrils. But what if it was
all a great machine of sorts and Grandmother merely one of the
better, improved features? *It's only a gap until it's filled,* Clemens—or was it his beckoning friend?—informed Tom.

Just as the motor manipulating the centrifuge groaned like a
dying beast, Margaret Leary started her song. Now—now, only!—
was she truly believed, absolutely and completely. Now—*at
last!*—there were other souls to join the chorus, share the
melodies they loved with Margaret.

Then Harold, drowsy with yesterdays, began to add his re-
frain—

And it did not matter that the flickering light inside the laboratory went out and ended the diversion, because kids were
yelling on yellow sand and balls bouncing almost high enough to
touch the arcing gulls. An ice cream store was opening for the
day, and everyone *knew* the cones and sodas would be even better than ever. Where unshadowed, golden beaches met blue waters, a family saw its reflections and then the faces of many
others, smiling up at them. A tall man in walking shorts wadded
a map between his hands, ready now for an easy climb to the
blue mists swirling just above the hilltops. Unzipping uniforms
and raising masks, a Martian and an Earthman hiked hand-in-
hand with a small, happily squealing girl over ravine trails, the
vacant lot behind the child.

A living ghost raised its solid arms—stretched them out to his
friend—and they clasped hands.

And a sun-metal face with a firm but gentle smile, delicate
nostrils, and the most beautiful eyes in the world—eyes the color
of the best aggies—met them all that evening with a platter of
fresh-baked warm cookies.

Sup on shadows, Reaper, and starve, starve, starve! Burn, Ice
Doctor. *Burn.*

The real banquet was beginning.

THE NOVEMBER GAME

F. Paul Wilson

He's a practicing New Jersey physician with a passion for science, literature, music, and medicine. As a science fiction writer, he began with a magazine sale in the early 1970s and saw three of his SF novels published by 1980. However, it is in the genre of horror that his talent has flourished. For this, he directly credits Ray Bradbury.

At the age of thirteen, Francis Paul Wilson picked up a paperback of Alfred Hitchcock's 13 More Stories They Wouldn't Let Me Do on TV *containing Bradbury's "The October Game." The central character is a cruel, angry father who disposes of his young daughter, Marion, in a particularly nasty way as an act of vengeance against his wife. Wilson declares that it was then, in that stunned moment after finishing Bradbury's classic shocker, that he decided that someday he, too, would write horror fiction.*

That goal has been brilliantly realized in novels such as The Keep, The Tomb, The Touch, Black Wind, *and in his superb short story collection,* Soft and Others.

When asked for a contribution to this book, Wilson eagerly responded with a chilling sequel to the story that had ignited his lifelong fascination with things horrific.

In "The October Game," Mich Wilder brutally murdered his eight-year-old daughter—and now, in "The November Game," F. Paul Wilson sees to it that he is paid back in kind for this dreadful act.

What goes around, comes around.

W.F.N.

Two human eyeballs nestle amid the white grapes on my dinner tray. I spot them even as the tray is being shoved under the bars of my cell.

"Dinner, creep," says the guard as he guides the tray forward with his shoe.

"The name is Mich, Hugo," I say evenly, refusing to react to the sight of those eyes.

"That translates into *creep* around here."

Hugo leaves. I listen to the squeaky wheels of the dinner cart echo away down the corridor. Then I look at the bowl of grapes again.

The eyes are still there, pale blue, little-girl blue, staring back at me so mournfully.

They think they can break me this way, make me pay for what I did. But after all those years of marriage to Louise, I don't break so easily.

When I'm sure Hugo's gone I inspect the rest of the food— beef patty, string beans, french fries, Jell-O. They all look okay— no surprises in among the fries like last night.

So I take the wooden spoon, the only utensil they'll let me have here, and go to the loose floor tile I found in the right rear corner. I pry it loose. A whiff of putrefaction wafts up from the empty space below. Dark down there, a dark that seems to go on forever. If I were a bit smaller I could fit through. I figure the last occupant of this cell must have been a little guy, must have tried to dig his way out. Probably got transferred to another cell before he finished his tunnel, because I've never heard of anyone breaking out of here.

But *I'm* going to be a little guy before long. And then I'll be out of here.

I upend the bowl of grapes and eyeballs over the hole first, then let the rest of the food follow. Somewhere below I hear it all plop onto the other things I've been dumping down there. I could flush the eyes and the rest down the stained white toilet squatting in the other corner, but they're probably listening for that. If they hear a flush during the dinner hour they'll guess what I'm doing and think they're winning the game. So I go them one better. As long as they don't know about the hole, I'll stay ahead.

I replace the tile and return to my cot. I tap my wooden spoon on the Melmac plates and clatter them against the tray while I smack my lips and make appropriate eating noises. I only drink the milk and water. That's all I've allowed myself since they put me in here. And the diet's working. I'm losing weight. Pretty soon I'll be able to slip through the opening under that tile, and then they'll have to admit I've beaten them at their own rotten game.

Soon I hear the squeak of the wheels again. I arrange my tray and slip it out under the bars and into the corridor.

"An excellent dinner," I say as Hugo picks up the tray.

He says nothing.

"Especially the grapes," I tell him. "The grapes were delicious—*utterly* delicious."

"Up yours, creep," Hugo says as he squeaks away.

I miss my pipe.

They won't let me have it in here. No flame, no sharps, no shoelaces, even. As if I'd actually garrote myself with string.

Suicide watch, they call it. But I've come to realize they've got something else in mind by isolating me. They've declared psychological war on me.

They must think I'm stupid, telling me I'm in a solitary cell for my own protection, saying the other prisoners might want to hurt me because I'm considered a "short eyes."

But I'm not a child molester—what "short eyes" means in prison lingo. I never molested a child in my life, never even *thought* of doing such a thing. Especially not Marion, not little eight-year-old Marion.

I only killed her.

I made her part of the game. The October game. I handed out the parts of her dismembered body to the twenty children and twelve adults seated in a circle in my cellar and let them pass the pieces around in the Halloween darkness. I can still hear their laughter as their fingers touched what they thought were chicken innards and grapes and sausages. They thought it was a lark. They had a ball—until some idiot turned on the lights.

But I never molested little Marion.

And I never meant her any harm, either. Not personally. Marion was an innocent bystander caught in the crossfire. Louise was to blame. It was Louise I wanted to hurt. Louise of the bleached-out eyes and hair, Louise the ice princess who gave birth to a bleached-out clone of herself and then made her body incapable of bearing any more children. So where was my son— my dark-eyed, dark-haired counterpoint to Marion?

Eight years of Louise's mocking looks, of using the child who appeared to be all of her and none of me as a symbol of my failures—in business, in marriage, in fatherhood, in life. When autumn came I knew it had to stop. I couldn't stand the thought of another winter sealed in that house with Louise and her miniature clone. I wanted to leave, but not without hurting Louise. Not without an eight-year payback.

And the way to hurt Louise most was to take Marion from her.

And I did. Forever. In a way she'll never forget.

We're even, Louise.

(*suck . . . puff*)

"And you think your wife is behind these horrific pranks?" Dr. Hurst says, leaning back in his chair and chewing on his pipe stem.

I envy that pipe. But I'm the supposedly suicidal prisoner and he's the prison shrink, so he gets to draw warm, aromatic smoke from the stem and I get pieces of Marion on my food tray.

"Of course she is. Louise was always a vindictive sort. Somehow she's gotten to the kitchen help and the guards and convinced them to do a *Gaslight* number on me. She hates me. She wants to push me over the edge."

(*suck . . . puff*)

"Let's think about this," he says. "Your wife certainly has reason to hate you, to want to hurt you, to want to get even with you. But this conspiracy you've manufactured is rather farfetched, don't you think? Focus on what you're saying: Your wife has arranged with members of the prison staff to place pieces of your dismembered daughter in the food they serve you. Would she do something like that with her daughter's remains?"

"Yes. She'd do anything to get back at me. She probably thinks it's poetic justice or some such nonsense."

(suck . . . puff)

"Mmmmm. Tell me again what, um, parts of Marion you've found in your food."

I think back, mentally cataloging the nastiness I've been subjected to.

"It started with the baked potatoes. They almost fooled me with the first one. They'd taken some of Marion's skin and molded it into an oblong hollow shape, then filled it with baked potato. I've got to hand it to them. It looked quite realistic. I almost ate it."

Across his desk from me, Dr. Hurst coughs.

(suck . . . puff)

"How did you feel about that?"

"Disgusted, of course. And angry, too. I'm willing to pay for what I did. I've never denied doing it. But I don't think I should be subjected to mental torture. Since that first dinner it's been a continual stream of body parts. Potato after potato encased in Marion's skin, her fingers and toes amid the french fries, a thick slice of calf's liver that didn't come from any calf, babyback ribs that were never near a pig, loops of intestine supposed to pass at breakfast as link sausage, a chunk of Jell-O with one of her vertebrae inside. And just last night, her eyes in a bowl of grapes. The list goes on and on. I want it stopped."

(suck . . . puff)

"Yes. . . . " he says after a pause. "Yes, of course you do. And I'll see to it that it *is* stopped. Immediately. I'll have the warden launch a full investigation of the kitchen staff."

"Thank you. It's good to know there's at least one person here I can count on."

(suck . . . puff)

"Tell me, Mich, what have you done with all these parts of Marion's body you've been getting in your food? Where have you put them?"

A chill comes over me. Have I been wrong to think I could trust Dr. Hurst? Has he been toying with me, leading me down the garden path to this bear trap of a question? Or *is* it a trap? Isn't it a perfectly natural question? Wouldn't anyone want to know what I've been doing with little Marion's parts?

As much as I want to be open and honest with him, I can't tell him the truth. I can't let anyone know about the loose tile and the tunnel beneath it. As a prison official he'll be obligated to report it to the warden, and then I'll be moved to another cell and lose my only hope of escape. I can't risk that. I'll have to lie.

I smile at him.

"Why, I've been eating them, of course."

(*suck* . . .)

Dr. Hurst's pipe has gone out.

I'm ready for the tunnel.

My cell's dark. The corridor has only a single bulb burning at the far end. It's got to be tonight.

Dr. Hurst lied. He said he'd stop the body parts on my trays, but he didn't. More and more of them, a couple with every meal lately. But they all get dumped down the hole along with the rest of my food. Hard to believe a little eight-year-old like Marion could have so many pieces to her body. So many I've lost track, but in a way that's good. I can't see that there can be much more of her left to torment me with.

But tomorrow's Thanksgiving and God knows what they'll place before me then.

It's got to be tonight.

At least the diet's been working.

Amazing what starvation will do to you. I've been getting thinner every day. My fat's long gone, my muscles have withered and atrophied. I think I'm small enough now to slip through that opening.

Only one way to find out.

I go to the loose tile and fit my fingers around its edges. I pried it up with the spoon earlier and left it canted in its space. It comes up easily now. The putrid odor is worse than ever. I look down into the opening. It's dark in my cell but even darker in that hole.

A sense of *waiting* wafts up with the odor.

How odd. Why should the tunnel be waiting for me?

I shake off the gnawing apprehension—I've heard hunger can play tricks with your mind—and position myself for the moment of truth. I sit on the edge and slide my bony legs into the opening. They slip through easily. As I raise my buttocks off the floor to slide my hips through, I pause.

Was that a sound? From below?

I hold still, listening. For an instant there I could have sworn I heard the faintest rustle directly below my dangling feet. But throughout my frozen, breathless silence, I hear nothing.

Rats. The realization strikes me like a blow. Of course! I've been throwing food down there for weeks. I'd be surprised if there weren't a rat or two down there.

I don't like the idea, but I'm not put off. Not for a minute. I'm wearing sturdy prison shoes and stiff, tough prison pants. And I'm bigger than they are.

Just like I was bigger than Marion . . .

I slip my hips through the opening, lower my waist through, but my chest and shoulders won't go, at least not both shoulders at once. And there's no way to slip an arm through ahead of me.

I can see only one solution. I'm not comfortable with it but I don't see any way around it. I'm going to have to go down head first.

I pull myself out and swivel around. I slip my left arm and shoulder through, then it's time for my head. I'm tempted to hold by breath, but why bother? I'm going to have to get used to that stench. I squeeze my head through the opening.

The air is warm and moist and the odor presses against my face like a shroud freshly torn from a moldering corpse. I try to mouth breathe, but the odor worms its way into my nose anyway.

And then I hear that sound again, a rustle of movement directly below me—a *wet* rustle. The odor grows stronger, rising like a dark cloud, gagging me. Something has to be behind that movement of stinking air, propelling it. Something larger than a rat!

I try to back up out of the opening, but I'm stuck. Wedged! The side of my head won't clear the edge. And the odor's stronger, oh God, it's sucking the breath right out of me. Something's near! I can't see it but I can hear it, sense it! And it wants me, it *hungers* for me! It's so close now, it's—

Something wet and indescribably foul slides across my cheek and lips. The taste makes me retch. If there were anything in my stomach, it would be spewing in all directions now. But the retching spasms force my head back out of the hole. I tear my arm and shoulder free of the opening and roll away toward the bars, toward the corridor. Who would have thought the air of a prison cell could smell so sweet, or a single sixty-watt bulb a hundred feet away be so bright?

I begin to scream. Unashamed, unabashed, I lay on my belly, reach through the bars and claw the concrete floor as wails of abject terror rip from my throat. I let them go on in a continuous stream until somebody comes, and even then I keep it up. I plead, sob, *beg* them to let me out of this cell. Finally they do. And only when I feel the corridor floor against my knees and hear the barred door clang shut behind me, does the terror begin to leach away.

"Dr. Hurst!" I tell them. "Get Dr. Hurst!"

"He ain't here, creep."

I look up and see Hugo hovering over me with two other guards from the third shift. A circle of faces completely devoid of pity or compassion.

"Call him! Get him!"

"We ain't disturbin' him for the likes o' you. But we got his resident on the way. Now what's this all—?"

"In there!" I say, pointing to the rear of the cell. "In that hole in the back! Something's down there!"

Hugo jerks his head toward the cell. "See what he's yapping about."

A young, blond guard steps into my cell and searches around with his flashlight.

"In the back!" I tell him. "The right rear corner!"

The guard returns, shaking his head. "No hole in there."

"It must have pulled the tile back into place! Please! Listen to me!"

"The kid killer's doing a crazy act," Hugo says with a snarl. "Trying to get off on a section eight."

"No-no!" I cry, pulling at his trousers as I look up at him. "Back there, under one of the tiles—"

Hugo looks away, down the corridor. "Hey, doc! Can you do something to shut this creep up?"

A man in a white coat appears, a syringe in his hand.

"Got just the thing here. Dr. Hurst left a standing order in the event he started acting up."

Despite my screams of protest, my desperate, violent struggles, they hold me down while the resident jabs a needle into my right buttock. There's burning pain, then the needle is withdrawn, and they loosen their grip.

I'm weak from lack of food, and spent from the night's exertions. The drug acts quickly, sapping what little strength remains in my limbs. I go with it. There's no more fight left in me.

The guards lift me off the floor and begin to carry me. I close my eyes. At least I won't have to spend the night in the cell. I'll be safe in the infirmary.

Abruptly I'm dropped onto a cot. My eyes snap open as I hear my cell door clang shut, hear the lock snap closed.

No! They've put me back in the same cell!

I open my lips to scream but the inside of my mouth is dry and sticky. My howl emerges as a whimper. Footsteps echo away down the corridor and the overheads go out.

I'm alone.

For a while.

And then I hear the sound I knew would come. The tile moves. A gentle rattle at first, then a long slow sliding rasp of tile upon tile. The stinking miasma from below insinuates its way into my cell, permeating my air, making it its own.

Then a soft scraping sound, like a molting snake sliding between two rocks to divest itself of old skin. Followed by another sound, a hesitant, crippled shuffle, edging closer.

I try to get away, to roll off the cot, but I can't move. My body won't respond.

And then I see it. Or rather I see a faint outline, greater darkness against lesser darkness: slim, between four and five feet high. It leans over the bed and reaches out to me. Tiny fingers, cold, damp, ragged fingers, flutter over my face like blind spiders, searching. And then they pause, hovering over my mouth and nose. My God, I can't stand the odor. I want to retch, but the drug in my system won't let me do even that.

And then the fingers move. Quickly. Two of them slip wetly into my nostrils, clogging them, sealing them like corks in the necks of wine bottles. The other little hand darts past my gasping lips, forces it way between my teeth, and crawls down my throat.

The unspeakable obscenity of the taste is swept away by the hunger for air. Air! I can't breathe! I need *air!* My body begins to buck as my muscles spasm and cry for oxygen.

It speaks then. In Marion's little voice.

Marion's voice . . . yet changed, dried up and stiff like a fallen leaf blown by autumn gusts from bright October into lifeless November.

"*Daddy* . . ."

THE OTHER MARS

Robert Sheckley

For almost four decades now, SF and fantasy readers have enjoyed the wild, witty, carefully-crafted fiction of Robert Sheckley— ex-aircraft worker, pretzel salesman, landscape gardener, charter boat operator, bartender, farmer, and jazz guitarist.

Bob grew up in New Jersey. After graduating from New York University in 1951 he determined to become a professional writer. His first SF story saw print in Imagination, *just a year later. That sale unleashed a veritable flood of short fiction—vigorous, urbane, and often sharply satirical—most of which appeared in a wide variety of SF magazines.* Untouched by Human Hands, *his first of many published collections, was issued in 1954, with* Immortality Delivered, *the first of some dozen SF novels, appearing four years later. (Sheckley has written an additional seven novels in the action-adventure vein.)*

Bob's 1966 book, The 10th Victim, *was also a popular film, inspiring two Sheckley sequels,* Victim Prime *and* Hunter/Victim.

When Ray Bradbury's The Martian Chronicles *was published in the summer of 1950, scientists knew much less than they do today about the planet Mars. But even back then, the book was considered more mythic fantasy than science fiction. In the 1990s, thanks to space probes and advanced computer technology, we know that the real Mars is far different from Bradbury's fanciful conception.*

What might a modern-day space crew actually find on the Red Planet? In "The Other Mars," Robert Sheckley answers that provocative question.

W.F.N.

It was a standing joke in the Mars Expedition base camp that whenever you saw Bernstein with a lot of equipment decked all over him, you know it was his day off and he was going exploring.

The NASA-Mars expedition had been on the surface of the planet for less than a week. They had barely gotten a feel of the place. Still, Mars was almost exactly what they'd expected from previous photo-recon surveys: a place of vast mountains, of winding canyons and endless miles of plains strewn with rocks, most of them covered with a thick, reddish-brown dust. And there was no water, of course, and no life. That had been known for quite a while, ever since the Viking and Mariner photographs. It was a thrill to be on another planet, especially one so famous as Mars. But it was a disappointment that no life existed there.

Bernstein was going further from the camp this time than ever before. He had promised to be extra careful. Everyone was afraid someone might wander off and break a leg and not be able to get back. It was dangerous to go wandering off alone. Official NASA policy discouraged solo ventures. On the other hand, there was no way they could stand each other's company for the year this visit to Mars was supposed to last. They needed to go off alone.

Bernstein was examining an interesting area that he'd looked at last week. The formations were just a little different from the surrounding jumble of rocks and volcanic extrusions. He came to the point he had gotten to last week. He'd marked his furthest progress with a bit of blue cloth. It was still there, the only blue thing in sight.

His spacesuit was keeping him warm and, more importantly, alive. It had a built-in air supply, more than enough for this journey and back. Of equal importance were the heaters built into the suit. Right here in this spot, the temperature was about 25 degrees Centigrade below zero. When he looked at his gauge,

the wind speed was around 35 kph. He knew it could gust suddenly up to a hundred, and go right off the scale at three hundred k an hour or more. The fine red brown dust blew incessantly.
Without a suit, it could flay the hide off a man.

He plodded past the spot he had reached last time. He was
moving almost due south by his magnetic compass, and trying
to keep careful note of what he was looking at. After half an
hour of picking his way through rock fields, he saw an unusual
feature ahead—two tall rocks that seemed to have been sculpted
into a rough arch. He moved toward it, finally stopping in front
of it.

The rock forming the right side of the arch was about twenty
feet high, the one on the left about fifteen feet high and just
touching the other. The formation didn't look quite the same as
the other rocks. It was paler and had more yellow in it.

He stepped through the arch. Even inside his insulated suit
this gave him an odd physical sensation, like a mild electric shock.
But he knew that had to be his imagination: stone arches don't
carry electrical charges. He passed through the arch and out the
other side.

Once through, he noticed that the scenery had changed. The
rocks had become fewer, the countryside, which had been cut
through by deep ravines, seemed to have turned into high desert
covered with low rolling hills. It was possible to get a little visual
perspective now. The sight of those low hills felt good to him.
And the wind pressure had dropped somewhat. He continued
forward.

The wind continued to diminish. There was a perceptible
clearing in the usually gritty atmosphere. He was moving among
tangled rocks, going up a slight rise. He reached the crest and
looked over. He was standing on the edge of a plain, and this
was strange because he didn't remember seeing this feature on
the maps. Still, Mars was a big place, and even this small part of
it hadn't been thoroughly surveyed.

The light was brighter here; the usual dust-haze had cleared.
He could just make out formations far ahead on the plain. One
in particular was interesting.

He set his visor for maximum magnification, and saw what
looked like a city. But what a city! He saw tall, slender, bone-

white buildings, some with crystal towers, some with domes and minarets.

He could just make out a road running in front of the city. There was something strange about that road. It was colored a sort of crystal, and it had bluish tones.

Then he realized—it was water.

But that was impossible.

Still, impossible or not, he was looking at a Martian canal, and beyond it was a Martian city.

There *were* no Martian canals. Schiaparelli and Lowell had been proven wrong. The Viking photographs of the 1970s proved beyond the shadow of a doubt that there were no canals, not even canal-like features on the planet. And there was no free-standing water. A little water was believed to exist under the polar caps, and there were plans to tap it for the use of future expeditions. But that would come later. For the present, the only free-standing water on Mars was what the expedition had brought with them. Water had made up nearly three-quarters of their payload.

Yet he was staring at something that looked like water. Something crystalline, sometimes green, sometimes blue. Something that acted like water.

He needed to check it out.

First he considered radioing back to the camp to report his discovery. Then he thought better of it. There could be no water on Mars! He'd sound like an idiot. "Bring us a sample," they'd say. And if he got to the canal and found it was an illusion—what then?

No, he'd investigate further before telling anyone anything. The chances were this *was* an illusion, some sort of Fata Morgana. When he got closer, it would fade away.

He passed through a crazy patchwork of house-sized boulders, then came into open country again. The water was much closer. The canal had been out of his sight for a while, but now he could see it again. It ran straight and true, and there were tall branchy things lining its sides. Trees? But trees were as impossible on Mars as water. These didn't seem to be in leaf. Were they petrified? No matter: trees had *never* grown on Mars!

He continued, and the land dipped again. He calculated that

when he crossed the next little rise he'd be just about at the canal, and not far from the city.

Was he ready for this?

He stood irresolute for a moment. There was still time to turn around, make his way back to the arch, pass through it, and return to the camp. He could just forget what he'd seen.

It was an oddly appealing thought. He had the feeling that if he turned back now, resolutely willing himself not to believe what he had just experienced, it would be as though it had never happened. Mars would be the way it was at the base camp— dusty, sterile, airless, and uncontaminated by anomaly.

This idea of turning back was tempting, but he couldn't do it. Bernstein didn't have the courage to turn away and go back to the camp as though nothing had happened. He would always wonder. He had to know.

He continued down the shallow declivity to the upward-tilting slope behind which lay the canal.

He scrambled up the embankment, sliding on loose sand and gravel. Then he came over the top and the canal was directly ahead of him. Its clear waters sparkled invitingly. It flowed in a channel that had been constructed with large stone blocks.

What he was looking at was quite impossible. But the canal was there. And flowing through it was what looked like water.

It was the surprise of a lifetime. But startling as it was, he had no time to react to it. The first thing he needed to react to were the four figures sitting on the bank of the canal.

They appeared to be men. Earthmen. The only kind of man there were, as far as Bernstein knew. They were lounging on the canal bank, happy as you please, paddling their feet in the water.

That was bad. But what was worse, they wore no space helmets. Yet somehow they were surviving in the oxygenless air, in the burning ultraviolet radiation of a planet without an ozone layer.

Either that, or he was crazy.

If you know you're crazy, does that make you sane? If so, what are you supposed to do when one of the forms you're hallucinating turns around, looks at you, and remarks to his friends, "Hey, guys, look what we got here."

The other three turned. They surveyed Bernstein with frank interest, their gazes attentive and unalarmed.

"He's not from our expedition."

"What expedition could he be from?"

"Maybe the Chinese got their rocket launched sooner than we expected."

"This guy doesn't look Chinese."

"Can't you talk, fella?" one of the men asked.

"Yes, of course I can talk," Bernstein said, his voice sounding strange in his own ear as he spoke through the suit's amplified speaker.

"He could be an American on a Chinese rocket," the second man remarked. To Bernstein he said, "What about it, Charlie? Is that how you got here? On a Chinese rocket? Or did the Rooskies finally make a launch?"

"Stop calling me Charlie," Bernstein said. "My name is Joshua Bernstein. I'm a member of the First NASA-Mars Project."

"Nasa? What's that?"

"It's the national space agency," Bernstein told him.

"Never heard of it," the first man said. "But of course there's a lot they don't tell us. Anyhow, welcome to Mars. It doesn't matter to me how you got here. But you're still in deep-space rig. I don't know what they told you, but you don't need it. The air's a little thin here, but an occasional sniff of oxygen takes care of that."

"What about exposure to ultraviolet?" Bernstein asked.

"Hey, no problem. This planet is a pussycat. This is one nice planet. Loosen up, stranger. Sit down and have a beer. Strip down and have a swim. Those little silver fish in there aren't going to bother you."

Peering over the side of the canal, Bernstein could see, deep in the blue-tinted crystal water, the quick-darting silver forms of fish. Goldfish! No, silverfish. But that couldn't be because silverfish weren't fish at all, but insects. But here were these silver goldfish, and here were some lads from Earth out having a picnic on the bank of a Martian canal that never existed, breathing air that couldn't be there, basking in the lethal ultraviolet and laughing at him because he was a greenhorn on their Mars and he didn't even know enough to take off his helmet.

When you're having a hallucination, Bernstein thought, and you can't do anything about it, you might as well relax and enjoy it.

And then, moving as though in a dream, he took off his helmet, expecting momentarily to fall down dead. But it was all right. The air was a little thin, as they'd said, but eminently breathable.

"How many of you are there?" Bernstein asked.

"About twenty of us back at headquarters on the other side of Mars City. Twenty miles over that way." His thumb jerked to the left. Looking in that direction, Bernstein recognized, beyond the glittering sands, the spired white city that he had seen before.

"That's a Martian city, isn't it?" Bernstein asked, striving to keep his voice casual.

"Yeah," the first speaker said. "One of the real old ones. Only a couple of Martians live there now. But sometimes at night, when the wind blows from a certain direction and at a certain speed—" his voice lowered and took on a mysterious tone—"you can hear them singing, those old Martians in their metal masks and long robes."

The others began to laugh. "He's a card, isn't he, Josh? No, no ghosts around here, though they do say some Martians still exist, up in the hills over that way." He pointed to a range of low blue hills just to the left of the sand dunes.

It was all impossible. And yet, it was strangely familiar. Bernstein searched his memory. And suddenly he knew who these guys were.

"Look, fellows," he said, "it's been great talking to you. I have to get back to my base now, but I'd like to have your names. Just for the record."

The first man said, "I'm Captain John Black. This is Lustig, our navigator. And this scholarly-looking fellow over here is Samuel Hinkston, the expedition's archeologist."

"Glad to meet you all," Bernstein said. "You flew here from Ohio, is that right?"

"Good old Ohio," Black said.

"Beautiful Ohio," Lustig said.

"See you soon," Bernstein said, and went back the way he had come.

He knew who those guys were. But he didn't want to think about it. As he returned to the camp, Bernstein tried to figure how he'd tell the others what he'd seen.

"*Hey, fellas, guess what? There's a whole other Mars just a couple of miles from here. A Mars with air, and water, and cities. There's a whole other expedition here, too. They came from Ohio in a rocket. Just follow me and I'll show you.*"

They'd lock him up and send him back to Earth at the first opportunity. He decided not to say anything about his discoveries. Not now. First he needed proof, for himself as well as for them.

Now that he thought about it, he was amazed that he'd gone through this whole thing without bringing back a shred of physical evidence. But what could he have brought back that would have proven conclusively what he's seen? *This is a bit of rock I picked up alongside the Martian Grand Canal.* No, the only way to prove anything would be with a camera. And that's what he'd bring with him tomorrow, when he went out again.

Should he ask one of the expedition members to accompany him when he went out next? If someone else saw what he'd seen, that would be proof, wouldn't it?

It was a tempting idea. But he didn't know any of the others well, and he wasn't especially friendly with any of them. They were Californians. He was the loner from M.I.T. And how would he ask someone to go with him? What reason would he give?

I saw something I'd like to check out again, but I think I might be hallucinating, so if you have nothing else to do . . ."

No, he couldn't, wouldn't do it.

And how could he explain the final incredible thing? He hadn't just seen people. That would have been bad enough. But these had been people from a story he had read long ago. These people, this Mars, was the place that Ray Bradbury had dreamed up in a book called *The Martian Chronicles.*

He'd have to go back by himself. For all he knew, he had just gone through an unaccountable hallucination, never to be repeated. Maybe he'd never find the stone arch again, never find the other Mars. It probably wouldn't be there next time. Then at least the strangeness would be over. He would know he'd had an unusual experience, and he wouldn't embarrass himself, or get himself into trouble, by claiming to have seen things that couldn't be.

The evening seemed very long. He thought at first he couldn't sleep, then fell off at last into troubled dreams. Morning came suddenly. He dressed, checked out a camera, loaded it, and started out.

One of the men called to him as he reached the camp perimeter, "Where you going, Bernstein?"

"I found some unusual rock formations yesterday. I thought I'd follow up on them."

"Don't get too far from base."

"Don't worry."

If they only knew how far away he was really going!

The rocks he followed this time didn't look familiar. But there was no reason they should. He'd be unlikely to have memorized their exact shapes and locations. It was the stone arch he was looking for. That was the sign he'd recognize, and he hadn't gone far enough yet to reach it.

Then, when he'd almost despaired of finding it, the arch was there in front of him.

He walked through, looking for familiar landmarks. He was annoyed at himself; he should have been more attentive when he came through yesterday. He should have taken notes with the little pocket recorder he carried in one of his zippered pockets.

As he moved on, he was sure he had dreamed up the whole thing. He seemed to be walking through some sort of canyon, and there were high stone walls on either side. It was like a maze, a maze of stone, and he was lost. He continued to go forward, and once he recoiled when a big monitor lizard scrambled hastily out of his path, rubbing its dry claws together, its tongue flicking.

It took Bernstein a moment to remember there was no life here, so he couldn't have seen a reptile. When he looked again it was gone. Had he really seen it? Or was it a hallucination?

Now he was coming to the end of the rock maze, and as he walked, moving with utmost caution, he heard a sound of tinkling laughter.

He spun around clumsily, and in the light gravity he turned right past the woman and had to catch his balance so that he didn't fall at her feet.

"My goodness!" the woman said. "Who are you?"

She was small, delicate, golden-haired, and she wore a gown of a shimmering metallic substance that changed color when she moved. Her features were elfin, and she was beautiful—but she was not human. Bernstein got an almost uncontrollable tremor in his hands for a moment when he realized that she was, she had to be, a Martian.

When he didn't answer she turned away from him, scanning the distant horizon. She seemed to have forgotten all about him, and he couldn't understand this at first, until he looked at her expression. She seemed enchanted, her violet eyes far away and filled with dreams, and she was singing something very softly in a high, clear voice. He listened, and after a moment he could recognize it:

> "Drink to me only with thine eyes
> And I will pledge with mine . . ."

She was singing that ancient song, just as Ylla had sung it in Bradbury's story.

Bernstein said, "Ylla?"

She turned to him, and seemed to take him in for the first time.

"Why, you are a spaceman from Earth, aren't you?"

"Yes, Ylla!"

Ylla looked at him. "I can't see your face," she said.

Bernstein took off the space helmet just as he had the previous day. She looked at him intently.

"Why are you so sad?" she asked.

Bernstein hadn't realized his unhappiness was so visible.

She asked, "Is no one waiting for you?"

"No, no one is waiting for me."

"Perhaps you'll find a nice girl here on Mars."

Bernstein felt himself drifting away into an impossible realm of magic. He pulled himself together. "I've got a problem," he told her. "I don't know how to tell my own people about you. Or about the other Earthmen here. Or the canal, or the city. None of it belongs, you see. Not in our construct. Not in our reality."

"I'm sorry to hear that," she said.

"In my world," Bernstein went on, "a conversation like we're having now would be impossible. In my world—the real world— Mars is a dead chunk of stone and sand."

"What a terrible world you must live in!" Ylla said. "You must get away from such a horrid world."

"I've thought that myself," Bernstein said.

Bernstein remembered Bradbury's story, of how Ylla had dreamed of Captain York's arrival on Mars before he actually arrived, how he had talked to her in dreams, how he'd promised to take her away from Mars, to visit Earth. And somehow Yll, Ylla's husband, had gotten wind of this. He had forbidden Ylla to go walking in the valley where she had foreseen York's ship would land. And Yll had gone there himself, with his gun. And it was pretty clear that Yll had killed York.

"York hasn't come yet," Bernstein told her. "You know what your husband is planning to do to him?"

"Yes, I know," Ylla said. "It is terrible. But perhaps it will be different this time."

"Where is Yll now?"

"He has gone to the south valley. He has gone hunting."

"But that is the valley where York will land his ship, is it not?"

"That's what I thought," Ylla said. "But I see now my dream was wrong. *Your* ship is there, isn't it?"

"Yes, it is."

"And there is some great mystery about you and the others who came with you. But where is York?"

"I don't know," Bernstein said.

He saw, in the far distance, a tiny figure trudging along slowly. Yll, no doubt. He carried a gun over his shoulder, a silver gun with a bell-shaped muzzle. There was no way of telling at this distance if he had fired it, and whether he'd hit anything if he *had* fired it. Bernstein decided he had to get away.

"Goodbye, Ylla! I hope to see you again."

He turned, but she was already gone. He realized too late that he hadn't taken a picture of her. He continued walking. Now he wanted to find the canal again, and go beyond it to the Martian city he had glimpsed yesterday. If he could take pictures of that, it would prove something . . . Wouldn't it?

The distant spires of the city came into view. Bernstein walked toward it steadily, and it grew larger and more distinct. It was a fairyland desert city, open to the sighing wind, and in front of it ran the long canal. There was a hint of moisture in the air, as though it might rain soon.

Was this the *true* Mars? Well, why not? Why should the version he knew be more lifelike or realistic than the one he was encountering now? Wasn't he being guilty of the sin of pride and intellectual arrogance, demanding that the universe conform to his opinion of it? Why should Mars be the way it seemed to him when he lived on Earth?

He entered the Martian city through a tall gate that pierced the wall surrounding it. Within the wall, he found himself in a magical place of tall thin buildings with crystal spires and golden columns. Marble walls bore the carvings of strange creatures— the gods of a world that never had been, perhaps. Bernstein sat down on a curb in the enchanted city, and he didn't know whether to laugh or cry.

Then a Martian came around the corner and sat down beside him.

"Is anything wrong?" the Martian asked.

"Something very strange is going on here," Bernstein said. "This isn't my Mars!"

"I'm bothered, too," the Martian says. "It's not mine, either."

"Then whose is it?"

"Perhaps it's the new version . . . the next thing that will be . . ."

"How could that be?"

"I wish I knew," the Martian said. "Maybe Mr. Xyx could tell you."

The Martian arose and drifted away. Bernstein forced himself to his feet. He needed to talk to someone who knew something.

He moved through the silent streets, beneath the strange, tall, old buildings, and after a while he saw someone else walking. It was a Martian, considerably older than the first one he'd met.

"You must be Mr. Xyx," Bernstein said.

"Who else would I be?" said Xyx. "And you're another, aren't you?"

"Another what?"

"Of those Earthmen. We had some here a while ago. I don't know where they went to."

"They were in a story," Bernstein said. "A story that never happened."

"Ah ... then it's all right. You see, if it *had* happened, that might be the end of it. But since it was only imagined, we can be sure it will go on."

"You mean that this dream civilization is actually still being created?"

"Yes, of course."

"Wait till I tell the others!"

"What others?"

"The men of the NASA expedition that I came with to this place. In our Mars, you see, there's no air to breathe and the climate is freezing cold."

"I'm sorry to hear that," Xyx said.

"Why?"

"Because the two constructs, your Mars and mine, cannot co-exist. There are too many anomalies, too much difference between the natural laws that the two are based upon."

"But what will happen?"

Xyx shrugged. "It's difficult to say."

Then Bernstein remembered the camera. He set his space helmet down on a doorstep and took it out.

Xyx asked, "What is that?"

"This is a camera," Bernstein said. "It takes pictures of what one sees. They can be viewed later, and they can prove what I'm seeing."

"Have you taken any pictures yet?"

"No. But I'm going to start with you."

"I advise you not to do that," Xyx said in a concerned tone.

Bernstein smiled. "It's perfectly safe. No harm will come to you."

"I'm not worried about myself," Xyx said. "The danger is to the one who takes the picture, not to the one whose picture is taken."

"That's crazy! Are you going to try and stop me?"

"Not at all. I was merely advising you for your own good. Do whatever you please."

The Martian strolled away.

Bernstein raised his camera, irresolute. He focused on Mr. Xyx's receding form, hesitated, scanned the buildings in the viewholder, poised the camera, then put it down again.

This was a very big moment. A moment of concern for human history. If he didn't take the pictures now, when he had the opportunity, he felt sure the whole thing would remain like a dream or a vision. Just another strange tale, like ten thousand other strange tales that men have dreamed up.

But if he brought back proof . . . maybe if he proved this place existed, it *would* exist.

He hesitated. There was the possibility that if he proved this place existed, the places *he* had known would no longer exist.

He didn't want to think about that.

Bernstein raised the camera and photographed the street he was standing on. He waited fearfully a moment. Nothing happened. He began taking more pictures.

Then he heard a sound behind him and he whirled.

A man was trudging down the street pushing a wide cart. He was a man of Earth. He wore a white apron and a straw hat. His cart was gaily colored in red and green stripes.

He was calling out something. As the man approached, Bernstein was able to make out what he was saying: "Get yer red hots!"

A hot dog salesman!

"Hi, I'm Sam," the hot dog man said. "Where are the others?"

"What others?"

"The others who escaped from Earth. The last pioneers."

"I don't know what you're talking about. Why should they want to escape from Earth?"

"Man, don't you know?" Sam asked, his voice incredulous. "Everyone knows what's happened to Earth."

"What are you talking about?"

"The atomics. A chain reaction. The whole planet is dead."

"Wait," Bernstein said, "that can't be right. In my world the Cold War is over, no one is threatening anyone with atomic bombs. Blowing up Earth has become inconceivable."

"Not here it's not. It's happened."

Bernstein couldn't stand this any longer. He backed away from the man, turned, started to run. He ran through the streets of the ancient city and out into the desert. Pushing himself as hard as he could, he moved rapidly across the stony ground. He should have remembered this outcome. It was foretold in one of Bradbury's stories, "There Will Come Soft Rains." But perhaps there was still time to avert personal doom.

Panting, out of breath, he reached the place where the high stone arch had been. But it wasn't there any longer. Two people were sitting on a pile of rocks nearby. A Martian and an Earthman.

The woman was Ylla. He had never seen the man before, but he knew it had to be Captain York.

"What happened to the arch?" Bernstein asked.

"I tore it down," York said. "Ylla helped me."

"But why?"

"To prevent your world from continuing."

Bernstein sat down on a rock near York and Ylla. He didn't have his helmet. He must have left it in the city. He didn't think he would need it any longer.

"So my world is gone?"

"It never existed," York said. "I made sure of that."

"It *did* exist!"

"Only as an unaccountable fancy. And frankly, it's no great loss. From what Ylla has told me, your world didn't sound especially nice."

"It was a fine world!" Bernstein said.

"But incompatible with this one," York said. "I don't want to live in a world in which Mars has no air and no life. Then there'd be no Ylla! And no me!"

"I see," Bernstein said. "I suppose this is a case of survival of the fittest hallucination."

"I suppose so," York said. He had his arm around Ylla's shoulder. He seemed pleased with himself.

"What about the other men of my expedition?" Bernstein asked.

"What men?" York said. "*What* expedition?"

Bernstein was numb.

"There's plenty of time for you to figure things out," York said. "For now, let's head for the Grand Canal."

"What for?"

"Just to sit beside it," said York.

"And watch our reflections in the water," said Ylla.

"And drink beer?" asked Bernstein.

York smiled.

Bernstein followed York and Ylla back to the Martian city. He was going to drink beer and throw his empties into the Grand Canal of Mars.

After that, he didn't know what he would do.

FEED THE BABY OF LOVE

Orson Scott Card

Orson Scott Card was born in Washington, grew up in Utah, and now lives in Greensboro, North Carolina. He was educated at Brigham Young University and served as a Mormon missionary in Brazil from 1971 into 1973. Returning to Utah, he ran a repertory theatre in Provo where he wrote and produced more than a dozen plays. In the late 1970s, through 1982, he was a teacher, first at the University of Utah, later at Notre Dame.

Card saw his first book published in 1978; he has become a major name in science fiction with such novels as Ender's Game *(1985) and* Speaker of the Dead *(1986), both of which garnered a hatful of prizes, including the Hugo and Nebula Awards.*

His theme as a writer embraces personal growth and transformation, and this theme is strongly echoed here in his contribution to The Bradbury Chronicles.

Orson Scott Card links Dandelion Wine's *boyhood world of 1928 with our present world of the 1990s in this sharply effective portrait of a woman who has reached a special turning point in her life.*

The longest story in this book—and one of the most creatively powerful.

W.F.N.

When Rainie Pinyon split this time she didn't go south, even though it was October and she didn't like the winter cold. Maybe she thought that this winter she didn't deserve to be warm, or maybe she wanted to find some unfamiliar territory—whatever. She got on the bus in Bremerton and got off it again in Boise. She hitched to Salt Lake City and took a bus to Omaha. She got herself a waitressing job, using the name Ida Johnson, as usual. She quit after a week, got another job in Kansas City, quit after three days, and so on and so on until she came to a tired-looking cafe in Harmony, Illinois, a small town up on the bluffs above the Mississippi. She liked Harmony right off, because it was pretty and sad—half the storefronts brightly painted and cheerful, the other half streaked and stained, the windows boarded up. The kind of town that would be perfectly willing to pick up and move into a shopping mall, only nobody wanted to build one here and so they'd just have to make do. The help wanted sign in the cafe window was so old that several generations of spiders had lived and died on webs between the sign and the glass.

"We're a five-calendar cafe," said the pinched-up overpainted old lady at the cash register.

Rainie looked around and sure enough, there were five calendars on the walls.

"Not just because of that *Blue Highways* book, either, I'll have you know. We already had these calendars up before he wrote his book. He never stopped here but he could have."

"Aren't they a little out of date?" asked Rainie.

The old lady looked at her like she was crazy.

"If you already had the calendars up when he wrote the book, I mean."

"Well, not *these* calendars," said the old lady. "Here's the thing, darlin'. A lot of diners and whatnot put up calendars after that *Blue Highways* book said that was how you could tell a good restaurant. But those were all fakes. They didn't *understand*. The calendars have all got to be *local* calendars. You know, like the insurance guy gives you a calendar and the car dealer and the real estate guy and the funeral home. They give you one every year, and you put them all up because they're your friends and your customers and you hope they do good business."

"You got a car dealer in Harmony?"

"Went out of business thirty years ago. Used to deal in Studebakers, but he hung on with Buicks until the big dealers up in the tri-cities underpriced him to death. No, I don't get his calendar anymore, but we got two funeral homes so maybe that makes up for it."

Rainie almost made a remark about this being the kind of town where nobody goes anywhere, they just stay home and die, but then she decided that maybe she liked this old lady and maybe she'd stay here for a couple of days, so she held her tongue.

The old lady smiled a twisted old smile. "You didn't say it, but I know you thought it."

"What?" asked Rainie, feeling guilty.

"Some joke about how people don't need cars here, cause they aren't going anywhere until they die."

"I want the job," said Rainie.

"I like your style," said the old lady. "I'm Minnie Wilcox, and I can hardly believe that anybody in this day and age named their little girl Ida, but I had a good friend named Ida when I was a girl and I hope you don't mind if I forget sometimes and call you Idie like I always did her."

"Don't mind a bit," said Rainie. "And nobody in this day and age *does* name their daughter Ida. I wasn't *named* in this day and age."

"Oh, right, you're probably just pushing forty and starting to feel old. Well, I hope I never hear a single word about it from you because I'm right on the seventy line, which to my mind is about the same as driving on empty; the engine's still running but you know it'll sputter soon, so what the hell, let's get a few more miles on the old girl before we junk her. I need you on the morning shift, Idie. I hope that's all the same with you."

"How early?"

"Six A.M. I'm sad to say, but before you whine about it in your heart, you remember that *I'm* up baking biscuits at four-thirty. My Jack and I used to do that together. In fact he got his heart attack rolling out the dough, so if you ever come in early and see me spilling a few tears into the powdermilk, I'm not having a bad day, I'm just remembering a good man, and that's my privilege. We got to open at six on account of the hotel across the street. It's sort of the opposite of a bed and breakfast. They only serve dinner, an all-you-can-eat family-style home-cooking restaurant that brings 'em in from fifty miles around. The hotel sends them over here for breakfast, and on top of that we get a lot of folks in town for breakfast *and* for lunch, too. We do good business. I'm not poor and I'm not rich. I'll pay you decent and you'll make fair tips, for this part of the country. You still see the nickels by the coffee cups, but you just give those old coots a wink and a smile, cause the younger boys make up for them and it's not like it costs that much for a room around here. Meals free during your shift but not after, I'm sorry to say."

"Fine with me," said Rainie.

"Don't go quittin' on me after a week, darlin'."

"Don't plan on it," said Rainie, and to her surprise it was true. It made her wonder—was Harmony, Illinois what she'd been looking for when she checked out in Bremerton? It wasn't what usually happened. Usually she was looking for the street—the down-and-out half-hopeless life of people who lived in the shadow of the city. She'd found the street once in New Orleans, and once in San Francisco, and another time in Paris; and she found places where the street used to be, like Beale Street in Memphis, and the Village in New York City, and Venice in L.A. But the street was such a fragile place, and it kept disappearing on you even while you were living right in it.

But there was no way that Harmony, Illinois was the street, so what in the world was she looking for if she had found it here?

Funeral homes, she thought. I'm looking for a place where funeral homes outnumber car dealerships, because my songs are dead and I need a decent place to bury them.

It wasn't bad working for Minnie Wilcox. She talked a lot but there were plenty of town people who came by for coffee in the morning and a sandwich at lunch, so Rainie didn't have to pay attention to most of the talking unless she wanted to. Minnie found out that Rainie was a fair hand at making sandwiches, too, and she could fry an egg, so the work load kind of evened out— whichever of them was getting behind, the other one helped. It was busy, but it was decent work—nobody yelled at anybody else, and even when the people who came in were boring, which was always, they were still decent, and even the one old man who leered at her kept his hands and his comments to himself. There were days when Rainie even forgot to slip outside in back of the cafe and have a smoke in the wide-open gravel alleyway next to the Dumpster.

"How'd you used to manage before I came along?" she asked early on. "I mean, judging from that sign, you've been looking for help for a long time."

"Oh, I got by, Idie, darlin', I got by."

Pretty soon, though, Rainie picked up the truth from comments the customers made when they thought she was far enough away not to hear. Old people always thought that because *they* could barely hear, everybody else was half-deaf, too. "Oh, she's a live one." "Knows how to work, this one does." "Not one of those young girls who only care about *one thing*." "How long you think she'll last, Minnie?"

She lasted one week. She lasted two weeks. It was on into November and getting cold, with all the leaves brown or fallen, and she was still there. This wasn't like any of the other times she'd dropped out of sight, and it scared her a little, how easily she'd been caught here. It made no sense at all. This town just wasn't Rainie Pinyon, and yet it must *be*, because here she was.

After a while even getting up at six A.M. wasn't hard, because there was no life in this town at night so she might as well go to bed as soon as it turned dark and then dawn was a logical time to get up. There was no TV in the room Rainie took over the garage of a short-tempered man who told her "No visitors" in a tone of voice that made it clear he assumed that she was a whore by nature and only by sheer force of will could he keep her respectable. Well, she was used to letting the voice of authority make proclamations about what she could and couldn't do. Almost made her feel at home. And, of course, she'd do whatever she wanted. This was 1990 and she was forty-two years old and there was freedom in *Russia* now, so her landlord, whatever his name was, could take his no-visitors rule and apply it to his own self. She saw how he sized up her body and decided she was nice looking. A man who sees a nice-looking woman and assumes that she's wicked to the core is confessing his own desires.

After work Rainie didn't have anywhere much to go. She ate enough for breakfast and lunch at the cafe that dinner didn't play much of a part in her plans. Besides, the hotel restaurant was too crowded and noisy and full of people's children running around dripping thick globs of gravy off their plates. The chatter of people and clatter of silverware, with Mantovani and Koste-lanetz playing in the background—it was not a sound Rainie could enjoy for long. And when she passed the piano in the hotel lobby the one time she went there, she felt no attraction toward it at all, so she knew she wasn't ready to surface yet.

One afternoon, chilly as it was, she took off her apron after work and put on her jacket and walked in the waning light down to the river. There was a park there, a long skinny one that consisted mostly of parking places, plus a couple of picnic tables, and then a muddy bank and a river that seemed to be as wide as the San Francisco Bay. Dirty and cold, that was the Missis-sippi. It didn't call out for you to swim in it, but it did keep moving leftward, flowing south, flowing downhill to New Or-leans. I know where this river goes, thought Rainie. I've been where it ends up, and it ends up pretty low. She remembered Nicky Villiers sprawled on the levee, his vomit forming one of the Mississippi's less distinguished tributaries as it trickled on down and disappeared in the mud. Nicky shot up on heroin one day when she was out and then forgot he'd done it already and shot up again, or maybe he didn't forget, but anyway Rainie found him dead in the nasty little apartment they shared, back in the winter of—what, sixty-eight? Twenty-two years ago. Be-fore her first album. Before anybody ever heard of her. Back when she thought she knew who she was and what she wanted. If I'd had his baby like he asked me, he'd still be dead and I'd have a fatherless child old enough to go out drinking without fake ID.

The sky had clouded up faster than she had thought possi-ble—sunny but cold when she left the cafe, dark and cloudy and the temperature dropping about a degree a minute by the time she stood on the riverbank. Her jacket had been warm enough every other day, but not today. A blast of wind came into her face from the river, and there was ice in it. Snowflakes like nee-dles in it. Oh yes, she thought. This is why I always go south in winter. But this year I'm not even as smart as a migratory bird, I've gone and got myself a nest in blizzard country.

She turned around to head back up the bluff to town. For a moment the wind caught her from behind, catching at her jacket and making it cling to her back. When she got back to the two-lane highway and turned north, the wind tried to tear her jacket off her, and even when she zipped it closed, it cut through. The snow was coming down for real now, falling steadily and sticking on the grass and on the gravel at the edges of the road. Her feet were getting wet and cold right through her shoes as she walked along in the weeds, so she had to move out onto the asphalt. She walked on the left side of the road so she could see any oncoming cars, and that made her feel like she was a kid in school again, listening to the safety instructions. Wear light clothing at night and always walk on the left side of the road, facing traffic. Why? So they can see your white, white face and your bright terrified eyes just before they run you down.

She reached the intersection where the road to town slanted up from the Great River Road. There was a car coming, so she waited for it to pass before crossing the street. She was looking forward to heading southeast for a while, so the wind wouldn't be right in her face. It'd be just her luck to catch a cold and get laryngitis. Couldn't afford laryngitis. Once she got that it could linger for months. Cost her half a million dollars once, back in '73, five months of laryngitis and a cancelled tour. Promoter was going to sue her, too, since *he* figured he'd lost ten times that much. His lawyer talked sense to him, though, and the lawsuit and the promoter both went away. Those were the days, when the whole world trembled if I caught a cold. Now it'd just be Minnie Wilcox in the Harmony Cafe, and it wouldn't exactly take *her* by surprise. The sign was still in the window.

The car didn't pass. Instead it slowed down and stopped. The driver rolled down his window and leaned his head out. "Ride?"

She shook her head.

"Don't be crazy, Ms. Johnson," he said. So he knew her. A customer from the cafe. He pulled his head back in and leaned over and opened the door on the other side.

She walked over, just to be polite, to close the door for him as she turned him down. "You're very nice," she began, "but—"

"No buts," he said. "Mrs. Wilcox'll kill me if you get a cold and I could have given you a ride."

Now she knew him. The man who did Minnie's accounting. Lately he came in for lunch every day, even though he only went over the cafe books once a week. Rainie wasn't a fool. He was a nice man, quiet, and he never even joked with her, but he was coming in for her and she didn't want to encourage him.

"If you're worried about your personal safety, I got my two older kids as chaperones."

The kids leaned forward from the back seat to get a look at her. A boy, maybe twelve years old. A girl, looking about the same age, which meant she was probably younger. "Get in, lady, you're letting all the heat out of the car," said the girl.

She got in. "This is nice of you, but you didn't need to," she said.

"I can tell you're not from around here," said the boy in the back seat. "Radio says this is a *bad* storm coming, and you don't walk around in a blizzard after dark. Sometimes they don't find your body till spring."

"Dougie," said the man.

That was the man's name, too, she remembered. Douglas. And his last name . . . Spaulding. Like the ball manufacturer.

"This is nice of you, Mr. Spaulding," she said.

"We're just coming back down from the Tri-cities Mall," he said. "They can't wear last year's leather shoes 'cause they're too small, and their mother would have a fit if I suggested they keep wearing their sneakers right on through the winter, so we just had the privilege of dropping fifty bucks at the shoe store."

"Who are you?" asked the girl.

"I'm Ida Johnson," she said. "I'm a waitress at the cafe."

"Oh, yeah," said the girl.

"Dad said Mrs. Wilcox had a new girl," said Dougie. "But you're not a girl, you're *old*."

"Dougie," said Mr. Spaulding.

"I mean you're older than, like, a teenager, right? I don't mean like you're about to get Alzheimer's or anything, for Pete's sake, but you're not *young*, either."

"She's *my* age," said Mr. Spaulding, "so I'd appreciate it if you'd get off this subject."

"How old are *you*, then, Daddy?" asked the girl.

"Bet he doesn't remember," said Dougie. He explained to Rainie. "Dad forgets his age all the time."

"Do not," said Mr. Spaulding.

"Do so," said Dougie. It was obviously a game they had played before.

"Do not, and I'll prove it. I was born in 1948, which was three years after World War II ended, and five years before Eisenhower became president, and *he* died at Gettysburg, Pennsylvania, which was the site of a battle that was fought in 1863, which was 127 years ago last July, and here it is November which is four months after July, and November is the eleventh month and so I'm four times eleven, forty-four."

"No!" the kids both shouted, laughing. "You turned *forty-two* in May."

"Why, that's good news," he said. "I feel two years younger, and I'll bet Ms. Johnson does too."

She couldn't help but smile.

"Here we are," he said.

It took her a moment to realize that without any directions, he had taken her right to the garage with the outside stair that led to her apartment. "How did you know where to take me?"

"It's a small town," said Mr. Spaulding. "Everybody knows everything about everybody, except for the things which nobody knows."

"Like Father's middle name," said the girl.

"Get on upstairs and turn your heat on, Ms. Johnson," said Mr. Spaulding. "This is going to be a bad one tonight."

"Thanks for the ride," said Rainie.

"Nice to meet you," said Dougie.

"Nice to meet you," echoed the girl.

Rainie stood in the door and leaned in. "I never caught *your* name," she said to the girl.

"I'm Rose. *Never* Rosie. Grandpa Spaulding picked the name, after *his* aunt who never married. I personally think the name sucks pond scum, but it's better than Ida, don't you agree?"

"Definitely," said Rainie.

"Rosie," said Mr. Spaulding, in his warning voice.

"Good night, Mr. Spaulding," said Rainie. "And thanks for the ride."

He gave a snappy little salute in the air, as if he were touching the brim of a nonexistent hat. "Any time," he said. She closed the door of the car and watched them drive away. Up in her room she turned the heater on.

During the night the snow piled up a foot and a half deep and the temperature got to ten below zero, but she was warm all night. In the morning she wondered if she should go to work. She knew Minnie would be there, and Rainie wasn't about to have Minnie decide that her "new girl" was soft. She almost left the apartment with only her jacket for warmth, but then she thought better and put on a sweater under it. She still froze, what with the wind blowing ground snow in her face.

At the cafe the talk was that four people died between Chicago and St. Louis that night, the storm was so bad. But the cafe was open and the coffee was hot, and standing there looking out the window at the occasional car passing by on the freshly plowed road, Rainie realized that in Louisiana and California she had *never* felt as warm as this, to be in a cafe with coffee steaming and eggs sizzling on the grill and deadly winter outside, trying but failing to get at her.

When Mr. Spaulding came into the cafe for his lunch just after one o'clock, Rainie thanked him again.

"For what?"

"For saving my life yesterday."

He still looked baffled.

"Giving me a ride up from the river."

Now he remembered. "Oh, I was just doing Minnie a favor. She never thought you'd stay a week, and here you've stayed for more than a month already. She would have reamed me out royal if we had to dig your corpse out of a snowdrift."

"Well, anyway, thanks." But she wasn't saying thanks for the ride, she realized. It was something else. Maybe it was the kids in the back seat. Maybe it was the way he'd talked to them. The way he'd *kept on* talking with them, even though there was an adult in the car. Rainie wasn't used to that. She wasn't used to being with kids at all, actually. And when she did find herself in the presence of other people's children, the parents were always shushing the kids so they could talk to *her*. "I liked your kids," said Rainie.

"They're okay," he said. But his eyes said a lot more than that. They said, you must be good people if you think well of my kids.

She tried to imagine what it would have been like, if her own parents had ever been with her the way Mr. Spaulding was with *his* children. Maybe my whole life would have been different, she thought. Then she remembered where she was—Harmony, Illinois, otherwise known as The Last Place on Earth. No matter whether her parents were nice or not, she probably would have hated every minute of her childhood in a one-horse town like this. "Must be hard for them, though," she said. "Growing up miles from anywhere."

All at once his face closed off. He didn't argue or get mad or anything, he just closed up shop and the conversation was over. "I suppose so," he said. "I'll just have a club sandwich today, and a diet something."

"Coming right up," she said.

It really annoyed her that he'd shut her down like that. Didn't he *know* how small this town was? He'd been to college, hadn't he? Which meant he must have lived away from this town *sometime* in his life. Have some perspective, Spaulding, she said to him silently. If your kids aren't dying to get out of here now, just give them a couple of years and they will be, and what'll you do *then?*

As he sat there eating, looking through some papers from his briefcase, it began to grate on her that he was so pointedly ignoring her. What right did he have to judge her?

"What put a bug up *your* behind?" asked Minnie.

"What do you mean?" said Rainie.

"You're stalking and bustling around here like you're getting set to smack somebody."

"Sorry," said Rainie.

"One of my customers insult you?"

She shook her head. Because now that she thought about it, the reverse was true. She had insulted *him*, or at least had insulted the town he lived in. What was griping at her wasn't him being rude to her, because he hadn't been. He simply didn't like to hear people badmouthing his town. Douglas Spaulding wasn't in Harmony because he never had an idea that there was a larger world out there. He was a smart man, much smarter than the job of small-town accountant required. He was here by choice, and she had talked as if it was a bad choice for his children, and this was a man who loved his children, and it really bothered her that he had closed her off like that.

It bothered her so much that she went over and pulled up a chair at his table. He looked up from his papers, raised an eyebrow. "This a new service at Jack & Minnie's Cafe?"

"I'm willing to learn," said Rainie. "I'm not a bigot against small towns. I just sort of took it for granted that small towns would feel oppressive to kids because the small town I grew up in felt oppressive to *me*. If that's a crime, shoot me."

He looked at her in wonder. "I don't have an idea on God's Earth what you're talking about."

"A minute ago when you shut me down," she said, really annoyed now. "You can't tell me that shutting people down is so unimportant that you don't even remember doing it."

"I ordered my breakfast is all I did," said Spaulding.

"So you *do* remember," she said triumphantly.

"I just wasn't interested in continuing that conversation."

"Then don't shut a person down, Mr. Spaulding. Tell them that you don't appreciate what they said, but don't just cut me off."

"It honestly didn't occur to me that you'd even notice," he said. "I figured you were just making small talk, and the talk just got too small."

"I wasn't making small talk," said Rainie. "I was really impressed with your kids. It's a sure thing *I* was never that way with *my* father."

"They're good kids." He took another bite and looked down at his paper.

She laid her hand on the paper, fingers spread out to cover the whole sheet and make it unreadable.

He sat up, leaned back in his chair, and regarded her. "The place isn't crowded, the lunch rush is over, so it can't be that you need my table."

"No, sir," said Rainie. "I need your attention. I need just a couple of minutes of your attention, Mr. Spaulding, because in your car yesterday I caught a whiff of something I've heard about but I always thought it was a legend; a *lie*, like Santa Claus and the tooth fairy and the Easter bunny."

He got a little half-smile on his face, but there was still fire in his eyes. "Since when is Santa Claus a lie?"

"Since I was six years old and got up to pee and saw Dad putting together the bike on the living room floor."

"It strikes me that what you saw was proof that Santa Claus was real. Flesh and blood. Putting together a bike. Making cookies for you in the kitchen."

"That wasn't Santa Claus, that was Dad and Mom, except that my Mom didn't make cookies for *me*, she made them for *her*, all neat and round and lined up exactly perfect on the cookie tray— Lord help me if I actually *touched* one—and Dad couldn't get the bike together right, he had to wait till the stores opened the day after Christmas so he could get the guy in the bike shop to put it together."

"So far you haven't proved that Santa Claus was fake, you just proved that he wasn't good enough for you. If Santa Claus couldn't be perfect, you didn't want any Santa Claus at all."

"Why are you getting so mad at me?"

"Did I invite you to sit at this table, Ms. Johnson?"

"Dammit, Mr. Spaulding, would you call me Ida like everybody else?"

"Dammit, Ms. Johnson, why are you the only person in town who doesn't call me Douglas?"

"Begging your pardon, *Douglas*."

"Begging yours, *Ida*."

"All I was trying to say, *Douglas*, when I brought up Santa Claus, *Douglas*, was that in your car I saw a father being easy with his children, and the children being easy with their dad, right in front of a stranger, and I never thought that happened in the real world."

"We get along okay," said Douglas. He shrugged it off, but she could see that he was pleased.

"So for a minute in your car I felt like I was part of that and I guess it just hurt my feelings a little when you shut me down back then. It didn't seem fair. I didn't think my offense was so terrible."

"Like I said, I wasn't punishing you."

"All right then. More coffee?"

"No thanks."

"Pie? Ice cream?"

"No thanks."

"Well, then why do you keep calling me over to your table?"

He smiled. Laughed almost. So it was all right. She felt better, and she could leave him alone then.

After he left, after all the lunch customers had gone and she was washing down the tables and wiping off the saltshakers and emptying the ashtrays, Minnie came over to her and looked her in the eye, hard and angry.

"I saw you sitting down and talking with Douglas," she said.

"We weren't busy," said Rainie.

"Douglas is a decent man with a happy family."

Now Rainie understood. In her own way, Minnie was just like the guy who rented her the room over the garage. Always assuming that because she was a good-looking woman, she was on the make. Well, she *wasn't* on the make, but if she was, it wouldn't be any of Minnie's business or anybody else's except her own. What *was* it about this place? Why did everybody always assume that sex was the foremost thing in a single forty-two-year-old woman's mind?

"I'm glad for him," Rainie said.

"Don't you make no trouble for that good man and his good wife," said Minnie.

"I said something that I thought maybe offended him and I wanted to make sure everything was all right, that's all. I was trying to make sure I hadn't alienated a customer." Even as she explained, Rainie resented having to make an explanation.

"Do you think I'm a fool? Do you think I'm such a fool as to think *you're* a fool? Since he first laid eyes on you he's been in here every day. And now you're going over sitting at his table arguing with him and then making him laugh. I've got half a mind to fire you right now and send you on your way, except I like you and I'd like to keep you around. But I don't like you so much I'm willing to have you making things ugly for people around here. You can make a mess here and then just walk away, but me and my customers, we'll have to keep living with whatever it is you do, so don't do it. Am I clear?"

Rainie didn't answer, just furiously wiped at the table. She hadn't been reamed out like that since . . . her *mother* was the last one to ream her out like this, and Rainie had left *home* over it, and it made her so *mad* to have to listen to it all over again. She was forty-two years old and she *still* had some old lady telling her what she could and couldn't do, laying down rules, making conditions and regulations, and claiming that she *liked* her while she was doing it.

Minnie waited for a minute till it was clear Rainie wasn't going to answer. "All right then," said Minnie. "I've got enough in the register to give you your pay. Take off the apron, you can go."

I don't need your money or your job, you poor old fool, I'm Rainie Pinyon, I sing and write songs and play the piano and cut albums, I've got a million-dollar ranch in the Horse Heaven Hills of eastern Washington and an agent in L.A. who calls me sweetheart and sends me checks a couple of times a year, checks large enough even during the bad years that I could buy your two-bit cafe and move it to Tokyo and never even miss the money.

Rainie thought all that, but she didn't say it. Instead she said, "I'm sorry. I'm not going to mess around with anybody's life, and I'll be careful with Mr. Spaulding."

"Take off the apron, Ida."

Rainie whirled on her. "I *said* I'd do what you wanted."

"I don't think so," said Minnie. "I think you got the same tone of voice I heard in my daughter when she had no intention of doing what I said, but promised to do it just to get me off her back."

"Well, I'm not your daughter. I *thought* I was your friend."

Minnie looked at her, steady and cold, then shook her head. "Ida Johnson, I can't figure you out. I never thought you'd last a week, and I *sure* never figured you for the type who'd try to hold on to a lousy job like this one after the tongue-lashing I just gave you."

"To tell you the truth, Mrs. Wilcox, I never figured myself that way either. But I don't want to leave."

"Is it Douglas Spaulding? Are you in love?"

"I used up love a dozen years ago, Mrs. Wilcox, and I haven't looked to recharge the batteries since then."

"You mean to tell me *you* been without a man for twelve years?"

"I thought we were talking about whether I was in love."

"No such thing." Minnie looked her up and down. "I'll bet you didn't wear a bra during the bra-burning days, did you?"

"What?"

"Your chest has dropped so low you could almost tuck 'em into your belt. I don't know what a man would find attractive about you anyway."

It was such an insulting, outrageous thing to say that Rainie was speechless.

"You can stay, as long as you don't call me Mrs. Wilcox. That just drives me crazy. Call me Minnie."

Things went right back to normal, mostly because Douglas Spaulding didn't come in again for more than a week, and when he did come back, he wasn't alone. He was part of a group of men—most of them in suits, but not all—who came into the cafe walking on the balls of their feet like dancers, like running backs. "You're all full of sass," said Minnie to one of the men.

"Time to feed the baby!" he answered.

Minnie rolled her eyes. "I know. Jaynanne Spaulding's gone out of town again."

"Dougie's Christmas present to her—a week with her folks up in Racine."

"Present to him*self*," said Minnie.

"Taking care of the kids for a solid week, you think that's a picnic?"

"Those kids take care of themselves," said Minnie. "Douglas Spaulding's just a big old kid himself. And so are you, Tom Reuther, if you want my opinion."

"Minnie, honey, nobody ever has *time* to want your opinion. You give it to us before we even have a chance to wish for it."

Minnie held up a ladle of her Cincinnati chili. "You planning to eat your lunch or wear it, Tom?"

One of the other men—a mechanic, from the black stains on his overalls—piped up from the two tables they had pushed together in the middle of the room. "He's already wearing every bit of food you ever served him. Can't you see it hanging over his belt?"

"Under my belt or over it, Minnie, I wear your food with pride," said Tom. Then he blew her a kiss and joined the others.

Douglas was already sitting at the table, laughing at nothing and everything, just like the others. He really *did* seem to be just a big old kid right then—there was nothing of the father about him now. Just noise and laughing and moving around in his chair, as if it might just kill him if he ever sat still for more than ten seconds at a time. Rainie half-expected to look down and see him wearing too-short or too-long jeans with holes in the knees, showing one knee skinned up and scabbed over, and maybe raggedy sneakers on his feet. She was almost disappointed to see those shiny sensible oxfords and suitpants with the hems just right. He didn't *not* look at her, but he didn't particularly look at her, either. He was just generally cheerful, being with his friends, and he had plenty of good cheer to share with anybody who happened to come along.

"You going to order separate checks and make my life miserable?" asked Rainie of the group at large.

"Just give the bill to Doug," said Tom.

"You can make one total and we'll divvy it up ourselves," said Douglas. "It'll be easy, because we're all having exactly the same thing."

"Is that right?"

"Beans!" cried Tom.

"Beans! Beans! Beans!" chanted several of the others.

"We gots to have our daily beans, ma'am," Tom explained, "cause we gots to feed the Baby of Love!"

"I got a double batch of chili with extra cinnamon!" called Minnie from behind the counter. "This time somebody had the *brains* to call ahead and warn me!"

Tom immediately pointed an accusing finger at Douglas. "What is this, Spaulding? A sudden attack of maturity and consideration for others? Malicious *foresight*? For shame!"

Douglas shrugged. "Last time she ran out."

"Chili for everybody," said Rainie. "Is that all? Nothing to drink?"

"What is the drink of the day?" asked one of the men.

"Whose turn is it anyway?" asked another.

"Tom's turn," said Douglas.

They turned toward him expectantly. He spread his hands out on the table and looked them in the eye, as if he was about to deliver the State of the Union address. Or a funeral prayer. "Seven-Up," said Tom. "A large Seven-Up for everybody."

"Are you serious?" asked Douglas. "And what's for dessert— toothpaste?"

"The rule is no alcohol at lunch," said Tom, "and beyond that we're free to be as creative as we like."

"You're giving creativity a bad name," said Douglas.

"Trust me," said Tom.

"If all we get today is Seven-Up," said the mechanic, "you are going to spend the entire evening as primordial slime."

"No, he's going to spend the night in *Hell*," said another.

At the soda machine, spurting the Seven-Up into the glasses, Rainie had to ask. "What in the world are they *talking* about?"

"It's a game they play," said Minnie. "It's notorious all over town. More satanic than Dungeons and Dragons. If these boys weren't so nice they'd probably be burnt at the stake or something."

"Satanic?"

"Or secular humanist or whatever. I get those two things mixed up. It's all about feeding beans to the baby and when you win you turn into God. Pagan religion and evolution. I asked Reverend Blakely about it and he just shook his head. No wonder Jaynanne leaves town whenever they play."

"Aren't you going to serve up the chili?"

"Not till they're through with whatever nonsense they do about the drinks."

Rainie loaded the drinks onto the tray and headed back to what she was now thinking of as the Boys' Table. Whatever it was that Douglas Spaulding and his friends had turned into, it was suddenly a lot more interesting to her now that she knew that at least some groups in the town disapproved of it. Evolution and paganism? It sounded like it was right up her alley.

She started to load off the glasses at each place, but Tom beckoned her frantically. "No, no, all here in front of me!" With one arm he swept away the salt and pepper shakers, the napkin dispenser, the sugar canister, and the red plastic ketchup bottle. "Right here, Miss Ida, if you don't mind."

She leaned over Tom's left shoulder and set down the whole tray without spilling a drop from any of the glasses. Before she stood up, she glanced at Douglas, who was right across from Tom, and caught him looking down the neck of her dress. Almost immediately he looked away; she didn't know whether he knew she saw him looking or not.

My boobs may have sagged a little, Minnie, but I still got enough architecture to make the tourists take a second glance.

There were other customers, but while she was dropping off their orders she kept an eye on the Boys' Table. Tom *had* been creative, after all—he had packets of Kool-Aid in his suitcoat pocket, and he made quite a ritual of opening them and putting a little of every flavor in each glass. They foamed a lot when he stirred them, and they all ended up a sickly brownish color.

She heard the mechanic say, "Why didn't you just puke in the glasses to start with and avoid the middleman?"

"Drink, my beloved newts and emus, drink!" cried Tom.

They passed out the glasses and prepared to drink.

"A toast!" cried Douglas, and he rose to his feet. Everybody in the cafe was watching, of course—how often does somebody propose a toast at noon in a small-town cafe?—but Rainie kept right on working, laying down plates in front of people.

"To the human species!" said Douglas. "And to all the people in it, a toast!"

"Hear hear!"

"And to all the people who only wish they were in it, I promise that when I am supreme god, you will *all* be human at last!"

"In a pig's eye!" shouted the mechanic joyously.

"I'll drink to that!" cried Tom, and with that they all drank.

The mechanic did a spit take, putting a thin brown Kool-Aid and Seven-Up fog into the air. Tom must have had some inner need to top that; as he finished noisily chug-a-lugging his drink, Rainie could see that he intended to throw the glass to the floor.

Apparently Minnie saw the same glint in his eye. Before he could hardly move his arm she screeched at him, "Not on your life, Tom Reuther!"

"I paid for it last time," said Tom.

"You didn't pay for all the lunch customers who never came back. Now you boys sit down and be quiet and let folks have their lunch in peace!"

"Wait a minute!" cried Douglas. "We haven't had the song yet."

"All right, do the song and then shut up," said Minnie. She turned back to the chili and resumed dipping it out into the bowls, muttering all the while, "... drive away my customers, spitting all over, breaking glasses on the floor ..."

"Whose turn to start?" somebody asked.

The mechanic rose to his feet. "I choose the tune."

"Not opera again!"

"Better than opera," said the mechanic. "I choose that pinnacle of indigenous American musical accomplishment, the love theme from Oscar Mayer."

The boys all whooped and laughed. The man next to him rose to his feet and sang what must have been the first words that came into his mind, to the tune of the Oscar Mayer wiener jingle from—what, twenty years ago? Rainie had to laugh ironically inside herself. After all my songs, and all the songs of all the musicians who've suffered and sweated and taken serious drugs for their art, what sticks in the memory of my generation is a song about a kid who wishes he could be a hot dog so he'd have friends.

"I wish I had a friend in my nostril."

The next man got up and without hesitation sang the next line. "In fact I know that's where he'd want to be."

And the next guy: "Cause if I had a friend in my nostril."

"Cheat, cheat, too close to the first line!" cried Tom.

"Bad rhyme—same word!" said the mechanic.

"Well, what else am I supposed to do?" said the guy who sang the line. "There's no rhyme for nostril in the English language."

"Or any other," said Douglas.

"Like you're an expert on Tadzhiki dialects or something," said Tom.

"Wastrel!" shouted the mechanic.

"That doesn't rhyme," said Douglas.

"Leave it with nostril," said Tom. "We'll simply heap scorn upon poor Raymond until he rues the day."

"You are so gracious," said Raymond.

"Dougie's turn," said the mechanic.

"I forgot where we were," said Douglas, rising to his feet.

The mechanic immediately jumped up and sang the three lines they had so far:

> I wish I had a friend in my nostril,
> I know that's where he'd really want to be,
> Cause if I had a friend in my nostril . . .

Rainie happened to be passing near the Boys' Table at that moment, and she blurted out the song lyric that popped into her mind before Douglas could even open his mouth:

> He could eat the boogers I don't see!

Immediately the men at the table leaped to their feet and gave her a standing ovation, all except Tom, who fell off his chair and rolled on the floor. The only people who didn't seem to enjoy her lyric were Minnie, who was glaring at her, and Douglas, who stared straight ahead for a moment and then sat down—laughing along with the others, but only as much as conviviality required.

I'm sorry I stole your thunder, Rainie said silently. Whenever I think of the perfect clincher at the end of a verse, I always blurt it out like that. I'm sorry.

She went back to the counter and got the chili, which Minnie had already laid out on a tray. "Are you trying to make my customers get indigestion right here in the diner?" Minnie hissed. "Boogers! *Eating* them. My land!"

"I'm sorry," said Rainie. "It just came out."

"You got a barnyard mouth, Ida, and it's nothing to be proud of," said Minnie. She turned away, looking huffy.

When Rainie got back to the table with the chili, the men were talking about her. "She got the last line, and it was a beaut, and so she's first," said Tom. "That's the law."

"It may be the law," said Douglas, "but Ida Johnson isn't going to want to feed the baby."

"Maybe I do and maybe I don't," said Rainie.

Douglas closed his eyes.

"Dougie's just sore because he could *never* think of a line to top Ida's," said Raymond.

"Retarded parrots could think of better lines than *yours,* Raymond," said the mechanic.

"Retarded parrot *embryos,*" said another man.

"What baby do you feed, and what do you feed it?" asked Rainie.

"It's a game," said Tom. "We kind of made it up. Dougie and I."

"All of us," said Douglas.

"Dougie and me first, and then everybody together. It's called 'Feed the Baby of Love Many Beans or Perish in the Flames of Hell.' "

"Greg had the idea in the first place," said Douglas.

"Yeah, well, Greg moved to *California,* and so we spit upon his memory," said Tom.

At once everybody made a show of spitting—all to their left, all at once. But instead of actually spitting, they all said, in perfect unison, "Ptui."

"Come on, Ida," said Tom. "It's at Douglas's house. The game's all about karma and reincarnation and trying to progress from primordial slime to newt to emu to human until finally you get to be supreme god."

"Or not," said the mechanic.

"In which case your karma decides your eternal fate."

"In Heaven with the Baby of Love!"

"Or in Hell with the Baby of Sorrows!"

"I don't think so," said Rainie. She was noticing how Douglas didn't seem too eager to have her come. "I mean, if Douglas's wife leaves town whenever you play, then it must be one of those male-bonding things and I've never been good at male bonding."

"Oh, great," said Tom, "now she thinks we're gay."

"Not at all," said Rainie. "If I thought you were gay I'd be there with bells on. The refreshments are always great at gay parties. It's you pick-up basketball-game types who think beer and limp pretzels are a righteous spread."

Raymond rose to his feet. "Behold our luncheon feast, Your Majesty," he said. "Do we look like the beer and pretzels type?"

"No, you actually look like the boys who always made disgusting messes out of the table scraps on their school lunch trays."

"That's it!" cried Tom. "She understands us! *And* she put a brilliant last line on the song. Tonight at seven, Idie Baby, I'll pick you up."

From the look on Douglas's face, Rainie knew that she should say no. But she could feel the loneliness of these past few weeks in this town—and, truth to tell, of the months, the *years*, before—like a sharp pain within her. Being on the fringes of this group of glad friends made her feel like ... what? Like her best days living on the street. That's what it was. She had found the street after all. Grown up a little, most of them wearing suits, but here in this godforsaken town she had found some people who had the street in their souls, and she couldn't bear to say no. Not unless Douglas *made* her say it.

And he didn't make her say it. On the contrary. She looked him in the eye and he half smiled and gave her a little shrug. Suit yourself, that's what he was saying. So she did.

"Okay, I'll be there," she said.

"But you should be aware," said Tom, "we probably aren't as fun as your gay friends' parties."

"Naw," she said, "they stopped being fun in the eighties, when they started spending all their time talking about who had AIDS and who didn't."

"What a *downer*," said Raymond.

"Bad karma!" said the mechanic.

"No problem," said Tom. "That just means she'll end up in Hell a lot."

"Do I need to bring anything?" asked Rainie.

"Junk food," said Tom. "Nothing healthy."

"That's Tom's rule," said Douglas. "You can bring anything you want. I'll be putting out a vegetable dip."

"Yeah, right," said Raymond. "Mr. Health."

"Mr. Quiche," said another man.

"Tell her what we *dip* in your vegetable dip, Dougie."

"Frankfurters show up a lot," said Douglas. "And Tootsie Rolls. Once Tommy stuck his nose into the dip, and then the Health Department came and closed us down."

"Ida!" Minnie's voice was sharp.

"I'm about to get fired," said Rainie.

"Minnie can't fire you," said Tom. "Nothing bad can ever happen to Those Who Feed the Baby!"

But the expression on Minnie's face spoke eloquently about the bad things that could happen to her waitress Ida Johnson. As soon as Rainie got behind the counter with her, she whispered in Minnie's ear, "I can't help it that it's at Douglas's house. Count the chaperones and give me credit for a little judgment."

Minnie sniffed, but she stopped looking like she was about to put a skewer through Rainie's heart.

The Boys' Table lasted a whole hour, and then Douglas looked at his watch and said, "Ding."

"The one-o'clock bell," cried Tom.

Raymond whistled between his teeth.

"The one-o'clock whistle!"

And in only a few moments they had their coats on and hustled on out the door. They might act like boys for an hour at noon, but they were still grown-ups. They still had to get back to work, and right on time, too. Rainie couldn't decide if that was sad or wonderful. Maybe both.

By the time Rainie's shift was over, Minnie was her cheerful self again. Whether that meant that Minnie trusted her or she had simply forgotten that Rainie was going to Feed the Baby with the boys tonight, Rainie was glad not to have to argue with her. She didn't want anything to take away the strange jittery happiness that had been growing inside her all afternoon. She had no idea what the game was about, but she knew she liked these men, and she was beginning to suspect that maybe this game, maybe these boys, were the reason she had stopped her wandering at this cafe in Harmony, Illinois. If there'd been a place in town that sold any clothes worth buying, Rainie would have bought a new outfit. As it was, she spent a ridiculous amount of time fretting over what to wear. It had to be that the sheer foolish immaturity of these boys had infected her. She was like a virgin girl getting ready for her first date. She laughed at herself—and then took off all her clothes and started over again.

She spent so much time choosing what to wear that she put off buying any refreshments until it was almost too late. As it was, all she had time to do was rush to the corner grocery and buy the first thing that she saw that looked suitable—a giant bag of peanut M&Ms.

"I hear you're going to Feed the Baby," said the zit-faced fat thirty-year-old checkout girl, who'd never given her the time of day before.

"How do these stories get started?" said Rainie. "I don't even *have* a baby."

She got back to her apartment just as Tom pulled up in a brand-new but thoroughly mud-spattered pickup truck. "Hop in before you let all the heat out!" he shouted. He was rolling before she had the door shut.

Douglas Spaulding's house was just what she expected, right down to the white picket fence and the veranda wrapped around the white clapboard walls. Simple, clean lines, the walls and trim freshly painted, with dark blue shutters at the windows and lights shining between the pulled-back curtains. A house that said good plain folks live here, and the doors aren't locked, and if you're hungry we've got a bite to eat, and if you're lonely we've got a few minutes to chat, anytime you feel like dropping by. It was an island of light in the dark night. When she opened the door of Tom's pickup truck, she could hear laughter from the parlor, and as she picked her way through the paths in the snow to get to the front porch, she could look up and see people moving around inside the house, eating and drinking and talking, all so at ease with each other that it woke the sweetest flavors in her memory and made her hungry to get inside.

They were laying the game out on the dining room table—a large homemade board, meadow green with tiny flowers and a path of white squares drawn around the outside of it. Most squares had either a red heart or a black teardrop, with a number. In the middle of the board was a dark area shaped like a giant kidney bean with black dotted lines radiating out from it toward the squares. And in the middle of the "bean" were a half-dozen little pigs that Rainie recognized as being from the old *Pig-Out* game, plus a larger pig from some child's set of plastic barnyard animals.

"That's the pigpen," said the mechanic, who was counting beans into piles of ten. Only he wasn't dressed like a mechanic anymore—he was wearing a white shirt and white pants with fire-engine-red suspenders. He was also wearing a visor, like the brim of a baseball cap. Rainie remembered seeing people wear visors like that on TV. In old westerns or something. Who wore them? Bank tellers? Bookies? She couldn't remember.

"What's your name?" asked Rainie. "I've been thinking of you as the guy in overalls cause I never caught your name."

"If I'd'a knowed you was a-thinkin' of me, Miss Ida, I'd'a wore my overalls again tonight, just to please you." He grinned at her.

"Three *Idas* in the same sentence," said Rainie. "Not bad."

"It's a good thing she didn't think of you as 'that butt-ugly guy,' " said Tom. "You're a lot better looking when you keep *that* particular feature covered up."

"Look what Miss Ida brung us," said the mechanic. "*M's.*"

Immediately all the men in the vicinity of the table hummed in unison. "Mmmmm. Mmmmm."

"Not just *M's*, but *peanut M's.*"

Again, only twice as loud: "MMMMMM! MMMMMM!"

Either M&Ms were part of the ritual, or they were making fun of her. Suddenly Rainie felt unsure of herself. She held up the bag. "Isn't this okay?"

"Sure," said Douglas. "And I get the brown ones." He had a large bowl in his hand; he took the bag of M&Ms from her, pulled it open, and poured it into the bowl.

"Dougie has a thing for brown M&Ms," said the mechanic.

"I eat them as a public service," said Douglas. "They're the ugly ones, so when I eat them all the bowl is full of nothing but bright colors for everyone else."

"He eats the brown ones because they make up forty percent of the package," said Tom.

"Tom spends most of his weekends opening bags of M&Ms and counting them, just to get the percentages," said an old man who hadn't been at the cafe.

"Hi, Dad," said Douglas. He turned and offered the old man the bowl of M&Ms.

The old man took a green one and popped it in his mouth. Then he stuck out his right hand to Rainie. "Hi," he said. "I'm Douglas Spaulding. Since he and his son are also Douglas Spaulding, everybody calls me Grandpa. I'm old but I still have all my own teeth."

"Yeah, in an old baby-food jar on his dresser," said Tom.

"In fact, he has several of *my* teeth, too," said the mechanic.

Rainie shook Grandpa's hand. "Pleased to meet you. I'm . . ." Rainie paused. For one crazy moment she had been about to say, I'm Rainie Pinyon. "I'm Ida Johnson."

"You sure about that?" asked Grandpa. He didn't let go of her hand.

"Yes, I am," she said. Rather sharply.

Grandpa raised his eyebrows and released her hand. "Welcome to the madhouse."

Suddenly there was a thunderous pounding on the stairs, and Rose and Dougie burst into the room. "Release the pigs!" they both shouted. "Pig attack! Pig attack!"

Douglas just stood there laughing as his kids ran around the table, grunting and snorting like hogs as they reached into every bowl for chips and M&Ms and anything else that looked vaguely edible, stuffing it all into their mouths. The men all laughed as the kids ran back out of the room. Except Grandpa, who never cracked a smile. "What is the younger generation coming to?" he murmured. Then he winked at Rainie.

"Where should I sit?" she asked.

"Anyplace," said Tom.

She took the chair at the corner. It seemed the best place— the spot where she'd have to sit back away from the table because the table leg was in the way. It felt just a little safer to her, to be able to sit a little bit outside of the circle of the players.

The mechanic leaned over to her and said, "Cecil."

"What?" Rainie asked.

"My name," he said. "Don't tell anybody else."

Tom, who was sitting next to her, said in a loud whisper. "We all pretend that we think his name is 'Buck.' It makes him feel more manly."

"What do I *call* you?" asked Rainie. "If I'm supposed to keep Cecil a secret."

"Now you've gone and told," said Cecil.

"Call him Buck," said Tom.

"Does anybody else really call him that?" asked Rainie.

"I will if you will," said Tom.

"Time for a review of the rules!" said Douglas, as he took the last place at the table, which happened to be in the middle of the table on the side across from Rainie, so she'd be looking at him throughout the game.

"I hate to make you have to spend time going over everything for me," said Rainie.

"They repeat the rules every time anyway," said Grandpa.

"Cause Grandpa's getting senile and forgets them every time," said Tom.

"They repeat them because they're so proud of having thought them up themselves," said Grandpa.

The game was pretty complicated. They used plastic children's toys—little robots or dinosaurs—as their playing pieces. The idea of the game was to roll three dice and get around the board. Each time they passed Start they were reborn as the next higher life-form, from slime to newt to emu to human; the winner was the first human to reach Start and therefore become supreme god.

"Then the supreme god turns over his karma cards. If he's got more good than bad karma, then whoever has the most good karma comes in second. But if the supreme god has more bad karma than good, then whoever has the most *bad* karma comes in second," said Douglas.

"So bad karma can be good?" asked Rainie.

"Never," said Tom. "What kind of person are you? No, if the supreme god turns out to have bad karma, it's a terrible disaster for the known universe. We all sing a very sad song and cry on the way home."

"The last time bad karma triumphed, Meryl Streep and Roseanne Barr released that movie *She-Devil*," said Douglas.

"So you see, the consequences can be dire," said Tom.

"She didn't even get to do an accent," said Cecil, his tone mournful and hushed.

"And . . . and *Ed Begley, Junior* had to play Roseanne Barr's husband," said Raymond.

"Only John Goodman is man enough to do that and live," said Cecil.

"So you see," said Tom, "our game isn't just a *game*. It has consequences in the real world."

Douglas continued with the rules. Every time you landed on a teardrop or a heart, you had a chance to pray to either the

Baby of Sorrows or the Baby of Love, depending. In order to pray, you had to make an offering of as many beans as the number shown on the square. "So beans are like money," said Rainie.

"Ugly money," said Raymond.

"Nasty money," said Tom.

"Filthy lucre," said Grandpa.

"We hate beans," said Cecil. "Nobody wants beans. Only *greedy, nasty, selfish people* try to get a lot of beans."

"Of course, you have no chance of winning unless you have a lot of beans," said Douglas. "But if it ever looks like you are too interested in getting beans, then we hold a bean council and punish you."

"I never did like beans," said Rainie.

"Good thing," said Cecil. "But watch out, because Tom is a miserable bean thief and he'll steal your beans when you're not looking."

"*If* I actually cared for beans," said Tom, "I'd be an excellent bean thief."

"If your prayer is granted," Douglas said, going on with the rules, "then you get a power card. There are evil powers and good powers, depending on which baby you pray to. When you use an evil power you get a bad karma card, and when you use a good power you get a good karma card. Good power cards are always played on other people—they never benefit the person who plays them. Evil power cards are always vicious and selfish and vindictive."

"That's not in the rules," said Cecil.

"But it's the truth," said Douglas. "Good people never use evil power cards."

"Dougie's just sore because of the time we ganged up on him and killed him every time he stuck his nose out of Hell," explained Tom.

"I tried to reason with them."

"He whined all night. It only goaded us to new depths of cruelty."

"They had no pity."

"We were nature red in tooth and claw," said Tom. "You were unfit to survive."

They went on with the rules, but at the end Rainie could

hardly remember half of them. "You just tell me what to do and I'll get the hang of it."

She started the game with five power cards. All of them were handwritten, the good powers in red ink, the evil powers in black. She had three evil cards and two good ones. One of the good ones said:

"BUTT-INSKI"
Allows you to
cause 2 other
players to swap
all power cards.

Two of the evil power cards said:

"UP THE PIGGAGE"
ADD 2 PIGS TO THE PEN.

and

"YOUR KARMA IS
MY KARMA"
ALLOWS YOU TO SWAP
KARMA CARDS WITH
ANOTHER PLAYER

The last two cards, one good, one evil, made Rainie laugh out loud. The evil one said:

**RELEASE
THE
PIGS!!**

The good one, on the other hand, said:

**RELEASE
THE
PIGS!!**

For the good of the
whole.

"What's funny?" asked Tom.

"Is there any difference between releasing the pigs on some-body from a good power card as opposed to an evil power card?" she asked.

"All the difference in the world!" cried Raymond.

"When you release the pigs for the good of the whole," said Cecil, "it's a noble act, a kind and generous sacrifice for the benefit of the entire community, without a single thought of personal benefit."

"Whereas," said Tom, "releasing the pigs from an evil power card is the act of a soulless, cruel, despicable human being."

"But I mean, is the actual pig attack any different?"

"Not a whit," said Douglas.

"Absolutely identical," said Tom.

"I'm betting that Ida has her a couple of Release-the-Pigs cards," said Raymond.

"How many beans are you betting?" asked Tom.

"Five beans says she does."

"Oh, yeah?" said Tom. "Well, *ten* beans says she *does*."

"That what *I* said," said Raymond.

"No, you said *five* beans," said Tom.

"Roll the dice, Ida," said Grandpa, "or we'll never get started."

"The fate of the world hangs in the balance," said the quiet guy at the other end of the table—Rainie couldn't remember his name. He looked very sad, even when he laughed.

"Because you are first," said Douglas, "and because you have never played before, you may use the lobster dice to begin."

The lobster dice were just like the other dice—there were about a dozen scattered around the table—except that they had a red lobster printed on the face that should have had the one-spot.

"The lobster dice have special significance," said Douglas. "And if you should be so fortunate as to have a lobster turn up on your roll, it changes your move. For instance, if you roll the three dice and get two fives and a lobster, the total isn't eleven, it's ten-lobster."

"How many do I move for the lobster?"

"One," said Douglas.

"Per lobster," added Tom.

"So that's eleven," said Rainie.

Douglas and Tom both made a show of looking stricken. "An unbeliever," said Douglas. "I never would have thought it of you."

Tom addressed the others. "If she can't tell the difference between eleven and ten-lobster, then what if she rolls, like, *four-lobster-lobster?*"

They all shook their heads and made mournful noises.

"I worry about you, Ida," said Douglas. "You seem to have an unhealthy grip on reality."

"Nay," said Cecil, "reality hath an unhealthy grip on *her.*"

"Maybe I'm not worthy to use the lobster dice," said Rainie.

"Ah," said Douglas. "That's all right then."

"What is?"

"As long as you think you might be unworthy, then you *are* worthy."

"Thinking I'm unworthy makes me worthy?"

"Here are the sacred lobster dice," said Douglas. "You found the perfect last line for the song. You served us our beans and brought us our drinks. No one is worthier than you."

He spoke with such simplicity and sincerity that, even though she knew he was joking, she couldn't help but be touched. "I'm honored," she said, and meant it. She took the dice and rolled.

Two of the dice showed lobsters. The other die showed an ace. Some of the men gasped.

"One-lobster-lobster," murmured Cecil.

"The first roll of the game."

"Surely good karma will triumph tonight."

"Tell me," said Cecil, "are you perchance a visitor from another realm, temporarily dwelling among us mortals in disguise?"

"No," she said, laughing.

"Have you not been sent by the Baby of Love," Cecil insisted, "to bring the blessing of healing to a world of woe?"

Rainie reached out her hand toward Cecil. "Flesh and blood, see?"

He touched her hand, cradled it gently in his, as if it were a porcelain rose. "Ah," he said, "she is real. I know it, for I have touched her."

"She's not a real person," said Grandpa. "She's a ghost. Can't you tell? We're being haunted here tonight. Ida Johnson is just a figment of her own imagination."

The others chuckled, and Rainie laughed. But as she took her hand back from Cecil, she felt strangely shy. And when she looked at Grandpa, she found him gazing at her very steadily.

"I'm not a ghost," she said softly.

"Yes she is," said Grandpa to the others. "She can fool you boys, but not these old eyes. I know the difference."

"One-lobster-lobster," said Douglas. "Let's get this game moving!"

The game got moving. It only took a few minutes for Rainie to get into the spirit of it. The game was about life and death, but what happened with the dice was almost trivial compared to what they all did to each other with the power cards. The game had hardly begun when the blond guy at the other end of the table—Jack?—played a card on her that said,

"THE GRASS IS ALWAYS GREENER . . ."
Allows you to swap power
cards with another player.

and in one moment she found herself with a handful of completely different cards. It wasn't Jack's turn, or hers—he just felt like playing it.

In a moment, though, she saw why. Douglas had landed on a square whose pigpath—the line connecting it to the pigpen— had only three dots on it. Jack played one of her former Release-the-Pigs cards, and they all whooped and hollered and lined up the baby pigs at the head of the pigpath, with Momma Pig last in line.

"This is pointless," said Douglas. "I'm still primordial ooze. I can't regress any farther than that."

"I want you in Hell," said Jack.

"But I won't go to Hell. I don't have any karma at all yet."

"You personally released the pigs on me twice last time. Tonight you're *never* going to be reincarnated."

"Grudge-holding is beneath you, Jack."

Jack burst into a country-music song.

> If I can't hold me a woman,
> Then a grudge will have to do.
> The woman I'd hold against myself,
> But the grudge I'll hold against you.

Rainie had never heard the song before, so she figured he had made it up. The tune was actually pretty good.

The pigs were about to start charging down the pigpath when Jack played her former card, adding two pigs to the pen. Now there were even more pigs on the path, and since they leap-frogged instead of taking turns, the pigs were bound to reach Douglas. Each pig that got to him would cost him two life-pennies, except for Momma, who would cost him four. Since everybody started with only ten life-pennies, he was doomed.

"I need the lobster dice," said Douglas.

"You need an angel from heaven," said Jack.

Tom handed Jack the two bad karma cards he got for playing evil power cards.

"Oh, these are bad," said Jack.

"Only what you deserve," said Douglas.

"Well, before we sic the pigs on you, Dougie, let's try *this*." Whereupon Jack laid down another of Rainie's old cards, the one that allowed him to swap karma with Douglas. Since Douglas had none and Jack had two bad karma cards, it meant that when Douglas died his karmic balance would be negative and he'd go to Hell.

"You are one seriously evil dude tonight, Jack," said Raymond. "I like your style. Let's see what happens with this one." He laid down an evil power card that said,

"ANGRY OINKERS"

DOUBLES THE DAMAGE OF

ALL PIGS ON A GIVEN PIG
ATTACK

"Hey, how dead can I get?" asked Douglas.

"We won't find out on this turn," said Grandpa. He laid down a good power card that said,

> "FAIR IS FAIR"
> Causes the person
> who released the
> pigs to take the
> damage from a
> pig attack (only
> when pigs are
> released on
> someone else)

"Son of a *gun!*" shouted Jack. "You can't do this to me!"

"Can so."

"I'm not even on a pigpath!" It was true. Jack's playing piece—the plastic triceratops—was on a square with no path connecting it to the pigpen.

"Doesn't matter," said Tom. "You're taking the damage from the attack on Douglas, so the pigs will still follow *his* pigpath."

"And since you just played that evil power on Douglas switching your karma, you get a new evil power card of your very own," said Grandpa. "So if you die, you'll go to Hell."

The pigs started down the path. As each baby pig advanced to a new dot on the path, Jack got to roll one die. If he got a one or a two, the pig was "popped" and returned to the pen. He wasn't lucky—he only popped two pigs, so five reached him and he was dead before Momma could even start her run down the path.

Just before the last pig reached him, though, he played the other Release-the-Pigs card that he had got from Rainie, and since this one was "for the good of the whole" he got a good karma card for it. "Ha!" he said. "It's a ten and my bad karma card was only a four. I'll go to Heaven, and Douglas *still* has to face the pigs!"

So once again the pigs were lined up and started down the path. Rainie looked again at the cards she had gotten from Jack. One of them said,

"PERHAPS I CAN HELP"
Allows you to heal
another player of
all damage.
(Will not work after
they have been
killed).

She waited until Douglas was down to his last two life-pennies, and played the card.

"You are my hero," he said.

"You're just too young to die," said Rainie.

"There's still some more pigs," Jack pointed out.

"Not enough to kill me," said Douglas.

"But," said Tom, "what if *Momma rides again?*" He slapped down an evil power card that said,

"MOMMA RIDES AGAIN"
CAUSES THE MOMMA PIG TO COME
DOWN THE PATH TWICE.

"This has gone too far!" cried Cecil. "I say Momma is drunk as a skunk." He laid down a good power called "SOUSED SOW" that was supposed to keep Momma home.

"I hate do-gooders," said Raymond. He laid down an evil power card that said,

"I HATE
DO-GOODERS"
Allows you to
cancel a Good

> power before it
> takes effect.

"So Momma rides twice," said Tom. "That'll be eight life-pennies if she makes it both times, and that plus the two babies and you *could* die, Douglas."

"Good to know," said Douglas. "Is this how you talk to your patients?"

"I'm a dermatologist," said Tom. "My patients don't die, they just put bags over their heads."

"Let's make sure of this," said Raymond, laying down another card.

"PIGS CAN FLY"
pigs move 2 squares
each step instead of 1.

"I'm dead," said Douglas. And it was true. The pigs came down the path, Momma twice, and all his life-pennies were gone.

"Dead and in Hell," said Jack cheerfully.

"Boy am I nice," said Grandpa, laying down a card.

"Not 'Boy Am I Nice'!" wailed Jack.

But it *was* the Boy-Am-I-Nice card. Grandpa took on himself all of the bad karma Douglas had gotten from Jack, leaving Douglas with no karma at all. "And that counts as good karma," said Douglas, "and so I go to Heaven."

"No, no, no," moaned Jack.

"I'm in heaven while you're in *Hell*, Jack," said Douglas. "Which is the natural order of the universe."

"Do people get to stay in Heaven if they gloat?" asked Rainie.

"Absolutely. It's about the only fun thing that people in heaven are allowed to do," said Grandpa.

"And you should know, Grandpa," said Jack.

"All my old friends have gone to heaven," said Grandpa, "and not one of them is having any fun at all."

"They talk to you?" asked Rainie.

"No. They send me postcards that say 'Having a wonderful time. Wish you were here.' They're all gloating."

The game went on, the power cards flying thick and fast, with everybody praying like crazy to get more power cards. When someone didn't have enough beans to pray, somebody would invariably lend him a few. And Rainie noticed that there actually was a remarkable amount of bean-stealing when people weren't looking. In the meantime, Douglas had eaten every single brown peanut M&M in the bowl. "It really does look more festive when you do that," said Rainie.

"Do what?"

"Take the brown ones out. It looks so much brighter."

"Sometimes he leaves only the red and green ones," said Raymond. "At Christmastime, especially."

Douglas got out of Heaven after three turns there, and before long he had caught up with the others—or rather, the others had been sent back or killed or whatever so often that he was about even with them. Jack, however, was never even able to get past the slime stage and up to the level of newt. "The game knows," said Douglas. "Slime thou art, and slime thou shalt remain."

"Makes me want to go *wash*," said Jack.

"That's a question," said Douglas. "If slime washed, what would it wash off? I mean, what seems dirty to slime?"

The game ebbed and flowed, people ganging up on each other and then, at odd moments, pitching in and helping somebody out with a good power card. Rainie began to realize that crazy as it was, this game really *was* like life. Even though people could only do to each other whatever was permitted by the power cards they randomly drew, it took on the rhythms of life. Things would be going great, and then something bad would happen and everything would look hopeless, and then you'd come back from the dead and the dice would be with you again and you'd be okay. They didn't take it easy on Rainie, and she played with the same gusto as everyone else, but the dice were with her, so that she seemed to make up her losses quite easily, and seemed to have exactly the power card she needed time after time.

Rainie prayed successfully to the Baby of Sorrow and the evil card she drew was an event, not a power.

"TAKE A BREAK"
EVERYONE RELAX, EAT SOME

FOOD (AT HOST'S EXPENSE)
CALL YOUR SPOUSES OR
WHATEVER. AFTER ALL,
WHAT'S LIFE FOR?

"About time!" said Tom. "I'm hungry."

"You've had your hands in the potato chips all night," said Douglas.

"That just means my hands are greasy."

"Nobody can eat just one," added Raymond.

They were already up from the table and moving toward the kitchen. "Should I draw another power card to replace this?" asked Rainie.

"Naw," said Jack. "When the card says take a break, we take a break. You can finish your turn when we get back."

In the kitchen, Douglas was nuking some lasagna.

"It doesn't have that revolting cottage cheese this time, does it?" Raymond was asking when Rainie came in.

"It's ricotta cheese," said Douglas.

"Oh, excuse me, ri*cotta* cheese."

"And I made the second pan without it, just for you."

"Oh, I have to wait for the *second* pan, eh?"

"Wait for it or wear it," said Douglas.

Rainie pitched in and helped, but she noticed that none of them seemed to expect her to do the dishes. They cleaned up after themselves right along, so that the kitchen never got disgusting. They weren't really little boys after all.

The lasagna was pretty good, though of course the microwave heated it unevenly so that half of it was burning hot and the other half was cold. She carried her plate into the family room, where most of them were eating.

"They'll call them 'the oughts,' " Grandpa was saying.

"They'll call *what* 'the oughts?' " asked Rainie.

"The first ten years of the next century. You know, 'ought-one,' 'ought-two.' When I was a kid, people still remembered the oughts, and people always talked about them that way. 'Back in ought-five.' Like that."

"Yeah, but back then they still used the word *ought* for zero, too," said Douglas. "Nobody'd even know what it meant today."

"People won't use *ought* even if they *ought* to," said Tom. Several of the men near him dipped a finger into whatever they were drinking and flicked a little of the liquid onto Tom, who bowed his head graciously.

"What about *zero?*" said Raymond. "Just call the first two decades 'the zeroes' and 'the teens.' "

"People aren't going to say 'zero-five,' " said Douglas. "Besides, zero has such a negative connotation. 'Last year was a real zero.' "

"Aren't there any other words for zero?" asked Rainie.

"I've got it!" said Tom. "The zips! Zip-one, zip-two, zip-three."

"That's it!" cried Raymond.

Douglas tried it out. " 'Back in zip-nine, when Junior got his Ph.D.' That works pretty well. It has style."

"I know what's happening, you young whippersnapper," said Cecil, putting on an old man's voice. " 'I remember the nineties! I didn't grow up in the zips, like you.' "

"This is great!" said Tom. "Let's write to our congressman and get it made into a law. The next decade will be called 'the zips!' "

"Don't make it a law, or they'll find a way to tax it," said Raymond.

"Fine with me," said Tom, "if I get a percentage for having thought of it."

Rainie noticed when Grandpa got up, set his plate down, and stepped outside. Probably going for a smoke, thought Rainie. And now that she thought of smoking, she wanted to. And now that she wanted to, she found herself getting up without a second thought. It was cold outside, she knew, and her coat wasn't *that* warm, but she needed to get out there.

And not just for the cigarette. In fact, when she got outside and looked into her purse, she realized that she didn't have any cigarettes. When had she stopped carrying them? How long had she not even noticed that she didn't have any?

"Nasty habit," said Grandpa.

She turned. He was sitting on the porch swing. Not smoking.

"I thought you came out here to smoke," said Rainie.

"Naw," he said. "I just got to thinking about the people I knew who remembered the oughts, and I liked thinking about them, and so I came out here so I could hold the thought without getting distracted."

"Well, I didn't mean to disturb you."

"No problem," said Grandpa. "I'm old enough that my thoughts aren't very complicated anymore. I get hold of one, it just goes around and around until it bumps into a dead brain cell and then I just stand there and wonder what I was thinking about."

"You're not so old," said Rainie. "You hold your own with those young men in there."

"I am *so* old. And *they* aren't all that young anymore, either."

He was right. This was definitely a party of middle-aged men. Rainie thought back to the beginning of her career and remembered that in those days, people in their forties seemed so powerful. They *were* the Establishment, the ones to be rebelled against. But now that she was in her forties herself she understood that if anything middle-aged people were *less* powerful than the young. They had less chance of changing anything. They seemed to fit into the world, not because they had made the world the way it was or because they even particularly liked it, but because they had to fit in so they could keep their jobs and feed their families. That's what I never understood when I was young, thought Rainie. I knew it with my head, but not with my heart—that pressure of feeding a family.

Or maybe I *did* know it, and hated what it did to people. To my parents. Maybe that's why my marriages didn't last and I never had any babies. Because I never wanted to be forty.

Surprise. I'm past forty anyway, and lonely to boot.

"I've got a question I want you to answer," she said to Grandpa. "Straight, no jokes."

"I knew you'd get around to asking."

"Oh, really?" she said. "Since you're so knowledgeable, do you happen to know what the question is?"

"Maybe." Grandpa got up and walked near her and leaned against the porch railing, whistling. The breath came out of his mouth in a continuous little puff of vapor.

He looked unbearably smug, and Rainie longed to take him down just a notch. "Okay, what did I want to know?"

"You want to know why I called you a ghost."

That was exactly what she wanted to ask, but she couldn't stand to admit that he was right. "That *wasn't* my question, but as long as you bring it up, why *did* you say that? If it was a joke I didn't get it. You hurt my feelings."

"I said it because it's true. You're just haunting us. We can *see* you, but we can't touch you in any way."

"I have been touched in a hundred places since I came here."

"You got nothing at risk here, Ida Johnson," said Grandpa. "You don't care."

Rainie thought of Minnie. Of Douglas and his kids. "You're wrong, Grandpa Spaulding. I care very much."

"You care with your heart, maybe, but not with your soul. You care with those feelings that come and go like breezes, nothing that's going to last. You're playing with house money here. No matter how it comes out, you can't lose. You're going to come away from Harmony, Illinois with more than you brought here."

"Maybe so," said Rainie. "Is that a crime?"

"No ma'am. Just a discovery. Something I noticed about you and I didn't think you'd noticed about yourself."

"Well ain't you clever, Grandpa." She smiled when she said it, so he'd know she was teasing him, not really being snide. But it hurt her feelings all over again, mostly because she could see now that he was right. How could anything she did here be *real*, after all, when nobody even knew her right name? In a way Ida Johnson *was* her right name. It was her *mother's* name, anyway, and didn't Douglas Spaulding have the same name as *his* father? Didn't he give the same name to his son? Why couldn't she use her mother's name? How was that a lie, really, when you looked at it the right way? "Ain't you clever. You found out my secret. Grandpa Spaulding, Gray Detective. Sees a strange woman in his parlor one November evening and all at once he knows everything there is to know about her."

Grandpa waited a moment before answering. And his answer wasn't really an answer. More like he just let slip whatever her words made him think of. "My brother Tom and I did that one summer. Kept a list of Discoveries and Revelations. Like noticing that you were a ghost."

Every time he said it, it stung her deeper. Still, she tried to keep her protest playful-sounding. "When you prick me, do I not bleed?"

He ignored her. "We made another list, too. Rites and Ceremonies. All the things we always did every year, we wrote them down, too, when we did them that summer. First stinkbug we stepped on. First harvest of dandelions."

"They got chemicals to kill the dandelions now," said Rainie.

"Stinkbugs too, for that matter," said Grandpa. "Very convenient."

Rainie looked through the window. "They're settling back down to play the game in there."

"Go on back in then, if you want. Haunt whoever you want. Us mortals can't determine your itinerary."

She was tired of his sniping at her. But it didn't make her angry. It just made her sad. As if she had lost something and she couldn't even remember what it was. "Don't be mean to me," she said softly.

"Why shouldn't I?" he answered. "I see you setting up to do some harm to my family, Ida Johnson or whoever you are."

It couldn't be that Rainie was doing something to tip everybody off how much she was attracted to Douglas Spaulding, to the idea of him. It had to be that people around here were just naturally suspicious. "Do you say that to every stranger in town, or just the women?"

"You're one hungry woman, Ida Johnson," said Grandpa, cheerfully enough.

"Maybe I haven't been getting my vitamins."

"You can get pretty malnourished on a diet of stolen food."

That was it. The last straw. She didn't have to put up with any more accusations. "I'm done talking with you, old man." She meant to make a dramatic exit from the porch, but the door to the parlor wouldn't open.

"That door's painted shut," he said helpfully. "You want the other one." He pointed around to the far side of the bay window, where the door she had come out of was open a crack. The noises of the men at the table surged and faded like waves on the shore.

She took two steps toward the door, stalking, angry, and then realized that Grandpa was laughing. For a moment she wanted to slap him, to stop him from thinking he was so irresistibly wise, judging her the way adults always did. But she didn't slap him. Instead she plunked back down on the swing beside him and laughed right along.

Finally they both stopped laughing; even the silent gusts of laughter settled down; even the lingering smiles faded. It was cold, just sitting there, not talking, not even swinging.

"What was your question, anyway?" he asked out of nowhere.

For a moment she couldn't think what he was talking about. Then she remembered that she had denied that he was right when he guessed her question. "Oh, nothing," she said.

"It was important enough for you to come out here into the cold, wasn't it? Might as well ask me, cause here I am, and next week you can't be sure. I'm seventy-four going on seventy-five."

She still couldn't bring herself to admit that he had been right. Or rather, she couldn't admit that she had lied about it. "It was a silly question."

He said nothing. Just waited.

And as he waited, a question did come to her. "Your grandson, Dougie, he said that there were some things that nobody in town knew, and one of them was his father's middle name."

Grandpa Spaulding sighed.

"You can tell *me*," said Rainie. "After all, I'm a ghost."

"Douglas has never forgiven me for naming him the way I did. And sometimes I'm sorry I did it to him. How was I supposed to know that the name would turn trendy—as a girl's name? To me it was a boy's name, still is, a name full of sweat and sneakers and flies buzzing and jumping into the lake off a swing and almost drowning. A name that means open windows and hot fast crickets chirping in the sultry night."

"Summer," she said. A murmur. A whisper. A sweet memory on a cold night like this.

"That's right," he said. "I named him Douglas Summer Spaulding."

She nodded, thinking that Summer was the kind of name a sentimental, narcissistic fourteen-year-old girl would choose for herself. "You're lucky he didn't sue you when he came of age."

"I explained it to him. The way I explained it to my wife. I wanted to name him for something perfect, a dream to hold on to, or at least to wish for, to *try* for."

"You don't have to try for summer," said Rainie. "You just have to have the guy come and service the air conditioner."

"You don't believe that," he said, looking appalled.

"Oh, aren't ghosts allowed to tease old eccentrics?"

"I didn't name him for just any old summer, you know. I named him for one summer in particular. The summer of 1928, to be exact, the perfect summer. Twelve years old. Living in Grandpa's and Grandma's boarding house with my brother Tom. I knew it was perfect even at the time, not just thinking back on it. That summer was the place where God lived, the place where he filled my heart with love, the moment, the long exquisite twelve-week moment when I discovered that I was alive and that I liked it. The next summer Grandpa was dead, and the next year the Depression was under way and I had to work all summer to help put food on the table. I wasn't a kid anymore after summer 1928."

"But you were still alive," Rainie said.

"Not really," said Grandpa. "I *remembered* being alive, but I was coasting. Summer of '28 was like I had me a bike at the top of Culligan Hill and from up there I could see so far—I could see *past* the edge of every horizon. All so beautiful, spread out in front of me like Grandma's supper table, strange-looking and sweet-smelling and bound to be delicious. And so I got on the bike and I pushed off and never had to touch the pedals at all, I just coasted and coasted and coasted."

"Still coasting?" asked Rainie. "Never got to the supper table?"

"When you get down there and see things close, it isn't a supper table anymore, Ida. It turns out to be the kitchen, and you aren't there to eat, you're there to fix the meal for other people. Grandma's kitchen was the strangest place. Nothing was anywhere that made sense. Sugar in every place except the canister marked sugar. Onions out on the counter and the knives never put away and the spices wherever Grandma last set them down. Chaos. But oh, Ida, that old lady could cook. She had miracles in her fingers."

"What about you? Could you cook?"

He looked at her blankly.

"When you stopped coasting and found out that life was a kitchen."

"Oh." He remembered the stream of the conversation. "No," he said, chuckling. "No ma'am, I was no chef. But I didn't have to do it alone. Didn't get married till I got back from the war, twenty-nine years old in 1945. I still got the mud of Italy under my fingernails, and believe me I've scrubbed them plenty, but there was my Marjory, and she gave me three children and the second one was a boy and I named him Douglas after myself, and then I named him for the most perfect thing I ever knew, I named him for a dream . . ."

"For a ghost," said Rainie.

He looked at her so sadly. "For the opposite of a ghost, you poor child."

Douglas opened the parlor door and leaned out into the night. "Aren't you two smart enough to come in out of the cold?"

"One of us is," said Grandpa, but he didn't move.

"We're starting up," said Douglas, "and it's still your turn, Ida."

"Coming," said Rainie, getting up.

Douglas slipped back inside.

She helped Grandpa Spaulding out of the swing. "Don't get me wrong," he said, patting her back as she led the way to the door. "I like you. You're really something."

"Mmm," said Rainie.

"And if I can feel that way about you when you're pretending to be something you're not, think how much I'd like you if you actually told the truth about something."

She came through the door blushing, with anger and with embarrassment and with that thrill of fear—was she found out? Did Grandpa Spaulding somehow know who she really was?

Maybe he did. Without knowing the name Rainie Pinyon, maybe he knew exactly who she was anyway.

"Whose turn is it?" asked Tommy.

"Ida's," somebody said.

"What is she, an emu?"

"No, human. Look, she's a human."

"How did she get so far without us noticing?"

"Not to worry!" cried Douglas Summer Spaulding. He raised a red-lettered card over his head. "For the good of the whole— Release the Pigs!"

The others gave a rousing cheer.

"Give me my good karma," said Douglas. Then he grinned sheepishly in Rainie's face. "You have only five life-pennies and there are seven piglets and the pig-path is only three dots long, so I sincerely hope with all my heart that your karmic balance is of a sort to send you to Heaven, because, dear lady, the porkers from purgatory are going to eat your shorts."

"Heaven?" said Rainie. "Not likely."

But she popped every one of the pigs before they got to her. It was like she couldn't roll anything but ones and twos.

"Grandpa's right," said Tommy. "She really *is* a ghost! The pigs went right through her!"

Then she rolled eighteen, three sixes, and it was enough to win.

"Supreme god!" Tommy cried. "She has effed the ineffable!"

"What's her karmic balance?"

She flipped over the karma cards. Three evils and one good, but the good was a ten and the evils were all low numbers and they balanced exactly.

"Zero counts as good," said Douglas. "How could anyone have supposed otherwise? So I bet I come in second with a balance of nine on the good side."

They all tallied and Grandpa finished last, his karmic balance a negative fifty.

"That's the most evil I ever saw in all the years we've been feeding the baby," said Tommy. He switched to a midwestern white man's version of black dialect. "Grandpa, you bad."

Grandpa caught Rainie's eye and winked. "It's the truth."

They all stayed around and helped finish off the refreshments and clean up from dinner, talking and laughing. Tom was the first to go. "If you're coming with me, Ida, the time is now."

"Already?" She shouldn't have said that, but she really did hate to go. It was the best night she'd had in months. Years.

"Sorry," he said. "But I've got to scrape some moles off people's faces first thing tomorrow, and I have to be bright-eyed and bushy-tailed or I accidentally take off noses and ears, and people get so *testy* with me when I do that."

"That's fine, I really don't mind going."

"No, you go on ahead, Tom," said Douglas. "Somebody else can take her home."

"I can," said Raymond.

"Me too," said Jack. "Right on my way."

They all knew where she was living, of course. It made her smile. Whether I knew them or not, they cared enough about me to notice where I lived. Small-town nosiness could be ugly if you looked at it one way, but kind of sweet and comforting if you looked at it another way entirely.

After a while she drifted away from the conversation in the kitchen and began wandering a little in the house. It was a bad habit of hers—her mother used to yell at her about it when she was a little kid. *Don't* go wandering around in strangers' houses. But curiosity always got the better of her. She drifted into the living room. No TV, lots of books. Fiction, biography, history, science—so that's what accountants read. I never would have guessed.

And then up the stairs, just to see what was there. Not meaning to pry. Just wanting to *know*.

Standing in the upstairs hall, in the near darkness, she could hear the children breathing. Which room is which? she wondered. The bathroom had the nightlight in it; she could see that the first two rooms belonged to the kids, one on the right, one on the left. The other two rooms had to be the one Douglas shared with his absent wife, and Grandpa's. A houseful. The extended family. Three generations present under one roof. This is the American home that everyone dreams of and nobody has. Dad goes off to work, Mom stays home, Grandpa lives right with you, there's a white picket fence and probably a dog in a nice little doghouse in the back yard. Nobody lives like this, except those who really work at it, those who know what life is supposed to be like and are determined to live that way.

Lord knows Mom and Dad weren't like this. Fighting all the time, clawing at each other to get their own way. And who's to say that Douglas and Jaynanne aren't like that, too? I haven't seen them together, I don't know what they're like.

But she did know. From the way the kids were with their father. That doesn't come out of a home torn apart with power struggles, with mutual fear and loathing.

She walked down the hall—just to see—and opened the last two doors. The one on the right had to be Grandpa's room, and she closed the door immediately. The one on the left had the big bed. Douglas's room.

She would have closed the door and gone downstairs at once, except that in the faint light from the bathroom nightlight she caught a glimpse of bright reflection from an old familiar shape, and suddenly she was filled with a longing that was so familiar, so right, that she couldn't resist it, not even for a moment. She snapped on the light and yes, it was what she had thought, a guitar, leaning against the wall beside the dresser that was obviously his—cluttered on top, no knick-knacks.

Pulling the door almost closed behind her, she walked to the guitar and picked it up. Not a particularly good make, but not a bad one. And the strings were steel, not that wimpy nylon, and when she strummed them softly they were perfectly in tune. He has played this guitar today, she thought. And now my hands are holding something that his hands have held. I don't share the having of children with him, I don't share this sweet impossible house with him, but he plays this instrument and I can do that too.

She didn't mean to play, but she couldn't help herself. It had been so long since she had even wanted to touch a musical instrument that, now that the hunger had returned to her, she had no will to resist it. Why should she? It was music that defined who she was in this world. It was music that gave her fame and fortune. It was music that was her only comfort when people let her down, which was always, always.

She played those old mournful melodies, the plucked-out ones, not the strumming tunes, not the dancy, frolicking ones. She played softly, gently, and hummed along, no words, no words . . . words would come later, after the music, after the mood. She remembered the hot African wind coming across the Mediterranean and drying her after a late-night swim on a beach in Mallorca. She remembered the lover she had had then, the one who yelled at her when he was drunk but who made love in the morning like no man had ever made love to her before—gluttonously, gorgeously, filling her like the sun coming up over the sea. Where was he now? Old. He'd be in his sixties now. He might be dead now. I didn't have his baby, either, but he didn't want one. He was a sunrise man, he was always gone by noon.

Tossing and turning, that's what sleep was like in Mallorca. Sticky and sweaty and never more than a couple of hours at a time. In the darkness you get up and stand on the veranda and let the sea breeze dry the sweat off you until you could go back inside and lie down again. And there he'd be, asleep, yes, but even though you were facing away from him you knew he'd reach out to you in his sleep, he'd hold you and press against you and his sweat would be clammy on your cold body, and his arm would arch over you and his hand would reach around you and cup your breast, and he'd start moving against you, and through it all he'd never even wake up. It was second nature to him. He could do it in his sleep.

What did Mallorca have to do with Harmony, Illinois? Why were tunes of hot Spanish nights coming out of this guitar here in the cold of December, with Christmas coming on and the little dying firs and pines standing up in the tree lots? It was the dream of love, that's what it was, the dream but not the memory of love because in the long run it never turned out to be real. In the long run she always woke up from love and felt it slip away the way dreams slip away in the morning, retreating all the faster the harder you try to remember them. It was always a mirage, but when she got thirsty for it the way she was now, it would come back, that dream, and make her warm again, make her sweat with the sweetness of it.

Maybe there was a noise. Maybe just the movement at the door. She looked up, and there were young Dougie and Rose, both of them awake, their faces sleepy but their eyes bright.

"I'm sorry," said Rainie, immediately setting the guitar aside.

"That's Dad's guitar," said Rose.

"You're good," said Dougie. "I wish I could play like that."

"I wish *Dad* could play like that," said Rose, giggling.

"I shouldn't be in here."

"What was that song?" asked Dougie. "I think I've heard it before."

"I don't think so," said Rainie. "I was making it up as I went along."

"It sounded like one of Dad's records."

"Well, I guess I'm not very original-sounding," said Rainie. She felt unbelievably awkward. She didn't belong in this room. It wasn't her room. But there they were in the doorway, not seeming to be angry at all.

"Can't you play some more?" said Dougie.

"You need your sleep," said Rainie. "I shouldn't have wakened you."

"But we're already awake," said Rose. "And we don't have school tomorrow, it's Saturday."

"No, no," said Rainie. "I have to get home." She brushed apologetically past them and hurried down the stairs.

Everybody was gone. The house was quiet. How long had she played?

Douglas was in the kitchen, making a honey sandwich. "It's my secret vice," he said. "It's making me fat. Want one?"

"Sure," she said. She couldn't remember ever having a honey sandwich in her life. She watched him pull the honey out of the jar, white and creamy, and spread it thickly on a slice of bread.

"Lid or no lid?" he asked.

"No lid," she said. She picked it up and bit into it and it was wonderful. He bit into his. A thin strand of honey stretched between his mouth and the bread, then broke, leaving a thread of honey down his chin.

"It's messy, but I don't care," he said.

"Where do you buy bread like this?"

"Jaynanne makes it," he said.

Of course. Of course she makes bread.

"Where is everybody?" she asked.

"Went home," said Doug. "Don't worry about a ride. They all had wives waiting for them, and I don't, so I said I'd take you home."

"No, I don't want you to have to go out on a night like this."

"I figured we'd leave a note on Minnie's door telling her you'd be late tomorrow."

"No," said Rainie. "I'll be there on time."

"It's after midnight."

"I've slept less and done more the next day. But I hate to have you have to drive me."

"So what would you do, walk?"

I'd sleep in your bed, Rainie said silently. I'd get up in the morning and we'd make breakfast together, and we'd eat it together, and then when the kids got up we'd fix another breakfast for them, and they'd laugh with us and be glad to see us. And we'd smile at each other and remember the sweetness in the dark, the secret that the children would never understand until twenty, thirty years from now. The secret that I'm only beginning to understand tonight.

"Thanks, I'll ride," said Rainie.

"Dad's out seeing to the dog. He worries that the dog gets too cold on nights like this."

"What, does he heat the doghouse?"

"Yes, he does," said Douglas. "He keeps bricks just inside the fireplace and then when he puts the fire out at night he wraps the hot bricks in a cloth and carries them outside and puts them in the doghouse."

"Does the dog appreciate it?"

"He sleeps inside with the bricks. He wags his tail. I guess he does." Douglas's bread was gone. She reached up and wiped the honey off his chin with her finger, then licked her finger clean.

"Thanks," he said.

But she could hear more in his voice than he meant to say. She could hear that faint tremble in his voice, the hesitation, the uncertainty. He could have interpreted her gesture as motherly. He could have taken it as a sisterly act. But he did not. Instead he was taking it the way she meant it, and yet he wasn't sure that she really meant it that way.

"Better go," he said. "Morning comes awful early."

They bundled up and went outside. They met Grandpa coming around the front of the house. "Night," Grandpa said.

"Night," said Rainie. "It was good talking to you."

"My pleasure entirely," he said. He sounded perfectly cheerful, which surprised her. Why should it surprise her?

Because I'm planning to do what he warned me not to do, thought Rainie. I'm planning to sleep with Douglas Spaulding tonight. He's mine if I want him, and I want him. Not forever, but tonight, this sweet lonely night when my music came back to me in his house, sitting on his bed, playing his guitar. Jaynanne can spare me this one night, out of all her happiness. There'll be no pain for anyone, and joy for him and me, and there's nothing wrong with that, I don't care what anyone says.

She got in his car and sat beside him, watching the fog of his breath in the cold air as he started the engine. She never took her eyes off him, seeing how the light changed when the headlights came on inside the garage, how it changed again as he leaned over the back seat, guiding the car in reverse down the driveway. He pressed a button and the garage door closed after them.

No one else was on the road. No one else seemed even to exist—all the houses were dark and still, and the tires crunching on snow were the only noise besides the engine, besides their breathing.

He tried to cover what was happening with chat. "Good game tonight, wasn't it?"

"Mm-hm," she said.

"Fun," he said. "Crazy bunch of guys. We act like children, I know it."

"I like children," she said.

"In fact, my kids are more mature than I am when I'm with those guys."

She remembered speaking to them tonight, their faces so sleepy. "I woke them, I'm afraid. I was playing your guitar. That's a bad habit of mine, intruding in people's houses. Sort of an invited burglar or something."

"I heard you playing," he said.

"Clear downstairs? I thought I was quieter than that."

"Steel strings," he said. "And the vents are all open in the winter. Sound carries. It was beautiful."

"Thanks."

"It was—beautiful," he said again, as if he had searched for another word and couldn't think of one. "It was the kind of music I've always longed for in my home, but I've never been good enough on the guitar to play like that myself."

"You keep it in tune."

"If I don't the dog barks."

She laughed, and he smiled in return. She couldn't stop looking at him. The heater was on now, so his breath didn't make a fog. The streetlights brightened his face; then it fell dark again. He's not that handsome. I'd never have looked at him twice if I'd met him in L.A. or New York. He would have been just another accountant there. So many bright lights in the city, how can someone like this ever shine there? But here, in the snow, in this small town, I can see the truth. That this is the true light, the one that all those neon lights and strobes and spots and halogens are trying to imitate but never can.

They pulled up in front of her apartment. He switched off his lights. The dark turned bright again almost immediately, as the snow reflected streetlights and moonlight.

I can't sleep with this man, thought Rainie. I don't deserve him. I made my choice many years ago, and a man like him is forever out of reach. Sleeping with him would be another self-deception, like so many I've indulged in before. He'd still be Jaynanne's husband and Dougie's and Rose's father, and I'd still be a stranger, an intruder. If I sleep with him tonight I'd have to leave town tomorrow, not because I care what anybody thinks, not because anybody'd even know, but because I couldn't stand it, to have come so close and still not belong here. This is forbidden fruit. If I ate of it, I'd know too much, I'd see how naked I am in my own life, my old life.

He opened his car door.

"No," she said. "You don't need to help me out."

But he was already walking around the car, opening her door. He gave her a hand getting out. The snow squeaked under their feet.

"Thanks for the ride," she said. "I can get up the stairs okay."

"I know," he said. "I just don't like dropping people off without seeing them safe inside."

"You'd walk *Tom* to the door?"

"So I'm a sexist reactionary," he said. "I can't help it, I was raised that way. Always see the woman safely to the door."

"There aren't many rapists out on a night like this," said Rainie.

Ignoring her arguments, he followed her up the stairs and waited while she got the key out and unlocked the deadbolt and the knob. She knew that he'd ask to come inside. Knew that he'd try to kiss her. Well, she'd tell him no. Not because Minnie and Grandpa told her to, but because she had her own kind of integrity. Sleeping with him would be a lie she was telling to herself, and she wouldn't do it.

But he didn't try to kiss her. He stepped back as she pushed open the door and gave a little half-wave with his gloved hand and said, "Thanks."

"For what?" she asked.

"For bringing your music into my house tonight."

"Thanks," she said. It touched her that it seemed to mean so much to him. "Sorry I woke your kids."

He shook his head. "I never would have asked you to play. But I hoped. Isn't that stupid? I tuned my guitar for you, and then I hid it upstairs, and you found it anyway. Karma, right?"

It took a moment for her to realize what it meant, him saying that. In this town she had never touched a musical instrument or even told anybody that she played guitar. So why did he know to tune it for her?

"I'm such a fool," she whispered. "I thought my disguise was so perfect."

"I love your music," he said. "Since I heard the first note of it. Your songs have been at the heart of all the best moments of my life."

"How did you know?"

"You've done it before," he said. "Dropped out. Lived under an assumed name. Right? It took a while for me to realize why you looked so familiar. I kept coming back in to the cafe until finally I was sure. When you talked to me that day, you know, when you chewed me out, your voice—I had just listened to your live album that morning. I was pretty sure then. And tonight when you played, then I really knew. I wasn't going to say anything, but I had to thank you . . . for the music. Not just tonight, all of it. I'm sorry. I won't bother you again."

She was barely hearing him, though; her mind had snagged on the phrase he said before: Her songs had been at the heart of all the best moments of his life. It made her weak in the knees, those words. Because it meant that she *was* part of this, after all. Through her music. Her songs had all her longings in them, everything she'd ever known or felt or wished for, and he had brought those songs into his life, had brought *her* into his home. Of course Dougie thought she sounded like his dad's records—they had grown up hearing her songs. She did belong there in that house. He had probably known her music before he even knew his wife.

And now he was going to turn away and go on down the stairs and out to his car and *leave her here alone* and she couldn't let him go, not now, not now. She reached out and caught his arm; he stopped on the next-to-top step, and that put them at the same level, and she kissed him. Kissed him and clung to him, kissed him and tasted the honey in his mouth. His arms closed around her. It was maddening to have their thick winter coats between them. She reached down, still kissing him, and fumbled to unbutton her coat, then his; she stepped inside his coat as if it were his bedroom. She pressed herself against him and felt his desire, the heat of his body.

At last the endless kiss ended, but only because she was ready to take him inside her room, to share with him what she knew he needed from her. She stepped up into her doorway and turned to lead him in.

He was rebuttoning his coat.

"No," she said. "You can't go now."

He shook his head and kept fastening the buttons. He was slow and clumsy, with his gloves on.

"You want me, Douglas Spaulding, and I need you more than you know."

He smiled, a shy, embarrassed smile. "Some fantasies can't come true," he said.

"I'm not fantasizing you, Douglas Spaulding."

"I'm fantasizing *you*," he answered.

"I'm real," she said. "You want me."

"I do," he said. "I want you very much."

"Then have me, and let me have you. For one night. Like the music. You've had my music with you all these years. I want the memory of your love with *me*. Who could begrudge us that?"

"Nobody would begrudge us anything."

"Then stay with me."

"It's not me you love," said Douglas. "and it's not my love you want."

"No?"

"It's my life you love, and my life you want."

"Yes," she said. "I want your life inside me."

"I know," he said. "I understand. I wanted this life, too. The difference between us is that I wanted it so much I did the things you have to do to get it. I set aside my career ambitions. I moved away from the city, from the center of things. I turned inward, toward my children, toward my wife. That's how you get the life I have."

Against her will, there were tears in her eyes. Feeling him slip away she wanted him all the more. "So you have it, and you won't share, is that it?"

"No, you don't understand," he said. "I can't give it to you."

"Because you're afraid of losing it yourself. Afraid of what all these small-minded people in this two-bit town will think."

"No, Rainie Pinyon, I'm not afraid of what they'll think of me, I'm afraid of what I'll know about myself. Right now, standing here, I'm the kind of man who keeps his promises. An hour from now, leaving here, I'd never be that kind of man again. It's the man who keeps his promises who gets the kind of life I have. Even if nothing else changed, I'd know that I was not that man anymore, and so everything would be changed. It would all be dust and ashes in my heart."

"You are a selfish bastard and I hate you," said Rainie. At the moment she said it, she meant it with all her heart. He was forbidding her. He was refusing her. She had offered him real love, her best love, her whole heart. She had allowed herself to *need him* and he was letting some idiotic notion of honor or something get in the way even though she knew that he wanted her too.

"Yeah," he said. He turned and walked down the stairs. She closed the door and stood there with her hand on the knob as she heard him start the car and drive away. It was hot in her apartment, with the heater on, with her coat on. She pulled it off and threw it against the door. She pulled off her sweater, her shoes, all her clothes, and threw them against the walls and crawled into bed and cried, the way she used to cry when her mother didn't let her do what she *needed* to do. Cried herself to sleep.

She woke up with the sun shining into her window. She had overslept. She was late for work. She jumped out of bed and got dressed, hurrying. Minnie will be furious. I let her down.

But by the time she had her clothes on, she knew the truth. She had overslept because in her heart she knew she was done with this place. She had no reason to get up early because working for Minnie Wilcox wasn't her job anymore. She had found all that she was looking for when she first dropped out and went searching. Her music was back. She had something to sing about again. She could go home.

She didn't even pack. Just took her purse with all her credit cards and walked to the post office, which was where the buses stopped. She didn't care which one—St. Louis, Chicago, Des Moines, Cairo, Indianapolis, any bus that got her to an airport city would do. It turned out to be St. Louis.

By the time she saw the Gateway Arch she had written a song about feeding the baby of love. It turned out well enough that it got her some decent radio airplay for the first time in years, her first top-forty single since seventy-five.

> Tried to walk that lonely highway
> Men and women, two by two
> Promising, promising they will be true
> You went your way, I'll go my way
> Feeling old and talking new
> Whatever happened to you?
> I wonder what happened to you?
>
> Spoke to someone in the air
> Heard but didn't heed my prayer
> Couldn't feed it anyway
> Didn't have the price to pay
> You got to feed the baby
> Hungry, hungry, hungry baby
> Got to feed the baby of love

She had her music back again, the only lover that had ever been faithful to her. Even when it tried to leave her, it always came home to her in the end.

THE DANDELION CHRONICLES

William F. Nolan

Creating an effective parody of an author's work is a very delicate and difficult business. In far too many cases, the resulting piece is cruel and barbed, deliberately designed to ridicule and put down its subject.

Not so with "The Dandelion Chronicles." It was written out of love and nostalgia, strictly to entertain, and it reflects my strong and abiding admiration for Ray's classic works.

I've been reading Bradbury since the early 1940s, when I was a teenager back in Kansas City (having first discovered him in Weird Tales). *Over subsequent decades, I've published two books and a number of shorter pieces on his work and career. We've been close pals for over forty years now.*

Ray has always employed his own unique style as a storyteller, and that special Bradbury style is happily echoed here in this wild parody, amplified, magnified, and exaggerated. "The Dandelion Chronicles" saw first publication as a limited-edition pamphlet in 1984, and I have completely revised and expanded it for The Bradbury Chronicles. *It was a joy to write, and I think it offers joy in return to readers of* The Martian Chronicles *or any one of Ray's other legendary works.*

Hop-skip-jump aboard the rocket and share the fun. I can guarantee you a surprising trip, with an ample supply of guffaws and giggles en route.

Up ship!

W.F.N.

"Look!"

"Hey!"

"Ah!"

The Waukegan crowd sighed, gasped, choked, cried out, the look of the great dream-colored climbing strawberry rocket in their round Illinois eyes, the thunder sound in their ears, mouths, on their pink tongues, all warm-ice and cool-fire and October carnival explosions, fading, fading . . .

Gone.

"Mom!" A bramble-headed boy shouted, yelled, pointed. "Are they going to Mars, eh? Is that where? All the way to Mars, Mom?"

"Yes," said the mother. "That is where they are going, Timmy. To Mars. All the way to Mars."

"Ah!" breathed the vast crowd, softly, watching and watching the calliope rocket fire away and away into the immense black velocities and depthless depths of Space.

Their ship was named *The Golden Dandelion,* and it was a good ship with a good crew, and it flew straight and true and did not slow down, ever. On board were Irish priests and simple Mexican peons and robust lightning-rod salesmen and rag-tag Dublin beggars and robots who cunningly resembled Irish priests and simple Mexican peons and robust lightning-rod salesmen and rag-tag Dublin beggars. And, of course, there was the crew: men named Littel and Bigg and Small and Able and Fine and Wright.

"Well . . ." said Captain Icarus Montgolfier Good. "So." He smiled. "Do you know what the old sun looks like from up here?" he asked, gazing and gazing through the strawberry porthole into Space, gentle hands folded behind his back. "It is like an immense dip of soft good lime sherbet, an immense dip of soft good lime sherbet indeed," said Captain Good, smiling and smiling through the strawberry port.

"Oh, you're *right,* sir!" agreed anthropologist Small. "It is like

the kind of sherbet Mom and Uncle Ned used to have heaped
and waiting on our plates when we'd come home for lunch, all
hot and tired and full of school, smelling of fresh-cut summer
grass and cool vanilla."

"And yet, sir—" marvelled Bigg, "—it is *hot!* It is as hot as ten
thousand furnaces going all at once and never stopping. It is as
hot as ten thousand wiener-fires on ten thousand picnic beaches."

"It is indeed," said the captain. He checked the gauge: Fahrenheit 451. "Ah," he said.

And they all stood silently, looking at the hot, hot sun.

"Jeepers, you know, Captain . . ." sighed crewman Littel. "I've
been thinking a lot about deep space lately, of how you have
to be crazy to voyage out here ten zillion light-years from
Earth—"

"Good grief!" exclaimed Captain Good, an exasperated tone
in his voice. "We aren't *nearly* that far out! I suggest you consult
your star charts before you indulge in wild metaphor."

"Anyway," stubbornly continued crewman Littel, "a person
still has to be *nuts* to fly out here, facing all the terrors and
dangers of space. Believe me, Captain, it's a graveyard for
lunatics."

"You're a big man, Littel," said the captain. "You can stand
up to it. We all must. We're a *team* out here in the void."

"Yet we die alone," said Littel.

"Yes, and it doesn't matter *where* we die," shrewdly observed
the captain, staring down at his tennis shoes. "On Mars, or on
some remote God-forsaken asteroid, or on good old Mother Earth
. . . death is always a lonely business."

The Golden Dandelion feather-drifted toward Mars, blown by
frosty polar winds and immense tidal moon winds and winds the
color of old wine, which smelled of Time and Eternity, winds
which blew and blew and never stopped blowing.

"Sound the solar foghorn," commanded Captain Good. "We
are rapidly approaching the Red Planet. Prepare—" said the captain, nervously cracking his knuckles, "—for dis-embarkation."

"May the saints preserve us every one!" sighed Father O'Faith,
the rusty old Irish robot priest.

The Golden Dandelion descended, feathered, dove-drifted,

hawk-settled, eased down from Space, balancing on a pillar of fire, baking the red dust of Mars with its angry furnace mouth.

The airlock hissed like a carnival snake, and they stepped out onto the waiting desert.

"Got a dime on ya, pal?" asked a greasy little rat-like man. He wore only a loincloth and his body was covered with illustrations that shimmered and writhed with a life of their own. Otherwise, he looked just like anyone else.

"Gollywhillerkers!" exclaimed crewman Bigg. "A humanoid!"

"Look," said the greasy desert rat, "you got no dime, you get no mirage. But—put a dime in my grubby palm, jump, hop, skip, run to the top of that rise, gaze out to your heart's content and sure as my name's Will Strange—you'll see Kubla Khan or New York or Port o'Spain. For a dime!"

"I'm all out of change," confessed Captain Good. "But I have a solar credit card. Or do you accept personal checks?"

But before Strange could reply, crewman Wright quickly fired seven deadly pellets from a bee-shaped hand weapon. Will Strange dropped to the red sand, twitched, gasped, choked, sighed, and said "Damn."

"There'll be *no* swearin'!" said Father O'Faith.

Then Will Strange died; all of his illustrations went dark.

"Sorry I had to waste him Captain," said crewman Wright sheepishly. "But that was probably no humanoid at all. That was, in my opinion, probably a hideous, ugly, revolting, spider-like, slithery, green, unnatural-looking, disgusting alien who hypno-tized us all, clouded our minds, warped and distorted our think-ing—all in an effort to entrap us, throw us off our guard, and destroy us to a man."

"Well, you're wrong, Mr. Wright," snapped Captain Good. "And frankly, I'm annoyed at you. Killing these aliens is *not* the answer. There *must* be another way to deal with them—and I intend to find it!"

Wright scuffed his toe in the sand. "Fooey!" he said.

"We don't have room for hotheads on board this ship," mused Good. "Remember, men, *we're* the aliens now!"

The captain looked down at his feet, and smiled. "It is good that I have on tennis shoes," he said. "Because they make my feet feel fine and good and there is a smell about them like going home after baseball."

All the men looked at the captain's fine black tennis shoes.

"Well, glory be!" breathed crewman Littel. "You know where I'd like to be right now, sir? I'd like to be out on the tippy-top of a tall, windy hill flying that old paper kite Dad made for me when I was ten and needed my backside switched."

"Me, I'd like to be running and running," cried Fine, "under the summer vanilla-night trees with the Illinois moon like a teardrop crystal in the sky."

The others joined in now, their voices blending, rising, surging, falling. And fire balloons were spoken of, and ripe lemon-yellow bananas, and Baby Ruth nut bars, and tall frosted cones fresh and dripping from the Ding-a-Ling wagon that came belling by each evening when it was warm-cool and the stars were winking on like so many yellow porch lights all up and down the long summer street. Like so many yellow porch lights, indeed.

And through it all Captain Good stood smiling down at his soft black tennis shoes, remembering and remembering.

Juan La Noche stepped like a dark shadow from the clockwork interior of the ship to stand beside the captain. He removed his broad, sweat-stained straw sombrero. "Maria, my common-law wife is big with child," he said. "She will soon honor me with a fine son or a miserable daughter, as the case may be."

"It is good to be a father," said the captain. "Each tiny tot forms yet another link in the universal cosmic chain. We must all grasp the rope of life and not allow it to slip through our fingers. Yet we dare not hold too tightly, lest it burn our hands. The way to do it is to kind of hold it loosely, and then you won't—"

La Noche slunk away, confused and bored, his eyes like dead coins in his penny-brown skull.

"A city! A city!" cried Billy Able, pointing to the horizon. "Hurrah! Hurrah!"

The captain put a long spy-glass to his eyes and peered at the distant strawberry hills rising like the back of a great white whale.

"It *could* be that greasy alien desert rat's mirage," he said.

"No! No! A city! A city!" cried Able. "Oh, hell, sir, we've *done* it!"

"Faith, an' willya stop the damn swearin'!" shouted the Irish robot-priest.

"Look alive, men," snapped the captain. "We'll soon see what's to be seen. Double-time! Hip-hup! Hop! Skip! Jump!"

The crew hop-skip-jumped into the city.

"Lordy!" breathed Fine. "It's—it's—"

"Greenboil, Illinois, on a Sunday afternoon in 1928," said Captain Icarus Good. "But it *can't* be!"

It was.

There, before them, was a maple-and-oak-shaded street, urine-colored dogs, legs defiantly raised near sun-red fire hydrants. Here, bellowing Stutz Bearcats full of dish-faced, flask-swigging college youths in long, foul-smelling raccoon coats. There, giant billboards advertising Carter's Little Liver Pills, and old, rotting rococo houses with senile grandmothers dozing on porch swings, spittle a-looping from their half-opened mouths—filthy kids in filthy knickers playing Mibs and emptying rancid garbage cans onto spotless front lawns.

"I don't like the look of this," mused Captain Good. He frowned darkly.

"Maybe," suggested crewman Small, "we've gone through some kind of time warp, ending up back in 1928 when things were clean and fine except for racial prejudice, and the stock market was booming."

Three odorous Irish beggars shuffled forward, all rags and open sores. "Let *us* go out an' make the test," they begged. "If nothin' terrible happens to O'Donnovan and Mike Fogarty and meself, Jamie O'Hennessey, poor blind dirty ignorant hoop-and-holler Dublin beggars that we are, then it'll be safe enough fer the rest a ya!"

"What these dirty ignorant Irish beggars are mewling makes good sense to me," said Fine. "Let's send them into the city."

"Fair enough, Fine," nodded Good. "Out they go!"

Yet, before they could slink an inch, crewman Wright rushed forward and began spraying the filthy kids and the urinating dogs and the drooling grandmothers and the flask-swigging college youths with deadly pellets from his bee-shaped hand weapon. Moaning, groaning, sighing, choking, clutching at their chests, they fell dead every one.

Silence.

"I was *afraid* of something like this," mused Captain Good. "Wright is, it seems, trigger happy. This sort of thing certainly won't win us many friends here on Mars."

Wright swung around, his bee-shaped hand weapon still smoking. "Don't you *see*, Captain? It was a trick. All a cunning, evil, not-so-good trick. They ran away with our minds. This street wasn't here, isn't here, not really, not truly really. It was all—"

"Mr. Wright, you may consider yourself under ship's arrest," snapped Captain Good. "Confine yourself to quarters. Double-time. Hip-hup! Hop! Jump!"

Wright hop-jumped back to the rocket, muttered "Fudge!" and slammed shut the airlock.

Good stepped forward, into the church-quiet corpse-littered blood-spattered maple-and-oak-shaded street. "Gosh!" he said, "What a mess!"

"Hey!" shouted Billy Able, waving excitedly from a distant corner. "Look! Hey! Over here!"

"Hip-hup, men," said Captain Good.

As they rounded the corner they all stopped, awed at what lay before them. . . .

An Irish cobbled thoroughfare, rattling carts drawn by phlegm-eyed sway-backed horses, old men in grime-stiffened caps and thick unwashed mufflers, clay pipes afire between toothless gums, thatched huts and tall stone churches, and drunken Irish songs drifting like gentle smoke from the pubs.

"Dublin!" breathed Father O'Faith. " 'Tis none other!"

Captain Good frowned darkly. "It doesn't make sense," he said. "It just doesn't add up."

Crewman Small ran to the swing door of Dooley's Pub. "Ale!" he shouted. "Stout! Black Irish whiskey!" He dipped his head inside the batwing door. "Shall we sample it, Captain? Oh, *shall* we, sir?"

"Poison!" A familiar voice announced behind them. It was crewman Wright again. He rushed past crewman Small and sprayed the pub's interior with a burst of deadly pellets from his bee-shaped hand weapon. "So," he said. "And *so*!"

The Irish songs had ceased. Inside, there was only . . .

Silence. The silence of an oh-so-deep Illinois ravine under a frosted Halloween pumpkin moon the color of orange sherbet when even the crickets have called it quits. *That* kind of silence.

"By golly, Wright," snapped Captain Good. "Didn't I just put you under ship's arrest and confine you to quarters?"

"But, sir, *someone* must protect you. I, therefore, chose to disregard your order."

"Then consider yourself under *double* ship's arrest," said Good. "Now, back to the *Dandelion*. Off you go! Hip-hup! Jump!"

Father O'Faith stepped up to Good. "They's one poor soul left alive in there," he said. "A fine broth of an old lady with a harp all silver like an angel's wing."

"Then drag her out," snapped Good. "We'll question her. Oh, and tell her she has nothing to fear from us. We come in peace."

"Aye!"

Father O'Faith fetched the old woman. She came side-blinking out into the soot-colored day, dragging a tall silver harp behind her.

She belched loudly. Again. And then again. And yet again.

"I am Captain Icarus Montgolfier Good, and this is my loyal crew and we have come all the way from Earth to you in a really neat spaceship—the first of many who will eventually descend upon your planet like so many silver locusts, like so many silver locusts indeed." He hesitated, out of breath. "Just who *are* you?"

"Me name's Molly Malone, yer honor," she said.

"Occupation?"

"Sure an' I play me harp fer a bit of drinkin' likker an' a pinch from a laughin' boy."

She dove-drifted a withered stick hand over the silver harp strings.

"Rain!" sighed crewman Bigg. "Sounds for all the world like a fall of clear and gentle rain."

"It sounds," said Tom Fine, "like ten thousand crystal drops on ten thousand sleeping roofs. It sounds like all the rain that ever was or ever will be!" And he burst into tears.

"Yes," said the captain, eyes closed. "And yes."

The old woman smiled toothlessly and danced her spider fingers through "Limerick Is My Town," "The Lovely Isle of Innisfree," and "Doin' it in Dublin."

"Hey, and do you know 'Laughin' on the Liffey'?" asked crewman Small.

"I do indeed!" The harp notes quivered on the cool air.

"Ah!" said Captain Good. And *he* burst into tears.

"Ah!" said Able and Fine and Wright.

"Ah!" said Littel and Small.

They *all* burst into tears.

Then the cheerful old lady pitched forward flat on her face to the street.

"Dead, an' gone to her sweet reward—mortally wounded by one a' them pellets from that pesky bee-shaped hand weapon," said Father O'Faith. "Sure, an' she was dyin' a little with every harp note, bless her withered old stick body."

"Darn!" said Captain Good. "I really *like* good music."

"Hey!" shouted Billy Able from the end of the murky Dublin street. "Come! Look! See!"

"Hip-hup, lads."

They ran. They stopped. They looked, mouths agape.

"Good God!" said Good.

"Maria!" cried Juan La Noche to his sweating wife. "See! Savor what your eyes tell you! Feast your sight like summer wine. We are Home!"

"Aa-eeee!" cried Maria, wobbling ponderously forward, her shawl close about her. A great quivering black hair grew ferociously from her left nostril. She was large with child and her hair was a color found long after midnight when the streets are black with things darker than old Mr. Death himself, but not as dark as the great pits of Space where there is no up or down or sideways, only the great pits. She burst into tears. "Juan speaks truth," she cried. "This *is* indeed our home. It is Guadalajara! Ae-eeeeee!"

Before them: sod shacks, crude roads of baked black adobe, a wedding-cake white graveyard, walls of hand-laid stones. And— next to the graveyard, the catacombs.

Juan rushed forward, yanking back the great wooden door sunk in rich earth.

He fell back, gasping. "Down there," he said softly, "the dead stand like so many frozen soldiers, wired to the walls, horror-mouthed and stark-socketed. Their screams are silent, but one can *hear* them; their skull sockets are eyeless, yet they see Death. Bone fingers claw fetid air; bone legs arch and writhe like so many breadsticks in an oven. Ayeeeee! The dead ones—the standing mummies of Guadalajara! It is good to be home!"

"I don't like the smell of things, Captain," said Tom Fine.

"Aye," breathed Maria, holding her nose. "The dead do not smell so sweet. Good grief, Juan, shut the door!"

The big door whammed down like a drum. Bang!

"There's something about all this I don't understand," said the captain. "This isn't . . ." He groped for the word. ". . . *normal.*"

At that precise moment, a withered old night watchman approached them.

"I'm a withered old night watchman," he said, "an' you fellas have got to get the hell off the lot and quit killin' the extras."

"Lot . . . extras . . ." breathed Captain Good. "Great Scott! I think I'm *beginning* to understand!"

The men all held their breath, waiting for their captain to figure things out.

Suddenly, the captain's eyes lit up. He hopped. He danced. He shouted. "Oh, men, don't you *see?* Don't you, each and every one, see the plain and simple truth?"

They all shook their heads, still holding their breath, each and every one.

The captain shouted out the words, the important words, the words that made everything plain and simple: "Mars . . . is *Hollywood!*"

"Waal," spat the old night watchman, "not exactly. This here is Television City. Me, I call it the Meadow of the World, but that's because I'm an old poetic night watchman. But Hollywood *proper* is a few miles off. Tell ya what—ya just take Fairfax up to Sunset, then ya turn right and go past La Brea an' then ya—"

"Good grief," exploded the captain. "Our enormously expensive and incredibly complicated space direction finder must have gone on the fritz. Men, in plain and simple words, we've landed back on Earth."

The men all began breathing again, knowing that their captain had finally figured things out.

"There's only one minor item which still continues to puzzle me," said Captain Good.

"Whazat?"

"Who in blazes was that greasy old desert rat we originally killed near the ship—the illustrated fellow with the mirage?"

"That was a plot complication," said the old night watchman, "an' *nobody* can explain plot complications. Ain't no way out of 'em."

The captain nodded, frowning darkly.

"Well, what do we do now, eh, Captain?" asked Billy Able.

Captain Good rocked slowly to and fro in his black tennis shoes, cracking his white, white knuckles.

Silence.

"Gee, I'm not sure what to do next," confessed the captain, biting his lower lip like a sullen child. "Yet . . . I've always wanted to act. To be a great star. To see my name in lights. To wear a gold Elvis coat and have packs of panting, swarming, full-bosomed young teenaged girls clawing at my body . . ."

The captain looked at his crew.

"What say you all—shall we *act?*"

"Aye! Aye!" shouted the crew. "So shall we all!"

The old night watchman yawned. "The casting office is 'bout half a block west of here," he told them. "Just say that Ed Poe sent you over. What with all the extras that crazy fella of yours killed with that bee-shaped hand weapon, they'll be needin' some replacements."

"Hurrah! Hurrah for Mr. Poe!" shouted Father O'Faith.

And Juan La Noche and Maria and the three dirty ignorant Irish beggars and Billy Able and Tom Fine and crewmen Bigg and Littel and Small, all of them shouted, "Hurrah! Hurrah!"

And they turned their backs on the great golden rocket and ran and rushed and arrowed in a tide, a drift, a freshet, a bright-running river—straight for the casting office.

And, watching them go, the withered old night watchman shook his withered old head.

"Damn bunch of fools!" he said, and spat into the silent dust.

Afterword: Fifty Years, Fifty Friends

Ray Bradbury

How can one look back at fifty years of living and writing and make any sense of it? The overwhelming memory, seen from this end of the tunnel, is a raving mediocrity carried about in a twenty-year-old body. Thank God, I did not know how truly bad I was as a poet, short story writer and playwright. Work, lots of it, and ego, delivered me from that knowledge. It is only now, when I prowl through the old files from 1939 and 1940 that I lay hands on my own ineptitudes and suddenly recall how I invaded the lives of so many Los Angeles writers with my awful tales. I was underfoot in Jack Williamson's apartment, only a few blocks away (unfortunately for Jack) from where I lived. I aged Henry Kuttner some few years by an amiable enforcement of my words. Robert Heinlein allowed me, on occasion, to watch him type. Arthur K. Barnes heard me knocking and ran for the exit. But finally they all took me under their wings in order to kick me around the block and knock some creative sense into the young fool.

I'll come back to these friends in a moment. But, first . . .

I'm still a great mystery to me. Even now, perhaps more of a mystery than ever. Come off it! you say, don't pretend. You *must* know something of how it happened. To which I would reply: I imagine it was a slow process, like a happy disease coming on and your temperature rising so slowly that you don't know you have a fever, and then suddenly you *got* it. *It* being able, at last,

317

to write a decent story, and then a better one than that, and at last a story that is very good indeed.

I guess the best description for myself, at seventeen, when I joined the Los Angeles Science Fantasy Society while still in high school, is that I wrote every day.

That sounds most moronic in its simplicity, but there you have it.

By writing each day I got all the clichés out of my system, to make room for better metaphors. Simultaneously, I introduced into my bloodstream metaphors from a variety of fields, most of them found in the library.

I remember going to parties with various older members of the L.A.S.F. Society, and being bored because I didn't drink, and wandering through some fan's house until I found an unoccupied typewriter and sitting down to write, or trying to write, a story.

While everyone else wasted their time (so I thought) I was advancing from terrible into awful, on my way to mediocre.

Mediocre is wonderful. Most people have forgotten what the word means: medium. To be medium is halfway on to being well-done. But it was a long journey and luckily the work itself puts a mask over how dreadful the product. You need only see the essays and low comedy I wrote for the fan magazine *Imagination* or my own publication, *Futuria Fantasia* paid for by Forrest J. Ackerman, bless him, to see how bad I was, and how hopeless my case.

Still, the affliction persisted. At times, in my late teens, I stumbled on the secret of creativity but, being unperceptive, didn't know that I had and veered back into the bad and the un-beautiful.

I have kept copies of stories typed in my last year in high school, in which I visited my hometown ravine and was frightened by it and my attic and basement, as well as the Lonely One, but lacked the intuitive sense to keep going back to the edge of the green abyss or below or upstairs in my house. I wandered off, typing madly, into imitations, far away from my true self.

It would take years of stenography to fill the stupid void in my head with photographs by the world's great photographers, poems by Shakespeare and Emily Dickinson, or films by Orson

Welles and others. They took up so much room, finally, that I must have been shoved into creativity. The clichés were thrown out as garbage. Finally, my memory, teased by word-association, locked away, fearful, hiding back in corners, began to creep out, a hint here, a hint there, bullied by the fine works of others and yearning to breathe.

I remember finding copies of *Coronet* magazine and ripping out pages of photographs by Steichen, Karsh and others to write prose-poems or demi-haiku on what I saw: mainly females in various states of undress, what else? I was at least responding to metaphor, while ingesting the illusion of motion, the film, eyeball upon eyeball.

During that time my best nesting place for many years was the downtown Los Angeles Public Library. My favorite room in the library, the jackdaw place, was the literature room with its scores and stacks of essays about writing, literature, and ideas from every country in the world.

I discovered that I loved picking up bright objects: concepts, fancies, notions by people I had never heard of. I found commonplace books which were collections of quotes, paragraphs, *pensees* covering hundreds of years: The Notebooks of Samuel Butler and F. Scott Fitzgerald fell under my eye. I made the right decision to live in and around and through the stacks of that room. Searching, selecting, opening, reading, and making notes while standing.

Sometimes writing stories, by God, on those little paper pads you find in libraries on which to note down titles or simple quotes. I became so ravenous that I used up scores of pads, fearing to leave to find my own pad to write on, because the idea might vanish. I rarely brought paper with me, for I never dreamed ideas would up and rape me unawares in the stacks.

People often ask me how it is that I was such a raving optimist in the face of, at times, abysmal surroundings. First of all, though I was raised poor, no one ever told me. We took it for granted we would have nothing so never missed it. I learned, while in high school, to get to know every movie house manager within three miles so that I could see as many as fourteen motion pictures a week. I ran errands for them, bought nightly newspapers, or simply begged entrance and got in. I rollerskated to Hollywood

Saturday nights to buy a pack of cigarettes for Roy Evans, the manager, who became a friend fifty years later, in order to cheap-bribe my way in to first run films at the Paramount. I ushered at the Biltmore Theater and saw all the major plays that arrived in L.A.

I had a family that if it didn't understand me let me run around Hollywood late nights on weekends, searching for famous people. Those were great years in L.A. Nothing bad ever happened to me. For that matter, nothing bad happened to anyone I knew in the thirties.

I soft-soap-bullied my way into George Burns' life, asking him to take me and Donald Harkins, my best friend in junior high school, into the *Burns and Allen* White Owl Radio Show. George did so. And the curtain went up to find an audience of two, Don and myself, watching and hearing George and Gracie. In the months following, Don and I wrote scripts, bad ones, and handed them over to Mr. Burns every Wednesday night. Whether or not he read the dreadful things, he never admitted. He just indicated that we were geniuses and should continue in our madness. When I brought my Mom and Dad down to meet Gracie, no one demurred.

At the same time, Louella Parsons entered my life. No, I barged into hers, asking her to take me in to watch her *Hollywood Hotel* broadcast. She took my hand and led me to a seat next to Gary Cooper and Franchot Tone, acting out their roles for radio in *Lives of a Bengal Lancer* in a smallish studio that contained an audience of eighty and an orchestra of, it seemed, eighty-five, led by Raymond Paige. During the following months Donald Harkins and I and three rowdy sisters, the Fredricksons, got to know Dick Powell, Frances Langford, and the stage crew for *Hollywood Hotel*, mainly because at the end of each broadcast, I ran up on stage and stole the scripts, which caused Dave, the stage manager, to kick my backside up the alley behind the theater. I still have dozens of *Hollywood Hotel* and *Burns and Allen* scripts in my files, fifty-five years gone and yellowing. Over the years, I lost contact with George Burns, but one night ten years ago at a Coconut Grove Awards show, I described my friendship with George and his kindness to the fourteen-year-old kid. When the show was over, George Burns came hurrying up to me, crying:

"Was that you? Was that really you, back in 1934? I *remember* you!"

And we embraced after a good part of a lifetime.

During those years I got to know Louella's chauffeur and rode around town with him on errands until Louella found out and I got the boot.

For one so shy, half of me was brass.

In those few short years, Don Harkins and I were tails to the Fredrickson sisters' comet. They ran around Hollywood, getting to know everyone. Bing Crosby took them to the horse races. Johnny Weissmuller invited them over to his home, after, of course, they had invited themselves. Through them I often encountered Bing, and forty years later, when I wanted to find the now lost sisters, the way to find them was: Bing.

I figured he would have kept in touch with them at Christmas. I was right. I wrote asking. Bing wrote back:

"I remember you and am happy for your life and work. Here are the Fredrickson sisters' addresses."

And when my crazy pals had gone off to live their lives, there was Forrest J. Ackerman to become my first editor and publisher, to put up money so I could publish my own fanmag, *Futuria Fantasia,* and finance my trip across country on a Greyhound bus in late June 1939 to attend the World's Fair and the first World Science Fiction Convention in New York. I took along a portfolio of Hannes Bok's drawings and paintings to agents to the fantasy and SF magazines, a typewriter, and some horrible stories which I showed to only a few editors. I sold Farnsworth Wright on the idea of hiring Bok to do covers for *Weird Tales* and, at nineteen, met just about every famous SF writer in modern history. I was in awe, being years away from my first real sale.

Again, optimism about my life and future, even when I had little but an old beat-up typewriter purchased over a period of months, a buck a week, from Perry Lewis, one of the amiably crazed inhabitants of that Little Brown Room in Clifton's Cafeteria in late 1937. I think I gave him twelve bucks, which I paid for by going without lunch, a quarter a day for most of the late winter, early spring semesters at L.A. High. I ate lunch only once a week, Fridays, when I spent the quarter on hamburgers and popcorn.

And then of course there was Laraine Day, a lovely actress in films at MGM. Watch her again in *Foreign Correspondent*, one of Hitchcock's better films, and you'll see why I fell in love and stayed in love with her. She sized me up when I came to try out for the Wilshire Players Guild in October 1939. Back from the World's Science Fiction Convention and the New York World's Fair, I read an item in Louella's column that Laraine was forming a theater group at the Mormon church only two blocks from my apartment. I arrived looking like the disreputable newsboy that I was, hair too long, clothes yanked at and untidy, but theater flames shooting from my eyes. Laraine resisted a look of distaste, shuffled through my pile of bad plays and glanced up at me.

"You've *got* to take me," I said. "I've already told my friends you *would!*"

Amazingly, she didn't throw me out the door but took me, under surveillance, into the group. Within months I was acting in a musical comedy with her and rewriting most of the lines. Incredibly, again, she didn't fire me off the stage. My sense of humor, pitiful as it was, was better than hers. And my jokes improved her script. Swallowing her bile, Laraine let me proceed. My pay was walking around the block with her during rehearsal breaks, in the moonlight, hoping that one day I would gather courage enough to grab and kiss her. I never did.

To continue:

Optimistic? Why?

Because of:

Jennet Johnson, my short-story teacher in Los Angeles High School, who confessed she didn't understand what I was up to, but that I wrote well enough, and who came out of high school to follow me through my life and ask me what I was reading, until she died at the age of ninety-two a few years ago.

Who else? Here are the L.A. writers and the number of my stories each read and knocked down and put together for me between 1939 and 1945:

Ross Rocklynne. Two dozen.

Jack Williamson. Six or eight.

Arthur K. Barnes. Three.

Henry Hasse. Twelve.

Henry Kuttner. Thirty.

Leigh Brackett. Ninety or one hundred.

These last three deserve special comment.

I had been writing to Henry Hasse because of his friendship with Hannes Bok up in Seattle. When he arrived in Los Angeles in 1940 we began collaboration on a half dozen stories, all of them dreadful, except "Pendulum" which had a decent if strange metaphor at its center. By mid-1941 I realized that we were a set of crutches with no human writer between. I told Henry it was time for me to go my own way. He flew into a rage. Our friendship ended there. I realized later that Henry was one of those writers who absolutely needed a collaborator. After that he wrote only a few stories, most of them with a co-writer. Years later, in the seventies, we met again and renewed our friendship.

Kuttner was incredible. He criticized in detail everything that passed under his eye. His ending for "The Candle" in *Weird Tales* remains there today. I could find no better way to finish it and asked permission to use his last 300 words. He shepherded my story "Chrysalis" through a half dozen rewrites and submitted it on at least three occasions to John W. Campbell, hoping to at last help me invade *Astounding*, the best magazine in the field. Campbell was sympathetic but gave a final rejection to the story, which appeared later on in *Amazing Stories*.

Kuttner's best advice to me, which helped my career blossom, was: "Do me a favor, Bradbury? Shut up! You go around raving your ideas, but never write them. Sew up your mouth."

I did, and never told another story out loud ever again in my life.

Leigh Brackett? Sit back. It's a long and beautiful story of friendship.

Leigh invited me down to play volleyball, or mostly watch, week after week, every Sunday, for five years, at Muscle Beach, Santa Monica, California—familiar territory to me. I had grown up there with my family from the age of thirteen on. It was where my football-playing-surfer brother Skip lived and survived best, among the bodybuilders. Through Leigh I re-acquainted myself with a world I could never take part in. Swimming was always my great love, but competing? Never.

So I arrived on Sundays, starting in 1941, with my terrible, cliché-burdened, outrageous stories and Leigh sat on the sand, read them, and wept with boredom and frustration at not being able to help me much more quickly. And I sat on the sand and read her incredibly neat, forceful stories about her brute heroes on Mars, or detectives who managed to stay clean in a dirty world. It was Leigh who introduced me to the work of James Cain, Raymond Chandler, and Dashiell Hammett, good influences and teachers, all. We formed what we finally called The Malts, Manuscripts and Ah, Bergman and Bogart Society. When we weren't talking story, we rehashed *Casablanca* at the center of our lives.

We were an odd couple, I must admit. My hair was longer than Leigh's, or was it that Leigh's was shorter than mine? A lot of people wondered about us, but never asked, so we never noticed. I think we were in love with one another, but only admitted if in an offhand, careless way. And so the Sundays progressed through to the end of the War. Due to a frightening and truly terrible eyesight, I wound up writing materials for the National Red Cross. Legally blind was the term.

In the early 1940s the editors of *Planet Stories*, Malcolm Reiss and Wilber Peacock, read some of my stories and refused to buy them. They were too good, they said, for *Planet*. They then proceeded to submit my stories, from their office, acting as friendly agents, to *Collier's* and *The Saturday Evening Post*. Only when those magazines rejected them, did *Planet* proceed to buy and publish them. What amazing editors they were!

And, during that time, I had a quite amazing agent, Julius Schwartz, who read and sold some ninety-odd stories of mine to the pulp magazines, at twenty to forty bucks apiece. When it came time for me to move on up into the quality magazines, Julie blessed me and sent me on my way to *The American Mercury*, *Harper's*, *Collier's*, and *The Nation*.

In the late 1940s–early '50s, two young men showed up on my doorstep.

Bill Nolan, or the Windmill, as we call him from his wildly flailing arms whenever he gets enthused, which is about two dozen times daily. He stayed on to become my Imperial Indexer, Critic, and friend. I have scores of his letters covering a forty-year period, analyzing my novels in the works. His advice on *Death is a Lonely Business* stretches over a number of years. When I began my TV series, Bill read and critiqued all of the first teleplays.

The second young man, a student at the USC Cinema School and still untried in films, was named Sam Peckinpah. Years later, when we sat down to lunch after he had become famous as a film director, Sam reminded me that he had hung around my Venice, California porch, asking permission to do a student film on one of my stories. Sam promised to do *Something Wicked This Way Comes.*

I waited at least two years for him to fulfill the promise. When he wandered off in an amiable daze of gin, I finally sold the rights to Chartoff/Winkler who never made it, then a free option to Spielberg, who never made it, and at last Disney and Jack Clayton.

Along the way, Peckinpah, provoked that I hadn't waited for him for another year, sent me as gift a cactus with a jar of vaseline, advising me to split the cactus in quarters so I could share it with Chartoff, Winkler, and Clayton. I could not help remembering that, years before, he was the only man who ever sent me flowers for my birthday. We had some wild fine times together. He was always pouring gin in my beer. I bear no malice. I miss him. I still love him.

John Huston . . . That's another entire book, which I am now writing. The entirety is love/hate. But I don't know which is skin and which is flesh and blood beneath the skin. He changed my life forever by giving me the job of writing *Moby Dick* for the screen. Everything changed after that. I didn't have to pick up the phone and ask for work. The phone rang, all by itself.

Bernard Berenson. Who read my defense of writing science fiction in *The Nation* and sent me a letter saying "this is the first fan letter I have written in 89 years," telling me that if "you ever touch Italy, come see me." And so the doors of the Renaissance were opened and he became a second father to me until his death in 1959.

Fellini. Who read my analysis of his films in the L.A. *Times* and wrote, inviting me to come visit. I wrote back immediately saying, "By a strange coincidence, we will be in Rome in August." So, meeting, we found to our joy that we were twins.

Margaret Booth and Miklos Rosza, film editor and film composer, from whom I learned more about film-making in a few weeks than in all the years with other directors, producers, and writers. I fell in with them when MGM asked me to provide an ending for a remake of *King of Kings*. I suggested that they should search the Bible for such an ending. They insisted I could do better. I took the job, and to my delight wound up with Maggie and Mickey. The friendship has lasted for thirty years.

Ron Miller. Former head of Walt Disney films. Who had the good sense to summon me back when the first production of *Something Wicked This Way Comes* was a disaster. He recalled the actors, had the sets rebuilt, ordered a new musical score, and allowed me to write an editing-outline and work with the film editor on the last reel of the film, thus saving us from the snorts and scoffs of disbelieving audiences. We mouth-to-mouth breathed a dead picture back to life, with Miller as guide.

Sir Carol Reed. We spent the best summer ever with him in 1957, writing the screenplay of my *And the Rock Cried Out*, which was never made. I would deliver six pages of screenplay to Carol's Kings Road home every afternoon at five. At midnight each night, Carol would telephone my hotel. His response was always the same:

"Oh, Ray! Ray!" he would cry. "Continue!"

His joyful shout banged me back to my typewriter. The screenplay was finished in six weeks. Carol sent it to Rome and Ingrid Bergman, hoping to cadge her for the lead.

Walking down the Via Veneto in August, my eight-year-old daughter Susan suddenly exclaimed, "Oh, look, Daddy, there's Ingrid Bergman!"

I walked over to the sidewalk cafe where she was sitting, introduced myself, and reminded her that Sir Carol had airmailed her my screenplay.

"Oh yes," said Ingrid Bergman. "I didn't like it."

I froze.

"I just don't understand fantasy or science fiction of any sort," she explained.

At least an honest actor. I shook hands, told her I loved her anyway, and departed.

Roy A. Squires. Who fulfilled my dream of one day having some of my stories or poems published with handset type and printed on the best quality paper.

Herb Yellin. Who continued where Roy left off, publishing a half dozen of my spare volumes, publishing acts of much love if small profit.

Norman Corwin. I sent him a copy of my first book of stories, *Dark Carnival*, with a note: "If you like these half as much as I love you and your radio dramas, I'd like to buy you a drink some afternoon." He responded with: "You're not buying me a drink, I'm buying *you* dinner!" It was Norman who suggested I go to New York on the Greyhound bus to meet editors. Result: *The Martian Chronicles.*

Stan Freberg. The funniest man ever to show up at a boring political rally. I took one look at him, chatted for five minutes, and it was love forever. Many years ago, he called and asked me to do a 1-minute television commercial. I said no, I didn't do that sort of thing. He said, "How about the Brave New Prune of the Future?" I said, "Stan, you *got* me."

Donn Albright. Who crept into my life month by month, year by year, until when I looked up one day there he was as Recording Angel, Personal Librarian, and Life Enthusiast. I'm leaving my body to him, in 2020 A.D.

Those of you who have been counting must realize I have not as yet listed fifty friends. They are there in time, but I have run out of space.

So there you have me. There I stand in the midst of a mob, a honeycomb of tolerant helpers for an early-on writer of intolerable prose. Take any one of them away and I am diminished. Add them back, and I am fulfilled.

I have saved to the last those four who were always, or almost always, first.

Alexandra/Zana, my daughter, who has suffered my creative company and run my notions through the typewriter for many years now. She is out when the sun isn't. She knows all the songs and jokes from the greatest and worst musical films ever made. Nuff said.

Marguerite/Maggie, the lady who took a vow of poverty to marry me forty-four years ago, and who has read every story and novel, play and poem I ever wrote, and what's more, back in 1947 through 1953, typed all our manuscripts. Maggie never advised me to sell out but just go on writing what I knew and loved best, never doubting that one day we might have an income, but meanwhile never talking about money, since there was none to talk about.

And Don Congdon, who married me as agent the same week I took the vows with Maggie, and who for the same forty-four years has read and advised on every single story and novel. A fine human being who knows literature and has often said, "What will this sale mean to your future ten years off? Let's not do it." And so has protected me from being a fool.

And finally Sid Stebel, who entered my life in 1948, and has stayed to read my stories and allow me to read his *The Collaborator*, a superb piece of work.

That's my sum with many individual substances.

So, you see, that my feeling of optimism came from the encouragement I got from all those listed, and some not, who caused me to write/work/play joyously every day and thus achieve the optimal behavior I am always yelling about.

To live at the top of your lungs, your genetics, the rambling and incoherent half-awake, half-asleep dreams just before dawn, or in the morning shower, or on your pillow during afternoon naps. To *not know* what you're doing but find out in the doing. To always be surprised and never damn or turn away from surprise. To love life while surrounded by so much that is annihilation. To answer, as I did one night not long ago at a lecture, when asked, "Why do you write so much about death?" To which I said, "Because I am alive."

I end as I began, nonplussed at my own history, but sure of certain aspects. I became what I became because I fed myself every day, a mild-mannered horse at the library trough, munching his Poe, Pope, Dickens, Dickinson, Shakespeare and Donne, minding his oats. And writing early morns or late nights, scribbling down the drivel to get rid of it to make welcome space for personal metaphors needing room and wanting out. And rushing to my much more than fifty friends for succor, aid, or tender loving care.

Beyond that, there is no me that exists. Only the books that have names. And those you know.